Enlightened

S.J. JENSAR

Don't Waste Your Business

© S.J. Jensar

All rights reserved. No part of this publication may be reproduced, stored in a retrieval system, or transmitted in any form or by any means, electronic, mechanical, photocopying, recording or otherwise, without the prior written permission of the author.

National Library of Australia Cataloguing-in-Publication entry

Author:	Jensar, S. J., author.
Title:	Enlightened / S.J. Jensar.
ISBN:	9780992447700 (paperback)
Subjects:	Fantasy fiction.
Dewey Number:	A823.4

Published with the assistance of www.inhousepublishing.com.au

ONE

It was the flash of teeth that caught my attention.

Glistening in the moonlight, they sank into the delicate skin of her throat.

I blinked to clear my vision.

I did not just see that.

My mind instantly went into reassurance mode, telling me it was the playful nip of a lover and definitely not the deadly bite of a vampire - a Kudlak, feeding on its victim. I dismissed the notion as ridiculous even as I gave chase, cutting through the thick crowd to get a closer look. It was impossible, a vampire, here?

My mind flicked to recent events and an uneasy feeling settled over me. Ignoring the annoyed grunts and words of indignation, I pushed against the surge, catching glimpses of my quarry here and there. With his arms wrapped around her, he backed them away from the well-lit street, edging towards the shadows of a nearby alley. The crowd pushed back and swallowed me up, I lost sight of them, and my heart skipped at the prospect of losing them altogether. I had no idea what I was going to do when I caught them, if I caught them. If it wasn't a vampire then the worst thing that could happen is I make an arse out of myself. If it was a vampire, then it was already too late. If it didn't kill her by completely draining her of blood, the venom would take what was left and turn her. In a couple of hours, she'd be one of them; either way I couldn't just stand by. I had to do something.

The crowd eased and I found them again. Her head had fallen to the side and her hands gripped at the sleeves of his shirt. Whether it was the delight of her lover's kisses or the ever weakening fight for life against the Kudlak as it drained her body of blood I couldn't tell.

"Ana, what are you doing?"

I turned at hearing my name. Pushing through the crowd after me was my best friend Natasha, concern clear on her face.

She called over the jumble of people. "What's wrong?"

I turned back to the couple just as the shadows of the alley swallowed them up and I barrelled forward, calling over my shoulder, "I think someone's in trouble."

I cleared the crowd and looked back for Tash. Popping out from behind a family she looked slightly dishevelled but hurried to me.

I motioned for her to follow, explaining as I rushed toward the alley. "Quick. I saw a guy drag this gi-"

My sentence was cut short as I ran into the larger half of a giggling couple exiting the alley in front of us.

"Whoa! Slow down there."

I stepped away from the steadying hand. "Sorry I ah, wasn't watching."

Was this the couple I'd seen?

I eyed her neck but her hair was brushed forward, it seemed much longer now.

4

My eyes flicked past them and into the gloom. "Was anyone else back there?"

The guy smiled down at his girlfriend, clearly smitten. "Nope." He tapped her nose and she giggled. "Just us."

I dismissed them as they started kissing noisily. Clearly they hadn't had enough of each other in the alley. Lips locked they stumbled away.

Tash let out an impatient sigh. "Seriously people, get a room." I was studying the sheer walls on either side of the alley when she came to stand next to me.

"Gross."

"How high do you reckon these walls are?"

"What?"

I stopped craning up at the stone to look at her. "The wall's; how high?"

She made a big show of patting her pockets. "Oh darn it. You know? I forgot to bring my tape measure."

I ignored her sarcasm. "Do you think a Kudlak could climb a wall like this carrying a body?" I cringed at how crazy that sounded, even to my own ears.

She rounded on me, "Are you serious Ana? A vampire."

The way *she* said it made it sound even crazier and I indicated lamely toward the alley.

"I thought I saw a guy biting a girl's neck and....and then dragging her into the alley."

She crossed her arms, her expression suddenly serious, and her tone no nonsense. "You did." She indicated in the direction of the kissing couple. "They just walked off to find another dark doorway to get gross in."

I followed the angle of her pointing finger and looked down the street but it didn't seem right. I slowly shook my head, "I could have sworn that his teeth...and her hair, it wasn't that long."

5

She cut me off, "Are you calm?"

I brushed at my fringe in frustration, "Yes I'm calm."

She stepped closer, "You know what I mean."

I met her level gaze, "Yes I know what you mean."

She was referring to my little incidents; sometimes when I get agitated I accidentally make things happen. And when I say *make things happen,* I really mean, blow shit up.

Her eyebrow rose speculatively, "Are you sure? Because we can't afford to have you losing it with all these people around, someone might see, or worse, get hurt."

"Yes Tash I promise, I'm fine."

She relaxed visibly, "Good." Her mouth kicked up a little at the edges. "In that case, the answer's no."

"No, what?"

"No, I don't think a Kudlak could scale either of these walls with a body."

We both looked up, she was right, the stone was two stories high and I was a crazy person.

I stood there for a moment looking up at the night sky beyond the walls. A storm was brewing on the horizon. The night was muggy and the anticipation of the oncoming storm seemed to electrify the air around me. Maybe that was why the hair on the back of my neck wanted to stand on end.

Tash bumped me with her hip, "C'mon, I want to do some shopping before the fireworks start."

I took a deep breath and dragged my eyes from the rooftops. She was smiling at me expectantly, excitement animating her features.

I relented, "Far be it for me to come between you and your shopping."

Tash smiled and I followed as she headed back into the main street. It was the Eve of the Daska Festival, an annual event, which runs for four weeks during the heart of summer. Traditionally it was a time to celebrate our God Daska, the creator of our race, the Kresniks. Yet these days, it's more about catching up with old friends and having a good time. Kresniks from all over the world were converging on our city for the celebrations and from the looks of this evening's Pre-Festival Party - they weren't going to be disappointed.

I heard the ominous rumble of thunder and looked up, lightning flashed in the distance, backlighting the building bank of storm clouds on the horizon. Movement across the rooftops caught my attention but when I shifted focus, it was gone. My breathing sounded overly loud in my ears as I concentrated and suddenly everything stilled. The feeling was unnatural, as though the night itself was holding its breath. Despite the humidity, a chill skipped up my spine, followed quickly by an overwhelming need to back away but I stood firm, staring hard into the darkness.

Nothing moved.

"Come *on* Ana!"

"Alright, I'm coming." Moving backwards, I eyed the rooftops one last time before turning my back on them. "Keep your pants on."

I ignored the dark feeling that clung to me and hurried to catch up with Tash.

We meandered through the rows of makeshift stalls, slowly making our way toward the centre of the park. Tash had already bought some beaded jewellery and was eyeing off some preserves when I got the unsettling feeling of eyes boring into my back. Turning I scanned the crowd slowly.

Everyone was going about the business of having fun and showing absolutely no interest in me.

Shaking my head I mumbled quietly to myself, "Your imagination is working overtime tonight Ana."

I turned my attention back to the stall of preserves where Tash was finalising her second purchase of the evening. Smiling she presented the jar of homemade chutney to me for inspection, before dropping it into her bag.

"Okay, so where to now?"

I opened my mouth to respond when I felt it again.

That is not my imagination.

I spun around just in time to catch a pair of old eyes narrowing on me before they ducked behind a tent flap. I took a step toward the tent but the bang of the first fireworks stopped me in my tracks. Gunpowder exploded in starbursts across the night and the crowd, suddenly drenched in hues of pink and purple, looked up as one.

Tash motioned to me, "C'mon, let's find a place to sit."

I followed, throwing one last look over my shoulder at the tent into which my observer's eyes had disappeared. It was larger than most and covered in deep coloured velvet cloth, the sign outside advertising Taro, Runes & Palm Readings by the famed Gypsy Vadoma. I decided that all of a sudden I felt a desperate need to know my future. It would be easy to convince Tash to come with me later. She loves all that mystical Hoo Haa.

Forty- five minutes and one spectacular fireworks display later I followed the Gypsy Vadoma as she ducked under the flap of heavy material separating her tent into two rooms. Tash had just received her reading, and gave me a Double-Thumbs-Up as she took her seat in the waiting area. I threw her a cross-eyed look before the tent flap snapped closed. Turning back I came up short, Vadoma was standing before me arms crossed. I looked down at the imposing figure that only came up to my shoulder (and that included the five inches of grey hair that stood on end). Her one good eye bore into me. I tried to avoid staring at the milky white one and gave an awkward smile that she didn't return. Which was probably a good thing, I didn't think her heavily lined face would take the sudden shift in direction.

She pointed a gnarled finger at me and spoke, her accent thickening the words. "Someding amusing you child?"

My eyes widened a little. "Ah…" I pointed at the tent flap we had just come through as if to blame it. "..I um. No, I guess…" I took in a lungful of hot tent air and tried not to gasp. "…No."

She started mumbling in another language and turned to limp her way further into the room. Reaching the small table in the centre she smacked the chair closest to me.

"Sit."

I didn't know if she was using her magic Hoo Haa on me or if she just had a very good way with people but I didn't want to disobey and quickly made my way to the chair. She paused to light a candle and placed it in the middle of the table next to an ornate black mirror. Moving back to avoid the heat from the flame I folded my legs into the cramped space under the table and watched as she wrestled with the folds of her shawl before taking the seat opposite me. How she wasn't melting under all those layers I had no idea.

She closed her eyes and took a deep breath. I looked around. Tash's reading had taken about ten minutes; screwing up my nose I gave a mental sigh and figured that was probably the standard. I tried to shift my legs into a more comfortable position but sweat had them sticking together, I shifted my weight to try and ease the velcro effect when my right knee shot up and bashed the underside of the table. Vadoma's eyes flew open and I quickly reached out to steady the teetering candlestick.

"I'm sorry I…"

"You got vorms gerl?"

I blinked at this question. "Uh, no."

"Vell sit still."

She closed her eyes again after giving me a warning look and I slapped a hand to my face, covering my mouth and pinching my nose in an attempt to stop the giggling that so desperately wanted to get me into more trouble. Closing my eyes I pulled myself together and lowered my hand, I took a couple of deep breaths and opened them to find her eye balling me again. I smiled internally, she saw right through me. I returned her glare with a serious look of my own which I guess satisfied her because she spoke again, her thick accent rolling her 'r's.

"Ready?"

I nodded and she turned her attention to the ink-like surface of the mirror, I remained as still as possible so as not to disturb her. Time seemed to slow and I sat there for what felt like ages, her breathing becoming deeper and slower. Leaning forward I thought she might have fallen asleep with her eyes open but then her breathing changed again, becoming sluggish and laboured. I leaned closer still, my hand hovering in the air between us, stuck between the fear of interrupting her again and the concern that she might be getting ready to keel over in front of me. She started mumbling quietly under her breath and I pulled my hand back quickly waiting for her to start talking to me but she kept on mumbling incoherently.

Feeling more and more uncomfortable, I started my escape plan. Twisting my neck around I looked back over my shoulder at the tent flap. If I could get up quietly enough, I had a shot at getting through the flap before she realised, then it was just a matter of grabbing Tash.

"PRRIMUMM!" Vadoma screeched.

My head twisted back around. "Whaaa?"

Her eyes snapped from the dark depths of the mirror to mine. There was something new there and I could have sworn it was fear.

"You must go. Go now. I vill not see for you. No more."

She blew out the candle and stood, covering the surface of the mirror with a piece of red cloth and turning to rummage through a drawer behind her. She turned back to me and pointed in a way that reminded me of an evil witch in one of the old Disney cartoons.

"You are cursed child."

My eyebrows skipped up, this was quite the show. I let her usher me with her bony fingers towards the waiting room. Halfway through the door she stopped and grabbed my hand pushing a worn cloth pouch into my palm and closing my fingers over it.

Eyes wide she pulled me close, "You must stay lost gerl, it is ze only vay."

The corners of my mouth twitched and she stepped back letting the tent flap fall closed between us.

"Okaaay." Turning on the spot I smiled at Tash and threw a thumb over my shoulder. "I think someone forgot their meds this morning."

"Shhh, Ana she will hear you!"

Tash gathered her shopping and we pushed our way through the opening flap of the tent and into the crowd. Thunder rumbled overhead and we both looked up, a fat drop of rain landed on my forehead. Blinking I wiped at it with my hand.

"Want to call it a night?"

Tash nodded. "That's going to be a big downpour."

Squealing, we burst through our front door just as the wall of rain hit. Tash dumped her bags and I made my way to my room to change. Kicking my shoes off into my cupboard I stripped and pulled my pyjamas out from under my pillow. Yanking my tank that doubled as a pyjama top on I heard a tell-tale rip.

"Crap." I twisted around like an unco ballerina to see what had given way. Lifting my right arm I found it. The side of my tank top had ripped from armpit to halfway down my ribcage. "Ah crap."

I shrugged my shoulders and headed back out into the lounge room, it was only me and Tash.

She smiled as I sat down on the couch next to her and pointed to the tear. "You okay?"

Leaning forward to grab a chip out of the packet she had just opened I nodded. "It's a new design." I popped the chip in my mouth and waved the sides of the tear. "Added cooling features."

Tash gave me a sideways look. "You're an idiot."

I grinned. "But you still love me; what does that make you?"

She gave a resigned sigh. "Some kind of sick masochist I'm sure."

She reached for the remote, and I pulled out my little pouch from Vadoma, emptying the contents into my palm. Five smooth stones fell out, catching the light and Tash's attention.

She paused in her button pressing. "What are those?"

I shrugged. "I dunno. Vadoma gave them to me. What was in yours?"

"My what?"

"The pouch thingy from the reading." I held mine up for inspection.

Tash shook her head. "I didn't get one." She let her jaw drop in indignation. "Why didn't she give me one?"

I tried not to laugh. "Tash, she's old, she probably just forgot."

"But that's not fair!"

I held mine out to her. "Want mine?"

She turned her attention back to the remote. "No, no. They were meant for you. I will, however be visiting Vadoma tomorrow and asking for *my* goodie bag."

She jabbed at the buttons and I put on a serious tone. "Want me to take her out."

She rolled her eyes and we both turned our attention to the television as "The Walking Dead" came on.

"Seriously Tash, I know someone that knows someone."

I gave her a sideways look and waggled my eyebrows. It had the desired effect and she giggled. "Shut up Ana."

Half way into the show I realised I hadn't taken anything in. I couldn't concentrate. My mind kept alternating between visions of teeth sinking into flesh and Vadoma's one-eyed glare. I grappled for rational thought and decided a good lecture was in order.

I did not see a Kudlak feeding from a woman in the middle of the street. It was dark and they had been a fair distance from me, so I definitely could not have seen what I thought I had seen.

The image of the bite flashed into my mind again and I dismissed it ruthlessly.

It was just a couple getting a little amorous. There was no-one else in the alley and absolutely nothing on the rooftops.

Satisfied I stared pointedly at the TV but it didn't take long for my thoughts to drift.

What if Vadoma knew there really was something different about me? That I wasn't normal, as normal as a Kresnik girl could be anyway. Maybe she's not the crazy. Maybe I am cursed.

I shifted in my seat but the questions kept rolling and I gave up all hope I had of watching the show.

If I am cursed then is there a way to get un-cursed? I would happily try anything, as long as it didn't involve getting naked and shaking my maracas in the light of a full moon.

I rolled my eyes at the image that conjured up and gave a self-deprecating smirk.

Who am I trying to kid? If getting crazed and naked was a sure-fire way to being normal, then pass the kooky sauce please and make it a double.

TWO

I pulled the pillow over my head in a vain attempt to block out the thumping sound that had woken me. Unfortunately, I hadn't purchased the pillow with any, "Early Morning Thump", sound-proofing features. Somebody should invent one of those. They would make a killing.

Blowing a few strands of hair from my face, I cracked one eyelid and squinted to check the time on the bedside table. The numbers 06:03 mocked me in eye-straining red. Snapping my eye shut I let out a sigh.

"May as well get up Anastasia, early bird and all that."

I didn't move.

It was Saturday and I don't actually eat worms, so there's no real value in being an early bird. The persistent thumping was impossible to ignore now. Rubbing a hand across my face I threw the covers back and heaved myself out of bed, shivering at the unusually cold morning. The rain last night had cooled everything down considerably and my shorts and singlet top where not going to cut it. My bare feet padded across the cold stone floor as I grabbed an over-sized jumper and pulled it on. Then, rummaging through my sock drawer, I retrieved a pair of long woollen socks that reached my knees. Pulling them on, I smiled and wiggled my toes in the soft warm wool.

Turning toward the window I caught a glimpse of my reflection in the full length mirror and grimaced. My ice green eyes looked groggy and I rubbed the sleep from them before fumbling through my drawer for a hair tie.

"Why do I always wake up looking like I have been shagging all night?"

My hair is and always will be the one thing that frustrates me about my appearance - long and dark with flashes of copper, it isn't straight but not curly either; like it can't quite make up its mind. Tash loves pointing out that it's just a reflection of me - a little bit wild, but I'm not buying. The rest of me is alright - my body is on the curvy side of fit and if I don't work out it has the tendency to get wide but I like running and working out with my two brothers, so that keeps things in check.

Finding an old elastic, I captured my hair back into a messy ponytail and made my way to the bedroom window, which was on the second floor of the old stone building where we lived. Tash and I have lived here for more than four years. The old building was one of the first in the region to have access to the internet and pay TV; two of the many perks from living in a military city with government funding. We live in Lumeer. Located near the Carpathian Mountain ranges on the Slovakian border (in the middle of nowhere) it's one of the oldest and most protected cities in Central Europe. Not to mention the most well hidden, thanks to the Department of External Affairs (DEA) and a few strings. Let's just say it's not on any GPS or Google Maps. Tash and I moved here from a neighbouring village after we finished College. Some people move out of the region altogether, the remoteness can be claustrophobic.

Kresniks who move away, settle into mainstream life with humans without any concern. Although physically dominant to humans, Kresniks are well educated and all find work within the communities in which they choose to live. I stayed in Lumeer because my family and friends are here and there is important work to do. Those that stay know what is at stake, and if everyone were to leave, well the consequences would be catastrophic.

I turned my attention back to the window. It overlooked the training ovals at the Kaul Military Barracks, just across the street. The Kaul, as our soldiers are known, train here every day, practising hand to hand combat and running through the ever-changing obstacle courses. I often sit here and watch them, even though for me, it is a bittersweet endeavor. I have wanted to be a member of the Kaul ever since I was a child and have emulated their training regime since moving to Lumeer. I'm fit but even if I could prove my physical abilities, it would be a waste of time. I can't change the fact that I am female and as such, I will never be allowed to be a member of the Kaul.

I rubbed at my eyes again.

"What the hell are they doing at this time of the morning?"

The thumping continued.

I was used to hearing the Kaul run through their training but this was totally different. Pushing the curtains aside, I leant forward and was stunned at the sight. It wasn't the imposing mountains that helped protect the region that was so impressive, although the remote and rugged landscape was spectacular even on a grey and misty morning such as this. It was the three Sikorsky Black Hawk Helicopters that were bearing down on Lumeer that had immediately caught my attention. Nose angled down and rotors blurred they were travelling at speed. The wing stubs had been deployed to cater for an armament of missiles and gun pods, the display of warfare was designed to intimidate and it worked.

Drawing level with the ovals they slowed their forward motion giving me a bird's eye view of the impressive machines; they were pitch black and had no markings or serial numbers that I could see. The tinted windows reflected the grey sky giving the impression of cold, stormy eyes. A shiver skipped up my spine.

"Lucky they are the good guys."

The steady thump of the rotor blades sent the trees surrounding the ovals into a wild bending frenzy, some of the younger saplings were starting to look more like Slinkies than trees. The morning mist swirled as the choppers started their descent. Intrigued, I sat on the smooth stone of the deep window sill. Reaching down I grabbed a couple of pillows off the floor for comfort - one to sit on and the other to put at my back so I could lean against the stone frame. Drawing my knees up to my chest I pulled the bottom of my jumper over my bare legs and waited. The lead chopper touched down and the side door flew open almost instantly.

"And who do we have here?"

As the second and third chopper landed to either side just behind the lead, several figures emerged from the belly of the first. All but one was clad in standard Kaul Battle Uniform. Smiling, I admired the men in their dark camouflage pants, black skin tight Tee's and big combat boots.

"Mmmm, I love that uniform."

I could make out five soldiers and one DEA Liaison. He was glaringly obvious in his dark suit as he struggled to keep his papers in order under the gust of the rotors.

"Well you're definitely human."

The occupants from the second and third chopper quickly grouped with the Kaul from the first. They all assembled in front of one Kaul, obviously of higher rank his stance alone screamed

Alpha which was eloquent, given the company he was keeping. His long arms were tanned, the strength in them obvious even from this distance. He addressed the group in what looked to be a very direct brief before giving a signal that had them all moving toward the Barracks. I leant forward, most Kaul were around six foot two or three but he was taller. I chewed at my lip absentmindedly and wondered what it would feel like to stand next to someone so tall.

My eyes flicked to the Liaison as he scurried to keep up with the group but he didn't hold my attention long. As if on their own accord, my eyes were drawn back to the lead Kaul, he was clearly dangerous and watching him was intoxicating. He covered the distance from the choppers in long powerful strides and there was a certain predatory edge to the way he moved that had me a little breathless.

"Who are you?"

At that moment he stopped and looked up in the direction of my window - almost as if he had heard me ask the question. The Kaul following obviously highly trained and alert, stopped instantly. One reached out and grabbed the Liaison by the collar to stop him from walking into their superior. My breath hitched but I didn't move from my perch. Surely there was no way he could see anything other than a dark shape at this distance.

Calling something over his shoulder he turned and continued. The Kaul instantly fell in step behind him. I watched as he disappeared into the Barracks, only then did I move again letting out my breath in a big whoosh.

"Wow."

Hearing Tash in the kitchen, I turned my attention back to the fact that it was just after six in the morning and I was awake. Sighing I turned to get off the window sill to search out some coffee. Too quick, I could feel one leg still trapped in my jumper as the other failed to find purchase. Arms flailing I hit the ground.

"Crap. Ouch!" I let my head fall back and glared at the ceiling. "I seriously should not be awake right now."

The door swung open and Tash came marching in wearing her Little Miss Clever pyjamas. "What on-," her expression instantly became one of amusement, as she tilted her head to the side and studied me. "Ana, why are you on the floor looking like a giant pretzel?"

I grinned, "It's a new style of Pilates. Wanna try it?" I patted the floor next to me in invitation.

Tash raised an eyebrow, "C'mon, the kettle just boiled."

I narrowed my eyes at her retreating form. "How anyone can be so chipper at this time in the morning is beyond me."

Disentangling myself I followed her into the kitchen. Flopping onto one of the seats at the breakfast bar, I rested my head in my hands and watched Tash flit about the kitchen, humming as she made the coffee.

Her long blonde hair was impossibly shiny and dead straight, the complete opposite of my own tangled mass. No matter what product Tash used, she had never been able to get body into it. There was an entire graveyard of failed curling irons somewhere, courtesy of that head of hair. Her face looked freshly scrubbed with just a hint of pink on her cheeks, giving her pale complexion a healthy glow. Tash was, as always, effortlessly beautiful.

"How do you wake up so, I don't know-" I waved my hand at her face, smiling in patient question. "Awake, every morning?"

Tash poured the coffee into two large mugs and pushed one across the counter at me. "Can't help it, I'm a morning person and you know what they say. The early bird catches the worm."

I smiled and reached for my mug, "I've discovered that's a flawed theory."

Tash stopped mid sip. "Huh?"

"Never mind!" I said shaking my head.

I wanted to see if Tash knew anything about the incoming Kaul. "Did you see the new arrivals?"

Nodding, Tash lowered her mug. "Mmm, yep. I didn't know they were scheduled, which is interesting."

I raised one eyebrow, "That *is* interesting."

Tash worked for the Council in the Archives Department. She had done so ever since we moved here. Her quick mind and good work ethic had seen her become invaluable to her superiors, so much so that they allowed her access to areas that were restricted to most. Her constant presence in these more secure areas tended to make her privy to conversations that perhaps she shouldn't be privy to. As a result, not much happened in Lumeer that Tash didn't know about ahead of time.

"Any ideas as to who they might be?"

She shook her head. "No, but it's definitely Elite Kaul with that kind of an entrance. And did you notice the Liaison?"

I scoffed, "How could I not, he stood out like a sore thumb." My curiosity was piqued. "Do you think this entourage was brought in as a result of what happened to Petar Lavric?"

Tash nodded as she turned to get some muesli from the pantry. "The Head of the Lavric Elite is murdered, within the city walls no less. The other Elite Families are more than a little concerned that one of their own could be picked off like that."

Tash held up the box of muesli in silent question. Shaking my head, I clutched my coffee and waited for her to continue.

She grabbed a bowl and poured some cereal for herself.

"We knew the Council was planning serious action and from the look of that, I would say that the big guns have just arrived at Lumeer."

21

THREE

Tash was rushing me out the door - again. "I know I had them on when I came home last night so they are here somewhere."

She moved into the room to help look. "What have you lost?"

"My sunnies and before you say that I won't -"

"They're on your head genius, now let's move it."

"Oh." I pulled them down, and grabbed my bag as she shooed me out the door. "We've got ages until the opening, stop stressing."

Tash pulled the door closed and threw me a look of disbelief over her shoulder. "You know that the fun starts well before the opening '*ceremony*'."

She made air quotes over the word ceremony and I couldn't help but smile. I love this girl like a sister but we are like chalk and cheese, it was just like her to work herself into a state over the opening of a Festival.

"I can't believe that you are not excited by the Festival."

We stepped out into the street heading for the Council Park.

"I didn't say I wasn't excited, it's just that I'm excited by the events as opposed to the politics."

She shrugged, "Fair enough."

The overnight rain had made the cobblestones slick in some parts and we picked our way around the wetter areas. The drains on this side of Lumeer weren't that great due to the extensive network of tunnels that snaked their way under the city streets and beyond. The Council were working on modernising the systems, as well as restoring some of the more neglected parts of town. The facades of the buildings had been the same for hundreds of years; all large and imposing medieval like stonework but over the last half century the insides had changed dramatically. The Kresnik people were embracing technology in all its wireless glory and loving it.

The streets were filling up with people making their way toward the festival activities, adults laughing and children splashing in puddles. The day promised to be fun for all. We joined the crowd and I couldn't help but let my mind wander to our early morning visitors. I might try and see if my brothers have heard anything about them. I was sure to bump into them at some point over the weekend. If I didn't, Tash would find out more about Petar Lavric's murder and the arrival of the mysterious Kaul when she got back to work on Monday. Patience wasn't one of my strong suits, but I could wait until then. Or at the very least make a genuine attempt.

Reaching the Park we collected a Festival Guidebook and I scanned the list of attractions. It looked as though the Council had gone to extra lengths to get people's minds off the recent tragedy. In addition to the usual stalls with hawkers competing against each other, they also had Kaul demonstrations scheduled throughout the entire four weeks. This news had me bouncing on the spot.

"How cool is this! The Kaul are doing demonstrations on just about everything." I stabbed at the page with my forefinger. "Look!

Look! They have everything here from cooking road-kill in a pit, to taking out your enemy from fifty yards."

"Ewww."

Tash leaned over my shoulder to get a better look at the guide as I quickly scanned the dates and times for anything with the word Kaul in it. My eyes skidded to a halt as they stumbled across my eldest brother's name - Kaul Archery Demonstration led by Lieutenant Dahrel Valinski. There was a blurb about how the Kaul still use the bow and arrow as one of their Impalement Arts but unfortunately it's not as popular these days due to the development of hardwood bullets that didn't splinter when fired from a conventional gun.

Tash must have read the same line as she gave a little groan. "Ana, don't start."

I love Archery, as does my entire family. Before my brothers left home to join the Kaul, we would spend most weekends in the forests surrounding our home practising. Once we were skilled enough, Dad let us hunt game for dinner. Not only was this physical, but the mental challenge could be intense. You need to be able to get close enough to your quarry to make a humane kill shot. When we didn't need to hunt for food, we would practise Combat Archery. This is kind of like Paint Ball but without the paint. We had special cushion-tipped arrows and light body armour but even with the cushion tips and armour, an arrow still hurts like a bitch.

When my brothers left to join the Kaul, I continued to shoot and hone my skills. They came home to visit a few times and were shocked when they realised I could kick their butts, or shoot their butts as was the case. My father gave me a beautiful bow for my twenty-first birthday. He hand crafted it and it is my most prized possession. He died almost a year ago now and if the house was burning down, my bow would be the first thing I would grab... after Tash of course.

"Ana?"

I knew what she was going to say. That there was no way the Kaul were going to let me compete and that I shouldn't draw attention to myself by kicking up a stink about it. I didn't want to hear it. I was already trying to figure out how I could convince Dahrel to let me shoot. The competition wasn't for a couple of weeks so I had time to work on him. I needed to give it my full attention which was something I couldn't do right now.

I turned to Tash who was eyeing me suspiciously and handed her the guidebook. "Okay, where to first?"

She ignored the book. "What? No rant about how The Kaul are sexist pigs and that they are doing the Kresnik society an injustice by upholding their archaic, 'No Women', rules?"

I shrugged and adopted a nonchalant pose, "They are a bunch of sexist pigs, as we all know. But there is nothing I can do about it right now so let's just enjoy the day."

Tash eyed me suspiciously but I guess she figured if I was willing to let the subject drop she should too.

Tash grabbed my arm and pulled me into the flow of traffic, smiling she called back over her shoulder to me. "The Official Opening will be starting soon and I want a good spot to see who's there."

Tash was always very interested in reading what was going on within Elite circles and she had a knack for knowing things before anyone else, sometimes even the Elite themselves.

We arrived at the centre of the park and found a stage had been assembled with seats arranged directly in front. The seated area had been roped off, obviously for Elite only.

The Elite are the Kresnik version of Royalty - carrying the genes that can produce male offspring with special powers. There were five Elite families originally, those born with the powers were referred to as Enlightened, or Veiled if you were old school. Enlightened Elite are all shown the utmost respect and as they are all born with iridescent icy blue eyes; they are not hard to spot.

I turned my attention back to the stage as a hush fell over the crowd, the Elite Lavric Family were arriving. The whispering masses parted as a sombre looking Travko, the new Lavric Head, led his family toward their seats. He was Enlightened and carried the Lavric families' power of healing living creatures, unfortunately for Travko's father, Petar Lavric, this power doesn't include bringing people back from the dead.

It was clear the new position of Lavric Head was weighing heavily on Travko. Shoulders sagging he wore what looked to be a very expensive suit, which didn't conceal his despair. He was mourning, whether it was the loss of his father, or the loss of his carefree, never-worked-a-day-in-his-life lifestyle, who knew. I had never been a big fan of Travko, all he had ever done was get drunk and flaunt his Elite position, basically behaving like a spoilt brat. His hair was oily and his Enlightened eyes, (which were always trying to find their way down women's tops) were just a bit too small for the rest of his head. It made my skin crawl.

If he had spent his time more constructively by joining the Kaul or becoming more involved in the Council, he may have been more prepared for what was to come. Still, I couldn't help but feel sorry him. His life has just been thrust into the spotlight and everyone was watching, eagerly waiting for him to fail in some spectacular fashion. Some of the Elite families could be ruthless with each other when they sensed weakness and the Lavric's are certainly not at the top of the food chain. Travko is the perfect example of a deer caught in the headlights, but I guess it's a Semi-Trailer of his own making.

His mother was dressed dramatically head to toe in black and I watched as Alexis Vidmar move to convey her sympathies while her husband, Drago, Head of the Elite Vidmar family, zeroed in on Travko. I heard Tash making a disapproving humming noise as Drago threw an arm over Travko's hunched shoulders and whispered in his ear.

Thanks to Tash I knew a little about the politics of Council and I knew that this wasn't the comforting support of a family friend but a play for power by one of the most manipulative family heads on the Council. The Vidmars were ruthless when it comes to climbing the proverbial ladder, and this was a golden opportunity for them to try and get a leg up. The driving force behind their deceitful behaviour was their power. The Vidmar Elite can gain impressions from touching objects or people to determine their history. Sounds pretty cool but when compared to the other family powers, this one was by far the weakest. Not that you would ever say that to a Vidmar.

Vladimir and Sonja Preseren arrived at the roped off area and the Vidmars instantly moved back, allowing them room to speak with the Preserens briefly before taking their seats in the front row. The subtle show of submission was evidence of the unspoken ranking within the Council and how control revolves heavily around each family's power. The Elite Preseren has the ability to create and control fire. This power makes them a formidable force on the battle field and their ability makes them highly valued warriors within the Kaul.

My favourite power by far was the Drevenseks. I say *was* because the last of their line died about twenty years ago. They had the power to change the appearance of objects and surroundings. This was how we initially kept wayward travellers from stumbling upon Lumeer. Now we use other methods to divert travellers, but with the advancements in technology and the assistance of the Department of External Affairs it is easy to make Lumeer disappear.

The Elite family member stood as one, I could just make out a couple moving slowly among them to take their positions.

The Bravnicas had arrived.

They have the scariest power of all, the ability of mind control. They can communicate using telepathy, completely wipe your memories or even insert their thoughts into your mind. There are crazy stories of people throwing themselves out of windows or getting lobotomised just by a look. Nobody has ever been able to back up these claims and anyone with a rational thought in their head knows it's a load of crap. But at the same time, the Bravnica's have never gone out of their way to quell any of the rumours. Either way no one messes with them. They are the most powerful of all the Elite families and as such they head up the Council and the Kaul. The Elite head of the Bravnica Family is our Emir - Ruler of the Kresnik people.

Tash bumped me out of my musings. She was on tip toes trying to see over the crowd. This is the part she really comes to see, the interaction between the Elite families. I am always amazed at what information she can gather by simply observing.

The day was heating up and the rain from the night before was making it steamy. I couldn't wait for this to be over so that I could get out of this jumble of sweaty people. I could hear the tech guys doing final sound checks on the stage and knew that we were running out of time. I spied one of the old park trees just to the left of the stage and made a beeline for it. Its base was encircled by an old stone ring people used to sit on to take advantage of the tree's shade. We climbed up to stand on the ring and get a better view. I smiled as a cool breeze hit us once we were above the crowd. Reaching up I quickly pulled out my ponytail and twisting my hair into a messy bun, let the fresh air tickle the back of my neck.

I couldn't help my sigh of relief, "Oh, that is so much better."

Tash's attention was on the roped off area. Travko was helping his mother to her seat. The rest of the families were settled and talking quietly amongst each other, some using their Festival guides to fan themselves. There was movement at the front and everyone's attention turned to the beautiful woman ascending the stairs to the stage. Tressilia Vidmar was the eldest daughter of Elite Head Drago Vidmar, Prom Queen, voted, 'Most Likely to Succeed' and complete bitch.

Our mutual dislike started years ago, when I dumped a bucket of horse shit over her head. She had been making fun of Tash's second-hand dress and so deserved it. Tash and I have been besties ever since and Tressilia our nemesis. Dramatic, I know.

I watched as she strutted across the stage flicking her hair so that it landed just so. Seriously, there must be some sort of school they send these girls to that teaches the art of the hair flick. If I were to try it, I would just end up with a mouth full. Not attractive.

Clearing her throat daintily, she did a quick finger wave to someone in the Elite area before pasting a brilliant smile on her face and turning her attention to the crowd.

I pulled my sunnies down from their perch atop my head and mumbled under my breath. "Seriously, those teeth should come with a UV rating."

Tash shooshed me as Tressilia started her speech.

"Esteemed members of the Elite, Ladies and Gentleman, thank you for allowing me to welcome you all to this year's Daska Festival."

Good lord this was going to be painful.

"My family, the Vidmar Elite, have the honour of hosting the Festival this year and we trust that you will enjoy yourselves during our month long celebration."

She paused to smile and acknowledge the applause from some of the Elite. I looked skyward.

"However, in all the merriment, it is easy to forget the true meaning behind the Daska Festival."

Here we go. She couldn't just cut a bloody ribbon could she?

"The Daska Festival is held in honour of Daska and the birth of the Kresnik people. In the days of the Gods, Daska our Sun God, loved to play in the underworld at night."

I smiled to myself. *My kind of God.*

"He danced and played with all the beings from the underworld and returned to the warmth and safety of the sun during the day."

Tressilia looked up to the sun and smiled adoringly, making her look even more beautiful. She was loving this attention.

"He was very powerful and soon his brother Draku, the God of Night, became jealous. Draku wanted to play on the other side as Daska so easily did and so began to plot against his brother to steal his powers."

Some small children squealed. They all knew the story and at what point they should be shocked.

"Daska discovered Draku's plans and became enraged that his brother would steal from him. So, to keep his powers safe he decided to hide them. Creating five men, he split his powers and instilled a fifth into each man. Charging them with the task of protecting the powers from the underworld at all cost and to destroy any that would attempt to steal them."

I couldn't help but roll my eyes. She was starting to work the crowd up, ensuring a big applause.

"The five men of Daska were our forefathers, the first of the Kresnik race." She waved a hand at the roped off area. "The Elite families are their direct descendants. We still hold the gift of

Daska's power and we still fight to keep them safe and we will destroy any who try to take them from us!"

The crowd cheered loudly, even Tash was smiling and clapping. I found it interesting that Tressilia had failed to mention the little part about Draku getting really pissed when he figured out that Daska had outwitted him. In retaliation, he created five beings of his own to scour the Earth at night in search of Daska's men and his powers. The five beings of Draku were the first of the Kudlak. vampires - mortal enemy of the Kresnik people and basically anything with a heartbeat.

I turned my attention back to the stage just in time to catch the last of Tressilia's performance.

"I declare this year's Daska Festival officially open!"

"Thank Daska." I let out a dramatic sigh that was drowned out by the cheering crowd.

Tressilia turned and pulled a string releasing hundreds of helium balloons into the atmosphere.

Way to keep a low profile guys.

I hopped off the stone bench as the crowd started to disperse. This was the part Tash loved, she would casually wait around to see if anything interesting happened between the Elite families but my stomach was making some serious demands. I rubbed it to ease the grumbling.

"Can we go? I have a hankering for a Hot Dog."

Tash pulled a face. "I don't know how you can eat those things. Do you know what's actually in them?"

"I don't think anyone does to be honest."

"You are seriously gross Ana."

She looked over to where the Elite were busy congratulating Tressilia.

"There's nothing going on here, we may as well go and have some lunch."

We turned back toward the centre of the park in search of a Hot Dog for me and something identifiable for Tash.

We cleared the narrow row of congested bodies and our attention was immediately caught by a large group of Kaul parading in full battle uniform. The steady thump of big booted feet marching in five impressive lines had the crowd parting before them. Each line represented one of the Elite families and was headed up by a flag bearer holding each family's crest aloft. A large crowd started gathering to watch and people bumped for position to get a better view. The flag bearers separated, leaving their respective lines and moved to form a large circle around the group of warriors who held the now silent audience captive with anticipation. As one, the flag bearers brought their staffs down, slamming the ground and on queue each Kaul turned to face another and an amazing display of sparring ensued. The crowd gasped and squealed as the Kaul circumnavigated the circle in an incredible display of strength and skill that was controlled but deadly. The suppressed power of the men as they moved around each other was palpable - it bubbled just below the surface of tanned skin and honed muscle. The efficiency with which they commanded their bodies was precise - not one step taken that hadn't been considered, not one blow delivered that wasn't calculated. It was clear that we were only seeing the very tip of what they were capable off.

I stood on my toes to get a better view and Tash was right beside me grinning broadly.

"Do we know any of them?"

"I think I recognised a couple of my brother's friends but they're moving so fast I can't be sure."

I felt her take a deep breath beside me. "Gosh it's amazing having so many Kaul in one place."

She was right. Lumeer was our Capital, the home of the Kresnik race but still, I had never seen so many Kaul in the city before. I had a feeling the current influx wasn't just down to the Daska Festival though.

Kaul are stationed in nearly every country on the planet. Some live on the fringes of society in small units protecting the general populous. Some are in the middle of large cities doing the same and then there are those posted on protection details with higher ranking officials and Elite families. Either way they are all brought up and trained to do the same thing. Fight the same evil. The Kaul warriors are the last line of defense in the battle against the Kudlak.

The flag bearers slammed their staffs into the ground again and the sparring instantly stopped. I was amazed when each Kaul turned from their opponent and the five lines were formed again. People in the crowd started clapping as the flag bearers made their way back to the front of the lines. Then, as one the procession marched off to the cheers of the wowed crowed. I moved closer to get a better view of the retreating butts and put my fingers to my mouth to let out an earsplitting wolf whistle.

"Ana!" Tash slapped me playfully, "Seriously, that is embarrassing."

"'Don't try and tell me you didn't appreciate that display of…. virileness."

"Ana, that isn't even a word."

I raised an eyebrow in challenge. "Oh that is *so* a word, and there was so much virileness going on there," I waved a hand at the exiting Kaul. "I can't even get my head around it."

She gave me a sideways look as we continued our way to the heart of the park. "Well there is a lot to be said about those big black boots."

I started laughing, "Ha! See!" I pointed an accusing finger at her. "You, Natasha Kovak, are a closet perve!"

She waved me off, "Don't be ridiculous."

I leaned in, "Your boot fetish is ridiculous."

The rest of the day was spent being entertained by talented musicians, magicians and weirdly flexible acrobats. By late afternoon my enthusiasm was fading fast due to my lack of sleep the night before. I left Tash with some work friends and headed home for an early night.

My head felt fuzzy as my mind dragged its way into consciousness the following morning.

"I need coffee."

Sitting up I swung my legs over the side of my bed and grimaced at the mirror across the room. Running my fingers through my hair I made a half arsed attempt at trying to make it look semi neat before shrugging.

"Whatever."

Entering the kitchen I realised we had company and instantly wished I had tried a little harder with the hair.

"Big night little sister?"

I rolled my eyes at my eldest brother Dahrel and grabbed a mug to fill with wake-up-juice.

"Why are you in my house?"

"Do I need to have a reason to visit you?"

"No, but there is a reason and it's too early to be beating around any bushes." I sat down at the breakfast bench and took a sip of coffee.

Waiting for a response, I regarded Dahrel over the rim of my mug as he raided the pots and pans cupboard and started helping himself to the fridge.

"You know there is a kitchen at the barracks."

He flashed me a cheeky grin and continued pottering about. Tash walked in the room looking like she had been up for hours. As she passed the lounge I realised my brother wasn't our only visitor. Regarding me lazily as he lounged casually on the sofa was Yari. My hand flew to my hair as he rose from the chair in one fluid motion and crossed the room.

"Oh. Hi Yari, I didn't realise you were here too."

He opened his mouth to speak but stopped and tilted his head to the side. Reaching out he hooked a finger through the tear at the side of my tank and let it skip lightly down my ribcage. I jumped off the stool. Face flush as I remembered the gaping hole in the side of my top. He raised a wicked brow as I grabbed the two sides and held them together.

"You need help with that 'Lil Bit?"

Dahrel made no attempt to hide his laughter as I crab-walked my way back to my room. Closing my door on their chuckles I heard Yari speak.

"So that's why they teach us to sew."

I rolled my eyes as their chuckles erupted to laughter.

Yari had been best friends with both my brothers since they were kids and we saw him at our place almost every week for dinner from as far back as I can remember. My parents welcomed him and loved him as if he were their own. From the boy who used to pull my pigtails, to the man that was now a trained warrior, our future together was planned well before we knew what being 'Promised' really meant. Our feelings on the matter were changing rapidly though and it kinda helped that he was drop-a-gallon-of-hot-sauce-down-my-pants gorgeous. He was over six feet tall with sandy brown hair and a face that was nearly too perfect. Then there was that grin, it was the epitome of cheek and sex and had the girls falling over themselves at his feet.

Rolling my eyes at the thought, I grabbed a loose T-shirt and pulled it over my ruined tank top before planting myself in front of the mirror to try and do something with the birds nest atop my head. After several failed attempts, I gave up and pulled it into a ponytail. I know the whole ponytail thing is a little juvenile, but when you have a head of hair like mine you take what you can get. Feeling much more presentable I walked back into the kitchen to find Dahrel cooking bacon and eggs.

"You had better be making enough for everyone."

Dahrel smiled as he reached across the bench and playfully tried to muss up my hair. I ducked out of his reach.

"You're getting slow in your old-", my retort was cut short by the wash cloth that I had not seen coming.

Having just turned thirty-four Dahrel was getting more and more sensitive about his age, not that he needed to worry. Being a Lieutenant in the Kaul Army kept you extremely fit. He was about half a foot taller than me and had dark hair and a crooked nose from too many breaks. It didn't deter the women though. Every time we went for a night out he had a new one on his arm. I gave up trying to keep track of their names years ago.

Picking up my coffee I turned to sit at the table where Tash was telling Yari about how she didn't get any Hoo Haa stones. Returning Yari's smile I sat down and sipped quietly at my coffee while Tash gave him a blow by blow of our visit with Vadoma. I felt his glance touch my face every now and again but kept my attention firmly on Tash. Her story came to an abrupt end when Dahrel arrived at the table holding one of Tash's china serving platters that are only used for VIP's.

The Valinskis are a lot of things - VIP's not being one of them. I watched as Tash's eyes nearly popped out of her head. Jumping up she gently removed the platter from Dahrel and placed it delicately on the table. Her struggle with the need to be polite to my brother who had just cooked us all breakfast and the compulsion to whisk her precious platter away and replace it with the plastic one we usually use, was obvious. I handed her the tongs so that she could serve the boys and make sure no one chinked the china while I turned my attention to Dahrel.

"So do we know any more about what happened to Petar Lavric?"

Dahrel and Yari shared a look. It was clear they were debating what to tell us and I raised my eyebrows in invitation.

Yari gave a shrug, "They're gonna hear about it sooner or later."

I put my cutlery down and stared at Dahrel. "What?"

Dahrel let out a long suffering sigh. "There are rumours circulating at the moment that Petar was killed by a Kudlak."

Tash dropped the piece of bacon she was serving to Yari. "That's impossible."

Yari grabbed the bacon off the table and took a bite. I felt his eyes search my face. He was waiting for my reaction but I was too busy with the memory of teeth and flesh to pay him much heed.

I heard Dahrel answer Tash, his voice sounded disembodied, as if speaking from a distance.

"Well the crime scene shows evidence of an attack. I don't want to go into detail with you two but let's just say it was violent. The injuries sustained by Petar, the strength it would take." He shook his head slowly. "Only a Kudlak could do that."

"Ana?" I looked up as Yari spoke. "You okay?"

Dragging myself back to the present I swiped at my fringe.

"Sure, I'm fine. That's just a bit crazy you know, a Kudlak running around the city."

Dahrel picked up a piece of bacon and waived it in my direction.

"Let's just be clear, there is no Kudlak running around the city. I don't want you girls to get hysterical over this, there are teams in place working round the clock hunting for Petar's killer and protecting the city, which brings me to my point." He looked directly at me.

And here comes the reason for breakfast.

"What are your plans for the next few weeks?"

I tried to look as casual as possible. "I actually have a pretty full schedule. Why do you ask?"

Tash cleared her throat and looked at me accusingly. I actually had no plans, but a girl is entitled to a little privacy. Dahrel dismissed my reply with the ease that only an older brother can master.

"I have some great news! You know how you got fired from your last job?"

Tash groaned as I choked on my coffee. "Uh, yeah."

It's kind of hard to forget the humiliation of being sacked in the middle of a restaurant full of people. Apparently slapping a plate of spaghetti sauce in the lap of a customer is not acceptable, even if said customer is a dirty old man with wandering hands.

Dahrel barely waited for my response. "Well I have managed to score you a temp position as an Admin Assistant for the Kaul."

Tash squealed and my mouth dropped open. This was not what I was expecting. Ignoring Tash's excited looks I eyeballed Dahrel.

"Ah, what exactly does an, 'Admin Assistant', do?"

"Oh it's nothing too hard. You will have no problems doing the job."

A smiling Tash got up from the table to remove her platter to safer grounds.

I raised my eyebrows and let sarcasm win. "Gee bro, thanks for the vote of confidence."

He gave me an annoyed look, obviously I was not supposed to interrupt his little spiel.

"With the arrival of so many Kaul Elite, the Council needs a few people to assist with errands and admin work. It's only until they are able to wrap up the Lavric investigation and head back to their postings, but it should be good experience. And you never know it might lead to something."

To say I was stunned would be an understatement. This was a fantastic opportunity and probably the closest I would ever get to become an actual member of the Kaul.

Tash turned to Dahrel. "Do you know if she will be based at the Barracks or at the Council?"

Dahrel shrugged. I hadn't even said yes yet, but there was no stopping her now.

"Oh how cool will that be if you're at Council, then we can do lunch and coffee." Her voice was rising an octave every second word. "Oh, my, Daska." Tash raced toward my bedroom. "We have to figure out what you are going to wear."

Sighing I listened as Tash rifled her way through my cupboard. As a girl I'm a bit of a failure, call me crazy, but I just can't get excited over clothes.

"Well, my work here is done." Dahrel dropped a card on the table and went out of his way to slap Yari on the back as he sauntered to the door. I inspected the card. It had details of where I needed to be on Monday morning and who I had to report to.

"Don't be late."

I looked up and caught his playful wink as he made good his escape.

I shook my head and leaned back in my chair smiling. "He always manages to leave without helping to clean up." The kitchen was a disaster. "Seriously, how many pots do you need to cook bacon and eggs?"

Yari's chair legs scraped as he stood and started gathering plates.

"Thanks."

I followed him into the kitchen with an armload and handed them to him as he rinsed them off in the sink and stacked them into the dishwasher.

"You don't have to do that."

He smiled at me and straightened from placing a plate in its rack. "I know."

He stepped closer and I backed up a little harder against the kitchen bench, looking up I wished I had brushed my teeth as he leaned closer. He reached one arm behind me and I smelt the spicy tang of his aftershave as he closed the gap between us, then giving me a cheeky grin he backed away, pulling a dirty plate out from behind me and stacking it in the dishwasher.

"But I figure you owe me now."

Face a little flush I cleared my throat, "Oh really, how so?"

"Well now that I have cleaned your kitchen for you, I think you should take me out to the movies."

I let one eyebrow raise in question and he moved toward me again, this time taking my hips in his hands and pulling me to him. Lowering his face he rested his forehead on mine.

"You know, as a way for you to say thanks."

This was typical Yari, all confidence and sex appeal. We were still in the very early stages of our courtship and so far I had spent most of my time trying to stop my head from spinning while he spent all of his time trying to spin it. I swear all he wanted to do was make me blush. Giving me his sexy half smile he leaned down and my breath caught as I realised he was going to kiss me.

"So Ana, what do you think of these colours?"

Yari let out a small groan as he turned his head toward Tash who was standing in the lounge room holding up a bunch of clothes. Oblivious to what she had just interrupted she continued on.

"I think the winter colours suit you best, which is good because bold colours like this are very powerful in the corporate world."

Yari let his hands fall from my hips and took a step back. "Anyone ever told you your timing is a little off?"

Tash looked up from a pantsuit. "Huh?"

He smiled and shook his head. "Nothing. I'll ah, leave you two to your clothing... stuff." He gave me a sucks-to-be-you look as I walked with him to the door.

"Yeah thanks for that."

Tash didn't miss the sarcasm. "Hey, you will thank me in the morning."

Yari gave a chuckle and ducked out the door.

"Deserter!" I muttered as the latch clicked behind him.

I suffered through the wardrobe shenanigans with good grace for over an hour. Tash had coordinated five outfits for the week and was very pleased with herself.

I voted for a break.

Pulling on my running gear and grabbing my iPod I passed her on my way back out the door.

"I need a run, will be back in an hour or so." I didn't wait for her reply as I inserted my earphones and pulled the door closed behind me.

Kelly Rowland sang *Work* as I rounded the final bend of my 10 kilometre track and could see the park ahead. My legs felt like lead but I commanded them to make one final push. I hit the stop button on my watch as I passed my tree and slowed my pace to a walk, looking down to check my time. 62:38. *Damn.* My chest heaved as I sucked in great lungfuls of air. Apparently beating an hour is only possible after having a huge fight with one of my brothers or being sacked in an embarrassing manner. Shaking my legs out, I made my way toward the centre of the park, smiling at the occasional runner on my way. Pulling the bottom of my t-shirt up I used it to wipe the sweat from my eyes. The park was abuzz with people walking their dogs and families playing games on the manicured lawns. I stopped under the shade of a tree, balancing on one foot and lifting the other behind me to stretch.

"Heads!"

I straightened up and my teeth clattered together as my brain shifted in my skull. The sound of the impact took its time to reach my brain and I blinked back starbursts to clear my vision.

"What the hell?"

FOUR

Grabbing the back of my head I spun to see what the projectile had been. A soccer ball was rolling to a lazy stop beside one of the park benches nearby. Anger flared and rationale fled as I yanked out my earphones and stormed over to the bench. Picking up the offending ball, I thought how satisfying it would be to puncture it.

"Sorry about that."

I turned ready to let loose on the irresponsible owner of the ball but the words caught in my throat. The figure approaching had broken away from a group of guys playing soccer. Clad only in a pair of shorts he casually jogged over, oblivious to the stares as he snagged the attention of every woman he passed. The way he moved screamed Kaul. He smiled and offered a casual wave as he drew nearer, causing my stomach to do a couple of somersaults. Giving myself a mental slap I planted my feet and took a deep breath. Steadying my temper I watched his approach and tried desperately not to be impressed. He was well over the average height for a Kaul, with dark hair and a physique that was the obvious product of some serious and regular workouts. I found myself wondering what kind of training could produce a body like that when I realised he had been speaking to me.

"Are you okay?"

It took a second for my brain to kick back into gear. Feeling like I was already on the back-foot I went on the offense.

Willing my voice to come out without squeaking, "What the hell are you guys doing?" A little bit husky, but certainly no squeaking. Given the circumstances I was quite pleased but cleared my throat all the same.

"Look, I'm really sorry." He indicated over his shoulder. "My guys were just…"

"Not thinking is what they were doing."

He looked taken aback and to be honest I was a little shocked at my own temper. I tried to hide it by brushing angrily at stray piece of fringe that was determined to get in on the action.

"Do you realise this is a public park?" He opened his mouth to speak but I cut him off unable to stop my little tirade. "There are children in this park. What if this had hit one of them?" I held out the offending ball for his inspection.

He looked at the ball and then back at me, hands palm up and out to the side he took a slow and measured step forward. The movement forced me to look up even further, it unnerved me a little but I refused to step back, instead I raised my eyebrow and glared at his dark sunglasses.

He smiled and lowered his voice to a soothing tone. "Look I am really sorry."

I nearly melted into a puddle of self-righteous goo.

"Some of my guys have been travelling for most of the day and I was just trying to give them a stretch before reporting for duty tomorrow."

I found myself becoming distracted, suddenly mesmerised by the journey of a little bead of sweat as it snaked it's way slowly down his tanned six pack, changing speeds as his lungs stretched his chest. Expanding and contracting it slipped and slid its way down, when it disappeared into the dark snail trail that was cut short by his waistband I realised I had been staring. Snapping my eyes up I caught the tail end of a grin that he quickly hid.

He took another step forward and raised a hand toward my head. "I hope you aren't hurt."

He was barely a foot from me now and I could feel the heat radiating from his chest.

Red faced I stepped back. "I'm fine."

He dropped his hand and retraced his step, obviously aware of my retreat.

Oh Daska could you please organise a sinkhole, nothing too spectacular, just big enough to swallow me whole?

I could hear his group of Kaul calling for him to hurry up so that they could continue on with their game. He waved them off without turning from me.

"Ok, well, I'm really glad you weren't hurt."

"Of course I'm not hurt, it's just a ball." I held it out to prove it.

He looked at the ball again and the edges of his mouth twitched. "Okay."

Swallowing hard I tried to regain some semblance of control and shrugged in a dismissive manner.

"Okay then."

His lips were full and looked soft in contrast to the harsh angles of the rest of his face.

Get a grip Ana.

Closing my mouth I sensed his amusement and felt my face flush brilliantly as those sinful lips turned into a full blown grin. I now had a new definition of sexy.

"So um, can I have my ball back now? Please?"

I gave myself a mental shake. *Oh Daska please, right now, sink hole, you can do it...*

Nothing.

Nodding in a self-deprecating manner, I formed a smile that felt more like a grimace and threw the ball back at him. Hard. He caught it with a satisfying exhale of breath and shot me a knowing grin.

I raised my eyebrows, daring him to say something but he took the higher road, raising the ball and smiling. "Thanks."

I wanted to say something that would wipe that melt-an-iceberg smile right off his face but realised that I should just quit, even though I wasn't ahead. So swiping at my fringe again I nodded a dismissal and made my retreat. Shaking his head he turned, I could hear him chuckle behind me as he re-joined his group.

I let out a breath.

Could you have made a bigger fool of yourself Ana? I think not. Well done girl.

I started for home ignoring the little thrill that had taken up residence in my belly.

Having spent the afternoon completely distracted, I gave up and decided there was nothing for it but a cold shower. Alas this did not cool my inner turmoil. A cluster of emotions were currently rampaging through my body and it seemed blind lust was heading up the riot. Determined to ignore it I dried myself quickly, pulled my pajamas on and wrapped my wet hair in a towel. Tash was cooking a stir fry and it smelt amazing. Food - the perfect distraction.

Smiling at me as I entered the room she indicated to my bowl. "You know Ana, when it comes to food your timing is impeccable."

She grabbed some chop sticks and I grabbed a fork before settling ourselves on the couch to eat while I told the story about my meeting in the park. When I got to the part where I got hit in the head with a ball Tash lost it.

I raised my eyebrow at her, "Seriously Tash, it wasn't that funny."

She looked at me with tears in her eyes and nodded. "I can just picture you standing there."

I rolled my eyes and finished the story, ignoring her little snorts as she tried to calm down. Smiling and dabbing her eyes dry with a tissue she turned to me.

"Oh, wow. Ok I'm good now." She cleared her throat. "So do you know who he was?"

I shook my head. "No idea. Never seen him before in my life and he's not someone you would forget in a hurry."

She cocked her head to the side in typical Tash style. "Okay, so he must be from out of town. Ooh ooh I know". She pointed at me with a chopstick. "Did he have an accent?"

"No, but to be honest I was not really paying too much attention to what he was saying."

Tash rolled her eyes. "I can't believe you told him off." She paused. "Actually scratch that - I can."

I groaned, "I must have sounded like a complete psycho."

Tash nodded.

I dropped my fork. "Uh, hello! Best friend, you are supposed to say 'Oh I'm sure it wasn't that bad' or something equally supportive."

She smiled at me. "No, I think you nailed it with 'psycho'."

I let my head fall into my hands. "Oh Daska how embarrassing, I am such an idiot!"

Tash gave me a sympathetic look. "Hey, don't stress about it. With the amount of Kaul in Lumeer at the moment, the chances of you actually seeing this guy again are very slim."

I nodded - it was no doubt for the best. I had enough going on in my life at the moment without throwing in a heart crushingly gorgeous Kaul.

"So did it hurt?"

I was busy with the memory of his sweat bead and missed her question. "Hurt?"

I looked up as Tash started giggling again. "The ball!"

I shook my head but couldn't help smiling. "Oh someone needs to slap the silly out of you in one hit."

Arriving for work at the Council Chambers the next morning I was totally awed. The building stood on a podium of deep stone stairs that encompassed its circumference. Two massive oak doors guarded the entrance, they looked like they weighed at least a ton each and I shook my head feeling for the poor sod that had to open and close those things at the beginning and end of each day. Taking a deep breath I looked down at the card Dahrel had given me for what must have been the hundredth time since waking this morning.

"C'mon Ana, you can do this." Straightening my shoulders I exhaled and crossed the imposing threshold.

The reception area did nothing to quell my nerves. I stopped dead as the staccato of hurried feet bounced from the gleaming tiled floors and reverberated around the room, which was as you would expect, massive. The ceiling was so high I had to squint to make out the ornate decoration that had been carefully carved into the stone hundreds of years ago. The history these walls had witnessed was so evident I could have easily closed my eyes and gone back in time. But now was not the time to stand around gawking like a star-struck commoner, I followed the flow of bodies as we made our busy way to the lifts.

The call button for the lift had already been pressed when I arrived so I stood against the wall and studied the jumble of suits. They all seethed with sophistication. There were businessmen and council representatives in Armani suits looking very slick and women who looked like they could bust corporate balls simply by raising an eyebrow. The lift arrived with a pleasant, 'ding', and we all hustled our way into the cramped space. I caught a glimpse of myself in the mirrored glass and was thankful for the effort Tash had made with my wardrobe. My charcoal suit may have been itchy, but I blended in well and so was happy to suck it up. As I squeezed myself into a corner I practically dislocated my neck trying to make sure that level 3 had been pressed before the doors closed. Whilst not meeting anybody's eye, I tried blending in. A sign above the floor buttons advised that this lift could hold 16 persons. I let out an involuntary snort and instantly flushed crimson as the gentleman next to me looked down his nose. I gave a weak smile and indicated toward the sign.

"Sixteen midgets with acrobatic tendencies maybe."

His lip curled, like literally curled as he rolled his eyes and tried to shuffle as far as the space would allow away from me.

Oookaay, note to self Ana, do not have any fun. The doors opened and closed and thankfully Mr. Serious and most of the other official looking people had exited the lift by the time it dinged on level three. I stood back letting everyone else exit first before stepping out into what looked like a scene from minority report. I groaned.

"Dahrel what have you gotten me into?"

I turned to my right and watched as my fellow lift passengers entered through a set of large glass doors. Quietly I waited till the door had closed behind them all and gathered my wits.

"Don't stuff this up Ana. Listen with your ears, not your mouth."

Lifting my chin I grabbed the handle and pulled. The doors refused to open and shook violently as I tugged and my already crimson face did the impossible and turned an even darker shade of what could only be described as complete mortification. I let go of the doors and stood back looking for a bell or something that I could ring. All I could see was some kind of strip that looked like you had to swipe a card through. Did I have a magic swipey card? No.

People moved about on the other side of the glass doors, all looking very busy and not so much as glancing in my direction. I started to wave frantically to gain someone's attention.

Nothing.

Looking at my watch again panic set in, it was after nine.

"Oh this has got to be one of your worst starts yet Ana."

Closing my eyes and wishing for a miracle I tugged one last time on the doors when a friendly looking girl, about my age glanced in my direction. I waved and she smiled giving a quick little nod to indicate that she had seen me.

"Oh thank Daska."

I tried to smooth down my hair and tugged at my skirt to make sure it was sitting properly. My saviour dumped a pile of papers on a desk and moved to the door. Extracting a magic swipey card from the folds of her very stylish jacket, she buzzed me in with a brilliant smile.

"Hi there! My name is Sierra. I am the Emir's Executive Assistant."

I was still a little dazzled by her welcome but shook the proffered hand.

"I'm Anastasia Valinski."

She stood there expectantly and I felt compelled to explain myself.

"My friends call me Ana… It's my first day."

She gave a little chuckle and then made a sweeping motion with her hand for me to enter. "Come on in Ana."

I liked her already. I followed behind as Sierra retrieved her stack of papers and navigated her way through the maze of desks and hurrying bodies. She looked back to make sure I was keeping up and smiled.

"I'll take you to the breakout room first. You can dump your bag and then I'll give you a quick tour."

I nodded but was only listening with half an ear. The main office was amazing. The opposite side to the tricky glass doors was flanked by a row of windows that had been shaded with block-out blinds. As we headed to one end of the rectangular shaped room, I glanced back to see a group of Kaul in full uniform studying LCD screens that showed maps with various locations marked with red dots. I was stunned to see them manipulate the screens with deft flicks of their hands. The technology in this room was incredible.

Bumping into Sierra I realised I should probably be watching where I was going. "Sorry."

She gave me an understanding smile. "It's cool." Her eyes flicked over my shoulder at the screens on the opposite wall. "I walked around here like a stunned mullet for the first few days. It is extremely impressive but like all things, you get used to it."

She dropped off the paperwork at a nearby desk and then headed through a door at the end wall.

"This is the kitchen area." She waved an elegant hand at one end of the room. "You're welcome to help yourself to Tea or Coffee, there are usually some nice biscuits too but you have to get in quick if you want the creamy centred ones." She gave me a conspiring look and lowered her voice. "The big tough Kaul have a curious penchant for them."

I returned her mock serious manner. "Oh I can be pretty quick when it comes to food."

She beamed, "Excellent, you will fit right in then."

She led me to the ladies and gave me a locker for my bag then we headed back out to the main room. She indicated to the open doorway on the opposite wall.

"That hallway leads to the debriefing room and some smaller meeting rooms. There is also a copy room there that you will no doubt become familiar with." She gave me a smile. "The Kaul love paperwork. And at the far end of the hall are Commander Bravnica's rooms."

I gave an involuntary gasp. "Commander Bravnica comes into this office?"

"Yep. You will meet him later."

I had never seen the eldest Bravnica, Dominik, before but I had heard a lot about him from my brothers as they rave about his courage and the respect he shows his Kaul. I'd heard countless times how his men would quite happily lay down their lives for him without batting an eye lid and that that kind of devotion can only be inspired by a truly great leader. Dahrel has served a couple of missions with him and has become friends with the Bravnica brothers, Anton and Taras. Being the Kaul Commander, Dominik Bravnica is also in line to become the future Emir and head up the council when his father dies. So, to sum him up in one word – *the* most powerful and eligible man within the Kresnik race. Well that's actually ten words, but you get the drift.

"These are the fire stairs. Don't stress yourself out about the evacuation plans though. We are in a room full of testosterone driven Heroes, you'll be flung over a burly shoulder and rushed to safety before you can ask *'does anyone else smell smoke?'*"

I was still chuckling when she introduced me to a Lieutenant who led me down the hall and into one of the smaller meeting rooms containing a low table surrounded by three comfy looking chairs.

"You will need to wait here."

He indicated to one of the chairs and left the room with no further explanation. He had closed the door so I couldn't even take a peek at the other rooms from the doorway. Sighing I sat down to wait, patience was not one of my strong suits but apparently Daska was determined for me to learn the art. My butt had barely touched the plush cushion when the door swung open and I bolted straight up again.

"Good morning, you must be Anastasia. I'm Anton Bravnica." He held out his hand and my jaw dropped. I couldn't believe I was standing here with Anton Bravnica!

"Anastasia?"

"Huh?"

"It's not cool to leave me hanging like this." He looked down at his proffered hand and wiggled it at me.

"Oh shit sorry." I grabbed his hand and shook it enthusiastically and then realising I had sworn slapped my free hand across my mouth. "Sorry, I didn't mean to swear." I mumbled around my fingers.

This was met by a roar of laughter as Anton slapped me on the back like a long lost friend. "Oh, you are going to fit in well here Anastasia."

Not sure if that was a good or a bad thing, I just smiled. He placed some paperwork on the low table in front of me and I caught a glimpse of his eyes. They were the brilliant icy blue the Enlightened were most recognised for; half the reason why girls went gaga for Enlightened guys. He caught me staring and grinned.

"You have very pretty eyes too." He cocked his head to the side as he studied me. "Unusual." He said it as a statement of fact rather than a compliment.

"Err, thanks."

He watched me for a second longer and then seemed to recall why we were there. Straightening up he was all business.

"As a civilian working for the Kaul, you must understand your responsibilities in terms of what you can and can't talk about when not at work. Particularly in your role, you will become privy to sensitive information."

I nodded as I tried to recall what exactly my role was. No idea, I had accepted a job without even knowing what the job was. I mentally rolled my eyes at myself.

Anton continued as he crossed the room to close the blinds, his movements were quick and efficient. "I have read your file…"

I couldn't stop myself from interrupting. "I have a *file?*"

His brilliant blue eyes twinkled at me as he returned to the cosy chairs. "Everyone has a file Anastasia."

I raised my eyebrows. "How very cloak and dagger of you and please call me Ana. I only get Anastasia when I am in trouble."

He chuckled as he settled himself in the chair opposite me.

"Okay, Ana. As I was saying, I have no reason to doubt your loyalty to the Kresnik People and can see no political persuasions that should be red flagged." He separated some of the paperwork and keeping the large file aside, pushed some forms across the table at me. "This is a confidentiality agreement that you must sign before commencing work with us. As you can see it is fairly detailed so take as much time as you need to go over it before signing."

I picked the papers up and started scanning the pages.

This agreement and statement are legally binding contracts between the Kresnik Council, Kresnik Council Chambers, Lameer and Anastasia Valinski of … I skipped a couple of paragraphs *…The contract signifies a confidentiality statement agreement between The Kresnik Council and Anastasia Valinski. It is initiated to safeguard the Kresnik Council and Anastasia Valinski's interests, related disclosures, that have been made and are to be made thereof.*

Blah blah! I flicked to the last page and signed the paperwork without reading the rest. Handing the signed document back I eyed the large file that Anton had kept aside, I was intrigued as to what exactly was in my file. Anton placed all the paperwork in the file and grabbed a remote control that was sitting on the table and dimmed the lights.

"What are you doing?"

He ignored my question. "I trust you know what the Bravnica power is?"

His Enlightened eyes bored into mine and I could feel myself getting heavy in the chair as I answered. "Mind control."

His eyes never left mine and I started to feel uncomfortable. I willed myself to break the contact but it seemed I lacked the capacity to do as much as blink.

He gave me a reassuring smile. "Relax Ana, I'm not going to hurt you. This is the security measure you just agreed to. All civilians working with the Kaul go through this when they start with us."

I kicked myself for my lack of foresight. I should have been expecting this. All civilians are implanted with a subliminal command that stops them from sharing sensitive information to anyone. Panic set in, what if he could read my mind and found out about my little incidents.

Oh man I really need to start reading things thoroughly before signing.

I made a desperate attempt to break the contact but everything was so heavy.

"Ana stop. I promise I won't hurt you."

He pushed then and I couldn't hold him back. I sent a little prayer to Daska hoping that Anton wouldn't find my secret and let go. A warm rush flooded my head and receded almost instantly, leaving me with pins and needles on my brain. Realising I had my eyes closed I slowly opened them. The room swam for a moment before righting itself. I was reclined back in the chair and I heaved myself forward to sit upright. The movement made me a little woozy so I rested my head in my hands to steady myself.

"I feel like I'm on my third round of shots."

"The effects will wear off soon. You get used to it."

"I'm not going to get brain cancer am I?"

He chuckled. "You know you're really stubborn."

I squinted at him through my lashes. "The same could be said about you."

He laughed at this and stood holding his hand out to help me up. I ignored the offer and stood albeit a little wobbly. I wanted to prove that I wasn't some weak little thing that needed coddling.

He raised an eyebrow and gave me a knowing look before collecting the paperwork. "Come with me and we'll get a drink. You'll feel better afterwards."

Nodding I followed him out the door. I knew what just happened was normal practice and I should have been prepared. I gave Anton a sideways glance. I would have to watch him to make sure he hadn't found out about my episodes. I turned from Anton and the room started to swim again. Without missing a step he reached out and grabbed my upper arm, steadying me, releasing his grip once I had righted myself.

"Next time don't fight it."

I looked up at him and smirked. "I can't make any promises."

Shaking his head he opened a set of large double doors and indicated for me to enter. I realised we hadn't headed back out to the main room and to the kitchen beyond but had worked our way in the opposite direction, further down the hall. I stepped through the doors and into the most opulent room I had ever seen with furniture that was definitely antique and window dressings that contained enough fabric to make my entire wardrobe three times over. The room was dominated by an oval table that sat dead centre. In the middle of the table there was a three dimensional hologram depicting Lumeer and its surrounds, this was obviously some kind of War Room.

We skirted the room and Anton ushered me through to a small kitchenette, he sat me down and handed me a glass of water and a biscuit. I said nothing as he sat opposite me and swallowed his own glass of water in one go, then started on his biscuit. I ate in silence. Finishing my water I felt much better, I swept up my crumbs and headed to the sink to brush them off my hands.

Anton placed the empty glasses in the sink and turned to me. "Better?"

I smiled, "Much."

"Ok, then let's get to work."

We walked back into the large room that was full of Elite Kaul. I scanned the crowd looking for a familiar face but found none. This was obviously the crème de la crème. The older Elite were in smart black slacks with white shirts that had been starched to within an inch of their lives. Over the top they wore regal black jackets with their Family Crest embroidered in rich colours over the breast pocket. The younger Elite and higher ranking Kaul present were wearing their battle fatigues, tight black fitted T-shirt's, camouflage pants with buttons and pockets in all the right places and boots that laced half way up their calves.

I seriously love that uniform.

"Ok, you ready to meet your new boss?"

My stomach did a double flip, I ignored it and smiled. "Of course. I can't wait to get started."

"Alright then, follow me."

We made our way around the massive table to what I assumed was the business end, where a cluster of formal uniforms were grouped around one individual. His back was to me but I recognised him as soon as we drew near. The alpha stance was unmistakable. Mouth suddenly dry I swallowed hard as chopper guy spoke to the group. "I don't care about the political ramifications, I want it done."

This was met by a chorus of. 'Yes Commander' as the group dispersed.

Commander?

There was only one Commander within the Kaul. My attention was snapped back when Anton spoke.

"Dominik, this is your new assistant Anastasia. Ana, this is Commander Bravnica. He will be instructing you as to your tasks, you are to do everything he asks of you."

The broad back turned and the professional smile I had practised so diligently slipped as I looked up at the Ball Guy from the park, only now he wasn't wearing his sunnies and I felt the full force of his Enlightened ice blue eyes.

FIVE

My hopes that he wouldn't place me as the psycho from the park were dashed as he stepped forward and recognition flashed in his eyes.

Damn it!

"Thanks Anton. Anastasia and I bumped into each other at the park yesterday but we've not been formally introduced."

I'm pretty sure the next words out of my mouth were unintelligible. I have no idea what I was trying to say and the brothers shared identical looks of confusion.

Anton opened his mouth to speak but the elder Bravnica beat him to it. "I have some things I need to discuss with my brother. Anastasia, could you please make me a coffee and meet me in my office?"

I was a little stunned by this request but I think I covered my shock well. "Uh sure, how do you take it?"

He had already turned toward Anton and barely glanced at me to respond. "Black. Thanks."

Great, so I'm the coffee girl.

I figured I was allowed to drink coffee too so made two cups and after asking for directions, eventually found his office. It was smaller than what I expected with no grand architecture or plush décor. There was one large desk in the centre of the room with a matching leather chair that looked very comfy. The chair faced the entry way and at its back was a large bookshelf with windows on either side. I put the coffees down next to some neat piles of paper on the desk and was contemplating doing a couple of spins in the chair when the door opened and Bravnica walked in.

"How's the head?"

Embarrassment flared. "It's fine, I told you I was fine."

He raised an eyebrow. "I meant after the security check." He tapped his temple and I realized he had not been talking about the ball.

"Sorry. Um, it's fine."

His eyes never wavered from mine. "Anton told me you put up quite a fight. I think you impressed him."

Uncomfortable under his gaze I felt my face growing hotter. I so wanted to make a good first impression but was failing miserably.

"Well I'm not your average girl." This bordered on a snap and I regretted the tone instantly. He seemed to bring the worst out in me without any effort at all.

Waiting till my eyes met his, he spoke. The words were clipped and left me in no question as to his mood. "Sit down please."

I sat and thanked Daska I was on the correct side of the desk.

"If you are trying to prove yourself to me then you are wasting time." He moved to the other side of the desk and pulled out his chair but didn't sit. "I know who you are and I know what you are capable of and I also know your brothers. Your family has an excellent record within the Kaul, one that I am sure you will be eager to uphold." Placing his hands on the desk he leaned over, I had forgotten how big he was.

"Please do not insult my intelligence by insinuating that I would not run a check on a new member of my staff."

Yikes.

"Look, I realise that you may feel a little awkward because of yesterday but if you can't get past your own ego then you don't belong here and you need to say so - now."

I shook my head. "I don't have a problem. I'm sorry, it won't happen again."

He sat down and the timbre of his voice softened a fraction. "So we're clear?"

I nodded. "Crystal." I felt compelled to add, 'Sir', but refrained. He moved on and it was apparent that the dressing down was over.

"Ok then, I would like you to run over these reports so that you are up to speed on the Lavric investigation." He picked up one of the neat piles and placed it in front of me on the desk. "Once you're across everything I would like you to find out if the entry point has been established." He scribbled a name and number on a scrap of paper. "This is our contact. Tell him that I expect the report ASAP."

I took the paper and nodded. "Will do."

He paused for a moment and met my eyes, creating a small fire in the pit of my belly that I viciously stomped out.

Mercifully breaking the contact he turned back to his desk. "Any questions?"

"No." this came out as a little husky and so I cleared my throat and concentrated on the paperwork in front of me.

"Right, I have a few things I need to check up on so if you need anything you can ask one of the Lieutenants."

He picked up his coffee and walked out of the room. I waited until I heard the door click before letting out an explosive breath.

Well that was awkward.

I pulled the top pages off the pile of paperwork and began to read. The first page was a summation of the notes taken from the first responders.

> **Deceased's body was discovered in his study at approximately 0200 on Thursday morning by his wife (see statement file PL1:003).**
>
> **Initial examination by the ME suggests time of death was approx. 0100: Deceased's head had been torn from his body suggesting a Kudlak attack.**

I tapped my fingers on the page. The only thing strong enough to do that to a Kresnik - was a Kudlak. I tried not to conjure up any images and continued reading.

> **Deceased's wife was upstairs asleep and woke to find the deceased missing from their bed. The deceased's wife went to check on him and found his body in the study.**
>
> **Deceased was last seen by his wife when they went to bed around 2130.**
>
> **Deceased's wife also stated that the safe key was missing from the chain the deceased usually wore around his neck. (See further details in statement file PL1:003)**
>
> **The Deceased's eldest son Travko (see statement file PL1:001) was sleeping in a different wing of the castle and heard nothing until he was woken by members of the Lavric Kaul.**
>
> **The Deceased made no report of a threat to his life and his Kaul were on skeleton staff. Those on duty, were stationed at the front and rear gates. One was on his perimeter check when he heard the deceased's wife scream for help (see statement files PL2:001 & PL2:002).**

The reality of what I was doing finally struck home. Someone was dead and regardless of my personal opinion toward the matter, justice must be done. I had no idea what I would be doing when I walked through those doors this morning but I will admit to secretly hoping it would be something worthwhile. If I couldn't join the Kaul and fight for the Kresnik people in the towns and cities that the Kudlak had made their killing grounds, then surely this was the next best thing. Satisfied with my private little patriotic battle-cry, I took a sip of my coffee and read the final paragraph.

Entrance by the assailant into the Lavric residence is undetermined. The front and rear gates were not breached. Recommend grid search of the surrounds to ascertain point of entry.

Video surveillance tapes to be collected from Lavric Kaul (see video evidence PL3:001).

I put the pages back on the pile and flicked through the remaining documents but they were just statements taken on the night of the murder. I stopped when I stumbled across the photographs taken from the crime scene. Most showed the position and location of evidence before it had been collected for testing and the room looked like it had been painted in blood, smeared over the walls like jam on toast. Then there was Petar Lavric. His body lying prone on the floor of his study, two feet away his head rested against the leg of his chair, eyes wide in surprise. A shiver crept its way up my spine, I shuffled the pictures on the table until they were in a neat stack and then placed them gingerly back into the file, I'd seen enough. I stood to grab the contact details for the lab when I noticed a handwritten document sitting on one of the files Bravnica had kept to his side of the desk. I hesitated before reaching over and snatching it up to have a little snoop. It was a list of questions regarding the murder that pointed out some obvious contradictions, none of which I had even considered. The one that caught my eye was top on the list and circled aggressively in red biro,

Body was not drained of blood???

Kudlak and their need for blood is almost uncontrollable. So this begs the question, why was Petar not drained? It must have taken an immense amount of control not to feed from him and Kudlak are *not* known for any kind of self-control. They are an uncivilized race, more animal than anything else. Their base desires are what drive them and they have not been known to waver from this pattern, until now. Creasing my brow I chewed on my lower lip to see if that would help in solving the puzzle.

"Sorry Bravnica, I've got nothing."

Sighing I put the page back, careful to leave it just as I had found it and made the call on Bravnica's landline. After being transferred a few times I finally got through to the lead investigator who advised he was about to email them to the commander and the Emir when I rang. I hung up and figured I needed to get an email account set up, so I went in search of Sierra. I only made two wrong turns before finding her in the tea room, balancing a tray of freshly brewed coffees and biscuits.

She smiled and indicated to the tray. "Meeting for the big wigs."

I looked at the pile of biscuits. "Creamy centered?"

She grinned. "Yup. Now what can I do for you?"

Walking with her as she hurried out of the kitchen I explained my quandary. She promised to have an account set up for me by tomorrow and told me to wait by the printer and she would run off a hardcopy of the email for me. Watching her hurry off I decided to take a little self-tour while I waited for the print out. Wandering down a wide hall I gazed at the pictures hanging on the wall, the subjects were all of Elite Families with most of the photos aged in a sepia tone. A young lady standing in a group of five couples on the stairs of the Grand Ballroom caught my eye. She was heavily pregnant and had a smile that could rival Tressilia's. She stood snuggled under the arm of a man who must have been her husband. He had placed a hand tenderly on her swollen belly and was not looking at the camera, but adoringly down at his wife. I am not a romantic but that did make me smile.

"Lucky girl."

I stood on tippy-toes to get a closer look at the plaque underneath. All five Elite Families were represented. Vidmar, Lavric, Preseren, Drevensek and Bravnica. Intrigued by the happy couple I was trying to figure out which family they were from when raised voices started to penetrate the closed door to my right. I froze when one of the voices registered - Bravnica.

Oh help.

Looking for a quick getaway I turned the knob on the door to my left and peaked in. A boxy little stationary cupboard with a large printer, boxes of paper and walls lined with drawers full of pens and the like. The voices seemed to be calmer now so instead of high tailing it like any normal person would do, I plastered myself against the wall to listen a little longer. I could only catch every second word but it was clear he was arguing with someone about the murder investigation and the security of the city.

I was about to shuffle closer when the door to the office was flung open. I scrambled to get into the stationary room but was not quick enough to close the door all the way. Unsure of what to do now I gave up and struck a casual pose amongst the supplies and prayed I wouldn't be seen in the dark room. It was only a few seconds before Drago Vidmar stepped into view just outside the stationary door. Looking as superior as ever he paused, turning back the way he had come.

"Dominik, I suggest you follow the council wishes. This could have repercussions for you if you do not comply. You are to be the future Emir. You will need the support of the council if you wish to be a successful ruler."

My mouth dropped open at the veiled threat as the Head of the Vidmar Elite turned and threw a final tidbit over his shoulder as he retreated down the hall.

"Do not tarnish your reputation by being pig headed."

I didn't know what was more disturbing, the threat, or the detached manner in which it was delivered. I stood frozen at the printer not wanting to give my presence away when Bravnica appeared. He pushed the door open all the way he crossed his arms over his chest. Leaning sideways against the door jam, he raised one eyebrow and looked directly at me. The man was huge, his broad frame effectively blocked my view to the hall, I felt like a mouse that had just been discovered by a rather large cat.

Ok, so this is a little uncomfortable.

The printer chose that moment to come to life scaring the crap out of me. I whirled around letting out an involuntary squeak as it hummed to life, printing out the promised email from Sierra.

Turning back to the doorway to try and explain my presence I found it empty and shook my head.

That man has some serious Ninja skills.

Email in hand I walked into Bravnica's office not knowing what to expect, it certainly wasn't the eyeful that I got. He had removed the formal jacket and shirt of his official uniform and was in the process of pulling one of those tight black T's that I love so much over his head. The movements stretched his stomach and made his pecks tighten as his arms flexed working the T-Shirt down. I snapped my mind back to reality as the chest spoke.

"Anastasia. Can you take this and grab a pen, we are having a meeting." He rounded the desk and handed me a file.

I juggled the file and report. "I just got today's report. Do you want to read it first?"

"I will take a look at it later, this won't take long. Put it in my bottom drawer."

He was just about to disappear down the hall when he turned back, hanging onto the door frame. "Meeting room five, I need you to sit next to me. I put the report in the bottom drawer, scrounged a pen from his desk and went in search of meeting room five.

"Ok Guys, take a seat, this won't take long."

I sat in a chair at the front of the room feeling a little nervous as Bravnica stood next to me. The room was filled to capacity with Kaul and I didn't recognise any of them. Upon hearing their Commander speak, the room quickly fell silent.

"I have been advised by the council that while we are here to investigate the murder of Petar Lavric, we will also be required to participate in some of the higher profile events of the festival."

The room became restless and I looked down at documents that Bravnica had handed me. It had all the events that the council expected them to attend.

"Miss Valinksi has a list of events. She will take it around to all of you and you can nominate what events you will attend."

One of the Kaul raised his hand and Bravnica nodded at him to speak.

"Sir, we were advised that the Lumeer Kaul would be helping with the festival."

He nodded at this. "They are, however the council believes it will keep the general populous calm and lift the morale of the city if we are seen out and about. There are some major players in this room and the people of Lumeer want to know everything is okay and that they have nothing to fear."

He moved behind my chair and indicated to the file I held. Every fibre I had was honed in on his position at my back.

"I have already nominated myself for some activities and am certain you will ensure the duties are evenly spread amongst yourselves."

Then he grabbed the back of my chair and I could feel his movements as he shifted his weight and fought the desire to lean back.

"One event that is compulsory to all Kaul not absent due to field duty is the Underworld Dinner. That's all. Thanks for your time."

He let go of my chair and I felt the air behind me move as he left the room.

"Excuse me Miss. May I have a look at the list?"

I was stuck in the stuffy meeting room for a good half hour, signing grumbling Kaul up for the festival events. When the last one finally left, I walked back to the office to find Bravnica at his desk hands splayed on either side of a map.

Curiosity got the better of me. "You don't seem happy about being a part of the festival."

He sighed and sat heavily in his chair. "My only concern is for the security of Lumeer and the safety of its people." He watched as I lowered myself into my chair and seemed to abandon that train of thought. "My men are professionals. They will not be distracted from their mission. I can see why the council would want to have their finest on show."

I studied his face for any hints that would contradict his words but he had his game face on. He knew what I was doing though and stood to break the contact. I guess disagreeing with the Council in front of staff was a no-no.

"Did you have any trouble getting the form filled out?"

He turned the tables and was now studying me, I felt a little uncomfortable under his steady gaze.

"Uh, no. I wouldn't say they were happy about it but they all put their names down."

He nodded looking back at his map. "Good. You can go to lunch now if you like. I expect you back here at 1300."

"Ok, thanks." I put the list of names on the corner of his desk so as not to cover the map he was so intrigued by and walked quietly to the door.

"Oh and Anastasia?"

I spun and raised an eyebrow in question.

"That's 1300 sharp."

I smiled. "Of course."

The next few days passed in a blur of paperwork and meetings. The investigation was ramping up and Bravnica's frustrations were steadily increasing, not that anyone else knew as he never let his poker face slip outside the privacy of his office.

It was mid-morning on Wednesday and I had just been called into a meeting with him and a human Liaison. I didn't really do anything in these meetings, just take down notes and observe but I was excited about this one having never met a Liaison before. The Liaisons were our link to the human world, they represented the DEA, an assemblage of the most powerful human governments who, having knowledge of the Kudlak had joined together to assist the Kresnik people in our fight to rid the world of them. Being a much weaker race, they could not help on the frontline but assisted in other ways, supplying us with technology, military equipment and intelligence as well as all the cool perks from Western society. These activities were carried out without the knowledge of the general human populous, a mutual agreement to benefit both parties. They wanted our protection without mass panic and we wanted their technology without the rubberneckers.

Taking my seat on Bravnica's right I pulled out my paperwork and pen ready to start. The Liaison walked in and seemed to hesitate before crossing the room to where we sat extending his hand.

"Commander Bravnica."

"Agent Pike. Good to see you again. This is my assistant Miss Valinski." He turned and waved a hand in my direction. "You are free to speak openly in front of her."

The Liaison nodded his head at me and smiled offering his hand.

"Miss Valinski."

I returned his smile and shook the proffered hand, surprised at the lack of strength in his grip. I knew Kresniks as a race were superior to humans in terms of physical ability but had never experienced it until now. With the formalities over, Agent Pike took his seat and Bravnica started briefing him on the current state of play.

"I must say Commander Bravnica, what you have presented is somewhat contradictory. You are sure it was a Kudlak attack, yet the body was not drained." He narrowed his eyes and leaned forward. "If this is true then it would certainly be unprecedented but would also beg the question of why?"

Bravnica leaned back in his chair. "I have been asking myself that very question."

Pike contemplated this riddle for a moment before something clicked and his eyes widened. "Has the Lavric Aurora been accounted for?"

"Unfortunately not at this stage. The Lavrics were reluctant to reveal it was no longer in the family vault when initially questioned, so we have only received this Intel in the last few hours. They were unsure if Petar had moved it before his death so they have been searching their castle for it. There is no evidence at this stage to suspect that it has been taken by the intruder but we are mindful of this possibility. I have every available resource searching for it as we speak."

This was news to me too. Bravnica did well to remain so calm. The Auroras were the Kresnik life blood, each said to contain the blood from one of Daska's five original Kresniks. They were considered more valuable than life itself. There were five in total one for each Enlightened family. I didn't know too much about their power but to lose them would definitely be bad. The legends suggest that the Auroras were what Draku was after when he created The First, his five original Kudlak.

Pike's face had grown steadily redder and I was wondering if steam was about to come hissing out of his ears.

"I want to be updated on this matter the moment there is any word."

His stubby fingers started poking at the tablet he cradled awkwardly in his lap.

"I will advise the DEA board. We need to keep our ears low to the ground." He raised his eyes from the tablet to give Bravnica a knowing look. "If *it* makes a move, we need to be ready."

Bravnica nodded, speaking from behind his steepled fingers, "Of course."

Pike seemed to calm a little under Bravnica's steady gaze. "Is there anything else?"

Bravnica nodded and lowered his hands to rest on the desk "Despite a thorough search we have been unable to ascertain point of entry and are in the process of expanding our search grid."

Pike seemed very interested in this. "Lumeer is believed to be impenetrable. Do you think there might have been assistance from inside the city walls?"

Bravnica dealt the Liaison a very direct glare before lowering his voice. "No I most certainly do not."

Pike was not a stupid man and had noticed the subtle shift in Bravnica's voice, so he wisely let the subject drop.

Bravnica stood. "That is all the information I have at this stage, is there anything else you need Agent Pike?"

Pike scrambled to his feet. "No, I have a lot to report back to my superiors. Let me know if there are any changes."

The two men exchanged pleasantries and I escorted Agent Pike out of the building.

Walking back to Bravnica's office I mused over the details of the meeting so I could complete the minutes after lunch.

Finding him still at his desk I took the opportunity to question him. "Hey, what did Agent Pike mean when he said "If it makes a move we need to be ready." Does he mean the Kudlak?"

Bravnica looked up at me, the question clear in his eyes.

"So I can put it in the meeting minutes."

Leaning back in his chair his eyes bore into mine. "Yes. He was referring to a Kudlak. Callisto."

"Oh, Okay."

Uh, I don't think this is okay.

He watched me, waiting for my reaction. Not sure how he wanted me to react I asked the obvious.

"So how come we know this Kudlak by name, why is he so important?"

Leaning forward in his chair he took a moment to answer. Taking a deep breath he looked up from his desk and gave me a grim smile. "Anastasia." He paused. "Callisto is one of The First."

SIX

My blood ran cold. The First. Was he serious?

I tried to hide my shock as he spoke.

"I have a few things that need finishing before we leave today so was going to suggest we grab something and eat in the office."

It wasn't a request.

"Ok, uh.'"

I followed Bravnica out of the office, struggling with the idea of The First being more than just a story. They were supposed to have been wiped out centuries ago, leaving only the Kudlak created by The First. There had always been legends that one of them still walked the Earth, fixated on its dark mission and that if it were to succeed then all bets were off. Some of the older generation still hold to the old ways and believe in the tale wholeheartedly but the general feeling is that it's just a scary story handed down through the generations to scare little kids. It never occurred to me that the story could actually be true.

Reaching the glass doors I pulled out my magic swipey card and ran it through the scanner.

Bravnica held onto the door handle waiting for the lock to release before pulling it open for me. "What do you feel like?"

I gave him a smile of thanks and walked through the door.

"I don't know, we will see what looks…oh crap!" I turned back toward the door. "I forgot my purse."

He pulled the door closed behind him.

And I faltered. "It'll only take a sec."

He waved me off, moving past me to press the call button for the lift. "No, Ana its fine. I'll get lunch today."

I shook my head automatically. "Thank you but no, I would rather pay for my own lunch."

The lift binged and he smiled. "Too late, you can buy me lunch tomorrow."

I was about to insist when the cooing of Tressilia Vidmar cut me short. "Dominik Darling."

I sensed Bravnica tense beside me as she sauntered out of the lift and descended on him with a barrage of swaying hips and air kisses.

"Tressilia, you're looking well."

I moved to the side as she stepped between us and wrapped an elegant arm around his waist. Lowering her voice she practically purred.

"So are you Darling but tell me…" She paused and levelled me with a look that was meant to humiliate. "…Why are you socialising with the help?"

I cocked my head to the side and smiled before shifting my weight to take a step forward. Seeing my movement, Bravnica extracted himself from her clutches and stepped between us effectively blocking my path as he ushered her through the glass doors.

"Tressilia, I would love to stay and chat with you. Unfortunately I have a lot of work on at the moment but we will catch up soon."

Licking her lips she leaned forward and kissed him on the corner of his mouth, watching me over his shoulder the whole time.

Bitch.

"Of course Dominik. We will be together soon."

The instant she turned her back and entered the office he pulled the glass door shut. "Let's get out of here."

I raised my eyebrows. "Sure, but I'm feeling kind of nauseous all of a sudden."

He ignored this and reached past me to press the call button for the lift again. When it arrived he stood back to let me enter first and I watched our reflection as he stepped in behind me wiping the side of his mouth with the back of his hand. I tried not to smile as we rode in silence to the ground floor. Bravnica seemed to be in a bit of a rush and I had to hurry to keep up with his long strides. We settled on a couple of sandwiches but didn't return to the office as planned. I wondered if this was because of Tressilia but was not going to complain as he led me outside to sit in the surrounding gardens. I filled my lungs with the fresh air and raised my face to the sun. I loved being outside on days like this, working in an office all day had confirmed that I was definitely an outdoors girl. We sat down on one of the garden benches and unwrapped our lunch. I had just taken a bite when Bravnica spoke.

"So how are you finding working for the Kaul?"

My eyes widened and I covered my mouth with my free hand trying to chew faster. This was the first time he had actually asked me a personal question and I was keen to have a conversation with him that wasn't based on a dead Elite.

He smiled at me as I struggled to swallow. "Sorry."

I finally got it down and held up a placating hand. "No, it's fine. I'm really enjoying it. I like doing something that is worthwhile."

He gave me a strange look and I realized that me running around with bits of paper, was very different to him running around decapitating Kudlak.

I tried to backpedal. "I mean, it's not as important as what you guys do of course." I trailed off realising how lame this was all sounding and took another bite of my sandwich to shut myself up.

"Anastasia, the meeting with Agent Pike, I don't want you to worry about that ok? We have no evidence to prove any theories at this stage. It's all just conjecture." He gave a rueful smile. "And there's a lot more of it to be thrown around before we'll be done."

His smile caught me by surprise and I was also taken aback that he was trying to reassure me but I guess it's the Kaul mindset - Always the protector. I don't know why I didn't expect that of him.

I looked up, still chewing and nodded to confirm I had heard his request.

He stared at me for a moment longer before changing the subject. "Ok so the work we have to get through this afternoon is in regards to the Lavric funeral tomorrow." He took a sip of his drink and continued. "We need to go over the logistics for the day and I am going to need you to check a few things for me in regards to the rosters."

We finished our lunch and I spent the rest of the afternoon working with high ranking Kaul confirming each of their roles for the funeral. By the time I got home I was exhausted. Closing the front door I leaned against it to kick off my heels, mumbling about Bravnica the Slave Driver. Picking up my shoes I padded my way across the lounge to my room, calling out to Tash.

"Honey I'm home!"

The next morning was chaos. I had arrived early for work as directed and hit the ground running. I hadn't even had time for my second cup of coffee. The payoff was that I only had to make it through to midday and then I could escape. On my way back from picking up Bravnica's Dress Uniform at the Dry Cleaners I checked my watch to confirm what I already knew. We were behind schedule by at least half an hour.

Shit

I picked up the pace and nearly toppled when the heel of my pumps jagged the edge of a cobblestone. Catching my balance I paused to take a breath and calm down before continuing. The list of things I had to do was steadily growing and the amount of time with which to do it all rapidly diminishing. Stepping onto the smooth pavers of the forecourt that led to the building I broke into a run, not slowing for the stairs I took them two at a time. Catching my breath at the lifts I hammered the call button until the doors Binged open. Taking stock on the ride up I absently congratulated myself for my impressive run in heels. Arriving at the third floor I swiped myself through the glass doors dodging the harried staff on the main floor and flew into Bravnica's office to find it empty.

"Crap, where has he gone now?"

I checked his desk to see if there were any clues as to his whereabouts but found none.

Ok, not a lot I can do about that now.

I laid his uniform out and picked up my check list when Sierra flung herself halfway through the door.

"Where is he? His father's car has arrived to pick him up."

I screwed up my face, before letting out a rush of air and confessing. "I have absolutely no idea." I looked at my watch. "The Emir wasn't supposed to be here for another fifteen minutes, he's early isn't he?"

I looked at Sierra hoping for confirmation that it was okay to make the Emir wait but the look on her face said it all.

I rolled my eyes and answered my own question. "No he isn't, he's right on time. The Emir can arrive whenever he bloody well likes, you just have to hope to hell that you are ready when he is."

Oh Daska.

I was scrambling now. "Let me try his mobile." Spinning around I picked up the desk phone and dialled Bravnica's number waiting to hear the ring.

Damn

I shook my head at Sierra. "Voice mail."

I hung up. There was no point leaving him a message, I'm pretty sure he already knew the whole time management thing was screwed right about now.

I rounded the desk. "I'll go look for him."

She gave me a brief nod. "Ok, when you find him, tell him his father is waiting at the back entrance." She left in the same manner she had arrived and I knew she was having the same kind of day as me.

"No worries." I rolled my eyes and marched out the door groaning to myself. "Oh, this is going to be a very long morning."

Glancing up and down the hall I wasn't sure where to start.

He could be anywhere.

After searching every nook and cranny of the third floor and even asking one guy heading for the gents to send him out if he was in there, I headed back to the Kitchen deflated and parched. I needed some water. After a few sips I turned to lean on the bench and spotted a flash of black dart past the door. I moved to investigate when it was back before I could put down my glass.

"Anastasia, we don't have time for leisurely breaks, come with me now." With that the black was gone again.

"Bravnica!" I yelled after him as I dumped my drink in the sink and dashed out of the kitchen. "I have been looking everywhere for you. Where were you?"

He was waiting impatiently for me at his office door reminding me of Tash when we were on our way to the Festival opening.

As soon as I entered he pulled the door shut. "I need you to help me."

He stalked across the room and started rifling through his desk giving me a chance to take in his appearance. His clothes were filthy. He had a smear of dirt across his chin and brown dirt all over his shoulders.

"What have you been *doing?* You're a mess!"

He didn't respond, instead bent over his desk and scribbled hurriedly on a scrap of paper before locking said paper in his safe. When he finally deigned to look at me I had my arms folded and hip cocked in an unmistakable what-the-hell-have-you-been-doing pose. He saw my arm fold and raised me an eyebrow. Giving a mental shrug, I abandoned my inept interrogation. You can't intimidate a Bravnica so don't bother trying.

"Your father is waiting."

"I know. Where's my uniform?"

He pulled his black T-shirt over his head spilling dust all over the floor, oblivious to the mess he shook it some more and used it to wipe his face. I suddenly needed more water as I scurried past the tanned six-pack to grab his newly pressed white undershirt. I held it out for him and he turned around, inserted one arm at a time into each sleeve causing all manner of wonderful muscle movements. After getting his arms through he turned pulling the shirt into place before dropping his fatigue pants.

"Have you got the list of Platoons in marching order?"

Still reeling from the whole pants down thing, I fumbled through the pile of clothes for his dress pants and tried to remember my lists. "Uh, I um." I cleared my throat and tried again. "Yes, everything's under control."

Found them!

Holding the dress pants out in his general direction I stared intently at the opposite wall and tried to breathe while ignoring the little voice that popped into my head daring me to look. I heard his fatigues hit the floor and then a subdued chuckle as the dress pants were tugged out of my grip.

"Are my gloves here?"

Turning back I caught a glimpse of thigh and swallowed hard before picking up his black jacket in search of the gloves. Deciding he must be decent by now I risked a look as I handed them over, pleased to see him with his pants done up.

Well that is just the most ridiculous thing Ana. Seriously? You're GLAD he has his pants on?

I imagined the echo of retreating footsteps and then a door slamming as the owner of the little voice left the building in disgust.

"You've been in contact with each of the Lieutenants?"

Ignoring my weird imaginings I attempted to concentrate on the task at hand. "Yes, I spoke with all of them and they know their positions."

He nodded as he concentrated on fitting his gloves. "Okay good, do you have any final questions?"

I picked up his jacket and held it out. He shrugged it on and turned holding out his glove encased hands. "Would you mind?"

I let out a tiny breath and stepped forward to do his buttons up, trying not to think about the intimacy of the task.

"I should get a raise for this."

His stilled and gave me a knowing smile. I could feel my cheeks going pink as my fingers fumbled unsuccessfully on the final button at the top of his chest. He placed his hands over mine and I instantly froze as he lowered his face to mine.

"Thanks Anastasia, I'll get this one on the way."

Too scared to speak in case my voice betrayed me I simply nodded and stepped back as he smiled and placing his hat under his arm, turned to leave the room. I held my breath as he hesitated at the doorway and I was sure he was about to turn back when a voice called to him from down the hall. He straightened his shoulders and an instant later disappeared from view. About a minute passed before I moved. I don't know what the hell had just happened and I was pretty sure I would be analysing it from every conceivable angle in the middle of the night but I didn't have time for it now. I turned back to the desk and picked up my check list determined to ignore the discarded clothes that littered the floor.

I waved weakly with a false smile plastered onto my face as the last of the Kaul left the main floor and silence descended on the office. As the lift doors closed I fell heavily into a nearby chair and closed my eyes letting my head fall back onto the headrest.

"Well, if I never have another day like this it will be too soon." I kicked my shoes off stretching my ankles and pushing my toes into the plush carpet. I blew a sigh into my fringe making it jump and land in my eye. Shaking it out, I heaved myself up and left the building carrying my shoes.

After going home for a quick change into casual gear I arrived at the Festival grounds and was surprised to see people still milling about. I had assumed that everyone would be going to see the Lavric Service, or at the very least the Funeral Procession. I wove my way through the maze of tents determined to get Tash her own Hoo Haa stones. Instead of the red velvet tent flaps, I found an elderly couple selling crocheted teapot cozies and antique clocks. Turning on the spot I confirmed my surrounds, this was definitely where we had our bizarre run in.

So where the hell is she?

I approached the elderly couple. "Excuse me. Do you know where the lady that had her tent here before you went?"

The elderly man squinted up at me but kept his mouth shut as the woman held up one of the tea cozies. "There's a special today. Twenty-five for you my Darling!"

I shook my head. "No, I don't need one of those. I'm looking for the people that were in this spot before you. Do you know when they left or where they went?"

Her wrinkled lips creased into a smile as she observed me through her cloudy eyes. "I have many colours." She spread her hands wide but did not break eye contact.

I shook my head and began to ask again but let my sentence drop as I spotted the old man's barely contained amusement. Looking back at the woman I noted a shrewd gleam.

Great! I am being screwed by a tea-cozy-crocheting nana and her old man. This could be a new low for you Ana.

I glared at the old woman. "Five."

Her expression didn't change. "Twenty-two."

I raised my eyebrow but will confess to being entertained by the old girls pluckiness. "Ten."

"Twenty."

Mumbling I shook my head and yanked my bag open to retrieve my purse. "I cannot believe I'm doing this." I slapped fifteen on the table. "I'll take the purple one."

Her eyes lit up and she pushed the purple tea-cozy at me before pocketing the cash.

"So what do you know about the people that were in this spot before you?"

The lady raised her shoulders in a slow motion shrug and showed me her palms. "I only know that they left here on Sunday morning before anyone was up. Rumour has it that they didn't pay the rent for the site, but you can't believe everything you hear."

I cocked my head to the side. "So that's all you know?"

She looked up as though there might be another detail hiding in the corner of her bushy grey eyebrows. She pointed a crooked finger at me and lowered her voice. "What I think is that they must have been running from something pretty serious to give up prime position at the biggest money spinner of the year."

She had a point - there were only a few Kresnik fairs throughout the year, the Daska Festival being the main event. Someone would need a pretty good reason to just up and leave. An uneasy feeling lodged itself in the pit of my stomach.

Maybe it wasn't a something that they were running from?

"Would you like to look at a clock dear?" The old woman stood and moved to the other side of the bench and was in the process of picking out a clock for me, all the while my thoughts were busy tumbling down a path I didn't want to travel.

SEVEN

"This does not prove anything Ana."

I only just managed to stop myself from spraying beer across the table and into Tash's calm face, as it was I felt some go up the back of my nose. It never fails to surprise me how much shooting beer out your nose actually hurts. We were at Reds, our local bar and place to go when nothing was officially planned. It was also the closest bar to our place and as a result - the Barracks. Thankfully though, most Kaul chose to drink at the Barracks Bar, apparently they get drinks at half the price. There was an unwritten rule that the higher ranking Kaul would steer clear of the Barracks Bar, giving the Privates and Corporals the freedom to relax and blow off steam if need be. So it was only the Lieutenants and Colonels that frequented Reds.

"Tash, please don't tell me I am reading too much into this."

She opened her mouth to do just that but I cut her off with an eloquent sing song. "La la la la la la not listening."

I smiled as she relented and fell back into her chair with an eye roll that had me wincing.

"Ouch Tash, you should not do that to your eyes."

She raised a neatly plucked brow but kept her mouth shut tight, so I teased some more.

"Seriously girl you could strain something. Then you would probably have to wear one of those ugly patches and…"

"Ana please! I know it's a stretch but can we please just stay focused here."

I leaned forward and lowered my voice. "Do you think she left because of me, you know the curse?"

Shaking her head she opened her mouth to reply when my other brother Garrick slid into the booth next to her knocking her sideways in his enthusiasm.

"Thought I might find you lovely ladies here, so what are we drinking?"

Wrapping an arm around Tash's shoulders he leaned forward in the booth to inspect our glasses. Tash poked him in the rib and he shifted away releasing her in the process.

She smiled at him and gave him a shove. "We're fine, go and get yourself something."

Garrick stood and leaned over the table to grab the back of my head so I couldn't escape and planted a noisy kiss on my forehead. I batted him away in smiling protest and he made his escape. Tash had her back to the bar so missed the typical show as he stood hip cocked leaning casually over the bar at the young barmaid who didn't stand a chance.

"Oh no, he's at it again."

Tash turned around in her chair and looking over the backrest let out a laugh. "Honestly that boy has no shame."

I turned my attention back to Tash as she righted herself in the booth. "We will chat about Vadoma later okay?"

She gave me a brief nod and tipped her head toward the door. "The formal stuff must be over now."

We watched as a group of Kaul we didn't know came sauntering in. I curled my lip as they made no effort to hide the fact that they were sizing up every woman up in the room. Some of them looked like they had been drinking already, which was a concern - given the fact that they would have only just knocked off work. My anger flared as one of them slapped the arse of an unsuspecting lady on her way to the toilets. Her squeal of surprise led to raucous laughter from the group.

"Well that tears it." I pushed my drink aside and went to get up but Tash reached across the table and put her hand on my arm.

"Just leave it Ana. There will be some higher ranking Kaul here soon and that will quieten them down." She gave me one of her meaningful looks that I could never seem to decipher. "Just leave it okay?"

I relented and sat back down but was determined to keep an eye on them. "What a bunch of wankers."

Garrick scooted back in next to Tash. "Who's a wanker?"

I smiled at him. "You."

He returned the smile and whipped out a card with a name and phone number written in swirly writing with the "i's" dotted with love hearts.

"Don't need to be a wanker when you're as good as me."

He leaned back in his chair turning to give us a side profile while he smoothed his fingers through his hair.

Tash punched him in the ribs and I snorted… again.

Wow that is getting to be really embarrassing.

"So little sis, what's it like working for the Commander?"

I looked at my watch. "Well I must say I am very impressed, I had that question pegged at less than one minute. Turns out it was under two."

He narrowed his eyes at me. "Don't take the piss Ana."

Giving him a casual shrug I tried to play it down. "I don't know what the big fuss is about to tell you the truth."

Garrick's horrified look was comical and I struggled to keep my rogue snorting in check. He was about to reply with what I'm sure would have been a lecture on respect when Tash spoke.

"Well speak of the devil."

We turned as one in the direction of the front door. I spotted Dahrel first, standing with Anton and Taras Bravnica. Upon seeing us they moved forward through the bar clearing the doorway and revealing the fourth person in their party - Dominik Bravnica. My stomach gave a lurch as he shifted his weight to enter the bar not looking at ease but then he didn't look uncomfortable either. Silence momentarily engulfed the bar as people realised who had just walked in. I saw the edge of his mouth twitch in response and found myself feeling a little sorry for him. The wankers stopped talking and put their drinks down all but saluting as he strode by. They were rewarded with a brief nod as he passed them on his way to our booth.

"Well this should be interesting."

Garrick couldn't hide the excited gleam in his eye and he didn't even look at me to reply. "What was that Ana?"

I shook my head lowering my voice. "Quick, sit next to me."

He turned and gave me a blank look. "What?"

Too late. They were at our table. I looked up as Dahrel made the introductions to Tash, Bravnica gave me a quick smile and I returned it with one just as brief. Anton slid in next to Garrick and Bravnica, being closest to my side hesitated for a second and then slid in next to me. His thigh pressed against mine causing alarm bells to ring in my ears, I sucked in a lungful of air at the contact and he pulled away quickly. I pressed myself as far from Bravnica's body parts as the wall on my other side would allow before turning back to the group.

I smiled at Taras - the youngest Bravnica, as he sat down on the other side of his older brother. I hadn't officially met Taras but had seen him a few times in the office. The group settled as Dahrel grabbed a nearby chair and pulled up to the end of the booth. I tried to catch Tash's eye to give a 'we're trapped' look but she barely glanced at me as Anton engaged her in conversation about her work. I gave a mental sigh, the Bravnica brothers were smooth, I'd give them that. Taras nodded at me briefly and I raised my hand to give him a little wave but he had turned to speak with Dahrel before I could so much as wiggle my fingers so I let my hand drop. I slumped back in the booth and started playing with my beer coaster. Dahrel was listening intently to what Taras and Bravnica were telling him and it seemed that the excitement level was rising by the minute. I turned my ear to catch what they were saying but the conversation turned suddenly casual as Garrick's pretty little barmaid walked over with a tray of beers, deftly placing one in front of each of the newcomers. They thanked the girl and Garrick gave her a cheeky wink before she hurried back to the bar, I was impressed as the conversation returned to work as though there had not been an interruption and I tried to listen in.

The place was filling up as more people arrived from the service and the general noise was rising. Bored, I tried to engage Bravnica in small talk. "So how was the service?"

He turned to me with an unsure look and leaned in close to my ear. "Sorry did you say something."

His breath felt warm as it brushed my neck sending little happy sparks dancing through my body. Inhaling sharply I had to blink away the memory of him slipping into his dress shirt.

I swallowed hard shaking my head. "Ah, no. Nothing."

He turned back to Dahrel and I let out a breath retreating to the wall again. *Ok, way too close proximity to try and hold a conversation with him.*

This was not how I had planned on spending my afternoon. I leaned over and tapped the table to get Tash's attention, she looked up at me and I nodded toward the bar.

"Come get a drink?"

She smiled and started shuffling her way out of the booth when I realised I would have to do the same.

Didn't think that one through did you?

There was nothing for it now but to go with it. Bravnica had already seen what we were about and was trying to turn sideways in the booth to allow me more room. I gave him a quick smile of thanks. As far as I was concerned the least amount of contact the better. The boys carried on with their conversation oblivious when Bravnica faltered as my butt drew level with his face. I allowed myself a little smile and resisted the urge to shake it, before throwing an apology over my shoulder.

Clearing the booth Tash grabbed my arm. "OMD, now *that* is an incredible specimen!"

I risked a quick look over my shoulder at the subject in question. He had shifted over in the seat and was tapping the edge of my beer coaster on the table. No longer interested in the conversation he contemplated the crowd. He even did brooding well.

I felt a gentle hand on the small of my back. "Hey there 'Lil Bit." I smiled and leaned back into Yari as he whispered in my ear. "Now how did I know I would find you here?"

I looked up and met his cheeky grin. "You been looking for me?"

He gave a casual shrug. "Maybe."

Turning around I threw him a knowing smile.

He stepped closer and let his hand rest on my hips. "So, can I get you ladies a drink?"

Smiling I shook my head. "I'm a working girl now. It's my shout."

"Hmmmm, a kept man." He leaned forward and planted a deliberate kiss on the side of my neck. "You know I could get used to this."

Conscience of our surroundings and the proximity of my new boss I pulled away slightly. Laughing nervously I placed my hands on his chest to give me little distance.

"Ok then, I'll be back." I gave him a gentle shove and he raised his eyebrow, I indicated over his shoulder and he relented.

Letting his mouth fall into his trademark sexy half smile he took a couple of steps backward, eyeing me the whole time. I was getting the full Yari Experience. He broke contact and winked at Tash before turning to saunter toward to others.

Tash headed for the Ladies and I waited at the bar for service as there was a queue now, the number of patrons had surged in the last half hour. I caught the eye of a no-nonsense barman and shouted my order across the bar. He gave me a quick nod to indicate he had heard me and was quick to get our drinks. Tash arrived just as I was pocketing my change and I handed her drink over before raising my glass to take a sip. Suddenly the wind was knocked out of me as I was grabbed from behind with enough force to send my drink flying. I vaguely remember lamenting the waste of a full drink before the adrenaline kicked in. Unfamiliar arms coated in dark hair wrapped around my body like a vice and a chin rough with stubble scratched at my right cheek. I tried to pull away from the assault on my face but he just leaned further over, bending me at the waist.

"Do you like flowers pretty girl?" I was sure it was a rhetorical question and was too busy trying to free myself of his grip to bother answering. "Well how about you put your tulips around this."

I saw red as he thrust his pelvis forward. Anger flared instantly and it was all I could do not to fly into a rage, he had me in a bear grip and there was no way I was going to be able to force my way out of it. Letting a sultry laugh escape my mouth I pushed back into his embrace, he automatically loosened his grip and I raised my arms to turn slowly. Flashing a disengaging smile I licked my lips and assessed my assailant. Kaul - out of Towner, large and powerful but drunk and swaying on his feet.

I leaned forward and purred. "Hey Big Boy."

Predictably his eyes were drawn to my cleavage and I took advantage as he bent over to get a better look. Curling my hand into a fist I channelled all my anger and slammed it into his face, his head snapping back and he stumbled into his mates who stopped him from falling. Gingerly touching his nose his shock turned to rage as he pulled his hand away to see it covered in his own blood. My own anger had been let loose though and there was not a lot that was going to stop it. Without letting the opportunity slip away I advanced before he could and landed a powerful kick between his legs.

Bulls eye!

I knew the Kaul was no longer a threat but I couldn't stop the rage that was now flowing through me. It was like someone had opened a floodgate and I could literally hear it roaring in my head. Smiling I moved to land one more hit for good measure but before I could satisfy the urge my arms were yanked behind my back in a painful grip that had me growling. I swung my head around to try and see who had me pinned but they raised my arms high forcing me to bow forward and effectively disabling my attack. The noise of excited patrons increased as the bar was plunged into chaos but it was nothing to the steady roar of anger that was flooding through me. I could feel myself begin to shake and knew I had to get out of the bar before something happened. I squeezed my eyes shut and tried to relax taking deep breaths one after another but it wasn't working. I had to get Tash to get me out of here. I looked up at the bar where I last saw her but she was gone. A red haze clouded my vision momentarily before a stack of beer coasters launched off the bar in front of me, scattering madly as though someone had taken to them with a powerful hairdryer.

Oh Daska, I am losing it.

A wave of nausea hit me and the bar tilted violently before righting itself just as quick. I tugged at my arms in a desperate attempt to get away.

"Get the hell off me."

I was pulled upright and a familiar voice growled in my ear. "Ana, calm the fuck down."

"Dahrel, please, you have to get me out of here."

Suddenly weak I leaned back against my brother for support. The crowd in front of us parted just in time for me to see my boss crouching over the now cowering Kaul who was lying prone on the floor. I'm not sure how the Kaul had ended up on the floor but from the look on Bravnica's face, I'd safely bet that he had helped him get there. I watched as he hauled the Kaul and half dragged half marched him out the back door. Taras followed them out and Anton closed the door behind them, turning to lean on it he smiled at the suddenly disappointed crowd that were no doubt eager to see just what was in store for the misbehaving Kaul. While the bulk of the crowd was distracted by Bravnica's exit out the back door, Dahrel marched me out the front.

I welcomed the fresh air and let the gentle afternoon breeze calm my ragged emotions. We continued to the edge of the gravel that surrounded Reds and stood under one of the large park trees. Dahrel planted me against the tree and turned to pace in an attempt to calm himself down, his face looked as though it was about to explode.

Damn it.

This was not going to reflect well on them.

I sighed and let my head roll to the side to find Garrick standing there with a stupid grin on his face trying desperately not to laugh.

"Remind me never to piss you off little sis!"

Dahrel rounded on him. "You think this is funny Garrick?"

Garrick smiled but the inevitably smart mouthed response was cut short.

"Do you think that our baby sister, being accosted in a bar and then getting into a fist fight with a Kaul twice her size..." Dahrel seemed to lose track as he dragged his hand through his tousled hair. He looked around as if an explanation might appear in the air around us then turned back to Garrick and pointing violently at the bar. "...And all of this in front of Commander Bravnica."

At this point I wanted to step forward and tell him to back off. After all it was me he was pissed off with not Garrick. I wanted to shout that I'm the one that embarrassed him by getting myself accosted in front of his beloved Bravnica. I wanted to know if my big brother even cared that I might have been hurt. But I was so weak from my little episode that I was finding it hard just to keep myself upright.

"Ana!" I looked toward the frantic voice to see Tash spilling across the gravel with our bags slung over her shoulders. "Ohmigoodnessareyouokay?"

She pushed passed Dahrel but before she could reach me was cut off by Yari's large form. "Did he touch you?"

I was trying to figure out how he got across the car park without me seeing him when he spoke again. "Ana, did he touch you?"

I was completely deflated. "It's over Yari, Just…"

He didn't wait to hear the rest and straightened, turning back toward the car park. "Where is he?"

Garrick and Dahrel both moved forward, blocking his path. Dahrel placed a hand on Yari's chest. "The damage is done, kicking his arse is not going to help matters."

Nor change the fact that I had lost it…in front of everyone.

Yari pushed at them and Garrick pushed back. "Whoa Man, she's cool, look." I watched as he nodded over Yari's shoulder at me. "Look."

Yari's back expand and contract as he took a deep calming breath before turning to look at me. He looked like he was ready to kill something, or someone.

Garrick threw an arm around him. "It's done. It doesn't need to go any further now. The Bravnicas have sorted it."

The air seemed to shift as Yari relaxed his shoulders and I realised we had all been holding our breath.

I still felt a little woozy and I whispered to Tash who had come to stand next to me. "I need to get home."

"I'll walk you home." Yari stepped forward but I waved him off.

"Please Yari, stay. You never got that beer. Go and hang out. I'll be fine." He looked like he was going to object. "Please Yari."

He must have heard the desperation in my plea and let it drop - I could see he wasn't happy about it though.

Relieved I gave him a reassuring nod as Tash turned to my brothers. "We are leaving."

Dahrel stepped forward to protest but Tash held up her hand.

"You can come by the house tomorrow morning if you would like to talk to Ana about this…" The hand that had held Dahrel in check so effectively now waved dismissively at the pub. She pulled our bags back into place on her shoulder and turned her back on the boys lowering her voice. "You okay to walk?"

I nodded, impressed by the way she had handled Dahrel. He didn't see that one coming. I pushed myself off the tree and Tash stepped back to give me some room.

"Not so fast you lot."

The boys groaned in unison as Red, the owner came barrelling toward us. A large burley man he was bald with a goatee that swept across his broad chest when he walked. His demeanour was usually enough to stop any serious conflicts and any that do arise are dealt with quickly. I leaned back against the tree and watched as he huffed his way toward us. Dahrel and Garrick moved to stand on either side of me, sending a clear message to Red. I smiled inwardly knowing my brothers had my back, no matter how pissed off with each other we may be, we were blood and the Valinskis always looked after blood. I took a breath and braced myself, for the berating I knew was coming.

He stopped in front of me and pointed his stubby finger. "I know you are local Ana and you and your brothers are nice customers."

He waved his finger at my brothers before swapping it for his thumb and pointed that stubby digit over his shoulder. "But that shit is not on."

I took a breath to defend myself but Red was having none of it. "We are gonna have a lot of new people around over the next few weeks and if you can't control yourself, then I don't want to see you here until the Festival is over."

I found my voice. "Red, did you see what that guy did? He deserved a lot more than what he got!"

His goatee bounced off his chest as he became more animated. "And I would have sorted that out if you had been able to control your temper. You do not go around picking fights with Kaul you do not know Ana. You are not stupid, so stop acting like you are."

This was a low blow and I wanted to say so but in a rare show of clarity, I held my tongue. After all, Red's was our favourite bar and I like beer. Taking my silence as agreement, Red glared at each of us in turn before turning his back and stomping back to the bar.

We breathed a collective sigh of relief. I pushed off the tree again but Yari blocked my path. "Show me your hand."

I had been ignoring the pain that was radiating from my hand in short sharp bursts until now. "It's fine, don't worry about it."

He reached behind me and grabbed it causing an explosion of pain that I hadn't been ready for. I cried out and was instantly surrounded by four very concerned but unqualified self-appointed doctors.

I winced as they gingerly turned my hand this way and that. "Seriously guys, it's fine." I took a sharp intake of breath as someone probed a swollen knuckle. "Argh, please is this really necessary?"

They ignored me and Tash who doesn't do blood very well, gave her diagnosis. "She needs stitches."

Garrick shook his head. "No, but look at this swelling, I think it could be broken. We should get it checked out."

"What?"

This was getting out of control. Ignoring the pain I yanked my hand out of their grip before they pronounced me dead.

"My hand is not broken. I just need to get home." I pushed past them, conscious of taking it slow so as not to fall flat on my face. I was still feeling pretty weak.

They let me go and Tash came up quickly beside me.

Yari called out behind us. "Make sure she ices that hand."

Tash waved back at them. "I can handle this."

We didn't stop, but both let out a relieved sigh when we heard the gravel under their big boots scrunch as they made their way back toward the bar.

We walked home in silence, I occasionally had to grab her arm for support but she didn't say anything, just slowed the pace. She helped me up the stairs and I collapsed on the couch. Tash looked down at me with sympathy in her eyes.

"So this one really took it out of you huh?"

I closed my eyes and nodded, "Do you think anyone noticed?"

Tash scoffed. "Ah no, luckily when you started blowing up beer coasters, the Commander had broken free of Taras and literally flew through the air taking out that Kaul." She narrowed her eyes and headed toward the kitchen. "I wonder if the Bravnica's have some kind of Matrix powers that they haven't let on about."

Suddenly very interested I pulled myself to a sitting position and interrupted her musings. "Sorry, what did he do?"

She pulled a bag of frozen peas out of the fridge and made her way back over to the couch. "As soon as Mr Gropey got hold of you I got pushed out of the way and couldn't get back to you so I stood up on a chair to call to Garrick for help. I saw you punch the guy, and can I just say that you looked awesome from where I was standing." She gave me a little wink and I laughed. "By this stage the boys were already in action. Dahrel was halfway across the room, Garrick was heading straight to me, Yari was heading towards the Gropey and Taras was holding back the Commander yelling at him to let the others handle it. I guess he didn't want the future Emir getting caught up in a bar room brawl."

She plonked herself on the couch next to me and handed me the peas. "Anyway the Commander broke free and just sort of flew." She made a sweeping motion with her hand and followed the trajectory of an imaginary Bravnica as he flew super hero style through the air. "He passed Yari and landed on the guy, I heard you cry out and then the coasters exploded. I jumped off the chair to try and get back to you again but bloody Garrick threw me over his shoulder like some conquering Neanderthal. He hustled me back into the booth growling at anyone that came near until I slapped him across the back of the head, telling him to go and help Dahrel get you out of the bar and that I would meet you all outside."

I smiled at the image of Garrick getting slapped by sweet little Tash.

She placed a hand on my forearm and gave it a little shake, compelling me to look at her. "So do you know what triggered it this time?"

I shook my head. "Tash, I don't know what came over me." I could feel panicky tears start to heat the back of my eyes and I blinked them back. "The rage just flowed and I couldn't stop it. I didn't *want* to stop it." I looked up at the ceiling in desperation. "I'm becoming more and more volatile."

I sniffed and Tash handed me a tissue. I wiped my nose and smiled as my best friend tried her best to reassure the both of us. "We are going to figure this out Ana, I promise."

I nodded. "I know. I'm going to bed now okay?"

She gave me a knowing smile and let the subject drop. We were both too worked up to discuss this rationally, besides I already knew that Tash would try and play it down and then go back over all the useless research we had done so far. I was in no state to be rehashing all of that stuff especially when the only lead we have had in years had just up and left for no logical reason. Amongst all the confusion of the day there was one thing that was now settled in my mind. Vadoma was right.

I am cursed.

EIGHT

I had been tortured by the clock all day. After last night's events at the pub I hadn't been able to escape the scrutiny of my brothers who had come pounding on the door at a very uncivilised seven am. After half an hour of serious evasion I finally scared them from probing any further by announcing that it could very likely have been due to Ladies Problems. They both looked suitably horrified and confused at the same time, quite a feat I might add.

Tash took over, distracting them with a couple of fried eggs and some crispy bacon which they wolfed down in under a minute before heading out the door, Dahrel giving me a dark look before pulling it closed. My relief was short lived. Tash had pulled out her old reference books in a token effort to explain my little episodes. We knew there was nothing in them. We had searched each one from cover to cover numerous times. I knew that she was just trying to make me feel better but it was having the opposite effect. I just wanted to forget the whole thing ever happened, I was going on my date with Yari tonight and would have much preferred to talk about that. Eating breakfast quietly I listened while she flipped through the familiar pages throwing around theories and possible explanations.

An hour later I dragged my butt into the office. I was dreading seeing Bravnica. I loved this job and hoped to hell that that stupid Kaul and my stupid temper hadn't blown it. Swallowing my humiliation I put my big girl panties on and headed for his office, reasoning with myself along the way that this job was worth grovelling for and if I had to, I would beg to keep it.

Pushing his door open I let out the breath I had been holding, his office was empty. A sticky note stuck to the back of my chair explained his absence.

Anastasia,

At Laurie Castle. Won't be in today. Please start on preparing the report for Council.

DB

I looked to the ceiling and mouthed a little Thank You to Daska. "Awesome."

I threw myself into the task and the day passed quickly. I only stopped briefly to feed my growling stomach. By three o'clock I had to call time, I had been ignoring the throb in my hand for a couple of hours but it was unbearable now. It was swelling again and I figured I wasn't going to get anything else done today so collected my stuff and headed for home. I wanted to have time to ice my hand before my date.

When the little hand finally dragged itself to the six, I jumped in the shower to start getting ready. What to wear wasn't an issue. I'd had my outfit laid out since this morning. I squeezed myself into my black skin tight jeans and turned to make sure my butt looked alright before grabbing my shimmery silver halter neck. This was one of my favourite tops and it never failed to impress. Turning on the harsh bathroom light I applied my make-up using a little more eyeliner than usual and shading my eyes with dark grey and a little silver. My hair was as always a bit wild, but I figured it went with what I was wearing and gave it a little shake for good measure.

I caught Tash's reflection in the mirror as she poked her head around the door and gave a low whistle. "That poor boy doesn't know what he's in for."

Smiling I turned and scrunched my hair. "Oh I think Yari can handle himself, he's a very popular boy you know."

She nodded, "Alas his love had only ever belonged to one." Tash clutched her chest dramatically. "Oh, the hearts that will be breaking across Lumeer tonight!"

I shook my head as I passed her and headed back to my room. She chuckled as I closed my door to put on the final touches.

I just finished putting on my silver hooped earrings when there was the awaited knock at the door.

"I'll get it." Tash yelled and I heard her thump through the house in her haste.

I let out an exasperated breath and asked my walls. "Would it be too much of a stretch to ask for a little subtlety?"

I heard her open the door to greet my 'date', there was a muffled conversation before she raised her voice. "He's here. Are you ready?"

"I guess that answers that question."

I could just picture her grinning at Yari like a Cheshire Cat.

I took one last look in the full-length mirror, giving myself the once over before placing my feet into my new six-inch patent black stilettos, completely impractical and totally gorgeous. Happy with the result, I reached for the glass bottle on my dresser containing my favourite perfume. Garrick had brought it home for me on his last trip to France. He found this little shop full of trinkets and gifts on a small back street in Paris. The bottle was exquisite - with its long elegant gold lid and its fat round belly covered with hand painted butterflies. It was the girliest thing I owned and I loved it. Applying two small dabs on either side of my neck I grabbed my purse off the bed and headed for the lounge room.

I was greeted by a beaming Tash, who was trying very hard to contain her excitement but failing miserably, she may as well be bouncing on the spot. Yari looked super-hot in his jeans and black dress shirt. Oh, what half the female population of Lumeer would give to be in my sexy but uncomfortable shoes!

Crossing the room toward me I watched as his eyes slowly travelled from my mussed hair all the way down to my toes and back again, finishing his lazy perusal with a raised eyebrow. "Maybe I should get my gun."

His tone was low and my body reacted like a tuning fork.

Wow.

Tash looked from one of us to the other, like a spectator watching a tennis match as she waited for my reaction.

"Uh, maybe we should make a move?"

Yari grinned and stepped to the side, clearing my way to the door. "After you."

Throwing my head back I met his grin with my own raised eyebrow and stepped forward, when I drew level with him he threw an arm around my waist, letting his hand rest a little low on my hip as we moved toward the door together. Tash smiled shamelessly in the kitchen as Yari opened the front door and ushered me out.

Closing it behind us with a resounding click I heard Tash call out from behind the solid wood. "I won't wait up!"

I rolled my eyes and moved down the stairs quickly to get out of earshot for fear of what other parting words she might call out.

We rounded the corner to find Yari's Ducati waiting impatiently in its brooding Superbike manner. I couldn't hide my excitement, I loved Yari's bike and he knew it. It was much bigger and a lot more powerful than my Fireblade so naturally I was a little jealous. I walked straight up to the bike and threw my leg over. Straddling his baby I settled my weight and stretched forward to grab the handle bars. I heard Yari's sharp intake of breath as it hissed between his teeth and realised the picture I must have created. Smiling I glanced back over my shoulder.

"So when are you gonna let me ride this bad boy?"

I knew I was being a tease, but it was Yari. We both knew our destiny and over the last year had started to do a little bit of harmless flirting. Harmless because he always backed down - which was why I was a little surprised when he didn't. Instead he held my gaze and stepped forward. Leaning over me he placed his hands on either side of the tank, his thumbs resting dangerously close to my breast I could feel the heat radiating from his rock hard chest as it pressed against me from behind.

With his mouth a mere inch from mine. "You'll get your turn when I'm sure you'll be able to handle the power."

I swallowed as my stomach did a little flip flop at the innuendo. Wow, ok so I guess this is why he is so popular with the ladies.

I didn't know how to respond and he let me off the hook, breaking the charged moment by stepping back. "C'mon, we'd better get moving."

I jumped off the bike a little too quickly and he gave me a knowing smile as he handed me my helmet, I made the mistake of reaching out with my right hand, giving him an eyeful of swollen knuckles.

He grabbed my hand. "Shit, Ana."

"It's fine."

I tried to pull away and it took a couple of tugs before he released me. Working his jaw he turned his head to the side and glared at a tree, obviously trying to cool his jets. Letting out a sigh he turned back to me causing one of his wavy locks to fall rakishly across his brow.

"I know you don't want to talk about this and I'm pretty sure you've already been lectured by Dahrel on the merits of taking on a Kaul but..."

I pulled a face, "Yep."

He gave me a shut-up-and-listen look before he continued.

"But I want you to stay away from that guy, and if you ever see him again..."

I laughed, "What, you gonna beat him up for me?"

He didn't share my amusement. "I'll be doing more than that." His stony look had me at a loss.

I pulled my helmet on to break the contact and waited as Yari secured his before reaching up and knocking on the top of his helmet a few times. He grinned and returned the favour. I have no idea how this little ritual started between us but whenever we rode together, the trip always started with a few good taps on each other's helmets. It felt good to do something familiar and it broke the tension between us.

Giving me a quick wink he jumped on, pulled the hulking machine upright and kicked the stand. His eyes crinkled with his grin as he hit the ignition and the bike growled to life. I waited as he backed out of the drive before jumping on, the seat forced me forward and I was very aware of the intimate contact. If this had been any other situation I wouldn't have thought twice about it but Yari had shown me a side of him that up until five minutes ago I didn't know existed and to be honest, it was kinda hot!

Not sure where to put my hands I grabbed the handlebar at the back of my seat out of habit. This was my standard hold when doubling. This however was not a standard ride, this was an official date. Taking a deep breath I shifted my weight, wrapped my arms lightly around Yari's waist. I felt him stiffen slightly and instantly regretted the move, embarrassed I loosened my grip and was about to pull back to resume my normal handhold when he grabbed my hands.

Holding them in place he turned his head sideway and called out. "You ready?"

His voice was muffled by the helmet but I knew what he was asking. Giving a quick nod I shouted. "Let's do it!"

He gave my hands a quick squeeze before letting go to shift the bike into gear and giving it a little extra throttle he lifted the front wheel slightly before the streets became blurred by speed.

Our ride was disappointingly short, even though the restaurant was on the far side of town - I guess that's what you get for living in a city that you could walk across in a few hours. Still, it was the best way to start whatever classification this night was supposed to be.

Laying my cutlery side by side on my plate I folded my napkin and placed it neatly over the top.

"Oh, that was so good!"

Yari regarded me over the top of his beer glass before taking a sip and placing it back on the table, allowing one corner of his mouth to lift.

"I'm glad you enjoyed it."

His gaze was a little unnerving, he looked hungry but I don't think what he had in mind was on the menu. I cleared my throat and checked my watch in an attempt to break the tension.

"So what time does the movie start?"

He smiled as though he knew exactly what I was trying to do.

It had been a great date so far. The conversation flowed easily, although it might have been a little one sided as we had ended up on the topic of women serving in the Kaul. I tend to get a little fired up about this issue because I am usually told to drop it before I can finish my sentence. Yari had heard my rants a million times before and I think it was sweet of him to indulge me.

I was stunned when he revealed that he thought some of my arguments were valid. He believed that whilst females may not have the physical strength to fight against the Kudlak, they definitely had something to offer the Kaul. I was surprised at this somewhat radical opinion coming from a member of the Kaul and maybe even more surprised that I never knew of it. Had I been that oblivious of Yari?

I looked up from my musings to find him signalling the waiter for the bill. I took the opportunity to actually look at him, not just see him as something on the peripheral as I had always done. His smile was quick and tended to kick up higher on one side than the other, I could see why girls would find this sexy as hell. His eyes sparkled when he engaged people. It was kind of like he was always up to something mischievous and was daring you to join in. I never took any notice as I always thought I knew what he was up to. Maybe I was wrong?

After signing for the bill he looked back at me and gave me one of his lopsided smiles. "You ready to go?"

Yep, there was definitely something to that sexy as hell theory. I nodded and we left the restaurant strolling through the busy street toward the only movie theatre in town, the Festival and perfectly balmy weather brought everyone out of hibernation. We joined the queue that snaked its way to the ticket booth and entertained ourselves while we waited by making up outrageous back-stories for people in the crowd. Yari purchased our tickets and we ordered some drinks and popcorn. Taking our seats in the dimly lit theatre I eased my feet out of my heels and silently thanked Daska that I could take them off without anyone noticing.

It takes pain to be beautiful.

Smiling I remembered this was my mother's favourite saying when she brushed my hair when I was little. She would have been happy to see Yari and me get together.

"You okay?" Yari was looking at me through his lashes, concern etching creases across his forehead.

I shook the melancholy mood away and gave him a brilliant smile. "Just wondering if you are gonna hog my arm rest for the whole movie."

He didn't move his arm, just leaned back in his seat and raised an eyebrow. "That's not what you were thinking about."

I lowered my eyes and dismissed the subject by picking up his left hand to examine his Kaul ring. Kaul receive one of these rings when they are promoted to Lieutenant and they are a coveted piece. The chunky band made from white gold has a square face depicting the sun, the light that protects and a symbol of our race.

"I remember when you got this."

He eyed me knowingly but went along with the sudden subject change. "It was one of the proudest moments of my life."

Pleased that he let me win I smiled. "I know that Garrick is hanging to be promoted later in the year. I'm not sure if it is for the ring or for the fact that he would get laid more as a Lieutenant."

Yari chuckled. "I'm betting on the latter."

The lights dimmed indicating the beginning of the show and we settled into our seats with the popcorn between us. I didn't take in much of what followed. My brain was too busy trying to get a handle on this new side that Yari was showing me. It was hard to believe I had known him my entire life but had never even had a glimpse of it. He had obviously been very careful about what he showed me, maybe saving this side for when he knew we were going to get serious.

Walking back to his bike we kept it light, joking about the movie. I tried not to think about the heat of his hand as it found its way back to my hip. The evening had cooled and the crowds had thinned but there were still a few revellers about. Most had made their way to the Festival where there was more entertainment to be had. I waited for him to ask if I wanted to go to the festival grounds, I was enjoying the night and didn't want to cut it short just yet.

Yari handed me my helmet. "C'mon then Cinderella, I'd better get you home before you turn into a pumpkin."

I tried not to let my disappointment show. "Ah, I think that was the coach that turned into a pumpkin."

I looked pointedly at his bike and he feigned horror. "We had better get a move on then!"

The bike growled to life and I didn't hesitate to wrap my arms around his waist this time. The night whizzed past and the ride was too short. Pulling up at my house he killed the engine and waited for me to slide off before kicking the stand out. Removing his helmet he rested it on the seat and smiled as I handed mine over. I ran a hand through my hair to make sure I didn't have helmet hair and stepped back as he rounded the bike, herding me up the stairs.

Suddenly very nervous I tried to think of something witty to say but came up with nothing. We reached my door and I turned to smile, jumping a little at how close he was. He smiled and I realised he knew exactly what he was doing. I don't know how it happened but somewhere during the last couple of weeks he had turned the tables on me, completely. He was staring at my lips and I knew what he was going to do.

Suddenly breathless I tried to wrench back some semblance of control. "Well I had a great time tonight."

Never taking his eyes off my lips he smiled that sexy half smile and leaned in a little closer, crowding me against the door. "Me too."

The air around us was thick and my entire body was on edge, like it knew it was perilously close to being devoured.

"So um..."

He leaned in a little closer, his breath mingling with mine. "Ana."

I took a shaky breath. "Yes?"

His lips hovered above mine as he spoke. "Stop talking."

NINE

"He kissed me."

Tash let out a whoop. "I knew it!"

She poured our morning brew with a little too much gusto, spilling some over the rim of my cup. Handing her a paper towel to mop up the mess she took it and gave me a sideways glance. "So is he a good kisser?"

My mind flew back to the moment our lips touched, the gentle tug of his teeth on my bottom lip as he coaxed my mouth open, the playful way his tongue flirted with mine, the way he teased me, pulling away too soon, deliberately leaving me breathless.

"Well?"

I cleared my throat. "Tash, I'm not going to give you a blow by blow account!"

She dropped the now soaked paper towel on the bench and moved my coffee out of reach. "Like hell you're not."

I giggled at her obvious attempt at extortion. "Tash seriously, I don't have time." I glanced at my watch. "Shit, I'm late."

I threw my heels in my handbag and raced passed her, ignoring the disappointed look.

"Are you sure you don't have time for a coffee?"

Hopping on the spot I shoved my stockinged feet into my runners and looked back at the cup she was holding out to me.

Shaking my head I straightened my suit jacket and hoiked my handbag up over my shoulder.

"No, I'll grab a cup on the way. Apparently working for Bravnica means you don't have the luxury of enjoying a cup of coffee in your pyjamas on a Saturday."

Bastard

She pulled a face, "Sucks to be you."

With a self-depreciating smile I grabbed the door handle and yanked it open. "Well this morning it does anyway."

She smiled and toasted me with what was my coffee, taking a sip and closing her eyes. "Mmm, oh that's good."

In an incredibly grown up move I poked my tongue out at her and pulled the door shut before she could respond.

I jogged toward the centre of town hoping that the café near work would be open. There was something fundamentally wrong with getting a phone call at six in the morning - especially from your boss. By the time my sleep fogged brain had realised I was talking to Bravnica, I had apparently agreed to meet him at the office in twenty minutes. I'm sure my only input to the conversation was a few mumbled sounds as he ranted about a break in the investigation but here I am, jogging along the street at stupid o'clock in a skirt suit and sneakers. Relief flooded me as I spotted tables and chairs set up outside the café, they were open! A couple of people had already taken advantage and were sitting quietly reading the paper and sipping their coffees. Seriously, does no-one sleep in this town? I paid for my triple shot long black and walked the rest of the way to work clutching my coffee and pondering my boss. I guess the upside to this early morning torture is that I still have a job. I like to try and be a glass is half full kind of girl but whichever way I looked at this meeting with Bravnica, one thing was for sure. It was going to be very, very embarrassing. But I'm glad I can get it over and done with now when no one was around, instead of later in the morning with an office full of people. Climbing the stairs surrounding the council chamber I squinted up at the third floor and took a deep breath.

"Let's just get this over with."

This early the main doors and lobby areas were locked. I found the small side door Bravnica had told me about during his impressive I-haven't-drawn-breath rant this morning and swiped my access pass. I heard a little click as the locking mechanism released and couldn't help humming the theme song to Mission Impossible as I slid through the door Charlie's Angel's style. My humming stopped as the door slammed shut leaving me in a dimly lit corridor, narrow enough for one person to walk down comfortably but two people would have to turn sideways to pass each other. The small space made me feel a little claustrophobic and the sense of emptiness of a large building with no-one else around, it made me a little jumpy. I was glad that I was wearing my sneakers so that I could walk quickly without making a racket. The corridor ended at the foot of what I assumed to be fire stairs and so I started to climb, passing shadowed doorways on my ascent I found myself eyeing them warily.

You're being ridiculous Ana.

I quickened my pace and by the time I reached the top I was a little breathless. Unsure of where to go from here I turned and looked back down the stairs when a hand reached out of a doorway. I didn't even see it. It tapped my shoulder.

"Miss Valinski?"

I squealed and my heart rammed itself up against my ribcage before instinct kicked in and I started swinging my coffee-less hand in the general direction of the voice, please when I connected a few times with the owner of the disembodied voice.

"Miss Valinski… I must ask you to stop."

Another hit making him grunt.

Yes!

"Please."

The fact that I wasn't being attacked finally registered and I paused in my frenzied one-arm-windmill-attack. A startled Kaul stepped slowly out from the shadows, his hands held out in front of him as though trying to calm a wild animal.

"Miss Valinski, I'm Sergeant Rakevich." He pointed to his chest to indicate himself.

"Commander Bravnica requested I come and fetch you."

A rogue curl had escaped during my deranged attack and draped itself across my face. I blew at it ineffectually before responding. "Oh" was all I could muster as my face turned scarlet.

The Sergeant turned and disappeared into the shadows. "This way please."

Shaking the curl out of my face I quickly fell in behind him, staying close so as not to get lost.

Bloody Bravnica. Fetch me? What am I some chewed up tennis ball?

Sergeant Rakevich led me down a number of twists and turns before opening a small door that led to the lift entrance on the third floor. I had never taken any notice of the door before, from the outside it just looked like a maintenance cupboard. I raised my eyebrows and nodded at the door in silent approval, hard not to be impressed by that. Rakevich held the glass doors and waited for me to pass before heading towards a cluster of Kaul gathering at the kitchen end of the main room. Taking a sip of my coffee, I

116

turned and headed in the other direction to face the inevitable Bravnica lecture.

I found him in his office, hands splayed on either side of a large map covering his desk. Completely engrossed in his task he didn't look up as I entered the room pulling my heels out of my bag. It was clear we had not agreed on today's dress code. He was looking very toned and casual in his tight black T shirt and black fatigues. Me - head to toe corporate.

Great.

I shoved my heels back into my bag and pulled off my suit jacket. The movement caught his attention and he looked up from the map. I gave him a little wave before dumping my things on the floor.

"Thank you for coming in at such short notice. I appreciate it."

He looked me up and down, taking in the skirt-and-shirt look topped off by sneakers.

If he was amused by my appearance he didn't let on as he rounded the desk. "And you brought me coffee." Smiling, he reached for my triple shot of wake up juice.

I hesitated for a fraction of a second before rationalising. If this sacrifice was going to help win him over and prevent another humiliating sacking, then I would just have to suck it up. I surrendered my cup.

He took a sip and turned to walk back to the desk making a satisfied 'Ahhhh' sound.

"Thanks."

I swallowed hard. "No worries."

He placed my coffee at the edge of his desk and addressed the map again.

"How's the hand?"

I froze. I thought the coffee had helped us move passed this. Head still bent he considered me through his thick lashes.

"Ummm...." I cleared my throat before raising my chin a notch. "It's fine."

"That's good." He worked his jaw as his gaze dropped to my now only slightly swollen hand before taking a deep breath and turning his attention back to the map. I knew he wanted to say something else, his posture was screaming it. But nothing came.

The suspense was killing me and I couldn't help but ask. "Why do you want to know about my hand?"

And promptly gave myself a mental uppercut. I really needed to learn how to let sleeping dogs lie.

He raised his ice blue eyes and held my gaze in what seemed like a physical battle that I was helpless to retreat from. The atmosphere in the room became thick and I found myself holding my breath before he finally released me.

Letting his eyes fall back to the map I was surprised by his response. "You need to be able to type."

What? No lecture about how ridiculous it was to take on a Kaul? Let alone dangerous? Or how it probably goes against one of those silly clause thingies that I unknowingly signed because I was too lazy to read them when I first started?

Brow creased he started taking notes from the map, apparently over the conversation. Relieved and I must admit rather surprised I let it drop. I was more than happy to take this gift horse and tape its mouth shut - tight!

I crossed the room and stood on my side of his desk. "So, you mentioned there were some new leads?"

"Yes." He looked up at me and grinned causing a warm tickle to rush through me. I automatically returned his smile as he beckoned me around to his side of the desk.

"See here?" He pointed to a spot on the far side of the map.

On tippy toes I leaned forward to see what he was pointing out, bracing my thighs against the edge of the hardwood desk to stop myself from toppling onto the map. He moved to stand behind me, pointing at things that were more than likely, very important. However I was a little too pre-occupied with our proximity to give the map the attention it was due. My entire being was completely focused on him. The hard length of his body poised inches from mine. All I needed to do was lean back a fraction. I closed my eyes and took a deep breath trying to focus on the task at hand but all it did was fill my lungs with his scent, making me giddy. I quickly opened my eyes to stop the sudden room shift.

Really inappropriate Ana.

"So what do you think?" I stepped away from the desk to find Bravnica looking at me expectantly.

Oh crap.

"Um, I'm not sure."

"Look you will be fine, I promise." He smiled at me and at that moment, I would have done anything for him. He could have told me he was the Queen of Sheba and I had to build a machine to get him back to his own time and I would have agreed to it.

I smiled. "Okay."

He wheeled his chair forward. "Okay, so I need you to sit down."

I looked at his chair and then watched him move around the desk and pull the other, less comfortable chair around to this side.

He looked at me optimistically. "Are you going to sit?"

I snapped out of my Bravnica haze. "Yes! Of course!"

A nervous little laugh escaped my lips as I sat down in his chair. Oh Daska. What the hell have I just agreed to?

He pulled his chair close and sat, then leaning forward he grabbed the arm-rests of my chair and pulled me slowly toward him. Our knees were touching and I was suddenly very aware that I was wearing a skirt. Clamping my knees tightly together I tried to keep my cool. Or at the very least give a good impression of it. I looked up and it was clear he wasn't fooled.

Giving me a warm smile he moved back a little. "All you need to do is relax and I will do the rest."

I nodded, returning his smile until he spoke again. "'I'll get the lights."

Huh? Ok, now I'm a wee bit concerned. I watched him return through the darkened room to resume his seat, debating whether or not I should confess my ignorance. I don't want him to think I'm stupid, but then again why do we need to be in the dark? He sat back down and pushed forward in his chair so that our knees were best buddies again.

"I need you to pay attention to the details, in case there is something I didn't see. And then you will need to put together the report for tomorrow."

Ok so I have missed something big here. I opened my mouth to speak but he continued.

"Just relax, I will look after you." He smiled at me and his eyes twinkled mischievously. "Who knows you might even enjoy yourself."

What?

"Do you trust me?"

My mind was racing, just when exactly did I board this runaway train? I knew he wouldn't hurt me. But I am a certified control freak, I have no idea what he is about to do and he is asking me to just hand over the reins. Like it's no big deal! On the other hand, what could go wrong?

Letting out a steady breath I nodded slowly and leaned back into the chair watching as he took my hand in his. I drank in the sight, his hand was large and tanned compared to mine and his grip was strong and reassuring. Closing my eyes I sank further back as the warmth from his touch radiated up my arm and slid down my spine. I managed to suppress a shiver.

"I'm going to project the memory now, just remember that this is from my perspective and whatever you see can't hurt you. Okay, Ana?"

I opened my eyes and met his steady gaze.

"I need you to relax. Don't try and fight me. I am not going to take anything from you."

He gave a nod of reassurance and I relented. Letting go of the anxiety that wound itself tightly around my chest, I allowed my eyelids to fall closed and let out a slow breath.

"Okay. I'm ready."

Instantly I could feel it - a tingle on the inside of my head searching, branching out like an overgrown vine. The touch was more tentative than Anton's, almost a caress and like a cat I wanted to curl myself around it. Suddenly the air shifted around me, everything surrounding me disappeared and I was in a very large, very dark place. Before I could become alarmed I felt his presence, his warmth enveloped me and I clung to it.

His steady voice soothed me. "Good Ana. You're doing really well."

Glowing under his praise I felt myself become warmer still as I tried to figure out whether he was speaking or I was hearing his words in my head. Distracted by this puzzle I didn't notice at first when a grayish light appeared on my peripheral. Curious, I turned toward it.

"That's it." Buoyed by his reassurance I wanted to look closer and as if waiting for my will, it started moving towards me.

Fascinated I watched it draw nearer as though being pulled across a smooth black lake via some invisible rope. "That's my girl."

The light became larger and larger until it closed itself around me. I was standing in the grounds of the Lavric Castle and I could hear a familiar voice speaking. Turning toward the voice I found Anton addressing me.

"Ok big brother, we're here. Now could you tell us what it is we are looking for?"

I realized he was showing me a memory.

Cool! Bravnica Cam.

Dominik dragged a hand through his hair in a surprising show of frustration.

"We are here because a member of the Elite has been slaughtered and all we have managed to produce in the way of answers is more questions."

Anton and Taras shifted uncomfortably. Dominik knew that they were as unhappy about having a murderer on the loose as he was. He took a step back and glared at the entry way to one of the outbuildings.

"Did any of the Units search these buildings?"

Anton turned and leaned back to peer through the open doorway while Taras flicked through some papers before finding the answer.

"No. This one and the one to the right weren't searched."

Dominik let out a sigh. "Does the report say why not?"

Shaking his head Anton looked up at his Commander squinting his eyes to combat the sun. "They are empty. There isn't anything in them."

Dominik glanced at his watch. "Ok we still have time before the funeral so let's get in and get this done. Anton you take this one." He indicated to the closest outbuilding. "I know we are limited on time but don't rush it, be thorough."

Turning back to Taras he slapped his shoulder. "You're with me little brother."

Taras gave a quick nod and led the way. The interior was like that of a disused barn. Following Taras in, Dominik sniffed at the air, surprised to find it fresh despite the state of neglect. The wooden floor was covered with dirt and straw and the timber walls looked like they would collapse without much persuasion.

Dominik scanned the back wall, weighed down with rakes and shovels but nothing appeared out of place. "So this is what? The garden shed?"

Concentrating on his papers, Taras joined Dominik at the far wall and squatted to find the page denoting this particular building's use when it lifted gently, as if there was a breeze inside the barn.

Dominik stilled. "Did you see that?"

"I did." Taras rolled up the paperwork, shoving it into his backpack and held his hands out, searching for movement. "Which direction did it come from?"

Dominik joined him. "I think it was closer to the corner."

Taras stood to shift an old manual mower that had been discarded in the corner. With the space now free, Dominik moved closer, brushing away at the dirt and straw to expose the wooden floor. Both men crouched low holding their hands over the now empty space.

Dominik stopped suddenly. "Here."

The source was just to the left of the back corner. Taras grabbed a crow bar from the wall to leaver the planks up but there was no need. They were not secured and just rested against the joists. Dominik started pulling them up two at a time revealing a very large hole. Pulling the last plank away he sat back, leaning against the wall and stared into the black hole.

"Radio Anton and let him know what we've found. I'm going in."

Listening as his brother informed Anton of their find Dominik drew his gun, it settled in his hand reassuringly while he flicked his torch on and slowly lowered himself into the dirt hole. About eight feet deep, it was freshly dug and big enough for at least two Kaul to stand in. Scanning the dirt walls, Dominik spun in a slow circle, stopping when he came to a cement wall that had been chipped away at and now lay as rubble at his feet. Stepping through the centuries old wall his worst fears were realised.

"Shit."

Taras called back. "What is it?"

Dominik took a steadying breath before calling back. "Tunnels."

'Shit.' was all the reply he heard as he peered down the length of the tunnel, the torch light couldn't penetrate the inky black expanse and there was no way of telling how far the tunnel ran in either direction.

"Shit."

The Kudlak gained access by penetrating the cities underground tunnel system. Dominik stepped back through the collapsed wall and into the hole, blinded as his eyes adjusted to the glare of daylight outside. Looking up into the concerned faces of Anton and Taras, Dominik grimaced and held up a hand.

"We have to get back for the funeral."

Anton grabbed Dominik's proffered hand and hauled his brother out. "What's down there?"

Finding his feet Dominik dusted off his hands. "Tunnels." Indicating over his shoulder he continued. "This is where the Kudlak gained access."

Taras shook his head. "This isn't good. If it has access to the tunnels then it has access to the entire city!"

Dominik nodded. "We'll meet up after the funeral and go over logistics, then come back at first light. Agreed?"

The brothers nodded. "Agreed."

They replaced the planks of wood and gathered their belongings.

Taras turned to his brother. "Do you want me to set a guard?"

Dominik nodded. "Organise a team to stand guard for tonight."

Taras nodded. "Anywhere else?"

Dominik raised his hands palms up in a show of helplessness. "Where would we start? The tunnels are everywhere. I can't set a Kaul on every drain in the city."

Taras worked his jaw. "This is a nightmare."

My surroundings shifted, the edges of my vision became black and the view of Taras and Anton became smaller as it drew further away. I could hear muffled sounds and felt myself being dragged into consciousness. Hold on, have I been unconscious?

"Ana. Ana. How are you feeling?"

Blinking against the glare I slowly opened my eyes and watched as the dark blob in front of me turned into Bravnica. Feeling very groggy, I groaned and closed my eyes again rubbing my face with my hands in a sleepy gesture before cracking open one eyelid for another peak. He sat, hunched forward watching me intently as if he were peering into a window.

"Ana, are you okay?"

I straightened up. "Yeah. I'm good. That was just a little crazy. I didn't know you guys could do that." He smiled and I continued lamely. "Put memories in people's heads I mean."

He gave me a look that bordered on playful. "You might be surprised to hear this Ana, but there is actually a lot about the Bravnica Power that you don't know!"

I raised my eyebrows, "Apparently so."

Recalling what I had just seen, the questions flared, followed quickly by a sickening dread. There was a Kudlak roaming free in the bowels of our city. Every hair on my body stood on end and I looked to Bravnica for reassurance.

"This is worse than we thought isn't it?"

Unfortunately he wasn't in a very reassuring mood. "This has the potential to be catastrophic."

Great! We're all gonna die in out beds, not to be hysterical or anything.

He leaned back in his chair. "There is more I need to show you, would you like to have a drink first or can we continue?"

I still felt a bit groggy and was desperate for a coffee but figured my addiction could wait. It's not like I would ever have to deal with something this big again.

I shook my head and let out a deep breath, "No I'm okay, let's keep going."

He nodded and moved toward me again. Touching my knee I felt the tingle straight away and relaxed my body. I was getting the hang of this. I allowed a little mental pat on the back as I turned toward the light and let it engulf me once again.

Dominik stood before Anton and Taras in the tunnel just beyond the crumpled wall.

"I know it's daytime, but keep your eyes open. We don't know what's down here." He raised his eyes to the ceiling. "And the condition of this tunnel is not so great."

Anton and Taras nodded in unison. Anton then rolled up his map and checked his handgun, confirming he had a full clip of wood tipped bullets before ramming it home.

"Ready when you are big brother."

Taras rolled his eyes before flicking on his torch. "Rambo."

Dominik gave them both a hard stare. "Let's go."

Torch and gun held out in front of him, Dominik led the way down the southern arm of the tunnel. After fifty metres the tunnel ended in a T intersection, they had hit the border wall. As per their brief, Anton and Taras were to stick together and head east. Dominik double checked their route on his map before addressing them.

"Don't deviate from the plan. I don't want any hero shit. If you find something, radio it in."

Anton smiled, "Ah, bro. It's nice to know you care so much."

Dominik raised an eyebrow. "It's not you that I'm worried about. It's having to face our mother if anything did happen to you."

The boys both made 'Ahh' faces and nodded, conceding the point.

Anton elbowed Taras in the ribs. "C'mon little brother let's see if we can get Dominik into trouble."

He turned and winked at an unimpressed Dominik before they disappeared down the eastern arm. Dominik shook his head and headed west, focused on what was in front of him - kilometres of cement walls and hopefully no surprises. He had been travelling for about fifteen minutes when his radio crackled to life.

"Fox, this is Scorpion do you read?" It was Taras.

Dominik paused. "I have you Scorpion, go ahead."

"We've located an unmapped hole heading North back toward the city. Gerbil is going to investigate."

Dominik smiled at the call sign they had given Anton, this was a serious mission but they were still brothers and that's what you get for showing up two minutes late.

"Roger Scorpion. Gerbil, keep me informed."

Dominik waited five seconds for Anton's reply. Nothing.

"Gerbil please respond."

The radio crackled to life. "Roger that Fox…" There was a pause and Dominik could hear Taras chuckling in the background before Anton continued in a not too pleasant tone. "Gerbil out."

Knowing that the boys had split up made Dominik uneasy but he knew what they were capable of. They were trained killers and he trusted them with his life. Plus they were not new to crawling around in the tunnels. The Bravnica boys had played in them as young kids and were familiar with the ones that were underneath their own castle and the Bravnica grounds.

The tunnels had not been used since the turn of the century and due to a lack of maintenance had become unstable. Council deemed them too dangerous and they were sealed just over a decade ago. Each underground entry at the city's borders had been bricked up and any entrances within the city walls were barricaded. After that, the tunnels were quickly forgotten about by most.

Dominik neared what should have been the bricked up hole that sealed the old tunnel opening to the South West of the city but was greeted instead by a white light. His stomach dropped and he picked up his pace halting only when he reached the gaping hole leading out into the forest. Standing amongst the pile of bricks that used to be a solid wall, Dominik reached for his radio.

"Scorpion, this is Fox, what's your status?"

"Copy Fox. The Scorpion has the Gerbil and we are continuing on per original brief."

Dominik's eyes darted around the immediate area as he continued. "Copy that. I've located a breach in the South West tunnel entrance. I am going out to have a look around. Out."

Dominik stealthily picked his way through the rubble allowing his eyes to adjust to the glare when Anton responded.

"Copy that Fox. Take care Man."

Dominik executed a slow and steady search, working his way methodically out from the breach. Flicking over stones and checking the branches of every bush his frustration was beginning to show. Resigned to one last sweep of the external perimeter something caught his eye. A small clump of what looked like hair at the base of a broad tree. Moving quickly he bent down and picked up the clump, turning it over in his hand to reveal a piece of scalp still attached. Swearing under his breath he rounded the tree, my breath caught with his as he looked up at the girl. Nailed upside down to the trunk by her feet, it was obvious that her death had been incredibly violent. Her naked body, an unnatural gray, contrasted in spots by the dark spatter of dried blood. Feet ripped and red at the anchor points and the gaping hole that was once her slender neck, now slashed leaving a grotesque hole that exposed tendons and limp arteries.

It was clear the girl had been drained of blood. Bravnica shook his head - it would have been an agonizing way to die. Following the ribbons of dried blood, to the unstained earth beneath her hanging form it was clear the blood had not had a chance to hit the ground.

Kudlak.

This was the nail in the evidence coffin. Not only did he have a point of entry, but a drained body to prove it. The Council would have to accept his findings now. He took some photos with his phone and marked the position on his GPS before heading back toward the tunnel for a shovel.

TEN

I sipped my coffee ignoring the little tremor that rocked my mug as I cupped it between my shaking hands. Bravnica had insisted I get something to eat and drink as soon as he ended the memory mind show. We had resumed our places at respective sides of the large desk and I was trying to erase the memory of the girl's feet and the thoughts that maybe I had seen her before. I couldn't stomach the toast but the coffee was chasing away the chill that had sunk into my bones since seeing her.

A quiet understanding had settled over us. It wasn't just seeing things from his point of view, but knowing what he was thinking while I was in there. I felt nauseated from what I had learnt but figured I could puke later, for now I had a zillion questions and a report to write up. Bravnica wanted to take the evidence to the council that evening so that he could arrange for the immediate release of three full Kaul Units to search the tunnels. In addition to the report I had to obtain the co-ordinates of stipulated areas of interest and all known maps of the tunnels and South West forest.

Finishing my coffee, Bravnica watched me as I tried not to shake while placing the empty cup on his desk. "So do you have any questions or observations in regards to what you saw that you would like to discuss before we get started?"

Desperate to show that I could cope I pushed the sickening images from my mind and replaced them with professional cool.

"Does a bear shit in the woods?" Okay, maybe not *that* professional.

A chuckle escaped him. "Okay, stupid question."

I cocked my head to the side. "Ah kinda, yeah!"

He leaned back in his chair. "Okay, fire away."

I leaned forward propping one elbow on his desk. "Right, so starting at the beginning. The mower thingy that was on top of the planks in the shed. There's no way that anybody could have replaced all the planks and then put the mower on top from in the tunnel. So is the Kudlak still in Lumeer?"

Bravnica looked impressed. "Good observation." And like a lizard on a hot rock, I basked quickly in the glory of his praise, listening intently as he continued.

"I'd say after the attack it would have found another exit. There's no way a Kudlak would have gone undetected in the city for so long, especially with the increased number of Kaul milling around. Even so, we will be doing a thorough search of the Lavric tunnels as soon as it can be approved."

I felt reassured by this. I don't think I could have ever felt comfortable at night in the city knowing there was a Kudlak within its walls. With that concern ticked off my mental check-list I continued.

"From what I can gather, this is not your garden variety Kudlak."

Leaning back in his chair, Bravnica steepled his fingers and regarded me over their tips. "What makes you say that?"

I spread my hands out. "Well the point of entry for a start. If the Kudlak had the patience to sit there scratching away until that wall came down then that just doesn't add up to the mindlessness that we credit them with. We have always regarded them as opportunistic killers, not meticulous planners."

I held my hand out and ticked off my fingers. "That's one. Two is the fact that only one person within the city walls is dead. It makes my skin crawl, thinking about it creeping past bedroom doors where people were asleep. It must have had ample opportunity to prey on the rest of the family at the very least before being taken down by Lavric Kaul - why didn't it?" Bravnica acknowledged my point with a nod and I ticked off another finger. "Three, it didn't drain him. We all know that to a Kudlak, their thirst for blood can never be quenched. So why the hell didn't it drain him?"

Dominik opened his mouth to speak but I was on a roll.

"And then there is that girl! Even more proof that Petar's murder wasn't some random attack. It fed before it went in. Could this have been a precaution? Just in case a twinge of hunger sent it over the edge and it did drain him in a moment of weakness? Daska help us if it was! Our mindless enemies are now smart enough to think about precautions? And why not drain him? I mean, it was gonna kill him anyway. Why hold back?" I sat back in my chair, shaking my head slowly at the possibility of what I was voicing. "I guess this all boils down to what it wanted from Petar." I looked up into Bravnica's ice blue eyes. "And did Petar give it what it wanted?"

Bravnica raised an eyebrow as if conceding a point. "I've been asking myself the same questions."

"Could it be The First? Callisto?"

"That's a hard question. This Kudlak is very calculating I will give you that but to say it is the actions of one of The First? That's a big call." He took a deep breath. "I don't have all the answers yet, but I will."

There was a very determined edge to that last statement and I had no doubt that he would get his answers, one way or another. I still had questions and was going to press for as long as I could get away with it.

"So how many tunnels are there under the city? Do they all need to be checked?"

He leaned forward and spread his hands over the map of Lumeer. Letting out a sigh he shook his head.

"The tunnels are everywhere. It's a maze that would take weeks to check thoroughly. There are some tunnels that are still in use under certain high profile buildings, but the rest..." Rubbing his forehead he let his sentence die.

"There are tunnels under the chambers here aren't there? Where do they lead?"

He looked up from the map and narrowed his eyes at me. "Well they are not tunnels as such. More like passageways, similar to that which you used this morning, secret ways to get from one room to another."

Resolving to allocate a little time for research on the tunnels later in the week I let the subject drop and started working on the report.

Council had granted permission for three Units comprising of twenty Kaul to search the surrounding mountains for signs of Kudlak activity and one Unit to begin sealing the breach and scour the tunnels below the Lavric castle for any more holes. Bravnica's request for three more Units to search the tunnel network below the city was denied, frustrating the hell out of him and scaring the hell out of me. Council cited that as no solid evidence supporting the claim of a Kudlak residing below the city had been put forth, they could not justify the manpower a search of that magnitude would entail; nor could they risk the panic that would no doubt ensue.

To me it just smacked of head in the sand behaviour. While I will admit that the sight of Kaul jumping in and out of every drain in the city has the potential to scare people, it's much better than what could happen if they're wrong. What if the Kudlak is still down there? Wouldn't it be better to know either way? The Council is so concerned with the Festival and keeping up appearances with all the international visitors that they are willing to risk our safety.

Bunch of tossers.

The Units heading out of the city left the breach, on foot, that afternoon and were to travel no more than two days on their designated course. One unit going South, one South West and the other due West. I spent the evening in the barracks courtyard, handing out coordinates and running messages. The courtyard was a large open air rectangle surrounded on all four sides by the stone walls of the Barracks, kind of like the hole in a not so round doughnut. At each end of the courtyard was a large stone archway that led back out to the city and the walls along either side held doors that allowed access in and out of the Barracks. The area held several heavy wooden tables with matching bench seats and hard packed gravel on the ground. Kaul would meet socially here in the warmer months or, like today, before deployment. Bravnica had already briefed them on their missions, ordering the teams to travel no more than two days on their designated courses before returning, keeping radio silence, and sleeping in shifts during the day. The basic 'don't get yourself killed' kind of stuff.

Yari was leading the team heading south. They were to run parallel with the only access road to Lumeer and would be the most exposed. I watched him as he spoke with each member of his unit quietly while they were getting ready and was impressed by his ease. Even more impressive was his timing. I had been surrounded by Kaul all night, yet he somehow had managed to get me alone, or as alone as one could be in a courtyard full of Kaul about to deploy. The steady thrum of their low voices created enough background noise for us to speak without fear of being overheard. Holding the coordinates for his command in front of me for security, I let my guard down briefly.

"Make sure you come home in one piece okay?"

His steady regard held mine as he stepped forward and plucked the coordinates from my hand, closing in to fill the empty space between us. We were toe to toe, I could smell the soap on his freshly scrubbed skin and I had this crazy urge to lean into him. He must have read my mind as he did that sexy one sided smile of his and moved a hair's breadth closer, my lungs felt constricted and I lowered my gaze to hide my embarrassment but he was having no part of it. Reaching out he took hold of my chin, raising it slowly until I was forced to once again meet his eyes.

"I like that you're worried about me." He let go and gently ran the back of his fingers along my jaw line. The contact was incredibly distracting, I tried to backpedal but my voice came out sounding a little huskier than I would have liked.

"I'm not…" I cleared my throat and tried again. "I'm not, it's just that you're supposed to take me to the Underworld Dinner and I would hate for you to miss out on an awesome night with me."

His grin widened and without breaking eye contact, he let his hand fall so that the back of it rested against the back of mine.

"I'm a big boy Ana. I can take care of myself. I don't want you to worry about me, just make sure you're ready on time." Moving his hand he entangled his fingers in mine. "I promise I will be there to sweep you off your feet."

Giving my fingers a final squeeze he stepped away and moved back toward his command. Forcing myself back to the task at hand I let out a steadying breath. Hoping the flush had left my face I raised my head and went to turn back to the table piled high with paperwork and rations, only to have my eyes land on a set of icy blue ones. Hard and flat they met mine without reserve, there was no emotion behind them so I couldn't be sure how much of my exchange with Yari he had seen. Flustered I took a step back, unfortunately I didn't have anywhere to go and backed into the table, hitting it hard enough to leave a bruise and topple all my neat little piles of paper.

"Crap."

I frantically tried to save the piles while muttering some not too pleasant things about Bravnica under my breath. Why the hell does that man have the ability to unsettle me so badly without even saying a word?

I gave myself a mental shake and stopped my nervous fumbling. Squaring my shoulders I turned to challenge Bravnica's superior gaze with my own, daring him to say something but my efforts were wasted, he was gone.

Suppressing the urge to kick at the ground and ruin my shoes, I smiled at the Kaul standing in front of me waiting patiently for a ration pack. When it came time for the units to head out I watched as Yari lead his team through the Southern Archway. I could tell that he wanted to do more than give me a polite nod goodbye but standing next to Bravnica kind of made a more intimate farewell impossible. I watched as they moved out and found myself wondering where they would sleep tonight and hoping they had enough warm clothes.

I struggled through the rest of the weekend.

By Tuesday I had ditched my heals and opted for ballet flats, a decision that my feet were incredibly grateful for, although it irked me a little having to crane my neck at the Kaul still in the office.

Bravnica had been working on another request to gain approval for a search of all the tunnels and was going to the Great Hall to present his case to the Council. Reading over his report I felt reassured by his determination, he wasn't going to let this slide. I had just finished prettying up the documents for him when I heard him outside the door having a muffled conversation with someone. I stuck the documents back into their folder and stood to face the door as he stalked in. Thankfully Bravnica was too distracted as he entered to notice me falter.

"Ana, I'm due at The Great Hall." He looked tense as he crossed the room.

I handed him the folder and bit the bullet. "I know this is a big ask, but I was wondering if I could attend the hearing with you?"

Distracted he shook his head. "I don't have time to argue with you right now."

I stepped forward, catching his eye. "So don't."

Smiling he let out a sigh. "Fine."

Fine? Yes!

I did a mini fist pump and he reached out to stop the motion putting a halt to my celebrations.

"However…"

He fixed me with a very stern look and I made a good show of being serious.

"You must remain seated, at the back, near the exit at all times until I collect you. And you are not to say anything…" He gave me a suspicious look. "Or make any noises."

I smiled, "Done."

He fixed me with a final warning look before carrying on.

"Right. With me then." Folder in hand he turned and left the office, I scrambled for my handbag and hurried after him.

I was expecting to be impressed by The Great Hall and wasn't disappointed. It was a circular room situated at the back of the Council Chambers, accessed via the ground floor; the area was off limits to most and as a result there were numerous checkpoints. Four lead glass windows lined the opposite half of the room which protruded like a giant bay window from the building itself. Stretching from the floor to the three storey high ceiling they created a curved wall of brilliant light.

The windows were divided by five massive bookcases, on which sat row upon row of leather bound books. The books were no doubt older than dirt and worth more than the contents of Tressilia's designer wardrobe. In front of each bookcase were two levels of tiered seating that were not that wide and could probably only accommodate three people across both rows. They looked reserved for VIP's only, all five seating area's had a frame surrounding them like a four poster bed. Hanging from the frames were shear curtains that could be drawn, for privacy I guess. I seriously don't get the Elite.

Ahead of the curtained seating areas stood incredibly ornate desks, each of which was decorated with an Elite Family's crest. The desks created a rather confronting semi-circle for the unadorned desk and chair that sat facing them in the centre of the room. I guess that's where one would go to plead a case. I raised an eyebrow but remembered my promise and swallowed my scoff, instead settled for an eye roll which then drew my attention up.

A suspended gallery made of ornate wrought iron clung to the curved wall about six metres up. It was useful as well as beautiful, providing access to the higher tombs on the bookshelves. I followed the platform around looking for a set of stairs but found only a dark doorway standing directly above the one I had just entered. I was wondering how one could gain access to the dark doorway when Bravnica caught my attention.

Pushing me to the side he indicated to one of the wooden benches against the darkened back wall. "Do not move from that spot until I come and get you."

I gave him a casual salute and grimaced as my butt hit the unforgiving hardwood surface.

"Daska! Not all of us have layers of overindulgent fat for padding…" Bravnica threw me a shut up right now look. I lowered my voice and indicated toward the bench seats surrounding us. "Well, they could at least provide cushions."

Narrowing his eyes in a final warning he turned on his heal and headed to a large group of people gathered in the centre of the room. They seemed in no rush to start the proceedings, so shifting my weight in search of a more comfortable position I settled back to people watch.

The Lavrics, Preseren and Vidmars had already arrived and were mingling with each other. Each Elite family held two council seats. These were given to the two most senior males and were a coveted position. Of the five Elite Families only four would ever be present at council again. The last of the Drevenseks were murdered in a vicious Kudlak attack years ago, while visiting a Kaul outpost in the South of France. I remember it clearly as my parents were devastated by the news, the loss of the Drevensek bloodline was a tragedy. Their crest was still represented on one of the large desks. A nice show of respect to still have it there, although the cynic in me was thinking it had more to do with the fact that it wouldn't be as intimidating if the semi-circle was a little lopsided.

Scolding myself for being so cavalier I was surprised when as one, every person in the room stood and turned to face me.

Shit, did I say that out loud?

As my mind scrambled for an explanation, my heart seized as I realised too late that the Emir must be in the doorway. The only thing that separated him from where I sat frozen was an ornate wooden panel.

Red faced and painfully aware that I was in clear view of the entire room I held my breath and subtly tried to stand. The room moved as one as he entered, heads bobbing respectfully, the crowd separated to make way for The Emir. A long cloak of dark red hung from his broad shoulders, it billowed behind him as he strode into the room and rounded the desks. I caught sight of his face and smiled, the stubborn jaw line and steely gaze left me in no doubt of his paternal connection to Dominik. A hush descended as he took his seat behind the middle and most elaborately adorned Elite desk. As if by silent command and with much shuffling and scraping of furniture everyone else took their seats. Fascinated I sat and waited. Bravnica approached the desk, placed the folder down and nodded to the Emir.

"Father."

The one word was infused with respect, but also held an edge of determination that got the other Council Members looking up.

The Emir smiled, "Son."

Bravnica made a deliberate show of meeting each of their gazes, ensuring he had the attention of the room before he began.

"Emir, Elite Bravnica, Vidmar, Preseren and Lavric." He nodded at each house in turn. "I wish to raise my concern at the council's recent decision to formally deny a thorough search of the city's underground tunnels."

He paused to let his intent sink in and I watched as a couple of the Council members openly showed their annoyance. Issues were seldom heard twice at Council and I had a feeling that Bravnica was stomping on a few toes, albeit with the utmost respect.

"As stated at the previous hearing we have no evidence to confirm that the Kudlak responsible for Elite Petar Lavric's death has vacated the area."

Mikos Vidmar muttered, "And none to deny it. You still cannot prove it was a Kudlak that has committed this crime."

Bravnica turned his attention to the Vidmars.

"It is our responsibility as protectors of the people to scour every inch of this city and ensure those we love are *safe* in their beds."

The emphasis on the word safe had the Lavric Council members nodding in agreement. Drago Vidmar's eyes flicked to the Lavrics and then back to Dominik.

Leaning forward he tapped his fingers heavily on the desk. "Commander Bravnica…" His tone dripped with condescension. "…how do you propose we allow our loved ones to sleep well at night if they see us searching for an imaginary Kudlak in the bowels of our city hmm? It is your role, is it not, to provide protection…" Eyebrow raised, Drago looked pointedly at Petar's widow sitting in the curtained area behind her son, looking broken and a little pathetic. Bravnica's stance became rigid and I narrowed my eyes at Drago as he continued. "…and peace of mind to our people?"

Spreading his hands wide he encompassed the room, a dramatic look of concern on his face, while cousin Mikos picked up the gauntlet.

Tag team.

"Yes Commander Bravnica, how do you propose we do this without creating wide spread panic? And have you even considered the implications this would have on the Festival?"

Turning in his chair he dismissed Bravnica with a casual flick of his hand.

"This idea is just absurd. We won't be changing our vote and you are wasting Council time."

I willed Bravnica to go over to the Vidmars and knock their heads together just to see if they sounded hollow. Unfortunately I didn't have the power of mind control so had to sit and visualise it instead. I smiled.

Yep, definitely hollow.

The Emir's rugged baritone brought an instant stop to my pleasant musings.

"I'll thank you not to assume an opinion for me and my fellow council members Mikos."

Mikos squirmed under The Emir's censure.

The Emir pointed at the Vidmars' desk. "Drago, you made your opinion perfectly clear at the last hearing." He turned to his son and I was expecting his expression to soften. It didn't. "Commander Bravnica do you have any further information that The Council should be aware of?"

Bravnica lowered his voice and the Council leaned in as one to compensate.

"There is more at risk here than losing patronage at the Festival. The implications of Petar's murder have not yet been fully realised. How do you suppose the Department of External Affairs is going to react when they hear that we have failed to kill, let alone capture, the murderer who breached our walls, waltzed into the Lavric castle, tiptoed past the Kaul Guard and removed the head of the Lavric Elite?"

The room plummeted into chaos, every person in that room knew what he was suggesting and those that were not panicked were outraged.

Bravnica raised his voice and fed the flames. "Do you think that they will keep their end of the bargain if we do not keep ours?"

The Emir stood and the room hushed slowly. Once the mutterings had stopped he spoke.

"Commander Bravnica, I'll thank you not to insight panic." Bravnica received a look that reminded me of the way my Dad looked at me when I was being cheeky. "Now I would like an answer to my question."

Even though he had just been told off by The Emir, a situation that would certainly change the colour of my underpants, he spoke with confidence and my admiration for him jumped up a few notches.

"No further information. However I do believe there is a compromise to be had here."

The Emir held out his hand in invitation. "Then let it be heard."

Bravnica bowed his head quickly before continuing. "After the search of the Lavric tunnels have been completed and the breach sealed, I propose that we search the more significant areas at night and in smaller units."

He paused, to let this alternative breathe. No one jumped in to shoot him down so he pushed on. "Starting with the tunnels under the other Castles and the Chambers, if we are able to search these without incident, we can then look at expanding the search parameter. I also propose we install a number of closed circuit television cameras so we can monitor specific areas remotely."

Taking half a step back he opened his hands palms up and let them have at it. The Council argued back and forth for nearly an hour and with all the grunting and moaning going on one could be forgiven for thinking they were watching a Women's Finals at

Wimbledon. The negotiations were settled and Council took a vote. We needed six votes for the motion to be passed and I held my breath as hands started to rise, shifting in my seat to get a clear view. An official looking person walked into the centre of the room and made a big show of counting before turning to the Emir and bowing low.

"The Fore's have it your Excellency, six to two."

I let a little "Yes!" hiss through my teeth as the Emir turned his attention to his son.

"Commander Bravnica, your request has been granted with the provisions agreed upon by Council."

Bravnica was handed a sheet of paper, he thanked the council and turned toward the door flashing me a quick smile that made my lungs seize. I stood just before he got to the door and slipped out before him. When the doors closed behind us I let out a whoop of excitement and practically skipped down the hall, he let out a chuckle and looped an arm around my shoulders. The contact was surprising and I gave a little start. He instantly stepped back and muttered something that could have been an apology, or a drink order.

I'll have a double thanks.

I swallowed hard and got back to business. "So what are these provisions?"

Bravnica handed me the documents and we headed back toward the office while I scanned the summary page. The basic gist was that we could set up the CCTV cameras in the unsearched areas within the tunnels but we could only have one Unit searching at a time between 2400 and 0500 hours under the key buildings.

We rounded a corner and were chased down by an out of breath runner. In between gasps the poor guy managed to explain that the Unit ordered to seal the breach had completed the job and that the sweep of the tunnels directly below the Lavric Castle had been completed. Bravnica tasked one of his men to map out the locations for the CCTV cameras and headed off to inspect the seal, leaving me to return to the office and organise the logistics of our night time searches. Before heading home, I heard news that some of the search parties had returned home safely, unfortunately Yari's was not one of them.

I got little sleep that night, tossing and turning between thoughts of Yari and wondering what was happening with the search below the Council Chambers, as a result I was feeling very bearish the next day. Walking to work I gave myself a silent pep talk, refusing to give in to my mood.

Thankfully on my arrival, there was good news, progress with the night time searches had been positive and so far, the tunnels below Council Chambers and the Bravnica castle had been cleared. Although I would never ask, I'm pretty sure that Bravnica had been in on the searches, either that or he had been up all night doing other things. My mind instantly went to Tressilia and the way she had been parading herself around the office before I gave myself a mental slap. There was no way that Bravnica would be playing up all night when there was so much at stake. Pushing the unpleasant thoughts from my mind I plastered a smile on my face and swiped myself through the glass doors to the main floor.

Happy thoughts Ana.

That was easier said than done. Yari's group still had not returned and Bravnica was not happy. He had arranged some scouts to head out and search for them just before dawn but they had returned with no news and the Comm's team had not been able to raise them.

Adding to this Tressilia had seemingly taken up residence in the office insisting she be there to help Dominik. She was so full of her own self-importance that I could barely stand to be in the same room with her. But I figured if Bravnica had to suffer through her company, the least I could do was to stick by him.

Her attention span could be likened to that of a goldfish and as a result she was bored in under a minute and would take to trying to distract Dominik with talk of upcoming festival events. Her topic of the day was tonight's Underworld Dinner. It was incredibly frustrating to watch; here is this guy trying to ensure the safety of our entire bloody city and all she wants to do is bat her eyelashes and file her nails. I was impressed by his resolve as he had the patience of a saint and never once let the inane chatter get to him. I on the other hand am no saint and by mid afternoon had had enough.

"Has anyone ever told you that you talk too much?" My question was met by stunned silence and I was amused to see Bravnica's lip twitch ever so slightly. Tressilia slid off her perch on the desk and cocked her hip, raising an eyebrow at me.

"Are you going to let your staff get away with that kind of insubordination Dominik?"

Behind her Bravnica threw a frustrated glance skyward before pushing his chair back and rounding the desk. Smiling I waited for him to give it to her.

"Ana, can I have a word with you please?" My stomach dropped, I didn't hide my shock as I rounded on him.

"What?"

He moved to take my elbow but I jerked my arm out of his reach. Letting his hand drop he lowered his head and held my eyes. "We can do this here with company…" He indicated over his shoulder at Tressilia who had resumed her perch and was flashing her trademark brilliant smile. "… or we can do this in private." He nodded toward the door.

My stomach was still in free fall. I couldn't believe he was taking her side over mine! My temper was starting to simmer and I figured I'd better get out while I still could. Shaking my head I turned and stalked out of the room, heading for the small meeting room across the hall. Entering, I turned on my heel, crossed my arms and waited for him. I watched him take a deep breath as he shut the door and turned to face me. I lifted my chin in a show of defiance but for once in my life I kept my mouth shut.

"Ana, I cannot allow you to speak to a member of the Elite like that."

Allow?

I swallowed hard and willed my mouth to remain shut. Smiling sweetly I invited him to continue.

"You and I have a less formal relationship because we work together every day, however you must respect the class distinction with other Elite."

Working so closely with him over the last few weeks had brought a subtle shift to our relationship. It was very natural and easy being in each other's company and when we were alone, there was definitely no Elite verses Non-Elite formality. It hurt that the friendship I thought we had formed was based on ease rather than genuine mutual respect.

I was speaking before I realised I had opened my mouth. "So we are friends because it's more convenient for you, when working closely with commoners to forgo all the bowing and scraping?"

He cocked his head and lowered his voice. "Ana, that is not what I said."

Eyes wide I feigned shock. "Isn't it?"

Raking a hand through his hair he let his frustration show. "I don't have time to run around after you putting out spot fires." He spread his hands wide as if to indicate a mass of misdemeanouRS.

I let out an exasperated breath but he didn't give me a chance to respond.

"I want you to take the rest of the day off."

"What?" My shock was genuine now.

"And use the time to get your emotions in check. I pay you as a professional Ana and at the moment you are anything but."

I narrowed my eyes and threw him a filthy look.

Fine.

I swallowed the lump that had formed in my throat and squared my shoulders. Managing not to tell him where he could stick his spot fires I left the room. Heading straight outside I gulped in lungfuls of fresh air and paced, waiting for my temper to calm.

Five minutes later my hands had stopped shaking and I felt capable of walking home without screaming random curses at passersby. I decided to take the roundabout way and pass by the Barracks to see if there had been any news. When I drew parallel with the ovals, the back of my eyes were still stinging with unshed tears. Blinking fiercely I held them at bay and looked skyward, hands on hips.

"Hey 'Lil Bit."

Whirling around I let out a little cry of relief before running toward Yari and throwing myself into his arms. He dropped his tattered duffel bag just before catching me. Arms wrapped around his neck I buried my face in his shoulder and relished in the solid warmth of his body. It was all I could do not to bawl when his arms firmed around my waist, holding me up so that my feet dangled a foot from the ground. He smelled of sweat and dust but I didn't care. At that point there was nowhere that I would rather be.

I smiled as I felt his chuckle rumble through his chest. "Well if I'm gonna get this kind of a welcome every time I go on a mission I might have to put my hand up for more."

I wasn't ready to move from the comfort of his arms and didn't trust my voice enough to speak so shook my head in response. Angling his head toward mine he gave the shoulder I was using as a pillow a wiggle in an attempt to catch my eye but I squeezed them shut.

I do not cry.

His concerned tone didn't help. "Hey."

I could just imagine his brow creasing as the reality of my emotions hit him. Realising this I tried frantically to find my big girl panties.

Ignoring the low wolf whistles coming from his Unit as they passed us by, he loosened his grip and letting my feet touch the ground he took my face in his hands.

"Ana, what's going on?"

I sniffed and took a step back, out of his reach and rubbed my eyes. "Wow that is some serious dust you have on your shirt."

He wasn't buying, I pleaded with him, shaking my head ever so slightly. He did that half smile thing that I love and played along. "Yeah it's special Kaul dust, designed to get in your eye."

I sniffed again and swiped at my eyes.

"You okay?"

Daska I must look like shit.

"Never better."

He relaxed a little, letting his swag return.

Ah my bad boy was back. He took a step forward and pulled me into his arms as one of his unit called out.

"Sir, would you like me to speak with the Commander?"

Closing his eyes Yari took a deep breath before responding. "No, I'm coming." Still holding me his eyes found mine, I could see that he was torn. "Ana, I have a lot that I need to debrief the Commander on and I have no doubt he is going to want my report finished this evening." His expression looked pained and I realised what he was saying. "I know the Underworld Dinner is on tonight, but I'm not sure how long this is going to take."

I jumped in quickly to reassure him. "Oh look, it's fine. I can go with Tash and meet you there if you like?"

He gave me a little nod. The last thing I wanted was for him to worry about me, he must have been exhausted. I felt his body shift and his arms loosen. I don't recall the thought process that went in to my next move, but I tightened my hold and stood on tip toe, lifting my face to his and capturing his mouth with mine in a quick and tentative kiss.

Pulling back I waited for his reaction and watched as surprise gave way to satisfaction. When he spoke his voice was low and gravelly. "I am *definitely* putting my hand up for more missions."

ELEVEN

"So what do you think?"

Tash stood before me grinning in a not so subtle fire engine red knit mini-dress. Coupled with black leggings and some ballet flats, she looked fantastic as always, even with black snakes from the Medusa wig she wore swinging about her head.

"You look great."

Smiling she turned back to the mirror to adjust her snakes.

The annual Underworld Dinner was starting in half an hour and everyone had been having heaps of fun planning their costumes, even the boys were getting into it. Tash, being the eBay queen that she is, managed to procure the wig for her Medusa costume online. She also got the black angel wings that went with my Dark Angel outfit. Pushing Tash out of the way I took another sip of my wine and checked myself out in the mirror. I *love* my dress - black, strapless and fitted down to my hips before flaring out in layers of shear fabric, each layer landing just above my knee and cut at different lengths and angles, being modest one moment and flashing thigh the next. I swung my hips making the layers dance around my legs.

Look - Out - Yari.

Tash piped up behind me. "Don't think you can ignore the subject of Yari's kiss forever Ana. We live together, you can't escape me."

I looked at her reflection in the mirror, sitting patiently as though she didn't have a care in the world. Frankly I was impressed - this must have been killing her.

Turning to her I pulled my knee high boots on and relented. "It just sort of happened."

Tash threw her nonchalant air and my angel wings to the side as she jumped out of her seat and broke into a happy dance. At least I think it was a dance. She could have been convulsing so I thought I'd just wait it out to see if she hit the deck or not. I guessed it wasn't the latter when, finishing on a spin, she picked up her glass of wine and held it up to me.

"Here's to Yarna." She went to take a sip but stopped to explain. "That's your Hollywood couple-name."

I choked on my wine as she finished hers and picked up her handbag and my wings. Slinging the bag over her shoulder she tossed the wings at me.

"Wing up hussy, we are late and I want details."

Giggling like a pair of fourteen year olds we picked our way through fellow party goers and headed toward the Barracks where we were going to meet up with my brothers and hopefully Yari. The dinners at the Barracks always resulted in a big party, so that's where most tended to end up.

"Ana, your recounting skills leave a lot to be desired."

I scrunched up my nose. "I don't know what else you want me to say! We kissed, it only lasted a couple of seconds and then he pulled back. That's basically it."

"Did your toes curl?"

I raised my eyebrow, "Are you serious? People's toes don't actually curl Tash that would seriously hurt. You need to cut back on the historical romances."

She narrowed her eyes and threw me a warning look. "Don't knock the romances Ana. Not all of us are promised and a girl's gotta have someone, even if he is a fictional character who leaves me with unrealistic expectations for actual men."

I threw my arm around her shoulder, being careful not to snag any snakes. "I know I'm sorry. I won't knock your romances."

She humphed but threw her arm around my waist as we approached the barracks.

"Watch the wings Medusa."

The sun was just setting and candles all around the Barracks were being lit by figures in dark robes. We followed the crowd to the mess hall which had been transformed to a formal dining room full of round tables and candelabras. The volunteers had done a great job. Wispy black fabric hung from the ceiling at varying intervals around the edge of the room creating shadowy alcoves, some of which were already getting put to good use. Grabbing a drink each we scanned the crowd looking for the boys and found them amongst a group of Kaul dressed identically in Devil costumes. Blood red capes hung from their shoulders and hoods kept their faces in shadow.

Tash was not impressed. "Well so much for imagination and individuality." She practically stomped her foot at them.

Looking around the crowd I found more and more Kaul wearing the Devil costumes. The effect was eerie, with the crowd coloured here and there with hooded figures. Turning my attention back to the group I heard Garrick explain the outfits to Tash.

"So I got onto the manufacturer and bought a whole heap for next to nothing and then sold them in the Barracks for what one might call a tidy profit." Smiling he flicked an imaginary dust particle off his shoulder, obviously well pleased with his entrepreneurial skills.

Tash shook her head and turned her back on him. "Let's find our table before I hit your brother again."

Dahrel pointed us in the right direction and told us to behave as he eyed the skirt of my dress with obvious misgivings. We made a quick escape before he could make a scene in the name of brotherly protection. Finding our seats Tash turned to chat with a work colleague on the next table leaving me to people watch. A rowdy group surrounding a table near the front of the room let out a sudden cry of laughter catching my attention. I watched the group as they mingled and moved, slowly revealing the occupants of the table. My heart seized as Anton and Taras Bravnica came into view.

Daska please don't let him be here. Please, please, please.

As if hearing my little mantra and wanting to teach me a lesson in appropriate prayer use, the crowd suddenly parted, revealing a lounging Dominik Bravnica.

Thanks big guy.

A lump the size of a golf ball lodged itself in my throat and I took large swig of my drink to try and shift it. He was, like me, dressed in head to toe black and damn him if he didn't look hotter than usual with his air of disinterested superiority.

I let out a resigned sigh. *How is that even possible?*

Ignoring my stuttering heart and the sting of this afternoons reprimand, I turned my attention back to my table and forced a smile, silently wishing Yari would arrive and stubbornly ignoring the Bravnica half of the room.

I made it through entrée and main without really tasting my food. It looked fantastic and had Tash and my brothers exclaiming. Demolishing her desert Tash threw her napkin down with a sigh and turned to me.

"I need to go to the ladies, you coming?"

Jumping at the chance of a distraction I pushed my untouched soufflé toward Dahrel and left the table. Unfortunately the toilets were located at the front corners of the room so I had little choice but to see and be seen by the Bravnica table. Not surprisingly Tressilia sat in the seat next to Bravnica, whose hair had been disheveled by her persistent fingers. She was leaning over him, exposing ample cleavage that was desperately trying to escape the tight confines of the red PVC devil outfit Tressilia had poured herself into.

I pointed the pair out to Tash who narrowed her eyes to study them. "Oh she needs to ask for her money back, that outfit's two sizes too small."

Our mock concern turned into amusement at Bravnica's valiant efforts to keep Tressilia's hands off him, kind of like trying to keep an octopus in a cereal bowl - not easy.

"It must suck being so predictable."

Tash made a noise of agreement as we pushed through the door marked with a She-Devil. Having checked our hair and re-applied our lippy, we weaved our way back through the tables to our seats. The heat of eyes touched my back and I knew Bravnica was watching. Slowing my pace, I let my hips sway deliberately and refused to look at him.

Stick that in your Elite pipe and smoke it Bravnica.

People had abandoned their tables and were now milling around chatting and checking out each other's costumes, waiting for the bar to open. A beat started up and as one, the crowd moved toward a set of stairs that led into the bowels of the building. Tash started to move with the crowd, but I held her back.

"Just wait a minute. Let the crowd go ahead, we can follow once it's clear."

Tash nodded and we slowed our approach to a meander. I eyed the doorway leading down with a sense of unease even though I knew that the basement had been checked thoroughly and had seen the report myself. Bravnica and his posse disappeared down the staircase and as the crowd thinned, we had no choice but to follow. The staircase was narrow and dark and the sound of heavy base pulsated around me, forcing my body to move in time. A strobe light indicated the end of our descent and we entered a large smoke filled room surrounded by walls made up of shadowed archways. I noted that at the entrance to each archway stood a Kaul in black fatigues, Bravnica had left his group and was talking to one of them. I relaxed when, seemingly reassured he returned to his group and Tressilia's clutches. Nursing our drinks at the makeshift bar Tash and I stood under the overly protective glare of my brothers who, with their aggressive posture and scowls, managed to segregate us from the rest of the room.

I let out a heartfelt sigh. The night was not turning out like I had planned. I looked across the bar at Bravnica's group and froze when he chose that exact moment to look up and catch me watching him. An amused expression played across his face and it was all I could do not to storm over there and slap it off.

Fuming, I turned back to Tash. "This is ridiculous. I did not spend all this time creating this…" I moved my hands up and down my body and around my head, vigorously indicating my outfit and hair. "…To have it wasted at the bar with Tweedle Dee and Tweedle Dum." I pointed at Dahrel and Garrick in turn, just in case it wasn't obvious enough who I was referring to.

She narrowed her eyes. "Ana you need to take a breath. The last thing you want is to have another…" She made an explosive gesture with her hands and mouthed 'Kapow…moment.'

"I know and I am going crazy cooped up in the corner like this wondering when Yari's going to arrive. I'm going to dance and work off some of this energy."

I knew that this would get me away from the group as neither my brothers nor Tash were keen to cut a rug. Tash eyed the gyrating bodies on the dance floor and I knew she was considering taking one for the team and joining me. She opened her mouth to speak but I jumped in and cut her off.

"Tash, I'm cool. There's no better place for me to work it off than on the dance floor!" I smiled reassuringly and took a few steps back.

She didn't look convinced. "Ok then but just remember to breath and if it doesn't calm you down come straight back and we will leave."

I nodded and turned toward the pulsing crowd, smiling when I heard Tash call after me. "And don't do anything you wouldn't want to explain to the paramedics."

I'd usually be dancing with Yari at these kinds of events. He moved really well and no matter how wild I got, he was always along for the ride. The crowd parted before me as I grooved my way into the mix. The heat on the dance floor was intense and I threw myself into the moment with reckless abandon. I needed this. I needed to just forget about all the shit that was going on in the world and have fun. Forget about the Kudlak attack, forget about Bravnica and forget about my unexplained kapow moments. Just dance and have fun.

Half an hour later my hair clung to the sweat on the back of my neck and I could feel little beads of perspiration forming on my skin. Contemplating leaving the dance floor for a drink, I let out a whoop when one of my favourite hip grinding songs came on. I grabbed the nearest guy, who, judging from the look on his face was only too pleased to be grabbed. Smiling we found a mutual rhythm and our dance became gradually more and more risqué.

I was being watched again.

Continuing the dance I turned in my partners embrace to scan the crowd, possessive hands held my swaying hips close as I spotted my quarry.

Bravnica.

Drink in hand he leaned against the bar with one foot casually crossed over the other, giving the appearance of being relaxed, bored even. But the look in his icy blue eyes as he stared directly at me held something very different, something barely contained. My heart thudded in my chest and I fought a ridiculous urge to run for my life. Giving myself a shake I raised my chin in defiance.

I will not be intimidated by the likes of you Bravnica. Your Elite arse doesn't know what it's missing.

A smile touched my lips. Maybe it was the burn of this afternoon's dressing down, maybe it was the bottle of wine with dinner, whatever it was I wanted to get one over on Bravnica. Badly. I let my smile turn seductive.

Hold on to your throne honey, you might want to sit down for this.

There was one thing I could do well and that was move my body so holding Bravnica's gaze I turned up the raunchometre with some serious lower body action. My partner's hands were becoming more and more confident and I encouraged him boldly with my body. Holding my hands up high over my head, his hands played down the length of my arms to make their way slowly down my sides, just brushing the outer swell of my breasts. Watching Bravnica through my eyelashes I was enjoying the sight of him shifting restlessly, his expression had changed, hardened. I held his gaze ruthlessly and rolled my hips, pleased at my choice of dance partner who was holding his own. The heat surrounding me had risen again and I felt like I could burst into flames but I was determined to finish the dance. Closing my eyes I gathered my hair up off of my neck to let the cool air touch it and was hit by a force that knocked the breath out of my lungs. Shocked I opened my eyes for an explanation and inhaled sharply.

What the hell?

I wasn't on the dance floor anymore. Frantically turning on the spot I could hear the beat of the music, muffled as though from a distance but the room was dark and from what I could see, empty.

Shit, Shit, Shit.

I took a deep breath.

Ok, calm the fuck down Ana and figure this out.

I stood very still and got my breathing under control as my eyes swept slowly from left to right. Before I did anything I wanted to be sure that wherever the hell I was, I was alone. My eyes took their sweet time to adjust, as darker shapes slowly revealed themselves, shade by agonizing shade.

A large four poster bed.

A table with matching chair.

A large body moving toward me.

Checking the urge to scream I saved my energy for escape. Forcing my legs to move back I came hard up against a wall, followed an instant later by a pair of large hands slamming the stone on either side of me. I caught the familiar scent of his body as it kept coming, stopping just short of contacting mine. Both frozen, the air between us crackled with tension and I knew before looking up who stood over me.

"Ana."

He uttered my name in a strained tone and I looked up meeting the intense stare. He was leaning heavily over me as though wounded and my body was already responding to the close proximity of his, even though we didn't touch. His breathing was laboured and I found myself straining for air as we held each other's gaze, unable to look away. I was trapped in every sense of the word. The space between us electric, my skin prickled and I felt like there was an imaginary piece of string attached to my lower belly and I was slowly being reeled in toward him. I didn't fight it. I probably couldn't if I tried. I knew this wasn't possible, that this couldn't be happening, but I just didn't care. Oh Daska help me, with every fibre of my being I wanted this. He moved closer and my body screamed for contact as he lowered his lips to hover over mine. Every breath intermingling I was helpless with anticipation.

He spoke again, low and gravelly. "You should be more careful who you toy with."

I opened my mouth to speak but my words were swallowed as his open mouth met mine in a deliberate and carnal kiss that had me reeling. My hands grabbed at his shoulders. I wasn't sure if I was trying to push him away or pull him to me but I grasped at his solid frame all the same. He let out a low groan and crushed my body with his, deepening the kiss and changing the tempo to a slow and deliberate rhythm.

I let my eyelids fall as the weight of his body pressing against mine set my nerve endings thrumming, his scent swirled into my lungs and suddenly the breath was knocked out of me again. Stumbling sideways I fell to the floor. Confused I watched the dancing feet surround me as they twisted and turned to the beat of the music.

Well it's official. I am completely out of my fucking mind.

I made to stand up but just managed to flop my legs around ineffectually. Stunned I watched them betray me. Panic rising I looked around for help and nearly cried out in relief when I spotted Yari, standing aggressively over the guy I had been dancing with. The guy backed away holding his hands up in a gesture of retreat and Yari turned to me. Wrapping his jacket over my shoulders he scooped me up and charged off the dance floor toward the exit. Touching my swollen lips I looked over Yari's shoulder to search the crowd for Bravnica but his place at the bar was empty. Shaking uncontrollably, I tried to calm myself as Yari muttered profanities under his breath. We hit the stairs and I was about to tell Yari to find Tash first when she came careening around the corner, snakes flying. I relaxed as she clambered up the stairs in our wake throwing out questions like a piñata spewing lollies.

Yari laid me down on my bed as though I were a china doll. I felt shakey but I knew that was more to do with emotional turmoil than physical weakness. The question of whether my next fashion purchase should be a straitjacket was tumbling relentlessly through my head. Do they come in red? My style choices were interrupted as the bed dipped under Yari's weight. Sitting on the edge he watched me intently.

"Are you sure you're okay?"

I nodded and made to sit up but he grabbed hold of his jacket that was still wrapped around me and pushed me back onto my pillow.

"Ah, you need to keep that on for a sec."

Now I was really confused. "What?"

Yari stood and backed out of the room. "I'll wait out here."

He then lowered his voice and turned to Tash. "You get her cleaned up and then I want to know what the hell happened."

Tash gave him an exaggerated curtsey and closed the door. I sat up and threw my legs over the side of my bed.

"Tash, this is really, really, really bad."

She made her way over to me making shooshing noises that only made my panic worse.

"No Tash, you have to listen."

"No Ana, first we need to get you decent."

"What?"

She reached over and unwrapped Yari's Jacket, revealing a rip in my dress and half my left breast. Mortified I jumped off the bed to get out of my dress.

"How the hell did this happen?"

"Well I think your dance partner had a hold of your dress when you fell and that's how that…" She pointed at the tear. "…happened."

"Oh how embarrassing." I tugged at my now ruined dress until it hit the floor. Kicking it toward my door I let out a sigh. "I'm gonna have to burn that now."

Tash held out my dressing gown. "C'mon, let's get you showered and into bed. I'll tell your knight in shining armour that you passed out, then once he's out the door you can tell me what happened."

Head thumping I lay tucked safely under my covers and lied to Yari. "I think it must have been the heat." I picked at my sleeve feeling guilty. I knew I couldn't tell him the truth and I hated that. "I just kind of passed out."

Lie complete I met his gaze, he was pissed but his concern over my welfare was winning out at the moment. I had no doubt he was planning on tearing me a new one once he deemed me fit to fight. I knew he wanted to know how I got myself into a situation like that and I didn't have an answer for him. Or me. He let out a resigned sigh and leaned over me, gently cupping the side of my face he stroked my cheek with his thumb.

"Don't you ever do that to me again Ana."

Uncomfortable under his honest stare I made to nod and make light of the situation when his hand stilled, a muscle twitched in his jaw and I shut my mouth.

"I'm serious..." His tone was a little harsh and he cleared his throat and started again. "I'm serious, Ana. I don't know what the hell is going on with you lately, but you have no right to take your life for granted when I can name three men who would happily give theirs for yours, without hesitation."

Well that sobered me.

He straightened and turned to leave. "I'll be around tomorrow to check up on you."

He stalked out of the room followed by a speechless Tash. I listened to the deep rumble of his voice as he said goodbye then the sound of the front door opening and closing.

I let out a sigh and sat up as Tash made herself comfortable at the end of the bed. "Okay, so was it another 'incident'?"

"No, it was nothing like what usually happens." I shook my head as Tash waited for an explanation. "All I can say is that one minute I was on the dance floor and then the next..." Tash raised her eyebrows and motioned for me to finish. "And then the next I was in a dark room with um."

Oh Daska I sound like a lunatic.

I took a deep breath, "With Dominik Bravnica."

TWELVE

Tash weaved her way through the lunchtime crowd, reaching the small outside table I had reserved she dumped her bag and let out a dramatic sigh.

I smiled. "Thanks for meeting me for lunch. I've reached my limit of report writing for the day."

I had escaped the office after downloading all the reports from the deployed units. There were plenty of photos and possible leads but nothing the Council would buy as Kudlak activity. I filled Tash's glass with water and took a sip from my own.

She narrowed her eyes at me. "Thanks. Soooo, how is it?"

Feigning ignorance I studied the menu. "How is what?"

Tash plucked the menu from my fingers forcing me to look up.

"The Commander."

I sank back in my chair and rubbed at my temples. "He's fine, everything is business as usual. Sometimes I swear I can feel his eyes on me but when I look up he's totally engrossed in his work." I shook my head. "If anything did actually happen then he's not letting on but to be honest I'm beginning to think I imagined the entire thing. Besides I'm still pissed about the whole, convenient friendship Elite Non-Elite crap." I let out a sigh. "I just don't think I can handle another confrontation with him today. I mean he is just so damn..." Struggling for a word I looked skyward but nothing came and I let the sentence drop when a perky waitress arrived at our table pen poised over her little pad.

We both ordered, Tash waited for the waitress to leave before speaking. "Things will settle down, you just need to keep cool."

She was right. I was letting frustration get the better of me. I thought Bravnica and I had become friends. I thought wrong. No biggie. For my own sake, the best course of action now was to just lay low. I'll admit, some will say that's kinda impossible for me but I plan on giving it a red hot crack.

"I guess I'm just gonna have to stay out of trouble. Keep a level head and avoid the Looney bin." I chewed at my lip. "Speaking of, did you find anything more in your books about visions or hallucinations?"

Tash's brow creased as she shook her head.

Our drinks arrived and in silent agreement, we both settled in to enjoy our lunch and stop stressing about the endless drama that was my life.

I rounded the corner into the kitchen where Anton and Taras were deep in conversation. I didn't want to interrupt them so quietly pulled a cup down from the top shelf. Reaching for the coffee I stopped when I heard Bravnica's name, tilting my head toward them I tried to decipher their hushed tones.

"Could you imagine having Tressilia as a sister-in-law?"

What?

"I think father only said he would consider the offer out of courtesy, there is no way he would accept it."

"More to the point will Dom?"

"Well they have been spending a lot of time together lately."

A searing burn in my hand had me crying out in pain. I had overfilled my cup.

"Crap."

I heard chairs scrape behind me as the boys jumped up to help. "You right Ana?"

Hissing air through gritted teeth I jammed the cold tap on full and held my hand under the flow.

Idiot.

"Ana?"

"It's nothing, I'm fine. Just stupid, I burned my bloody hand. It'll be fine."

Taras reached me first and grabbed my hand to inspect the damage. "It'll be right, just keep it under the water for a few minutes."

I turned to face him. "Well thank you Captain Obvious!" Taras raised an eyebrow and I instantly regretted my smart mouth.

"Sorry, I'm just a little... distracted."

Handing me a clean towel he smiled. "That's cool Ana, it takes a little more than that to scare me."

He winked at me before turning to leave. Anton was chuckling as they left. "Ha, Captain Obvious."

I waited until the echo of their footsteps had faded down the hall before turning the tap off. Standing over the sink I took a couple of deep breaths, my eyes were burning.

Oh Daska this should not affect me.

Swallowing hard I tried to ignore the sick feeling that had settled in my stomach.

I don't care about Bravnica getting promised to Tressilia.

The fact that I was now lying to myself made me feel even worse. Pulling myself together I dumped my coffee down the sink and headed back to Bravnica's office. I still had to go down to the ovals to help set up for tomorrow's soccer games and I needed to grab my stuff. I had made it half way down the hall when I was almost mowed down by a hurrying Sierra.

"Whoa, slow down!"

She had obviously been looking for me. "Ana!" She gasped. "Commander Bravnica has to send an email to the Department of External affairs with the findings from the missions but he needs to attach these documents. They just need to be scanned in. I have to get back to the Emir so can you please look after this for me?"

That girl talked the way she walked - at full speed and out of breath.

Pushing a folder into my hands she smiled. "You're a gem, thanks so much." Then she was off again down the corridor leaving me in her wake.

I shook my head slowly.

That is a nervous breakdown waiting to happen.

I headed to the stationary room to scan the docs onto my thumb drive. It was a slow process. There were several photos that I had already seen this morning as well as a number of typed reports, Yari's being one of them. I pulled it out and skimmed the pages looking for anything else that they may have discovered. Nothing I didn't already know although my breath did catch when I read about the young man who was missing. They could not confirm he had been taken but there was no evidence to state otherwise. The local authorities were still looking into his disappearance. I flicked through the reports until I came across Bravnica's debrief. His concerns with regard to the tunnels were justified. The Kudlak didn't leave the way it came in, so where was it? We know it couldn't have left in a different direction, the other units found nothing. My heart froze as the realisation hit home.

It's still here.

Unsettled I headed back to Bravnica's office but pulled up short when I was confronted by a closed door. I contemplated it for a full minute before knocking quietly, holding my breath listening for a response.

Nothing.

I smiled. I could leave the thumb drive on his desk with a note and get back to the business of avoiding him. Pushing the door open wide I had made it halfway into the room before realising that I was not alone. I froze midstride. Tressilia was sitting on Bravnica's desk, leaning over him in a pose that exposed more of her skin than I ever wanted to see. I made a mental note to scrub my eyeballs and disinfect his desk later. They were both staring at me, Tressilia with a triumphant smirk and Bravnica with an impatient scowl. I had obviously interrupted something. I guess that confirms what Taras and Anton were talking about.

Tressilia was the first to speak. "Oh look, it's the coffee girl."

I could feel my face begin to colour as Bravnica shifted uncomfortably in his chair. "Yes Ana?"

It was at that moment that my brain decided to stop communicating with my vocal cords. I wanted to say something witty and cutting. "I um, the email." I held up the thumb drive and they both stared at it.

Tressilia made a noise as though she was trying to stifle a laugh and Bravnica looked back at me, eyebrow raised in question.

"For you. I mean the email from you."

His expression didn't change.

Ana, just give him the damn thumb drive and get the hell out of this room.

"Sierra gave me the files to scan for the email you need to send to the DEA." Pleased that I was now making sense I stepped forward and placed the files on his desk. "So here's the soft copy and the originals."

Bravnica's face registered what I had been trying to say. "Thank you."

I took a step back and tucked a wayward strand of hair behind my ear. "If there isn't anything else I'll head to the ovals to finalise the set up for tomorrow?"

Tressilia preened next to him and he gave me a quick nod. "That's fine."

Obviously bored with our exchange the paperweight stretched up, arching her back and yawning dramatically. I forced my eyes not to roll and quickly gathered my things. Slinging my bag over my shoulder I left the two love birds alone. Pulling the door closed firmly behind me I let out a groan.

Well, that was mortifying.

Ominous blue grey clouds rolled in that afternoon trapping the heat of the day and complementing my unsettled mood. The air was still and expectant. I didn't know if it was the oncoming storm or the possibility of a Kudlak still being in the city but the hairs on the back of my neck were prickling to attention. Shaking off the creepy feeling I raced home to change out of my corporate gear as the heavy clouds would break before I got home again and I didn't want to ruin my good clothes. Tash promised to cook something warm for dinner as I dashed out the door and jogged back to the ovals.

All the tents had been erected and there were people milling around, putting final touches here and there. This was usually one of my favourite events of the festival but I just wasn't in the mood today. Dumping my bag in the canteen area I came back outside to help assemble the portable bleachers. It was physical work and I threw myself into it, straining with the heavy metal poles and benches. A sweaty hour later, we were done and most of the helpers headed for home to beat the rain but I had one more job to do.

I headed back to the canteen to grab a drink and check on the catering. Finishing my water I eyed the stock list before grabbing a pen and making my way to the freezer. It was one of those massive chest freezers that could hide six bodies - more if you got creative. Opening the lid a billowing cloud of chilled air escaped, cooling my skin. I pushed it up waiting for it to catch but it kept falling every time I tried to let go. Grumbling I looked around for something to chock it open with.

Nothing.

"This is ridiculous."

I had a check list that I needed to mark off but couldn't do that and keep the door open at the same time. There was nothing for it but to bend from the waist and insert the top half of my body into the freezer. I took a deep breath and got to it, taking a break every minute or so to defrost. I only had the hot dog rolls to go but they were located at the bottom far corner. I was on tip toe and still couldn't quite reach.

"Stupid lid that won't stay open!"

I let out a foggy sigh and lifted one foot off the ground, bracing my opposite hand against the back of the freezer I slowly lifted the other foot using it as a counter weight as I balanced on my hips.

"Oh Daska, its freezing in this thing."

"Funny that."

I let out a squeal and teetered slightly. My hips slipped forward but before I ended up doing a handstand in the freezer, a warm hand caught my ankle, forcing it down and allowing me to seesaw and regain my balance. I went to stand but saw stars when the back of my head connected with the lid of the freezer as it fell shut.

Ouch.

I grabbed the back of my head with both of my hands and spun around to find Bravnica, leaning casually against the counter top making no effort to hide his amusement.

I rubbed my head and didn't bother trying to hide my embarrassment. "You enjoy the show?"

His eyes flared for a moment but he ignored the question. "I didn't think you would still be here. Are you almost done?"

I hate it when people answer a question with a question. "Yeah I've just got to finish with the freezer of death here then I'm done." I gave it a little kick.

He smiled. "I'm expecting you to play tomorrow."

"Yes, I'm playing. I put my name down so I'm playing."

"Okay." I waited for him to leave but he just stood there, looking at me. I shifted nervously under his gaze and felt my face start to heat.

"Ana." The door swung open just as he started to speak and Yari strode in. "Ana, we need to talk about last night."

Bravnica cleared his throat. "I'll leave you to it." In one fluid movement he caught the door before it swung shut and disappeared.

Yari turned to look at the empty doorway and then back at me. "Working a little late?"

I sighed at the not so subtle hint. "Yari, I'm tired and cold and I really don't want to argue with you right now."

I watched as the hero in him warred with the side that was demanding answers, surprised when the latter won. "You owe me an explanation."

I stared at him for a moment but he didn't budge. "Fine. But can you at least hold this stupid lid open so I can finish this first?"

He stepped forward. "You hold the lid, I'll check the stock."

Relieved that I didn't have to stick my head back in the ice box I juggled the lid and ticked off numbers as Yari called them out, making my twenty minute job take only five. Having double checked the canteen door was locked properly, I gave it a quick tug just to triple check.

Yari stood behind me. "You can't avoid this conversation Ana, stop procrastinating."

Turning to meet his questioning gaze I held out my hands. "There's nothing to tell. The dance floor was hot, I had maybe had one wine too many. It's not like I ran through the streets naked. I don't know why you're making such a big deal out of this."

Yari's jaw clenched. "Ana don't make light of this." He turned away from me and raked a hand through his hair. "I come home from three days hunting Kudlak, the whole time thinking of you. I'm exhausted but I work my arse off to finish my debrief report so that I can come to meet you. I scrub myself of the after effects of my job so I can be with you." He let out a breath of air and shook his head. "And when I finally get to you..." I tried to stop the tears that were burning the backs of my eyes. "...I find you unconscious on the dance floor with your dress ripped open."

Oh Daska what the hell is wrong with me?

The tears pooled momentarily at the edge of my eyelids before cascading down in unstoppable streams.

"I'm sorry."

He pulled me to him and wrapped his arms around me. "I thought you were dead."

I buried my face in his chest. "I don't know what's wrong with me."

He tightened his hold on me. "What happened? It's not like you to just pass out. Maybe your drink was spiked?"

Shaking my head I sniffed inelegantly and tried to explain myself. "Yari my drink wasn't spiked.' I took a deep breath. 'It's something else."

I felt him still, waiting for me to confess.

"Yari, I think I'm cursed."

With my head still pressed to his chest, Yari's chuckle sounded muffled. "Ana, you're not cursed." He paused for a moment. "You just have a deficiency when it comes to making sound decisions." I smiled at his sweet attempt to stop my tears. Pulling back he wiped at a tear as it rolled down my cheek. "So there's no-one else. I don't need to go kill that guy you were dancing with?"

An image of Bravnica leaning over me in the dark room flashed before my eyes and I pushed it away ruthlessly.

I met Yari's questioning gaze. "No, he was just some random who happened to be on the dance floor. There's no-one else."

Yari cupped my chin, tilting my face up and forcing me to look into his eyes. "I won't share you Ana. You're promised to me."

I nodded, "And you to me."

His lips found mine in a kiss, gentle and overdue. The taste of salt from my tears was quelled by the relief at being held safe in his familiar arms and having him home safe in mine. He loosened his hold on me as we broke the kiss reluctantly, smiling as drops of fat rain started slapping the ground around us.

I blinked as a drop splattered across my forehead. "It's starting to rain."

Wiping the raindrop from my face he smiled and sighed wistfully. "So it is. C'mon, I'll get you home before Tash starts to panic."

I sat bolt upright in bed, brain scrambling for conscious thought. My room was pitch black and silent but something had woken me. I waited for my eyes to adjust before scooting off my bed and quickly checking the house for any uninvited guests. Finding nothing I let out a shaky breath and returned to my room, heart pounding despite the fact that the house was safe. I took a couple of deep breaths to steady myself and crossed to the window but hesitated before looking out. Instead of parting the curtains, I went to the right side of the window to peak out the edge. The street was empty. I realised I was expecting to see a Kudlak out there and the relief I felt at not seeing one was so consuming, I slid down the wall and just let myself shake for a few minutes.

How can we be planning to play a soccer match tomorrow like nothing is wrong? Pretending everything is okay when there's a Kudlak just waiting....

I gave myself a mental shake and pulled myself up off the floor.

There is no point in getting hysterical. Yes you are scared and with good reason but Bravnica would never allow us to be in danger.

I crawled back into bed, pulled the covers right up to my chin and watched the shadows on my ceiling.

I woke up the next day bleary eyed and with the realisation that I would have to trust Bravnica to do his job and keep us all safe. The council was right. There was no point in freaking out the entire city when we had no evidence to prove that there was a viable threat. We were safe during the day and Bravnica had Kaul walking the streets at night in addition to the tunnel searches and CCTV cameras under the city. There was nothing more he could do and even though he made me crazy I knew that when it came down to it, I wouldn't hesitate to trust him with my life.

I was tying my shoe lace when I heard Yari at the front door. "Hey girls are you ready?"

I smiled, "As we'll ever be."

I looked over at Tash who was throwing us a dubious look. This was not really her thing and she was more than happy to be considered more sideline support than an actual player.

Wrapping an arm around my waist Yari narrowed his eyes at me. "You didn't sleep?"

I rubbed at my eyes. "Uh, are they that bad?" He raised an eyebrow and waited for me to explain. "It was nothing. Something woke me and then I started thinking about the Kudlak and..."

I pulled away on a sigh and Yari grabbed my hand as it waived dismissively. "We're going to catch it."

"I know." I was just not good at waiting.

Tash walked into the room and he lowered his voice. "You should have let me stay last night. I would have distracted you." I met his gaze sceptically and he feigned innocence. "I would have slept on the couch, promise."

His grin contradicted his words as Tash gave us a sidelong look. "Come on you two, we have to get a move on or we'll be late."

I grabbed my water bottle and went to fill it in the kitchen. "Tash have you got water?"

She was in the process of pulling her hair into a ponytail when I asked and screwed up her nose. "Well I don't plan on doing any sweating but you can fill one for me if it makes you feel better."

Smiling, I filled two water bottles and packed them in my sports bag. Straightening I turned and busted Yari admiring my ensemble - three quarter length leggings and a singlet top that left little to the imagination. I raised an eyebrow and he smiled slowly meeting my accusing gaze unashamedly. I swung the bag at him as a distraction and Tash squealed as it flew through the air in front of her.

He caught the bag and slung it over his shoulder. "Righto ladies let's do it." Indicating the door he waited for Tash and I to leave the apartment before pulling it shut behind us.

The ovals were swarming with people as they made their way to the field for their allocated games. There were several heats to be played this morning with the winning teams playing in the afternoon's finals. A large crowd of spectators was starting to gather to support family and friends.

We found Garrick and Dahrel with the rest of our team which was mostly made up of Kaul. As the games were mixed there were a couple of girlfriends and sisters to make up the female numbers.

Dahrel whistled to get everyone's attention. "Okay listen up. We're in the first round, so grab a black T-shirt from the bag and put it on. Game starts in five minutes."

Everyone zeroed in on the bag to get themselves a shirt. Mine was far too big and looked more like a nightshirt than a T-shirt. I tied it in a knot at the base of my spine to make it fit a little better. The others had moved away and were kicking the soccer ball around giving me a view of some of the other players. My eyes slapped on Taras and Anton and I instantly scanned the crowd for Bravnica.

Crap.

I couldn't see him anywhere and relaxed when Anton and Taras ambled across the ovals to the refreshment tent, obviously not playing in this round.

"Ana I think you should go and warm up. Did you put sunscreen on?" Tash held the sunscreen out to me knowing full well I hadn't. I took the sunscreen to placate her and applied sparingly, screwed the lid back on the tube and looked up to find Bravnica wearing a black and white striped shirt talking to Dahrel and the captain of the other team.

Oh you have got to be kidding me!

He was our Ref. I turned to Tash with a look of horror on my face when all hell broke loose on the field. A fight had broken out.

I stood on my tip toes to get a better look. "Save it for the game boys!"

I watched as Dahrel and Bravnica entered the Frey, pulling guys out of their way to get to the centre of the huddled group.

Tash followed in their wake and I jumped in behind her. "Ana, I think it's…" On tip toes she angled her head to the side. "…it's." She spun around to face me, eyes wide. "Yari."

I pushed past her and caught a glimpse of his opponent. My heart lodged itself in my throat as recognition flared. It was Mr Gropey from Red's.

"Rip his face off Yari." Stunned I turned to see Tash red-faced and fists clenched beside me.

"What?"

She blinked a couple of times. "Ah. Sorry."

Within a second it was all under control, Mr Gropey had been led away by his team captain and Bravnica was standing in front of Yari with one hand, fingers splayed resting on his chest as if to keep him in check. I didn't want to go over while he was obviously getting his arse handed to him. So I waited just out of earshot and catalogued his injuries. A couple of cuts on his face, one deep above his eyebrow and his knuckles were pretty messed up. Dahrel approached the pair and started talking to Bravnica so I went to Yari.

He answered my question before I asked it. "I'm fine, I feel much better now."

His lip kicked up in that sexy half smile. Chest still heaving he dragged his shirt up over his head, forcing tanned skin to stretch over taught muscle. My hand reached out of its own accord and rested gently on his side enjoying the feel of his muscle moving under my fingertips. I blinked as he bunched up the shirt and used it to wipe the blood from his eyebrow, the movement enough to snap me back to reality. I yelled for Tash to fetch some ice from the refreshments tent but didn't move my hand. Instead I stepped closer to the heat radiating from his still taught body.

"Seriously? We haven't even been here for five minutes and you're already injured." I placed the thumb from my free hand on the gash across his brow to stem the flow and he chuckled pulling my other hand up to his lips and kissing it firmly.

"I'm fine honestly." He was still a little breathless, the adrenaline coursing through his veins evident in his cagey stance.

Dahrel walked past us heading back to the team on the sidelines, roughing up Yari's hair in support.

Bravnica was not so pleased. "I don't need to go into this do I Lieutenant Pavic?"

"No Sir." Yari stood firm.

Bravnica looked at me then back at Yari, he lowered his voice and leaned in close. "I don't want to see a loss of control on the field Pavic. You of all people need to be setting the example. Do you understand?"

Yari nodded his head and responded with a very firm "Yes Sir."

Bravnica looked beyond Yari to the other team half dismissing us already. 'You are going to sit this half out, use the time to get yourself under control."

Yari nodded, as Bravnica strode off to the sidelines. "Alright everyone, shows over. Let's play."

Yari replaced my thumb with his own and tapped me gently on the arse. "Give 'em hell babe."

I smiled weakly at him and we walked back to join the team. Passing Bravnica I threw a dirty look at the back of his head, childish I know but better than throwing a ball.

"Ana, you are now goalie." Dahrel pointed to my position on the field.

"What? Dahrel I'm Striker, you can't do that!"

"I can and I have, so quit complaining and get out there."

I looked to Yari for support but he was siding with Dahrel. Relief clear on his face as Garrick busily applied avitene and petroleum jelly to his laceration. The penny dropped and I realised that Yari's actions had just made me enemy number one. Dammit. The boys were banding together to keep me out of harm's way.

I stormed onto the pitch and headed for the goals. "I can look after myself you know and I am *not* playing goalie in the second half."

Reaching the goals at the far end of the pitch I felt eyes on me and looked across the field to the opposing team. Mr Gropey was obviously fit to play and eye balling me as he walked to the centre of the pitch. Yari had done some damage, he already had a fat lip and I could see a cut under his eye, which would be black tomorrow. Seeing he had my attention he blew me a kiss. I cocked my hip and flipped him off, determined not to be intimidated. He smiled with intent and I felt a little relieved to be playing goalie.

Dahrel stepped into view effectively blocking our little stare off. He jogged over. "Don't do anything silly. Just stay out of his way. It's been dealt with."

I nodded and he turned to take his position. Bravnica was giving what seemed to be a warning look to Mr Gropey. The testosterone on the field was palpable and I knew there was no way the boys were going to let me anywhere near the action. The whistle blew and the crowd cheered as the ball made its way to the opposite end of the pitch. I kicked at a tuft of grass and squinted to try and follow the plays. Five minutes ticked by slowly and I had run out of swear words when someone went down in back play and the other team's captain started to dribble the ball steadily toward me. Garrick sprinted after him, being matched for speed by Mr Gropey. I let out a deep breath and stood my ground, knees bent ready to launch myself to either side and protect my goal. The sudden rush of bodies, all over six foot, was daunting. Mr Gropey called for the ball and made a shot at goal. I flung myself to the left using my body as a shield just as Garrick intercepted the ball. I landed hard on my side the breath knocked out of my lungs as Mr Gropey's studded boots dug into the ground inches from my face spraying grass and dirt over my head. I rolled away but he followed me bending low.

"I'm gonna make you squeal you little bitch."

I kept rolling and smoothly came to my feet, ready to lay one on him but he had already turned his back and was following in Garrick's wake.

"Bring it Fucknuckle."

He laughed over his shoulder at me and I had to swallow my temper. Picking grass out of my hair I looked over to the bench where Yari was standing, rigid and unblinking as he followed Mr Gropey's progress up the field. If looks could kill then Mr Gropey would have dropped dead on the spot. Tash had a hold of his arm and was gently tugging him back to a sitting position. His long arm muscles bunched under the strain of inaction.

This was not going to end well.

The boys managed to keep the ball in opposition territory for the next few minutes giving me time to calm down. I watched as the dirty play started and noted the aggression level increase. A few players went down and then Mr Gropey broke free of the pack, steadily working the ball toward my goal. Dahrel caught up with him and they darted around each other, the ball was passed to another player on the opposing team and it drew nearer. I braced myself again to defend my goal. Suddenly it felt like every player on the field was rushing me, I knew that Mr Gropey was one of them but had to keep my eye on the ball. The players passed it back and forth between them, waiting for a shot. Dahrel moved to be closer to me as the other team closed ranks teasing me with the ball. Back and forth. I knew I shouldn't have allowed it happen but my impatience got the better of me and I moved forward. I could hear Dahrel yelling something but I ignored him and went after the ball, attempting some fancy foot work to extract it from the opposition. There was a lot of pushing and shoving and all of a sudden my feet were ripped out from under me. I landed hard on my back. The wind forced from my lungs and I struggled for breath when an immense weight landed on top of me. Gulping I strained, trying to take a breath, the weight on top of me shifted and I filled my lungs, taking as much air as I could lest the weight move again. Opening my eyes I wasn't surprised to find Mr Gropey's smiling face just inches from mine. Lifting my arms I tried to push at him, but I had no hope of moving the six foot plus frame. Letting out a chilling laugh he pushed his knee in between mine, forcing my legs apart. I looked around for help but we were surrounded by players pushing and shoving.

Panic flared. "Get off me you filthy son of a bitch."

He lowered his face to mine and I could smell his foul breath. "Not until you squeal for me."

I shook my head in an effort to escape the thick stench but he grabbed me by the chin and held my head still. Eyes watering a groan escaped my lips and he tightened his hold on my chin, pushing my head to the side he lowered his mouth to my face.

Oh Daska get him off me.

Bile rose in my throat as he opened his mouth and dragged his wet tongue from my jawbone to my temple. Anger flared and I aimed it all at him, giving an almighty shove. He laughed and rolled off me just in time as Bravnica broke through the crowd. He took one look at me and then grabbed Mr Gropey by the scruff of his neck and marched him away. The other players traded insults as they made their way back to their places.

Dahrel reached me as I pulled myself up off the ground.

"You okay?" He took one look at me and grabbed me by the shoulders. "Ana what did he do?"

Mouth shut tight I wiped frantically at my face, then shaking my head I stalked across the field to where Bravnica was speaking with Mr Gropey.

"Don't do it Ana." Dahrel called after me but I didn't stop.

Bravnica saw me coming and tried to warn me off with a look. I ignored it.

Garrick reached out and grabbed my arm, but I jerked out of his grip. "Don't be stupid Ana."

I knew I had the attention of the entire pitch and its spectators but I didn't care. Reaching Bravnica and Mr Gropey the crowd held their collective breath as I cocked my hip and held my hand out to Bravnica.

"I'll take a red one thanks."

Bravnica looked confused. "What?"

"A card. I want one of the red ones."

His eyes flared in understanding a moment too late as I stepped forward and kicked Mr Gropey in the crackerjacks.

Hard.

THIRTEEN

He went down like a sack of potatoes and every male in the vicinity let out a groan in sympathy.

I leaned over him and gritted my teeth. "Who's squealing now bitch?"

"Ana." Bravnica tapped me on the shoulder and I straightened to find him eyeing me, red card at the ready. "Was it worth it?"

I plucked the card from his hand and smiled sweetly. "Bet your arse it was."

"I'll expect an explanation for this Ana."

I shrugged and spun on my heel.

At this point I don't really care what you expect.

Strutting off the pitch I acknowledged my team mates' calls of support.

Yari stood to meet me, his eyes shining. "That's my girl."

I grinned and wrapped my arms around his torso, relishing the feeling of his arms closing around me. 'How does that feel?'

I squinted up at him, "Much better."

He leaned down for a quick kiss. Smiling, we broke the embrace, taking our seat on the bench with the others. The reserve had gone onto the field to replace me at Goal and Tash shifted into her seat next to me, handing me my bottle of water. I smiled my thanks and took a swig before settling in to watch what was left of the first half. Bravnica was not tolerating any more crap and so the dirty plays had slowed and by the time he called half time it was nil all. I was not going to be playing in the second half thanks to my poor show of self-control so I spent half time tending to minor injuries and rehydrating the team.

Dahrel was going through some final plays when Bravnica called time on. I grabbed Yari and kissed him soundly before he left the sidelines. Resuming my seat next to Tash I tilted my head to the side to watch Yari jog onto the pitch.

"Have you ever noticed how nice Yari's butt is?"

Tash giggled. "Ah no, I haven't."

We settled in to watch, the match was intense from the start as the ball was worked from one end of the pitch to the other. Ten minutes into the game Yari kicked a goal and we launched ourselves out of our seats, screaming our heads off and fist pumping the air. Yari was jumped on by Garrick and then the rest of the team. Laughing, he freed himself of their bodies, straightened, searching me out in the cheering crowd and pointing directly at me.

I felt my face pinken as Tash awwwwwed beside me. "That's so romantic!"

I raised my eyebrow, "Righto Jackie Collins, simmer down."

She smacked my arm and I gave her a grin as play started up again. The match ended with only one point scored sending our team through to the next round.

The day heated up and we made it to the semi finals but were taken out by Taras and Anton's team in the final round. Regardless of this our spirits were high as we celebrated the loss at Red's. For a moment it felt like we didn't have a care in the world. Dahrel and Garrick were busy chasing phone numbers at the bar and Tash was flipping through the song list on the juke box. It was nice to see everyone in a good place, even if it was only temporary. I realised I felt good too, despite a Kudlak on the loose and my curse issues. I looked at Yari across the table and smiled as he seemed relaxed despite the reprimand for brawling. I guess that comes with his military training, like water off a duck's back. He had done what he thought was right and didn't apologise for it.

Sensing my eyes on him he smiled and leaned across the table taking my hands in his. "Let's get out of here."

His eyes were sparkling with mischief and I couldn't resist.

"Sure."

I grabbed my bag and Yari stood, helping me out if the booth. I gave a wave to Tash to let her know I was leaving. She gave me a nod and smiled as Yari put his arm around my waist. The door swung closed behind us but not before I heard a number of catcalls being shouted from the bar.

I rolled my eyes. "Garrick, he's so subtle."

"Nah, he's just jealous you picked up before he did."

I laughed, "No doubt!"

Our conversation died out as we got closer to my house and was replaced by a feeling of anticipation, I was overly aware of his large frame as it stalked next to me. Reaching the door I fumbled with my keys, I could feel him behind me and my skin prickled against the tension that had grown as our conversation had petered out. I felt his heat as he edged closer. Taking my shoulders in his hands he lowered his lips to the nape of my neck and laid a gentle kiss there. His stubble rough against my sensitive skin sent sparks shooting down my body.

Where is that damned key!

He closed the gap between our bodies and slowly traced the length of my arms with his hands.

Wrapping his hands around mine, his voice came out gravelly as it tickled the hair next to my ear. "Let me do it."

I surrendered the keys and he opened the door smoothly. I stepped out of the circle of his arms and entered the apartment. Tossing my bag onto the couch I turned to find him locking the door, the click of the lock seeming unusually loud in the silent space. Turning slowly he met my gaze through hooded eyes.

We both stood dead still. Assessing each other in the rising tension.

I tried to defuse the situation before we ended up somewhere I wasn't sure we were ready to go. "Coffee?"

He blinked slowly and gave a knowing smile. "Sure."

I put the kettle on and he kicked his shoes off, making himself at home on the couch. Moments later I handed him his coffee and I sat next to him, turning sideways so that I could tuck my toes under his legs. Sipping coffee we talked quietly about the day. It was nice, being at home with him. There was no pressure to be anyone but me. Taking my empty cup, he placed it on the coffee table and shifted on the couch to face me, I took his lead and snuggled up onto his lap and smiled inwardly when he wrapped his long arms around me. Comfortable in each other's embrace we sat quietly together. I played unconsciously with the sleeve on his T shirt and thought about the game. He shifted and his sleeve bunched up revealing the Kaul tattoo that marked his muscular shoulder.

Sitting up, I turned to face him. "Can I have a look at your Kaul Tat?"

He smiled. "You just wanna get me out of my clothes."

I rolled my eyes at him and he relented, pulling his T-Shirt up over his head he moved gingerly and I heard air hiss quietly through his teeth. Something was wrong. Torso exposed I pushed him back onto the couch to inspect the damage.

"Ana, don't, it's fine." I pushed his arms out of the way, three ribs on his left side were badly bruised. He let out a resigned sigh.

"Yari you're hurt." I gently touched his ribs and heard his sharp intake of breath. "Sorry."

I left the bruised area to check the rest of him leaning over to inspect the other side gently with my fingers. His muscles shifted under my fingertips and he grabbed my hands trapping them in one of his.

"Why don't you try kissing it better?" His voice was a little strained and I looked up to find him eyeing me hungrily.

I gave him a taste of his own medicine, letting my mouth fall into a lazy half smile I held his gaze and lowered my lips to place a feather light kiss on his ribs. "Better?"

He groaned. "Not yet."

Smiling I moved closer, still holding his gaze I kissed his chest. "Now?"

He let out a slow breath. "Getting there."

I moved closer again, my body leaning over his I reached up to kiss the hard line of his jaw. "How about now?"

His arms snaked around my waist and pulled me down. My breath caught as he crushed my body against his hard frame and captured my lips in kiss that was filled with desire. I kissed him back, eager to explore and he responded instantly. His mouth became more demanding and he shifted on the couch pushing me back so that his body was now above mine, his weight pushing me into the couch. His hands had moved from my waist, one now cupped the side of my face and the other had moved lower, cupping my butt and pulling me up, pressing me against him. Hard.

The feel of him shocked me back to reality. We had skipped ahead of ourselves and things were going way too fast.

A breath shuddered through him and he pulled back. "Sorry."

I swallowed and shook my head. "No, it's okay. I just…"

He shifted his weight off me. "It's fine Ana. I can wait."

We both stood and I watched as he pulled his shirt back on. I pulled it up so I could look at his ribs again. "I think you should get this checked out."

He took hold of my shoulders and gently pushed me back. "Yep, it's on the top of my To Do list." He grinned as I raised my eye at his sarcasm. "You'll be okay if I go? See you tomorrow afternoon when I finish my shift?"

I nodded and we walked to the door where he levelled me with his sexy half smile again. "Sweet dreams."

I smiled and he leaned in to give me a gentle kiss, I moved closer and wrapped my arms around his shoulders but he took a hold of my hips and pushed me back gently, breaking the kiss.

"Goodnight Ana."

I smiled, "Goodnight Yari."

I closed the door and turned to face the now empty couch. Things were progressing steadily with our relationship and I knew that sooner rather than later, it would be changing on a very permanent level. There is no such thing as to what the humans commonly call "divorce" within our society. Once you have been promised to someone that is it, there is no turning back. I blew at a rogue clump of my fringe.

Trying to drag Tash away from work when she was in the zone was like trying to pry drugs out of the hands of an addict. Sitting at the breakfast table she nibbled at her toast without taking her eyes off the files she was reviewing. I looked out the window at the beautiful morning that was promising to become a spectacular summer's day.

"Are you sure you don't want to come? The work is not going anywhere."

She lifted her head in my direction and her eyes reluctantly left the page to touch mine before snapping back like an elastic band.

"Ah, no. Thanks." She waved at me with her toast. "You go have fun though."

I smiled and picked up my bag before pulling open the front door. "Okay, just don't work too hard alright?"

When I didn't get a response I gave up and closed the door.

"How she finds that stuff so riveting is beyond me."

I started toward the festival grounds where the Kaul were putting on displays all day showing off their bad arse skills. They had sparring, self-defense, cross-bows, tracking-demonstrations, basically all the good stuff and even though the boys were on shift and I was gonna have to go solo, there was no way I was missing out. I headed straight for the crossbow competitions, burying my frustration at not being able to compete and the image of my own bow sitting in a cupboard at home. Approaching the field I spotted Dahrel bent over a table covered with paper and tacked toward him. He was coordinating the "Kaul only" comp and knew I was pissed at not being permitted to compete.

He saw me approach and held his hands up in defense. "You know I can't do anything about it so please don't start on me."

I gave a look of mock hurt. "I just came down here to see if you needed my help with anything." I started backing away. "But if you don't need me…"

I ducked but wasn't quick enough to escape his big arm as it wrapped around me.

"Oh sis, what would I do without you eh?"

He squeezed and I heard a couple of vertebrae crack before he released me and started handing over work. We chatted about the conditions, both pleased at how still the morning was. The comps were always held early as the winds tended to pick up in the afternoon. Looking at the numbers I was surprised at the amount of competitors we had this year but I guess that's what you get when you jam so many Kaul into one city. They like to compete which should make for a good show.

I was sorting groups into timeslots when Dahrel spoke quietly at my side. "The Commander had that guy re-deployed this morning."

My hands stilled and I looked up, my relief palpable. "Really?"

Studying me intently he nodded slowly. "Yeah, he was sent to The Tibetan Plateau."

My eyes widened, "Wow, sucks to be him."

Silence stretched as his eyes bored into mine and I shifted uncomfortably. Finally he looked away. "Guess he should have known better."

Huh?

Before I could ask what he meant by that comment he moved off and started calling the groups in order. The first rounds took forever to get through due to the high numbers we had competing. I was helping Dahrel reset the targets for the second round when I noticed Bravnica warming up. I bristled immediately and knew I was being childish because if anything I should be thankful to him for getting rid of Mr Gropey. That's assuming he did it for me of course, which he probably didn't, so I should just keep my mouth shut. He looked confident and relaxed as he chatted with the other competitors. I found myself wishing that I could compete against him, this was my sport and as petty as it sounds I would have loved the chance to beat him.

We got through the next rounds quickly and as much as I hate to admit it, Bravnica was an excellent shot. He made it into the finals easily as I guess we all knew he would. There was a scheduled break for half an hour and after re-setting the targets with Dahrel I grabbed a bottle of water and settled myself under one of the drink tents. Scanning the crowd my eyes landed on Bravnica. They seemed to seek him out of their own will like some kind of homing beacon. He caught my eye and I wasn't quick enough to look away. Face red I watched as he excused himself from his group and started making his way over to me. Mirroring my previous move he grabbed some water and availed himself of the chair next to mine.

Great.

"So you wanna talk about the game yesterday?"

I turned in my chair to face him. "Look, I don't mean to sound rude, but shouldn't you be focusing on your shots?"

Shut up Ana.

Raising his eyebrows he settled back in his chair. "I'll take that as a no."

The corners of his mouth kicked up in a lazy grin and he brought the water to his lips. My mouth went dry and I couldn't seem to tear my eyes away as he worked at the bottle.

Oh Daska.

I jumped up and walked over to Dahrel at the Officials giving myself a severe talking to. My self-berating was cut short when

Dahrel stood to call the finalist over, time for the next rounds. Bravnica's first two shots were dead on but he surprised us all by landing his final shot slightly wide. He stepped away from the mark wishing the next competitor luck before coming to stand next to me. I kept my eyes on the target as the other two finalists took their turn. The second shooter caved, landing his first shot in the outer circle, automatically putting him last but the third finalist matched Bravnica's score. They would have to go to a tie-breaker.

"Guess I should have been focusing on my shots."

I didn't try to hide my I told you so smile. "Guess so."

He tilted his head to the side and narrowed his eyes at me. "Ana, if you've got something to say to me, why don't you go find those big girl panties that you so frequently refer to and just say it."

I instantly regretted my attitude. I let out a sigh and looked toward the targets. "I'm sorry. I'm just a little... testy today."

Bravnica followed my gaze. "Your brother mentioned that you wanted to compete today. I take it you can shoot?"

I gave a half nod and a little smile in answer. "It's cool." I flicked some hair out of my eyes. "I wouldn't want to make the future Emir look bad in front of all these people anyway."

He let out a little chuckle and was about to respond when Dahrel called out.

I looked toward the field. "You need to get ready for your shot."

He nodded but didn't move.

"You know I would be more than happy to go a couple of rounds with you. If you're up for it?"

I let out a laugh. "Your funeral."

He grinned back. "We'll see."

With the targets re-set the crowd fell quiet and the two finalists stepped up to the mark. This was becoming quite a show. One shot each closest to the target wins. The other finalist shot first, his arrow flying wide it hit the second centre ring. I smiled - Bravnica had this in the bag. He stepped up to the mark and steadied himself.

Daska that man has great form.

He let his arrow loose and it hurtled through the air imbedding itself perfectly in the centre ring. A cheer erupted and smiling I turned to find some other entertainment.

The heat of the day was steadily increasing as were the demands from my stomach, it must be lunch time. I headed out in search of food and after eating what could at best be described as a rather suspect meat pie, I wiped my sauce stained fingers with a paper napkin and tossed it with my leftovers into a nearby bin. Taking a greedy swig from my bottle of water I started heading toward the shade of the sparring pit. The tiered seating area had been fitted with a massive shade sale for the Festival and was proving to be a popular spot. Finding an aisle seat a few rows back from the ring I settled myself in to cool down and be entertained. Looking around it was clear that I had just missed a very entertaining match. The crowd buzzed with anticipation and I looked to see who would be up next. Bravnica was in the ring but clearly in an official capacity only. He stood to the side with a couple of other older looking Kaul. They must have been overseeing the pairing to ensure even match ups. I listened to the spectators around me who all agreed that topping the last display was going to be hard. Speculation was running rife as to who would be up next when Taras stepped into the ring sending the crowd into a frenzy of wolf whistles and wild cheers. I clapped with my overly excited neighbours as he strutted around the ring making a big show of taking off his tight black Tee. Laughing I rolled my eyes at his amateur strip show. Bravnica raised an all suffering eyebrow and leaned against the wall of the ring, arms folded and head shaking ever so slightly. Taras circled the ring once, swinging his T-Shirt at his side and shaking his booty all the way before stopping in front of his brother and tossing the discarded shirt at him. Bravnica made no move to catch the shirt as it slapped him in the face and fell limply to the dirt floor. The crowd went nuts and I closed my gaping mouth with a pop. Bravnica looked at the wadded up material lying at his feet and then at his brother who was doing a surprisingly good chicken impersonation. Resigned but with a smile he pushed himself off the wall and unfolded his long arms to acknowledge the cheering crowd with a wave. I found myself leaning forward in my chair as with quick efficient movements he removed his black T-shirt. The women in the crowd now had two incredible specimens to ogle. Neither had an ounce of fat on them, stomachs clearly defined by ripples of shifting muscle, the strength in their arms and beautifully sculpted shoulders was impressively obvious and both men had chests that just made you want to touch. A groan escaped my lips and I cleared my throat to try and hide it. I shouldn't have bothered though as all the women in the vicinity were too busy drooling to take any notice of me. Shrugging I let a guilty smile turn the corners of my mouth and went back to enjoying my cataloguing of the assets on display. Bravnica turned and tossed his shirt to land next to Taras' giving me a clear view of his back.

My breath caught and the smile fell from my lips.

The scar ran in a vicious line from his left shoulder blade across the valley of his backbone and came to a merciful stop just below the ribs on his right side. Faded white with age it was wide and deep and should have been fatal. There were a few gasps in the crowd but they were drowned out by the applause that had yet to die down. I was shocked by the graphic evidence of the brutal life he leads. The brothers started circling each other in the ring, moving with calculated strength. Giving myself a mental shake I tried to get back into the excited mood of the crowd but every time Bravnica's back turned toward me, my eyes were drawn to the scar. The noise of the crowd rose and fell around me as the brothers wowed them with an incredible show of speed and strength. I watched numbly, desperate to know what had happened, imagining a scene with him lying wounded and vulnerable. He was Dominik Bravnica, the future Emir and strongest Kaul I have ever known. How the hell did he allow himself to be hurt so badly?

I forced myself to focus on the brothers and the impressive demonstration that would no doubt be the hot topic for weeks. Both men were slick with sweat, chests working they had broken apart and were circling again, Taras feinted left but Bravnica wasn't buying and stayed steady, waiting for the real attack. Both men were smiling and looked relaxed but their ice blue eyes were watching.

Waiting.

Taras made his move and they re-engaged in a blur of attacking hits and defensive blocks. I squinted my eyes to try and follow, then legs were flipped into the air and Taras came down, landing hard on his back. The dirt billowed around him as Bravnica followed him to the ground with what would have been a fatal blow to the throat if he hadn't stopped short of making contact with his brother. Smiling Taras conceded and took the hand on offer, allowing his brother to haul him to his feet. Both men slapped each other on the back before giving the crowd a quick wave and moving to the side of the ring for their shirts and some water.

Bravnica was using his shirt to wipe the grime off his face when a uniformed Kaul rushed into the pit. I watched his demeanour change as the Kaul whispered urgently in his ear. I knew my boss well enough by now to see from his body language that this was not good. He gave a couple of quick nods to the Kaul and pulled his T-Shirt over his head. Smile still in place he waved at the crowd and started moving toward the exit. Taras fell in step beside him, still shirtless but minus the smile. Bravnica shook his head at something his brother said then turned and looked directly at me, indicating for me to follow. How he knew I was there I had no idea, but I wasn't going to speculate as I grabbed my bag and threw it over my shoulder pushing through the crowd to catch up with the fast moving group.

Crammed into a dark room with ten other Kaul and officials was not how I had envisioned my Saturday afternoon. But here I was squinting at a security monitor, paper and pen poised on my knees, trying to figure out just what the hell had gotten everyone so worked up. The guy working the monitors had just finished explaining that one of the CCTV's had recorded an, 'event'. The motion sensors had been triggered by a moving object just north of the city centre. He had indicated which tunnel system on an electronic map that covered one wall of the room. I knew that the area in question hadn't been searched yet.

Monitor Guy went on. "The cameras have motion sensors on them, so they are designed to follow an object. The object has to be big enough for the sensors to detect, so for example, a mouse or a rat would be too small for the camera to pick up – it would have to be something of a reasonable size, say a Kresnik, or a Kudlak." I watched his Adams Apple bob as he swallowed and continued. "It follows that object, alerting the observer and records what it finds."

He hit play on the monitor and all eyes turned to the screen. Watching the tunnels brick wall and dirt floor through the eerie green sea of night vision I held my breath, waiting to see something. I jumped when the camera started moving. Steadily swinging from right to left, someone swore under their breath behind me.

Bravnica turned to one of the officials. "Find Sierra and tell her that she needs to get the Emir to call an urgent meeting of council. Tell her to make sure he knows the request is coming from me and that I have proof."

I stood with the rest of the group. I didn't get it. All I had seen was bricks and dirt.

I turned to Bravnica. "But there was nothing there."

He swung around to face me and the look he gave me was unnerving. His brow creased and it was almost like he was sorry. "You didn't see anything because the Kudlak cast no image on film."

I felt the blood run from my face and took a shaky step back. Bravnica reached out, his long fingers wrapped themselves around my upper arms as he took a step forward, shielding me from the others in the room.

"You okay?" His voice was pitched low.

Shocked I swallowed hard, fighting the urge to move forward into his arms. I was scared, really scared and the thought of having him hold me was incredibly tempting. But as safe as his arms were, they weren't the ones I should be seeking shelter from.

I clenched my hands into tight fists to stop them from shaking. "Yeah sorry. That's just…. Well that's just pretty fucking scary."

He gave me a rueful smile, "That's one way of putting it."

I moved away from temptation. "So what do you need me to do?"

FOURTEEN

I was amazed at how quickly things could get done once there was hard evidence. Within two hours of viewing the CCTV footage Bravnica had presented his case to a shocked council who agreed to most of his requests. Security in and around the city was to be ramped up and a complete search to be conducted of the tunnels. The Grand Ball was the last official event for the festival and council refused to cancel. It was to go ahead in an attempt to allay speculation but was brought forward a few days to Monday night so that visiting Elite and dignitaries could vacate the city sooner rather than later. All Kaul were to be placed on duty the night of the ball, with the higher ranking officers attending the ball itself, with orders to dance and *make pretty* but to pack heat in case anything happened.

I sat opposite Bravnica as he finalised the new orders, signing the documents before handing them to a waiting officer to distribute.

As soon as the officer left the room he turned to me. "Thanks for your help today Ana."

I brushed at my hair that had become wilder as the afternoon had progressed. "It's no problem. I want to help."

He pushed back in his chair and stood up. "You had best get home before it gets too late. I'll have one of the officers escort you." He rounded the desk and called to a passing uniform.

Before I could protest he had expertly manoeuvred me out of his office and bundled me into the hands of one of his lieutenants.

"I really don't think that this is necessary, it's still full light outside."

He ignored my reasoning. "Can you come in tomorrow?"

I nodded but his attention was taken by a flustered looking official.

The walk home was a little awkward. I couldn't help but feel that resources were being wasted here. He didn't say anything and neither did I but he managed to keep that two pace distance the entire way, even with me speeding up and slowing down.

I was relieved when I made my front door, pushing it open I turned back to my shadow. "Ah, thanks for that."

Standing ramrod straight he gave me a quick nod. "Have a good evening Ma'am." He stood there staring at me so I gave him a weak smile and closed the door.

Ma'am?

Peeking through the peephole I watched him spin on his heal and disappear from view. "I am not old enough to be referred to as Ma'am."

I had planned on going for a run but after what I had just seen there was no way I was going to be out near dusk. I took to the kitchen to help Tash start prepping for dinner and explain my escort home. It felt weird doing something as mundane as tossing a salad given the afternoon I'd just had but I guess that goes with the territory. No matter how wrong it feels you have to keep doing the basics.

Tash and I were clearing the plates when Garrick let himself in. "You girls need to lock your door."

Tash and I stood side by side with equally stunned expressions as Garrick chocked the door open and pulled out a power drill.

Tash put her plate back on the table and stepped forward. "What are you doing?"

Producing a massive deadlock he started to line it up on the doorframe. "Just beefing up security. Dahrel and Yari have been asked to pull a double shift, so I got the job."

Tash placed her hands on her hips. "You can't just come in here and start vandalising our door."

Garrick responded by starting up the drill and affixing the bolt to the door. Tash picked up her drink and turned to me.

"I'm going to take a long bath."

She stormed off to the bathroom and I saw Garrick watch her progress out of the corner of his eye. I finished cleaning the kitchen and Garrick finished with the door.

He came and placed the keys on the bench top next to me. "Make sure you use it."

I smiled at him and nodded, "Thanks bro."

He gave me a stern look. "You know what is out there Ana. Lock your damn door."

"I will. I promise."

A lot of good that bolt's gonna do against a Kudlak.

He gave me another warning look and headed to the newly reinforced door. "I've gotta go. I'm in the tunnels tonight."

My stomach clenched and I followed him to the door to give him a hug. "Be careful."

He mussed up my hair. "That's my middle name."

I scoffed, "Yeah and the other one is delusional."

Smiling he pulled the door shut and called through the solid wood. "Now lock it."

I slid the bolt into place and fought back the tears that were threatening.

Keep it together girl, you can't fight the undead with puffy eyes.

The lift doors opened and I was surprised to see the office already teaming with life. I had woken up at stupid o'clock and hadn't been able to get back to sleep so decided to come in early. It seems a few other people had the same idea as the CCTV footage had really created a stir and everyone was on edge. Dumping my bag I headed to the kitchen to boil the jug and get the coffee going. The morning was crazy, no one seemed to care that it was a Sunday. Bravnica had back to back meetings and had left me to ensure each Lieutenant was given their group's search coordinates and patrol rosters. I had just issued the last of my morning tasks and sat down staring at my full coffee cup. I had managed one sip on the way back from the kitchen this morning before I got swamped with work. Not a cool morning. Picking up the cup I turned to refill it in the kitchen when Bravnica walked through the door.

"Ana, I'm pleased I caught you. I wanted to talk to you about your home security."

Expecting some directorate in regards to the investigation I didn't have time to check my stunned expression. "Huh?"

He ignored my eloquent response. "You might make arrangements for one of your brothers to stay at your apartment. I know the council has not agreed to a curfew, but it would be prudent for you to ensure you are in before dark."

Oh Daska, I couldn't think of anything worse than having my brothers stay overnight. Bravnica assumed my obedience and continued.

"I have a meeting to get to now with the heads of Council. I need you to take this down to Drago Vidmar's receptionist on level two." He handed me an official letter with the Bravnica seal neatly stamped on the back and grabbed some files pausing at the door to look at me. "I'll see you after lunch."

I nodded and he disappeared out the door, I narrowed my eyes at the now empty space. "You know your self-assurance is incredibly annoying."

The office slowly emptied as Kaul and senior officials made their way to the Barracks for the meeting and I finished a couple of outstanding jobs before heading down to level two. Walking the long corridor I counted off the doorways. I had managed to procure a map of the level and knew that Drago Vidmar held the North West corner office.

I studied the letter trying to figure out what business required an official letter from the Bravnicas to the Vidmars? My mind flew back to the conversation I overheard between Anton and Taras.

Oh Daska.

I turned the envelope over in my hands, my heart sinking, as realisation hit. He was making me deliver the acceptance letter of their union.

Jerk!

There was no one sitting on reception. They obviously didn't need to get out of bed on a Sunday. I walked and found Drago's office and knocked on the ornate door three times. No answer.

Taking a deep breath I grabbed the handle, shocked when the door swung open. Peaking back out into the hall to make sure no one was about, I walked into the room, surprised to find it furnished in the French Colonial Style, all creams and soft pinks. A day-bed sat underneath one of the corner windows, suffocating under a pile of over-priced and over-stuffed cushions. Beyond that the view overlooking the river was spectacular. I shook my head and let my lip curl as I made my way to the large cream desk that screamed Tressilia.

"You have got to be shitting me."

It should have been her father's, but I guess it's only the best for Daddy's little girl. I pulled open one of the drawers and nearly laughed out loud. It was full of pairs of shoes. I picked one up by its stiletto heal and fought the urge to snap it off.

"All style and no...." The words caught in my throat as I heard footsteps outside the door.

Shit.

I dropped the shoe and looked around frantically for a hiding spot. There was an ornate wardrobe at the far side of the room. I made a dash for it and used the tips of my fingers to close the doors behind me as the door to the office swung open. Through gritted teeth I cursed at the small gap that I had left. I held my breath and strained to hear movement. Peering through the gap I had a view of the desk and the drawer lying open with the shoe hanging out.

Crap.

My view was suddenly obstructed by a familiar large form.

Shit.

Stepping forward he bent to pick up the shoe and place it back into the drawer with its other half and push the drawer closed.

Do not look at the wardrobe. Do not look at the wardrobe. Do not....

He turned and looked directly at the wardrobe.

Fuck.

The click clack of heals approaching caught his attention and he looked over his shoulder briefly. Turning his attention back to my lame hiding spot he reached into the back of his cargoes and stalked toward the cupboard with an intent that made me step back. I hit the back wall of the cupboard and watched as with one smooth movement he swung his right hand back around and pulled the cupboard door open with the left.

My eyes widened as they stared down the black barrel of Bravnica's 9mm.

"Ana?"

I managed a squeak and he let out a couple of expletives. Looking over his shoulder he put the gun away and unceremoniously pushed me aside, squeezing in next to me. I was pressed up against the wall of the wardrobe on one side and a wall of Bravnica on the other.

Perfect.

No matter how I tried to move, I couldn't escape the contact of his body. Nor could I escape his scent, it was intoxicating and made me want to breathe deeply. I held my breath.

How long do you think you can keep that up genius?

I breathed.

"This was my hiding place." I hissed.

His response was to cover my mouth with his hand and lean forward to Shhhhhh at my ear.

I struggled between the automatic response of wanting to press a little closer and the desire to inform him not to shoosh me. Before I could make up my mind, Tressilia glided into the room. Bravnica pressed me harder against the cupboard wall so that he could see through the gap in the doors. I gritted my teeth and closed my eyes. Being this close to him was becoming overwhelming, my whole body felt like a metal detector that had just struck gold, every sense was honed in on him and I hated him for it. Sensing my regard, he turned to look at me.

Breath shaky I was glad for the dark, I had a good Poker Face but there was no way I could conceal my feelings at this point. He stilled and my panic rose, I hated the way he made me feel, the way he made my body betray me, betray Yari.

The atmosphere in the wardrobe crackled with electricity. I'm going to have to burst out of my hiding place and face whatever Tressilia had to dish out, or stay in here and slowly combust. I was just about to push on the doors when the breath was knocked from my lungs and the wardrobe shimmered before disappearing.

Oh Daska not again.

Pressed against the same wall of the same shadowy room I looked up and met Dominik's intense stare, instantly feeling like a juicy steak being assessed by a starved lion.

"I think I'm going crazy." I managed to whisper.

My words brought his gaze to my lips and I took an unsteady breath as they parted of their own accord. His smile was hungry and I couldn't deny the thrill it caused. The pressure of his body increased as he lowered his lips to take mine.

Rhianna started singing about being the only girl in the world and all of a sudden I was back in the wardrobe.

What the hell?

I heard Tressilia pull out her phone and answer with her fake daaaarling voice. Closing my eyes I steadied my breathing, concentrating on trying to get myself under control.

What is wrong me?

Bravnica was only inches away. I could feel his breath on my cheek. He was breathing heavily too and I could feel the strain in his body, held taught, an inch from mine. I was beginning to wonder if maybe it wasn't just me after all. I strained but there wasn't enough light for me to see his face. The sound of the exterior door brought me back to reality. I was still way too close to Bravnica and needed to get out now. Pushing Bravnica aside I ignored the feel of him under my hands and looked through the crack. Tressilia was leaving her office, the sound of her click clacking down the hall and fake giggle over the phone was enough for me. I burst from the wardrobe and stumbled into the plush office, turning to see Bravnica slowly stepping out behind me. He looked as cool and as calm as ever.

Dammit.

"Just what do you think you are doing in here?" he asked.

I was still reeling and struggled to get my wits.

"Listen Bravnica, I am not the only one who was hiding in the cupboard, so don't get all puritanical with me."

He shook his head. "I was in the cupboard saving your arse."

Daska I feel sick.

I raised a doubtful eyebrow, "You could have done that from out here."

He levelled me with a hard stare.

"The things I came here to do are not for public consumption, besides I had to make sure you stayed put."

I let out a scoff.

"Ana do you even get how serious it would be if you were to get caught snooping around in an Elite's office?"

I knew the consequences, it would end my family. I just hoped like hell that Bravnica wasn't about to turn me in. I looked him dead in the eye. "Lucky I didn't get caught then isn't it?"

He crossed his arms and studied me. I was valiantly trying to keep it together but I knew I looked as white as a sheet. I bent my knees slightly to help with the shaking.

He worked his jaw. "You need to go home."

I shook my head, as terrible as I felt right now I would rather get this argument over and done with.

His cool demeanour slipped a little. "This is not a game Ana. You need to get home now."

He took a step toward me and I took a wobbly step back. It was hard enough being this close to him let alone having him any nearer. Seeing me retreat he halted his advance, letting his hand drop to his side.

"I will have someone escort you."

"No."

His eyes narrowed and I could see he was struggling to contain his temper. I was not prepared to go another round with him right now so I started moving toward the door.

"I'll go home now but I don't need an escort." I held his letter out weakly, letting it slip from my fingers as he took it, I didn't meet his gaze.

He followed me to the lifts and pressed the call button. Waiting for it to arrive in silence I was relieved when it dinged on my floor. He reached in and hit the button for Ground before pulling his hand back. Standing outside the lifts I thought he was going to say more, but he let the doors close between us without saying a word.

Exiting the Council Chambers I sucked in great lungfuls of fresh air in a vain attempt to clear my head. I had managed to put the incident on the dance floor to the back of my mind, convincing myself that maybe it was just a one off thing. But now there was no ignoring it, I was officially going mad.

I was completely drained.

Ignoring the Corporal that had tailed me from the chambers, I used the last amount of energy I had and pushed through my front door. Stumbling past the kitchen and straight to my bedroom I fell, face down, onto the bed. The midday sun streamed through the window, warming me like a blanket.

I woke when I heard Tash come home. The sun had moved to the other side of my room and I dashed to the bathroom to quickly wash my face. I didn't want her to know I had been passed out all afternoon.

It was Laksa night and we headed out to our favourite takeway. Finding an empty table outside, we waited for our meal.

Resting her hands on the table Tash gave me her serious look. "Okay, what happened?"

"What do you mean?"

"Oh don't give me that crap - you look like hell."

I leaned back in my chair. "First you have to promise not to have me certified."

Tash gave me a look of surprise. "Of course I won't have you certified!" She narrowed her eyes. "Spill it."

Fingers rubbing at the ache in my temples I lowered my voice. "Remember what happened to me on the dance floor at the Underworld Dinner?"

Her eyes widened. "Oh my goodness it happened again?"

I nodded and was vaguely amused as Tash tried to control her reaction, that girl could never play poker.

"A huh, ok, err so when did this happen?"

"When we were hiding in Tressilia's wardrobe."

Tash's nodding head instantly stopped its empathic motion.

"You what?"

I had enough grace to look a little guilty. "Long story, but I decided to snoop around her office but I got interrupted and jumped into her wardrobe to hide. It was Bravnica and then he got interrupted and availed himself of my hiding spot. So we were both stuck in this stupid wardrobe with Tressilia outside, and then, it just happened."

Tash leaned back in her chair shaking her head, we were both silent for a moment. She spoke first.

"I'm going to see if I can find any reference to this at work." She levelled me with a hard stare. "Seriously Ana, we can't keep ignoring what is happening to you and I'm not just talking about these new developments either."

This was exactly the reaction I was dreading but expecting. Every few years she would get all gung ho about trying to figure out just what kind of a freak I really was. Scouring any reference she could find and re reading every book we had on the weird and wacky. I would then try to make things happen by will instead of by accident and we always ended up knowing nothing more than we did when we started. Eventually we would stop looking for answers and get back to life.

"So it's only ever happened with the Commander?"

"Yes and before you go there... Just. Don't."

I was feeling embarrassed enough as it was. My reactions to him were ridiculous and incredible and just... stupid. He is Elite, not to mention the whole Promised to Tressilia thing... not that I care. I'm Promised to Yari.

Tash caught me off guard. "You like him, don't you?"

My laugh came out so hard it was almost a snort. "Now you are the one who needs to be certified, talk about arrogance. That guy is so far up himself, I'm surprised he can draw breath."

"You don't mean that."

I ignored her. "You know I think he and Tressilia will be perfect for each other, there might be some issues with ego in the... OUCH."

I pulled my foot out from underneath hers, "Tash what the hell?"

"Ease up sister," she looked around pointedly. "This is our future Emir your bagging."

Opting to avoid arrest for treason, I lowered my voice. "I do not have feelings for Bravnica."

Tash shook her head. "You should stop being so hard on the guy. Yes, he is very driven, but with an upbringing like his who wouldn't be."

"Tash, he's had everything handed to him on a silver platter. I'd hardly call that a traumatic childhood."

"Growing up knowing that you will bear the weight of the Kresnik race on your shoulders and being scrutinized for it the whole time would not be easy." She pointed an accusing finger at me. "And I think that what happened with Nikoli would classify as *traumatic.*"

She air quoted me but I ignored it. "Who's Nikoli?"

Before she could respond our meals arrived, we gathered our bags and started the short walk home.

I asked again. "So, who's Nikoli?"

Tash gave me a 'you should know this' look. "There were four Bravnica brothers - Nikoli, Dominik, Taras and Anton."

What?

"Nikoli was the eldest son and the only brother not born Enlightened."

"Wow. Sucks to be Nikoli."

Tash nodded, "Yup, he thought so too and was, from all accounts a pretty bad egg, despite his family's complete devotion." Her brow creased in thought, "I think he was twenty-one when he left."

"So what? They just never heard from him again?"

Tash shook her head. "I'm not sure of the details but rumour is he was killed by a Kudlak. Dominik spent two years searching for him before he got his Overseas Posting."

I tried to think what I would do if that happened to one of my brothers.

"That's so sad."

Tash nodded. "The Commander blamed himself for what happened. I think that's why he's all work and no play."

We walked the next block in silence. I eyed the drains wearily but noticed a heavy presence of Kaul.

Apparently Tash noticed it too. "Well he got that through quick, it was only yesterday that they recorded the incident."

My mouth fell open. "Seriously? How do you know this stuff?"

She tapped her nose. "Archives babe. We 'nose' it all."

I rolled my eyes, "Oh Tash don't ever give up your day job."

I felt relieved though that I could at least speak to my best friend about what was happening. Keeping things from her didn't sit well with me.

The sun slipped below the mountains and we quickened our pace. Rounding the final corner we found Yari standing in the street. My face flushed instantly with shame.

Smiling he took some bags and gave me a kiss. "Cutting it a little fine aren't you ladies? I was about to start a search party."

I plastered a smile on my face and hoped that he wouldn't see straight through it. I didn't know what was happening to me or how to explain it but I hated it. I hated the way everything in me reacted to Bravnica and I was riddled with guilt. Yari and I had been promised to one another forever. We were going to spend the rest of our lives together. I should not feel like that about anyone but him, let alone Bravnica! Having no time to process what happened in the cupboard I shoved it to the back of my mind. I had to shake whatever I thought was happening and focus on reality; and my reality was Yari.

We shared out our meals between the three of us and sat on the couches to eat, discussing the Kudlak threat in between slurps of Laksa.

Yari tried to alleviate our fears, "There have been no further attacks, so there is no point in panicking the city by cancelling the last few events of the Festival. As it is they have brought the ball forward."

I shook my head. "But after the hit on the CCTV shouldn't we be telling people what's down there? We are just letting them walk around oblivious, it's not right."

Yari stood to collect the now empty bowls.

"The people aren't walking around unprotected, Kaul are on nearly every street in the city." He leaned forward in his seat. "If you were a Kudlak, right now Lumeer would be the last place you would want to be."

FIFTEEN

The next morning I found myself hiding in the stationary room moving stacks of things around to avoid seeing Bravnica.

Why did I even come in this morning?

I was annoyed that he had reduced me to this. If I couldn't get it together then I would have to think hard about my position here and this was the best job I'd ever had. I didn't want to quit.

"Ana, I heard you were in, I've been looking everywhere for you."

Oh for the love of Pete.

Turning I found Bravnica in a casual pose, his shoulder resting on the doorframe arms crossed over his chest. Studying his silhouette I found myself wondering how something so large could move so quietly, he cleared his throat and I realised it was my turn to talk.

"Hi, I was um…" I looked around for an out and my eyes landed on a pack of Post-it notes. "…just looking for these." I held them up triumphantly.

His brow creased in what I could only assume was confusion. We both knew his office was well stocked with stationery – including Post-it notes.

I tossed them back into their box. "Look, I just wanted to say that I'm sorry for having a go at you yesterday. I know why you did what you did and I know that you and Tressilia are none of my business, so…" I took a deep breath and met his bemused stare. "I'm sorry."

I counted five full seconds before he chose to speak.

"You're right it's not." Pushing off the doorframe he stepped into the tiny room, making the space even smaller. "So let's drop it okay?"

I nodded eloquently and he continued.

"I have something for you." He came dangerously close to looking nervous as he handed me an envelope with my name elegantly scrawled across the front.

"It's to say thanks for all your hard work."

I opened it carefully. I didn't want to rip the nice paper while he was standing right there in front of me.

Two cards fell into my hand. I opened the first and had to double check what I had read.

"Tickets to the ball?"

He looked pleased with my surprised reaction. "I had planned on giving them to you yesterday but didn't get the chance."

My face heated at the unspoken reason as to why he didn't get a chance.

"I didn't want to spring it on you at the last minute but with the ball being brought forward."

I was still staring at the invitation. "But I thought you were against the Ball being held?"

"I am and there is a risk. But considering the number of Kaul that will be in attendance, I think it's probably the safest place to be tonight."

He nodded at the cards. "Anyway that's just to say thanks for the last few weeks, even though your coffee is shit."

My mouth fell open. "Well I wouldn't say it was *that* bad."

He gave me a dubious look.

"Why did you keep asking for it if you thought it was shit?"

He hit me with a knee wobbling grin.

"Cause I knew you hated making it."

For the first time ever, we shared a laugh.

"Well who'd have thought you have a sense of humour?"

This sobered him a little and I wished I hadn't spoken.

"Do you have a dress to wear?"

I shrugged doing my best to seem unconcerned. "I'll be able to rustle something up."

"All right then, I'll just get you to drop some orders off at the Barracks and then you can go and do whatever it is that girls do to get ready for a ball."

I shook my head. "I want to work, it won't take me long to get ready."

Looking at me sideways he conceded. "I'm sure it wouldn't but that doesn't change the fact that there's nothing really for you to do. I'm going to be in back to back meetings the rest of the day and there's no point you hanging around."

"Oh, okay then. Thanks."

We walked back to his office in silence. I grabbed my bag and he handed me the orders.

"So I guess I'll see you tonight then."

He moved to stand behind his desk. "I'll be there for show only Ana, like all the other Kaul attending."

I gave a quick nod. "Of course and thanks again for the tickets."

I kept my excitement in check but once I reached the street my smile lit my eyes and I let out a whoop. Pulling out my mobile I dialled Tash's number, holding it away from my head as she let loose an ear splitting shriek and promised to meet me at the shops in twenty.

Standing in my bedroom I smiled at my reflection in the full length mirror. My green eyes sparked against the shimmering jade of the floor length material. Elegance at the front gave way to sexy at the back with spaghetti straps running over the dip in my shoulders and coming to rest at the curve of my waist. The scant amount of material that was at the back, clung dangerously low to the curve of my spine and my olive skin practically glowed against the material. Awesome find. It would take a couple of months to pay off the credit card, but what the hell, this dress was made for me and I couldn't help the extra roll of my hips as I entered the lounge. Tash stood, hands clasped over her mouth, I did a twirl and smiled at her sigh.

"Oh Ana it's stunning."

I turned around to face her. "This is gonna knock Yari's socks off!"

She nodded and tilted her head to the side. "I have a feeling it's going to do a little more than that!"

I flicked my hair in my best attempt at sultry and struck a Jessica Rabbit pose. "Why, whatever do you mean?"

Rolling her eyes Tash gave me a gentle shove and went to get her gown on while I poured two glasses of wine. Sipping gingerly so as not to spill anything on my dress I called out. "How long until our escorts get here?"

Her reply was muffled but I think she said six, Bravnica had sent a note saying that they had to arrive early to report in.

Trying to tame my wild mass was going to be tricky. I glanced at the straightening iron heating up on the breakfast bench. "Just do your job and nobody needs to get shoved down the garbage disposal."

"Are you threatening inanimate objects now?"

Turning I found Tash, hand on hip and looking stunning in yellow silk. Not a lot of people could wear that colour, but she pulled it off beautifully. Raising her eyebrow she tilted her head to the side.

"Huh. I think that's a new low for you."

Smiling, I waited for her to do a twirl before handing a glass of wine over and giving a low whistle. "I hope you packed a whacking stick, 'cause you're gonna need one!"

Toasting to our hotness we clinked glasses and let the wine work on the nerves before we set about straightening my hair and curling Tash's.

At exactly six the doorbell rang. Garrick barely looked at me as he crossed the threshold, heading towards Tash. The only reason I didn't stick out a foot and trip him was because I was worried he might damage my dress. I narrowed my eyes at him and started to push the door closed, surprised when it started pushing back. I stepped sideways to find Yari, looking amazing in his dress uniform and staring at me with an open mouthed smile.

"Well it looks like I'm just in time."

I tilted my head in question as he moved into the room and gathered me into his arms. "Daska knows what could have happened if you stepped out of the house looking like this without appropriate protection."

I smiled up at him and he dipped his head, kissing me gently and murmuring against my lips, "You're beautiful."

I snaked my arms around his neck and he groaned in the back of his throat and pulled away hissing air in through his teeth. "We better stop or you won't make it out the door."

"At ease soldier."

Yari raised an eyebrow at Tash who gave him a knowing look. Garrick stepped forward holding out his arm for Tash. I checked my clutch for the house keys and herded everyone out the door. With tonight being the last official event of the festival, there will be revellers and parties all over town. Usually held on what is called, "Everlight", celebrations would last until morning. With the moon full and bright it was the lightest and safest night of the year. Even if they hadn't change the date and the ball was still held on Everlight, I would doubt the *safest night* tag. As far as nights go these days, I don't think any can be touted as being safe anymore. Engaging the deadbolt on my door I shunted my fears to the back of my mind and set out to enjoy my night with Yari.

The evening was perfect although a little balmy and as we strolled along the streets I could feel my hair wanting desperately to curl. I sent a silent prayer to the hair gods and turned my attention back to Yari. I rarely saw him in full dress uniform and was enjoying the view.

He must have felt my eyes on him. Still looking straight ahead he grinned, "And it's all yours baby."

I laughed and he wrapped an arm around my shoulder, pulling me into his side. I loved the ease in which we were slipping into our new roles. Somehow I didn't think the transition from friends to lovers would be this easy.

"You look very handsome Yari."

He stepped in front of me and turned, blocking my path. "Ana." His voice was a little gravelly. "You really are the most beautiful woman I have ever known."

I chewed at my lip I knew that he had *known* a few.

Moving closer he lifted my chin gently with thumb and forefinger and took my lips with his. His kiss was gentle but I could feel the control he was using to keep it that way. Just below the surface was a need that had been kept in check for a long time. Now that we had started pealing back the layers of control there was an element of danger that I couldn't help but be excited by. Knowing it was there and that I was the cause sent goose bumps through my body and left me a little breathless. He broke the kiss and I reluctantly let him pull back.

"It's always been you Ana. Always was and always will be."

I opened my mouth to return the sentiment but nothing came out. Embarrassed my face flushed and I swiped at my fringe out of habit. Yari caught my hand and tucked it back under his arm, stilling my nervous movements. His eyes sparkled knowingly and he let his trademark half smile curve his lips.

"C'mon, let's get you to the ball before I do something indecent."

We quickened our pace to catch up with Tash and Garrick.

My stilettos clicked on the checked black and white tiles that led us into the immense square space of the Grand Ballroom. It definitely lived up to its name. Massive granite columns were spaced evenly around the outer edge supporting a circular mezzanine level which looked down onto the centre of the room where people were already dancing to the sounds of an orchestra, tucked neatly into one of the back corners. A grand staircase dominated the other side of the room giving access to the mezzanine and rooms beyond. Above the dance floor was a beautiful domed ceiling made from coloured glass that would be spectacular during the day and fairy lights that clung like ivy to the ground floor ceiling, twinkling above us. They created a scene that was just magical.

Yari tugged me forward. "If you break anything, just run. I'll provide cover fire."

Laughing I nodded. "Good plan."

We moved to the side of the room and bunkered down next to the Grand Staircase. Looking around at the spectacle of dresses and suits I couldn't help but feel a little intimidated.

I spotted a guy with a silver tray full of champagne flutes and pounced, relieving him of two. Sipping mine I turned and held one out to Yari.

"No Thanks. I'm on duty."

"Oh, sorry, I didn't realise you couldn't."

He gave me his half smile and took the glass, handing it to Tash.

"It's fine."

He looked around and I followed his gaze, for the first time noticing several Kaul in dress uniform spaced evenly along the mezzanine above. I tried to ignore the uneasy feeling that the reality check had brought on. I knew that everything had been done to ensure the safety of everyone at the ball and in the main parts of town. Unfortunately I also knew that Bravnica was pushing shit uphill trying to keep the place secure without the help of council.

Idiots.

With Tash and I now safely delivered to the ballroom, Garrick and Yari excused themselves leaving us to gawk at our surroundings.

"Ana, you look stunning this evening."

Turning me away from Tash, Bravnica expertly twirled me as he manoeuvred himself in between us. I was too surprised that I hadn't stumbled and made an arse out of myself to notice. Leaning over to Tash, Bravnica let a lazy smile touch his lips. "Will you excuse us?" Steering me away, we started a slow circuit of the dance floor. "You look very elegant this evening Ana."

"Uh, thanks. You look very…" I took in his full dress uniform, different from the others I had seen. His was black and came complete with a wicked looking sabre. "…Deadly."

He chuckled deep in his chest, the sound trickling over my senses like warm honey. I felt my face flush and scrambled for something to say that could be deemed at least half intelligent.

"So is that real or just for show."

Smiling he looked down as I indicated his sabre. "Oh it's real. And quite a lethal weapon, if in the right hands of course."

"And are yours the right hands?"

Did I just say that?

"Dominik darling there you are."

Points to Bravnica, he didn't even flinch as Tressilia's words grated over us. Stepping between us she gave him a kiss on the cheek and tucked herself under his long arm. He looked uncomfortable but made no move to distance himself from her.

I clicked my tongue, "Okaay, I'll let you get back to your date."

Turning I concentrated on my exit walk, head up and sway elegantly.

Tressilia's exaggerated tones followed me. "Gracious they let anyone in these days."

I let them wash by, there was no point getting into a slinging match. Better to take the high road.

Moving through the crowd I slowly made my way back to the base of the stairs, to find Yari and Garrick had returned. Garrick and Tash were deep in conversation, so I pulled Yari toward the swirling bodies on the dance floor.

"Are you allowed to dance?"

He grinned. "My orders are to 'Do The Pretty'." He moved closer and whispered in my ear. "And you my dear are very pretty."

Shaking my head at his boldness, I couldn't help but smile. "You are a hopeless flirt!"

It was a crush but we found our own little space amongst the elegance. Yari surprised me when he raised my right hand with his left and holding me close with the other at my lower back, we began to waltz. After one rotation of the dance floor I caught my breath and gave him an impressed look.

"Well this is new."

His smile was blasé. "I aim to please."

I enjoyed the feel of his muscles shifting as he pulled me in close for a tight turn. My head spun, I had no idea what I was doing, but Yari obviously did. He commanded my body to move with a confidence that was effortless and I was surprised at how easy it was to follow.

The mood was magical and as the night wore on I found myself forgetting about the threat that loomed over us. We twirled in amongst flashes of colour and jewels and laughed at our own attempts at snobbery. I had lost count of the number of songs we had danced too, but I was feeling flushed and a little breathless so I knew we had been at it for awhile.

Moving to the edge of the dance floor we tried to escape the crush in search of fresh air and refreshments. Waiting for a large group to pass we had come to a standstill and taking advantage I leaned back into Yari and looked up into his face as he smiled down at me. I was about to stand on tip toe and invite him in for a kiss when something flicked across my peripheral vision on the colourful glass of the domed ceiling, demanding attention. I pulled back and Yari frowned.

"What is it?"

"There's something on the roof."

Instantly alert he turned to follow my gaze. "Are you sure?"

"I don't know, I could have sworn I…"

A massive pane of glass shattered from the dome above, drowning my words and spraying glass through the air like confetti. Stunned I watched as a body fell, limbs fluttering lifelessly as it hurtled through the air towards us. I heard a sickening thud and then screams as falling glass tinkled around us and chaos erupted.

SIXTEEN

Yari crouched over me, protecting my bare back from spraying glass as people ran, stumbling over each other in their panic to get away. Their screams reverberated through my head and I gritted my teeth against the urge to panic.

I tried to move but Yari tightened his hold on me, growling in my ear. "Wait."

It felt like an eternity for the sound of the glass to stop falling but eventually it did. We moved slowly, straightening to assess the damage. Panic still dominated the room but the screams were now sporadic and had given way to the static of Kaul radios and the rapid fire of orders. Guests pushed at each other to get to the doors and every Kaul in the room scrambled to their posts with the higher ranking Elite being ushered out of the ballroom by their respective protection details.

Yari took my hand and started pulling me away from the dance floor. "Are you okay?"

I stepped over a large smear of blood that had stained one of the white tiles and swallowed hard. "Where's Tash?"

Stopping, he caught both my hands. They shook uncontrollably and I was glad for his steady grip. "She's fine, Garrick is with her. Are you hurt?"

I shook my head and took in the chaos that surrounded us. "I'm not hurt."

Happy with my answer he turned and gave the room a quick scan, stopping once he reached the spot where the body had landed. I followed his gaze and my breath caught. Standing over the lifeless form was Bravnica, blood trickled down the side of his face and his ice blue eyes flashed dangerously. Seemingly unaffected by the anarchy that surrounded him, he barked orders in a steady stream stopping only when Anton rushed to his side and spoke in his ear. Both men looked at the ceiling simultaneously before Bravnica nodded sending Anton racing up the stairs. As if feeling my gaze, he shifted his attention from the jagged hole above him and let his eyes fall on me. He moved towards us and my skin prickled as his eyes traced their way to touch my neck and then my shoulders, stopping briefly at my shaking hands and then passing quickly over the rest of my body. Satisfied with his inventory I was dismissed and he turned his attention to Yari who moved to meet him. The conversation was over by the time I reached them, Bravnica's eyes met mine one last time before he dismissed us both and turned his attention back to the body.

Yari started pushing me toward the door but my feet weren't quick enough, I tripped on my dress. Steadying me with a curse he yanked my dress up tearing a good two feet off of the bottom before resuming our hurried pace.

I looked at the discarded material. "What are you doing?"

Yari didn't stop in our rush for the door. "Following orders."

Garrick passed in front of us pushing Tash towards the exit. I yelled out to her but my voice was drowned by the din of panic and I lost sight of them as they were swallowed by the doors. The air was hot and thick as we pushed our way through the crowd. Yari had my upper arm in a vicelike grip that didn't loosen even once we were clear of the ballroom and outside breathing fresh air. He pulled me along, stopping once free of the crowd to scan the area.

"You can let go of me now."

Ignoring me he scanned the street quickly before starting to drag me again. I planted my feet and he turned and growled. "Ana..."

"Yari please you're hurting my arm."

His eyes soften a fraction and thankfully so did his grip. "Sorry."

"Ana!"

Tash was bolting toward us, followed by Garrick. Daska my brother looked fierce, his eyes flicked over the surroundings as he kept easy pace behind her. Tash threw her arms around me and I squeezed hard, pulling back only to check for damage.

"Are you ok?"

She nodded. "Yeah, a little shaky though."

Garrick pushed Tash along. "You can chat later."

We were moving again, me pulling Tash as she struggled to keep up with the quickened pace. Yari and Garrick were flanking us, scanning the crowds and the buildings above us as we hurried down the cobblestone streets. Two more streets and we would be home.

"Almost there Tash."

We rounded the corner only a block from the apartment and came to a skidding halt as Garrick grabbed Tash and Yari pushed me against a wall.

I heard him curse under his breath, his attention fixed on two figures at the end of the street. He didn't look at us when he spoke. "Stay here."

Garrick pulled out a 9mm pistol, ejecting the clip to check his ammo and ramming it home in one smooth motion.

Oh Shit.

Yari was talking rapidly into his earpiece but the words made no sense to me as I pressed myself against the wall and squinted at the far end of the street.

He turned back to me with a look so harsh I did a double take. "Do not move from this spot until I tell you to and if I tell you to run. You fucking run."

Nodding, I opened my mouth to speak but he pulled out his own pistol and my words lodged themselves in my throat. The two of them started down the street at full speed, their guns drawn and intent clear.

Shit shit shit.

Two Kaul rounded the corner from the direction we had just come. They stopped upon seeing us and raised their weapons, my eyes widened as I looked at the pointy end of their hand held crossbows. Instantly realising we were not a threat they took us out of their cross hairs and started to approach. Unable to speak I raised my hand and pointed to the end of the street where Garrick and Yari had just slowed their pace. They both started to sprint and our attention was drawn again to the figures at the end of the street.

The larger form stood, taking on a defensive stance and the smaller form slumped to the ground like a puppet that had lost its strings. My feet moved without permission and I took a few steps closer. Chest heaving I realised what I was looking at, Garrick and Yari, going toe to toe with a Kudlak.

They approached with caution. It was freshly fed now and would now be incredibly strong. Blood dripped from its lips and it smiled, twitching its long spindly fingers in a dare for the men to come closer. I didn't want to see it but I couldn't look away, this was what nightmares were made of, its marbled skin glistened as though wet and its red eyes reflected the light from the street lamp above. Tash made a distressing noise but I couldn't turn to her, I couldn't take my eyes off the horror that was unfolding before me.

My heart slammed against my ribcage as Yari made the first move getting close enough to fire two rounds into its right shoulder. The air around us reverberated with the shots and it stumbled backwards from the force of the bullets. Off balance, Garrick and another Kaul took advantage. Launching themselves they pinned its powerful arms behind its back and the other Kaul steadied his cross bow at its chest. Yari stepped in and bound its arms and legs with silver cuffs. The silver would slow it down but it wouldn't hold it forever and the wooden rounds from Yari's 9mm would have been fatal if shot through the heart. They obviously didn't want it dead, not yet anyway.

My heart was in my throat with Yari and Garrick being so close but the Kudlak didn't struggle.

I let out the breath I had been holding. "Holy fucking shit."

Yari glanced at our end of the street and said something to Garrick before running back to us.

My attention was drawn to the pistol he hadn't holstered. "Get back to the apartment. You'll have to circle around this block. We will come for you as soon as more backup arrives, but the two of you need to get off the streets."

Tash nodded and started moving back the way we had come.

My attention was on Yari, as he pulled me in for a quick kiss. "Get your crossbow out and don't open the door unless you know it's one of us."

I nodded and he pushed me toward the corner after Tash before turning his back on me. My entire body shook but I forced myself to move. I had just rounded the corner when I heard Yari yell out. Tash hissed my name but imagining the worst I ignored her plea and turned back.

The Kudlak was fighting, the scene horrifying and mesmerizing. Yari shot the Kudlak again and one of its legs buckled and the two Kaul took advantage of the opportunity and wrested it to the ground. I slid along the wall, my hands running over the smooth brickwork until I found an old doorway. Eyes glued to the scene unfolding, I stumbling up the stoop and pressed myself into the shadows. Garrick levelled his gun at the Kudlak's chest and began to speak. I couldn't hear what was being said, but Garrick looked like he was struggling to maintain control. As he spoke he jabbed at the Kudlak with the muzzle of his gun. One of the other Kaul placed a steadying hand on my brother's shoulder but he shook it off. The Kudlak watched the movement and threw its head back, laughing manically at the sky. Garrick stood and in one swift movement kicked the Kudlak's laughing face, snapping its head back with a force so violent I heard a distinct crack.

Bile rose in my throat.

Its head hung at an impossible angle, resting backward against its spine. Upside down its red eyes swivelled from side to side taking everything in. I pressed myself deeper into the shadows. The sound of crazy laughter now replaced with weird popping noises as the Kudlak shifted its shoulders back and forth, working its head back into position atop its shoulders. It smiled the whole time. Closing my eyes I pressed the side of my face against the cold, hard stone of my hidey-hole. If I puked I would draw attention to myself and that would be very, very bad.

Opening my eyes I made a point of not looking at the Kudlak, I could see in my peripheral that its head was back in place. Garrick was bending over the other form lying lifeless on the ground. I had forgotten about the victim. He bent low and gently rolled the figure over. I couldn't make out her features from this distance but I think she was about my age. A lock of black hair shifted in the breeze and Garrick caught it between his fingers. Yari approached Garrick, his concern obvious. They spoke briefly and Garrick confirmed something Yari had asked with a stiff nod.

Oh Daska he knew her.

Yari placed a hand on my brother's shoulder but he shifted away, rejecting the offer of support. I covered my mouth with my hands and blinked back tears.

Garrick.

Standing he stalked away, back rigid against the rasping of the Kudlak's laughter. Yari bent on one knee at her side and pressed his gun against her chest.

No no no.

I shook my head.

This is not happening.

I jumped as the gun kicked, the muzzle flash lighting up Yari's face, anger etched in every line. The girl appeared to come to life, lurching forward as the bullet penetrated her heart. Body lighting up from the inside, like lava flowing underneath skin that was turning black and pealing, the heat disintegrated her body to ash.

Oh Daska I'm going to be sick.

Moving gingerly I made to step out of the doorway but jumped back when a military jeep came screeching past. I watched as it pulled to a stop at the end of the street, the driver parking it at an angle and obscuring my view. Bravnica and two other Kaul jumped out and headed straight to Yari. I was too far away to hear what was going on and I couldn't see Garrick anymore. I strained my neck trying to get a glimpse. Bravnica had his back to me as he listened to Yari.

My heart rate slowed to a milder panic now that backup had arrived. I figured they would have the situation well under control. No one was paying any attention to my end of the street so I eased out of my doorway. Looking over to Tash's corner I could see she was still there. She tried again to get me to go with her, only peeking her head around the edge of the building and frantically waving me to her.

I shook my head and holding up a finger mouthed "One minute."

The look she threw me was lethal but I ignored it and turned back, sliding along the wall just a little further until I had a clear view and was within earshot. Bravnica now stood in front of the smiling Kudlak, his voice was low and controlled.

"Why are you here?"

The Kudlak smiled its bloody smile, eyes flashing, it replied in a raspy sing song. "You have no idea what's coming."

The hairs on the back of my neck stood to attention at the sound of its voice.

Bravnica drew his Sabre and the Kudlak fell silent as the blade sung through the air and brushed at its neck. The action could not be confused with anything other than a blatant threat. Bravnica ignored its animal like hiss and kept his voice low.

"You have allowed yourself to be captured. There is something you want us to know. Tell me what it is."

I was torn between sticking my fingers in my ears to block the horrible noise of it speaking and leaning closer to catch every word.

I flinched as it threw its head back and laughed again, spittle flying as it screamed. "It's coming, and when it arrives..." It shook its head from side to side and let out a deranged whoop. "Ring the dinner bell boys 'cause it's gonna be all you can eat!"

Its dialogue was cut off as Bravnica swung his blade and separated the laughing head from its body. The head made a heavy thudding sound as it hit the street and rolled a couple of times. A booted foot kicked it back toward the rest of its body moments before it all started to burn like its victim. The air, now empty of the horrid voice hung heavy with unanswered questions.

I ordered my feet to move and was relieved when they obeyed. Shuffling slowly I backed my way down the wall towards Tash, two more feet and I would be around the corner, then I could break into a full-fledged sprint for home.

Oh man, I just want to be home.

"Anastasia Valinski."

I froze, staring longingly at the corner I had nearly made it around and listened to Bravnica's footsteps as he approached like an oncoming storm. He came to a stop directly behind me, the skin on my back heating as he stood there, waiting for my full attention. I turned slowly to face him. He was livid. Jaw clenching his body was poised, held only just in check. I didn't move lest I trigger the throttling he so obviously wanted to give me. He kept his distance. Just out of arm's reach, hands fisted at his sides and dried blood smeared across the side of his face I had never seen anything look so fierce.

"I was advised that you were ordered home by Lieutenant Pavic." His tone was low and his words were measured.

Oh crap.

I looked past him at Yari who looked like he would like to throttle me too. Bravnica stepped into my field of vision, forcing me to look back at him as he continued. "So this begs the question." He paused and I felt my face flush. "Why are you still here?"

I swallowed hard. "I was going but then…"

He exploded. "But then *nothing* Ana."

He stepped forward and reached out, I thought he was going to shake me but he pulled back at the last moment and dragged the raised hand through his hair instead, the movement enough to set my body trembling.

Regaining control he pinned me with his eyes again. "You were given an order by Lieutenant Pavic and you chose to disobey it. You may not be a member of the Kaul, but when there is a *damned Kudlak* one hundred metres away you should know to obey."

He let out a frustrated breath, took a couple of steps back and placed his hands on his hips as he glanced at the end of the street where he had just beheaded the Kudlak. His radio crackled and he shook his head.

I watched his chest rise and fall as he took a deep breath. "This is pretty basic stuff Ana."

He turned without sparing me another glance and stalked toward Yari. "You deal with her and make sure she does as she's told this time."

"Yes Sir."

"Debrief at 0700."

I watched Yari as Bravnica passed him shouting orders into his radio. His jaw was set in a hard line and his eyes were fixed on me.

"Yari I'm sorry."

He took my arm. "Save it."

Marching me to the corner where Tash stood drying her tears. We reached her and she wadded up her tissue. "Don't ever do that to me again."

"I'm sorry Tash."

Yari shook his head and the stupidity of my actions started to hit home. Not only had I put myself at risk, but Tash too, knowing full well that she would never leave me there alone.

Yari growled as he stepped forward. "Move it."

I resisted the urge to cry. A curled piece of fringe fell over my eyes and I swiped at it, so much for the sophisticated look. Sniffing like the lady that I am, I bent down to pull off my shoes, my dress was torn to shreds, my hair was wild, my shin was bleeding and my make-up had long since slid off my face, I didn't think being shoeless was going to matter much.

Tash inserted the key into the lock and opened the door, Yari finally let go of my arm to bolt the door.

Tash had gone straight to her bathroom and I could hear the shower running.

"Do you want to die?"

I turned to face Yari who had moved to stand in the middle of the room.

"Because from where I'm standing you seem to be hell bent on getting yourself killed."

"Yari I…"

He held up a hand to cut me off. "What about Tash? And me and Garrick? How the hell do you expect us to bring down a Kudlak if we have to worry about you putting yourself in harm's way?"

I looked at my feet. "I hadn't thought about that."

"No, you haven't been doing a lot of thinking recently have you?"

His response stung. "Yari I know I fucked up. I said I was sorry so what more do you want from me?"

His hands encircled my upper arms before I realised he had even moved, the grip so tight I stood on tiptoes to try and compensate.

His response was explosive. "Self-preservation!"

"If not for yourself then for me at least, if that Kudlak had gotten a hold of you..." He gave me a little jerk. "I won't do this without you Ana I can't."

My tears spilled over and he pulled me to him, crushing me in a desperate embrace. We stood clinging to each other until my tears stopped flowing and his grip on me had eased slightly. Pulling back I accepted the hanky he held in front of me and wiped my face.

"Thanks."

I jumped as someone pounded on the front door. Yari drew his gun and pointed it at the door. "Identify yourself."

"It's Garrick. I'm stationed here tonight."

Ten minutes later we were all settled in the living room. Garrick was busy setting up my crossbow and Yari sat at the table methodically cleaning the disassembled components of his gun. Tash was on the couch eyeing my bloodied shin with a pair of tweezers.

"You scared me half to death Ana." She plucked at the glass shard in a not too gentle fashion. I jerked my leg away.

"Ouch!"

She rolled her eyes at me and pulled my leg back. Hissing through my teeth I winced as the glass mercifully came free. "I'm sorry Tash."

I had a feeling I would be well versed in the art of apology before the week was out. Dahrel was going to kill me.

Oh crap.

"Where is Dahrel?"

Garrick looked up from my crossbow. "He's stationed at the Chambers."

I nodded and wiped at the cut on my shin with a tissue. Of course he was, they needed every available Kaul in the city right now. I knew that Yari would have to get out there too.

I put a plaster over my wound. "Does anyone know who it was - the body from the ball?"

Yari stood as he spoke, his response matter of fact snapping the clip home on his reassembled gun. "Vladimir Preseren."

Elite head of the Preseren Family.

SEVENTEEN

"I have to get back."

Yari sat next to me on the couch watching me warily. "Are you going to be okay?"

The events of the evening had caught up with me and my body shook so hard I felt like I was sitting in one of those massage chairs in the mall. I was definitely not okay but I smiled and managed to nod without sending everything off kilter.

"Just the adrenaline I guess. Think I'll take a bath."

He rose with me as I stood and shadowed me to the bathroom. I leaned against the cool tiles and watched as he started the bath, wondering how he managed to complete such a mundane task after just putting a bullet through the heart of a girl. As though feeling my eyes he straightened. Slowly turning to meet my gaze he positioned himself at arms-length and waited, our reflections in the mirror beginning to disappear as steam filled the room.

"You shot her."

He worked his jaw. "You shouldn't have seen that."

I looked at my feet. "I wish I hadn't."

He opened the door. "Look, I don't have time to discuss this with you."

I swiped at a stubborn piece of fringe and nodded. "Of course. I know you need to go."

He tucked the lock back behind my ear and let out a sigh before giving me a quick kiss on the forehead and leaving, pulling the door closed without a another word. I stared at the closed door a little shocked. I had expected him to tell me everything would be okay and that he forgave me, like he always had. I half expected the door to open and for him to come back and tell me what I wanted to hear, but he didn't.

My heart sank.

Freshly scrubbed and wrapped in the fluffy bath robe that Tash had given me for my last birthday, I held what was left of my dress in front of me and made my way to the bin. There was nothing to be salvaged out of that sorry pile of material and it wasn't even paid for yet. The lights had been turned off and Tash had gone to bed. Garrick sat by the window with my crossbow.

"Garrick…"

"Go to bed Ana." He didn't even look at me.

"Fine."

This would usually be the time that I would sit on my windowsill and brood but the images of the Kudlak were way too fresh. I shook my head and pulled the curtains close, it didn't matter, my view would never be the same again anyway. I tucked myself under the covers and prayed for sleep - mercifully I didn't have to wait very long.

Tash had gone early, leaving me a note saying that there was an emergency at work and she had been called in. What kind of emergency they could have in the Archives Department was beyond me. Indulging in a little self-pity I sat alone at the kitchen table, stirring my coffee and staring at the radio. The morning newsreader announced that Lumeer was in lockdown and an evening curfew had been put in place until further notice. The Council would be making an address at 1100 hours to discuss the 'incident' and any further details would be released as they came to hand. I let out a sigh and thumped my way through the empty house to the bathroom. Garrick must have left as soon as the sun came up. Thankfully I didn't think I would be seeing any of the boys today, they would all be on assignment for the lockdown so I could avoid their condemnation for today at least.

I pulled off my pj's and turned the taps on in the shower, turning them straight off again when my mobile rang. I wrapped myself in a towel and bolted into the kitchen to find the bench empty.

"Crap, where did I put it?"

I spun back to the lounge room honing in on my ringtone. The single seater was playing the intro to AC/DC's Back in Black. Reaching down behind the seat cushion, I came up with the handset and a few coins.

"Hello?"

"Good morning, this is Victor from Triple A security. May I speak with Anastasia Valinski please?"

"This is Ana, how can I help you?"

"Anastasia, I have you down as a contact in case of emergency. We tried to get on to Dahrel Valinski, but we're unable to gain contact."

"Emergency? What emergency?"

"Ms Valinski there was an incident at your family's farm last night."

My mind instantly flew to the young couple who lived next door and looked after the place for us.

"What kind of incident?"

"There has been a break-in."

Relief that no one had been eaten by a Kudlak quickly gave way to anger that someone had broken into our family home. Mum and Dad were buried now but the boys and I decided not to sell. We still go home regularly and keep everything the way it was. The boys use it more than me now as a place for them to go on their days off to hunt game and play cards with their mates.

"What did they take?"

"We don't know. You will need to come to the house to see what damage has been done and what property is missing. It could have just been teenagers looking for a place to party for the night."

"Damage?"

"The door looks like it's been knocked off its hinges. To be honest the security at the house is pretty good. It must have taken a hell of a kick to get that door down."

I was already moving through the apartment. There was no way Garrick or Dahrel would be able to get time off. Bravnica would be in back to backs all day and after last night. I sure as hell didn't want to see him.

"I'll be there in a couple of hours."

"Excellent, I'll get the paperwork ready for your insurer."

I ended the call and typed up a quick text to Bravnica.

"Won't be in today. Family Emergency."

I tossed the phone on my bed and dressed quickly in jeans and a singlet. Shoving my feet into my riding boots I hurried out of the room and stuffed my purse and a bottle of water into my backpack. Racing through the house I grabbed my riding jacket, keys and helmet and was out the door in under a minute. Riding my Fireblade I blasted down the street and out of Lumeer, pleased that I managed to get away without seeing anyone.

Pulling into the drive of my childhood home, I felt horribly disconnected. I had spent the entire ride wondering what precious items and memories could have been taken or vandalised. As a result I had made the trip in record time. Victor was standing out the front and stepped forward when I pulled up. He waited for me to dismount and remove my helmet before introducing himself and bombarding me with questions while juggling a pile of paperwork. I listened with half an ear as I strode toward the house.

Taking the porch steps two at a time I stepped through the entry way and onto the front door that was lying on the ground where it had landed. The lounge room was a mess, the television lay broken on the floor and the couches had been de-stuffed, the contents strewn about the floor as though an indoor snow storm had hit. Empty chip packets and soda cans scattered here and there. Mums knitting lamp had been knocked over and I rushed across the room to right it.

I moved through the rest of the house methodically, the kitchen was pristine except for the liquor cupboard which had been relieved of its contents, the door standing open as a testimony to its violation. The downstairs bathroom was trashed as was the dining room. Upstairs the rooms remained relatively untouched and I held my breath as I moved to Mum's drawers. The jewellry box on top of the tallboy was a decoy Dahrel had set up when upgrading security. It had been rifled through but if anything was missing I couldn't tell and didn't care. The real treasures were in a false back in the bottom drawer, not that they had any monetary value but to us they were priceless. Heirlooms for commoners. I ripped the bottom drawer from the dresser and yanked at the false back, tears of relief flooding when mums small bag of jewellry fell out.

"Oh thank Daska."

"I take it this is good news?"

In my rush to check for mum's treasures I'd forgotten about Victor. Straightening I gave him a wry smile.

"Yep, good news."

He eyed the drawer behind me. "You people should look at going into security yourselves. I have to say this is an impressive set up."

I moved past him, holding the velvet bag tight. "Not impressive enough apparently."

My brain went into self-preservation mode and shut down once I had been handed the paperwork for the insurance claims. Rolling the thick pile up I shoved it into my backpack, Dahrel could deal with that. In the meantime I had a door to secure. It was coming up to lunchtime and I had to get a move on if I was going to make it back to Lumeer before dark.

With the frame broken the door was a lot harder to fix than first thought, even with the help of my neighbours. In the end we decided to board it up and use the backdoor until we could get the materials to fix it properly. No doubt Dahrel would want to reinforce the next door anyway. With the final nail banged in I thanked my good Samaritans. Waving them out the back door I waited till they had cleared the boundary gate before returning to the house to start the lonely job of cleaning. With downstairs being the mess that it was I decided to tackle upstairs first, which was really only Mum's dresser. Kneeling on the floor to line up the runners, a slip of white in the empty space where the drawer was supposed to be caught my eye. Pushing the drawer to the side I lay down on my stomach and stretched my arm into the dark space. Fingers clutching at the object I just managed to scrape it so that I could trap it between the tips of my index and middle finger. It was a sealed envelope, addressed to me.

My heart thudded a little harder in my chest as apprehension took hold. Why would there be a sealed envelope addressed to me, hidden in the bottom of my mother's dresser? I turned the rich paper over in my hands. I guess the question should be, do I really want to know?

"Well I can't *not* open it."

Standing, I went to Dad's office to grab his letter opener. Somehow, tearing the elegant envelope open in my usual manner didn't seem right. Letter opener in hand I went back to the master bedroom and sat cross legged in the middle of the big bed. Taking a deep breath I inserted the tip of the blade into the corner of the envelope and sliced it open.

The ornate paper inside was folded into thirds and matched the thick envelope in richness and colour. I unfolded it gingerly, revealing elegant hand writing that must have taken years to perfect. I read the first line and a feeling of foreboding crept over me.

To Our Darling Daughter Anastasia,

We know that you cannot possibly understand the necessity of our actions. Your father and I love you desperately and that is why we have had to let you go. Please know that if there was any other way, things would have been very different for us. Your new family love you and will care for you as one of their own. They will protect you and keep you safe from the world. We trust them with your life. We hope you understand and can one day forgive us. We miss you and think of you every day. Be brave our darling daughter. Ut Daska tueri et vigilabo super meam vobis velato.

All our Love,

A and M

I reread the letter over and over until the elegant hand began to blur through my tears. I folded the letter up and allowed myself to cry. I looked around the room and was flooded with memories of being here, in this room with my parents.

"This has to be a mistake."

Wiping my face I went looking for proof that this wasn't what it seemed. Pulling the attic door open, I released the ladder and a couple of year's worth of dust, coughing I waved at the dust and climbed. Feeling my way carefully to the middle of the room, I fumbled for the string that turned on the bare bulb perched on the center rafter. Finding it I tugged and fifty years of clutter was suddenly illuminated in overwhelming piles of disorder.

"Daska I'm gonna be here all night."

I started with the newer looking boxes. The first held school merit certificates and old projects and paintings. The second was full of old clothes obviously meant for goodwill. I hit the jackpot on the third, finding Birth Certificates for both the boys and my parent's Wedding Certificate. I rifled through the manila folders packed with important documents but found nothing for me. Reaching the end of the pile I fought the urge to cry and instead started again, this time pulling each piece out separately and placing them methodically into neat piles.

"There has to be something here."

Half an hour later I was surrounded by paperwork. The earliest documentation I could find that related to me was a medical report from blood-work taken when I was two. I folded the report up and put it in my back pocket groaning at the twinge in my lower back as I shifted position. I had been sitting on the floor for too long. Standing I put the rest of the paperwork back and moved further into the room. If I wanted to hide something (which maybe my parents did) it would be in the deepest, darkest corner I could find. I moved to the far end of the attic where the light from the single globe lost its battle with gloom. I never understood why Dad thought one light bulb was enough, it clearly wasn't. A floorboard groaned under my weight reminding me of how spooked I used to get up here when I was a kid. I felt the cobweb too late and it broke across my face and slapping at it I knocked one of Dad's piles of newspapers.

"Shit."

Turning around to steady the stack before it toppled, I only managed to keep the bottom half from falling. The mess was instant, each paper seeming to spew its contents in protest on its way to the dusty wood floor, papers fluttering, slipping and sliding over each other, spreading further and further out.

Still holding on to the bottom half of the stack I watched, waiting for the last piece of escaping paper to settle.

"Perfect."

Shifting I looked up and was surprised to find an empty space behind the stack. I always thought the piles had rested against the far wall. On tip toes I peered into the dark void but couldn't see anything. I looked at the mess that surrounded me and gave a shrug.

"What the hell."

Reaching forward I pulled the rest of the stack down and toppled the one next to it, creating a hole big enough for me to move through. Two steps into the shadows and my shin glanced painfully off something unforgiving. Feeling with my hands I made out a wooden chest with a curved lid. Fingers running over the ornate surface for the sides I grabbed a handle with two hands and used my weight to start pulling it back through the hole and into the light. It took several short sharp tugs to clear the papers and even more to get it across the floor to a reasonable amount of clear space. I stood back, letting the struggling globe illuminate my find. The chest was obviously old. I couldn't decide whether it was decadent, with its gold paint and brass handles or tacky, like the cheap knock off my family could afford to purchase. My money was on the latter.

I pulled some old cushions down and sat on the floor. Opening the chest I was surprised at the amount of pretty things that were revealed. Kneeling over the chest I ran my hands through the treasure. A couple of the pieces were gaudy and very over the top - I left them in the box. There was one piece that caught my eye though, a silver necklace with a small butterfly pendant. The wings were coloured with beautiful gemstones that caught the light at every angle. Holding the butterfly in my hand I ran my fingers over the intricate design and found myself wondering who wore it. My curiosity piqued I placed the trinket in my pocket and burrowed further, coming up with a photo of a tiny baby. Turning it over I was affronted by the same elegant hand as the author of my letter.

Anastasia - two weeks.

I sat in silence. My entire body felt like it had been super-heated. Head spinning I put the photo on the floor next to the chest and lay down on the hard wood. Pulling the cushion over and using it as a pillow I dug the butterfly out of my pocket. It was a stunning piece that sparkled brilliantly, glittering through my tears.

I didn't know how long I lay there, crying quietly but the house dragged me out of my memories and back to reality, groaning in its old age. Pulling myself up, I put the butterfly in my pocket and checked to make sure I still had my medical report. Stretching up I pulled the string to turn off the light and headed back down the ladder slowly.

I had lost track of time, the house was dark and I felt my way along the walls, downstairs and into the kitchen. No point starving. Heating up a frozen meal I grabbed a fizzy drink and headed to the dining room to eat. Sitting at the table I had a clear view of the bookshelf in the lounge. The family photo albums were there.

"Don't do it to yourself."

Feeling nauseous I left my meal uneaten, checked that the back door was secure and turned off the downstairs lights. Climbing back up the stairs, I walked down the dark hallway, stopping at the doorway to my old bedroom. Reaching into the room I turned on the light and was instantly bombarded with agonizing memories. It was still as I had left it. My stuffed dog - aptly named Dog, taking pride of place on the single bed. The posters on the wall, my desk, the pictures of me and Tash pulling faces, my brothers leaving on their first Kaul assignment and my mother in the garden. I couldn't bring myself to cross the threshold, it was like I would be tainting what was. I staggered back and leaned against the wall opposite my room. Sliding to the floor I curled into a ball and cried.

"Daska Mum, how could you leave me with this? I miss you so much."

Lying on my side I looked at the pictures in my room, letting my tears fall. Eventually there were none left but I didn't move. My body gave in to exhaustion and I fell asleep, huddled outside the door to my old bedroom.

The fog of sleep was being pulled away and I was trying to fight it. I didn't want to wake up. I didn't want to have to think.

"Ana."

Someone was shaking me by the shoulders.

"Go away." I swatted at the voice.

The voice became more insistent and the shaking got harder. "Ana."

Groaning, I cracked my eyes open to see what the hell was going on. It was dark, but I could make out a large silhouette bending over me. Screaming, I scooted backwards and out of his grasp.

"Ana, it's ok, it's me, Dominik."

Groaning again I tried to rub the sleep from my face and get my eyes to focus. "Bravnica? What the hell?"

His voice was urgent. "Are you hurt?"

I was confused. "Wha... no. What time is it?"

Bravnica let out a breath in frustration. "It's 0600, get up, we're leaving."

I sat up slowly. "You are waking me at six AM? Is the sun even up?"

He flicked his torch light towards my face and I shielded my eyes.

"Aarghh, what the hell is your problem?"

He didn't answer my question, but stalked down the hall, disappearing as he rounded the corner and descended the stairs. I muttered to myself as I stood to follow.

"Arsehole."

Taking note of my surrounds, the memories of the day before came flooding back, hitting me like a physical force. I steadied myself against the wall taking a few deep breaths before heading after Bravnica. By the time I had reached the bottom of the stairs I had worked myself up into a fine temper.

"Just what the hell do you think you are doing here?"

He turned to me incredulous. "You really don't know?"

His surprise annoyed me even more. "Look Bravnica, it's six in the morning, I've had a pretty rough night and I can assure you that guessing games is the last thing I want to do right now."

I could see his composure begin to slip.

Ha!! Well call the media. The ever poised Dominik Bravnica might actually show some genuine emotion.

I smiled, following him into the kitchen as he struggled for control.

"Ana, you broke curfew. I am here to take you back to Lumeer."

I started laughing, I couldn't help myself. Was he serious? My entire world had been ripped out from under me, everything I had ever known to be truth was now a lie, and he was worried about curfew? Tears were threatening but I held them back, better off laughing like a crazy person than crying for real in front of him. And laugh I did, throwing my head back like an over enthused clown at sideshow alley, waiting for a ball to pop into my mouth. The laughter switched to hiccupping bursts that shook my whole body and I tried not to snort.

Bravnica narrowed his eyes, and before I realised he had moved he was poised a bare inch from me. I craned my neck up as his barely contained anger swallowed up the air around me, leaving me breathless.

"People are dead Ana."

He turned, ripping himself away and I suddenly felt like I could breathe again. I watched him warily as he ran a hand through his hair and regained control. Turning to me his voice was low and condescending, like he was talking to a child.

"Laws are there to keep you and everyone else safe. You cannot just disregard them at will."

I had managed to keep my anger in check but his tone grated through me, I couldn't stop it. Like a fire being doused with kerosene I exploded.

"Oh that is just perfect. My entire world is in turmoil, everything I ever thought I had I don't. And you, *you* expect me to just play nice and do my duty as though nothing has happened?" Pointing my finger I advanced on him. "Dahrel and Garrick are Kaul, they have to obey you. There was a time when I would have given anything to have that right but I'm thanking Daska for your Boys' Club mentality now. Someone has to deal with the reality of this family and I guess it's going to fall to me. And as much as it might piss you off, I am not one of your underlings and I don't require, nor do I give a toss about your approval." My finger jabbed at his chest. "Now get the fuck out of my house."

Arms braced on either side of the kitchen bench, Bravnica raised his eyes from my jabbing finger at his chest to meet mine. Raising an eyebrow it was clear he was back in control. I removed my finger and when he spoke, his voice was low and clipped.

"If you think you can intimidate me with that mouth of yours, think again Miss Valinski. You are coming back to Lumeer with me this morning, whether you like it or not."

Leaning back on the kitchen bench he crossed his arms and tilted his head in a cocky pose that made me want to give him an uppercut.

He looked me up and down pointedly before continuing. "Now we can do this the easy way, or we can do this the not so easy way. Whatever you choose will be fine with me."

I moved to put the island bench in between us, I was dangerously close to losing control and I couldn't afford to do that. I took a deep breath to steady my voice and dug my heels in. "I'm not leaving without sorting out the house." I looked him in the eye. "You take me back to Lumeer and I will just leave again." I shrugged my shoulders. "I won't leave it in this condition. Anyone could just let themselves in. I can't leave until it is secure."

I could see Bravnica thinking, he knew I would do it. Finally he relented.

"Fine. I will organise a Team to come and sort it out. Now get your gear. I'll be waiting in the jeep."

I shook my head. "You go ahead. I'll catch up on my bike."

Bravnica rounded on me. "You will do nothing of the sort. You will be travelling back to Lumeer, with me, in the jeep."

I was flabbergasted. "How can you be so pig-headed? You won, I'm coming back, but I will be coming back on my bike."

Bravnica smiled like a cat that'd got the cream. "I guess we will be doing it the not so easy way then."

He pushed off the bench and started toward me. I could see he had every intention of throwing me over his shoulder and carrying me out to the jeep. The heat of the anger at what I had discovered mixed with the frustration of my current helplessness clashed, rushing through my body in waves, pulsing relentlessly until it was a deafening roar in my head. Panic setting in I scrambled for control but it was too late.

The pain was intense and my vision blurred. Clutching my head I screamed trying to get it out and was instantly rewarded as the roar ceased and the heat started to slowly recede.

I gasped taking in great lungful's of air. "Oh Daska." Realising I had my eyes tightly closed I slowly began to open them.

The kitchen was in ruin. Every cupboard door was flung open, one swinging precariously from its hinges, it gave a little squeak of protest before giving way and clattering to the ground, scattering a packet of dry cereal as it landed on the floor, which was now host to the food that once resided in the cupboards. I followed a trail of golden syrup to the middle of the tiled floor, where it draped itself artistically across Bravnica's boots.

Shit.

There was no way I was going to be able to explain this away. I slowly raised my eyes to meet Bravnica's. His gaze was unwavering as he brushed a couple of biscuits from his shoulder. "You have something you want to tell me Ana?"

I was petrified, but I knew I had to keep my wits in front of him. I promised myself that I could be as freaked out as I liked… later. Turning to grab my bag I answered his question.

"Yes. I'm happy to ride in the jeep with you."

And with that, I was out the door. Bravnica joined me in the jeep a few minutes later.

Resting his hands on the wheel he turned to me. "I understand that you're not going to talk to me about this now Ana but you and I both know that at some point, you will." When I didn't respond he turned the key to start the engine. "I will know how you did that."

EIGHTEEN

I spent the first ten minutes of the car trip trying to fight my body's exhaustion; the episodes always took it out of me. Waking as the Jeep stopped out the front of my apartment I realised I had long lost the battle with sleep.

"It takes it out of you huh?"

I ignored him as he got out of the jeep and came around to my side. I grabbed at the handle to open my door but it didn't release, I tried it a couple more times before realising there must have been some kind of childlock on the door. He was watching my futile movements and I glared at him through the windscreen as he rounded the front of the jeep. He pulled the door open and I exited the car with as much dignity as I could muster.

"A childlock. Really?"

His eyes flashed momentarily but I ignored it.

"Thanks for the ride." Squaring my shoulders I dismissed him and headed for the stairs. I could feel the backs of my eyes heating with tears and I blinked furiously, red faced, fumbling with my keys as I made the front door. I couldn't wait to see Tash, I needed a shoulder.

What I got was an arm crossed and foot tapping Tash. "How could you just leave and not call? I was beside myself when you didn't come home last night. Why didn't you take your phone?"

I opened my mouth to explain but she wasn't done.

"Of all the irresponsible things you have ever done, this has *got* to be up there with the best of them." She got her pointy finger out and slashed it through the space between us. I went to step back but the air behind me seemed to prickle.

"Now this might come as a shock Anastasia Valinski, but not everything is about you. Sometimes, you have to think of others. And you should have, at some point thought, *hey maybe I should give Tash a call, she might be worried.* Especially at a time where Kresniks are being picked off by Kudlak right under the noses of our Kaul!" She flicked her eyes over my shoulder. "Sorry Commander."

My stomached dropped but I resisted the urge to turn around.

Tash, unconcerned, barrelled on. "I understand that you had to go home, but for Pete's sake, a phone call, just to let me know you were okay, that you weren't lying in a ditch somewhere after coming off that monstrous thing you use for transportation, or having your head used in a Kudlak game of catch."

Cheeks flushed she came to a merciful stop. I closed my mouth with a pop. Trying valiantly to keep my shit together I spun around to address my shadow.

"I'm home now, you can leave." I was pleased my voice only wobbled a little.

His face remained unchanged and his voice as level as ever.

"Your bike will be returned tomorrow, as will you be to work."

Not trusting my voice, I nodded my head and turned breezing past Tash and escaping to my room. I could hear the steady tone of his voice out in the living room and glared at the door as I changed into my running gear with jerky forceful movements. I had way too much anger and hurt and worry whirling through me at the moment, I couldn't think straight. I needed to run. Picking up my iPod I paused at my bedroom door eavesdropping on the conversation that was going on in the lounge.

Bravnica's low rumble was muffled by the door. "The DEA are going to be asking a whole lot of questions now and they will want answers. The Lavric Aurora has still not been recovered and with this latest development, we can't afford to fall behind."

"If it's in the Archives Sir, I'll find it."

I heard the clicking of the front door and relaxed a notch. He was gone.

My curiosity over what they were discussing would have to wait. At the moment I was wound so tight I felt like the slightest thing would set me off, and Daska knew I didn't need any more explosions today.

I ran my usual course, needing the comfort of the familiar surrounds. I pushed myself hard but my mind wouldn't switch off, thoughts of my earliest memories, the sibling rivalry, Mum and Dad together on the porch. The fact that I wasn't one of them had never even entered my mind. Did the boys know? How was I going to tell them?

I stopped dead.

"Oh hell."

I hadn't even told them about the house. My lungs were heaving and I cursed under my breath, putting my hands on my hips I looked to the sky. They were all right; Bravnica included. I was impulsive and thoughtless and self-centred and how any of them put up with my crap for as long as they have is beyond me.

"Daska one of these days I'll do the right thing." I was physically and emotionally exhausted. I couldn't do this on my own. I needed my Tash.

After a long shower I changed into some fresh clothes and headed to the living room where I found Tash with her nose buried in a leather-bound book.

"Tash I owe you a huge apology. You know that I would never purposely *not* call you."

"I know." She let out a resigned sigh and closed the book. "It's just with everything that has been going on, I was really worried. Especially with the way you have been passing out and losing control lately."

I nodded conceding the point. "I know."

"The boys have been in lockdown and I didn't know what to do, I found your phone and saw the message you sent the Commander, which failed by the way. I was getting frantic so I called him from your phone. When I explained that you had left your cell here and that I hadn't seen or heard from you all day, well you know the rest."

I nodded. *Yeah, I knew the rest.*

"What happened?" She indicated for me to sit down. "I know there was a break in at the farm but the Commander said you didn't seem quite yourself."

I took a deep breath. This was my opening. It was time to let the Valinski Skeleton out of its proverbial closet. I started the kettle and reached up into the top cupboard for some Cat Out of the Bag chocolate chip cookies.

Tash watched me from the couch. "Is it that serious?"

I nodded. "Can you make a pot of tea? I have to get something."

Moving to the kitchen she watched me with apprehension as I made my way back to my bedroom. Grabbing my riding jacket free, I looked at the corner of the envelope protruding from my pocket.

Oh Daska this is really real.

I sat on the couch opposite Tash who sat on the floor, a look of disbelief on her face. The letter lay on the coffee table in front of her and her cup of tea had gone cold beside it. She looked up from the letter and shook her head slowly. "This can't be right. Ana, there has to be some kind of mistake."

Closing my eyes, I let my head fall back on the couch. "That's what I thought."

Tash interrupted. "Where's your birth certificate?"

I let out a self-depreciating chuckle and rubbed at the dull ache in my temples. "Apparently I don't have one."

"What do you mean you don't have one? Everyone has one."

I opened my eyes and gave her my best 'wanna bet?' look.

I could see her struggling with the concept. This was the girl that had the warranties for every electrical appliance she owned alphabetised.

Stretching across the table I handed her the medical record. "This is the earliest documentation I could find with any reference to me."

Tash took the paper and started scanning the page.

"I found it in a box full of important documents, including both the boys' Birth Certificates."

Her eyes flicked up at that information and then back to the paper. I waited while she went over it, looking up when at length she placed it on the table next to the letter.

"This is extensive blood works for a two year old. Do you think they may have been looking for something?" She tapped the report. "Maybe they suspected your condition?"

I gave a shrug. "No idea, but I do know one person who now suspects something."

Tash looked at me in query and I indicated to the front door where I had earlier been deposited.

Realisation hit. "The Commander?"

I screwed up my face in response.

"No way!" Watching her shocked expression I leaned forward in my chair.

I grimaced, "Afraid so. I exploded the kitchen right in front of him." I did the mini hand explosion move. "Kapow."

She fell back, resting on the front of the couch. "Oh Ana."

"I know."

"What did you tell him?"

I pushed harder on my temples. "Nothing."

"He's not going to let this drop."

"I know."

"We have to figure out a plan." She started scrambling for paper. "We need a list."

Tash's theory on lists was like my brothers' belief in duct tape - they could fix anything.

"Tash, I don't want to think about this right now. Bravnica's fine, I've bought some time there. What I'm worried about now is telling the boys."

She stopped and looked up at me. "Of course. I'm so sorry."

Coming over she gave me a hug and I fought back the tears her show of affection brought on.

"Oh don't hug me." I sniffed. "I'll just start crying."

She let me go and handed me a tissue. "Sometimes a cry is warranted." I nodded and blew my nose. Tash sat back down on the couch. "Call your brothers, maybe they'll know something."

I tried Dahrel first and then Garrick, both numbers went straight to voicemail and I left an urgent message on both.

Tash screwed up her nose. "Not answering."

I shook my head. "Voicemail."

"Do you want to talk about it?"

I sat myself down cross legged on the couch. "To be honest, I don't want to think about any of it. I need a distraction."

Tash raised an eyebrow. "Really?" She smiled. "You asked for it."

I watched as she picked up a heavy looking box and unceremoniously dumped it in my lap, ignoring my groans of protest.

"I know you have no interest in book work but you need a distraction and I need you to go through this box for me."

It smelled musty. "Ergh. What I am looking for?"

Tash resumed her position. "Well, while you were AWOL there were some updates in the investigation."

I sat up, giving Tash my undivided attention.

"This isn't common knowledge but I know you have the clearances and will probably find out tomorrow anyway." I nodded impatiently and motioned for her to get on with it. "They discovered that the Preseren Aurora was stolen."

I stilled, "Is that supposed to be a joke?"

She shook her head. "Unfortunately not and given this, we have to err on the side of caution and assume that the Kudlak are after the other three." Taking a sip of her tea she indicated to herself. "Enter Moi, the bookish heroine."

I grinned but didn't interrupt.

"Because the old ways have not been practiced for centuries, there are more legends and old wives' tales than actual fact. Most are so old no one's really sure if they are based on any kind of truth at all. So, I need to go through any ancient texts referencing to the Auroras to try and determine how it all works."

My eyes crossed at the thought of all that research but I wanted to make sure I understood completely.

"If I remember it correctly the legend is that if you drink the blood contained in all five Auroras or something like that, then you inherit all the powers and turn into some kind of unstoppable Super God right?"

"That seems to be the gist of it but if it was that easy, others would have tried before now. We believe there is more to it, a ritual of some kind. Search anything that mentions The First, Daska or the Auroras."

My mind boggled at the enormity of the task. "Well that narrows it down." I started to flick through a book, looking for pictures.

I felt her eyes on me and looked up.

"Ana, this is really important. They will need all five Auroras to pull off this end of the world thing and they already have two."

Her words hit home and the truth of what could be started to sink in. My mind flew back to the meeting with the DEA liaison and Bravnica confirming that some of the fairytales were real. A feeling of uneasiness that had taken up permanent residence in my belly swelled and I took a deep breath opening the first tome on my pile.

After twenty minutes and turning yet another page in the smelly old book, my eyes were starting to glaze over. I had no idea how Tash had been doing this day after day.

"I just don't see how you can find anything amongst all this." I threw my arm wide to indicate the masses of books, scrolls and loose documents that littered the living room floor.

Tash smiled. "Patience Ana, the information is here, the trick is to know you've found what you need when you find it."

I gave her a doubtful look over the top of the leather bound book that was my current torture. Returning my attention back to the page I had just turned to, I was surprised to find a faded sketching. It depicted a man poised with a knife standing over a woman. She was spreadeagled and bound on what looked to be a sacrificial alter. Her face was covered with a sheer fabric or cloth, so you couldn't see the look of complete horror that must have been there. Her long limbs were straining against the bonds as if in a last ditch effort to escape the inevitable.

I let out a low whistle. "Sucks to be her."

Tash looked up. "What is it?"

I turned the book around so that Tash could see the picture. She scooted over to take a closer look.

"Sacrificial Offering." She surmised.

I let out a scoff. "Bloody men. Bet she was a virgin too the poor thing."

Looking back at the sketching Tash shook her head. "Thankfully that's one ritual we didn't pass down."

Afternoon turned to evening and we took a break to have some dinner. Reading books all afternoon had made my eyes weary and I struggled to keep them open. Tash cleared the table and put on her Mother Hen hat, insisting I get to bed. I'll admit I didn't protest too hard and the feel of my pillow was bliss.

Tash poked her head around the door, the light behind her making her look angelic. "Do you need anything?"

I shook my head. "No thanks, I'll see you in the morning."

She smiled. "Okay, goodnight." The stream of backlight disappeared as she softly pulled my door closed.

I pushed gently with my toes, back and forth, back and forth. The slight creaking of my childhood swing was soothing. The breeze moved my hair playfully and the sun warmed my skin.

I was home.

My mother was in the distance hanging sheets out on the line to dry; she was too far away for me to make out her features, which annoyed me. I wanted to see the face of my mother. I wanted the reassurance from her kind features. As quickly as the unhappy feeling arrived, it disappeared. I smiled as my attention was drawn to a butterfly resting on some wildflowers, it was so peaceful.

The sound of a second creaking slowly registered by my side. I turned my head. Dominik Bravnica was sitting on the second swing, smiling at me as he matched my back and forth motion. He was wearing faded blue jeans and a white T-shirt. I had never seen him out of his uniform, he looked younger, relaxed even - as though the weight of the Kresnik world had been lifted from his broad shoulders.

I returned his smile and pointed to the butterfly, surprised when he spoke. "Change isn't always a bad thing." He nodded at the butterfly as it danced around the flowers. "That butterfly didn't always fly; it started out as something much different."

I stopped swinging.

"So I'm a caterpillar?"

Dominik laughed the sound rich and warm. "Maybe."

Resuming my gentle swing I watched him. He seemed so different like this, not the unattainable Dominik Bravnica - future head of the Bravnica line and Emir to the Kresnik people. He seemed like any other guy, I wanted to drink him in, memorize every subtle change. Even his smile was different, it was quick and natural and it crinkled his eyes a little. The effect was intoxicating.

He spoke again. "Are you okay?"

I brushed some flyaway hair back with my fingers and regarded him. He had stopped swinging and was watching me intently, waiting for me to respond.

Looking down at my feet I shook my head, "No."

Dominik didn't retreat as I had expected. Instead he held out his hand to me, I automatically took it and we began to swing again. It felt very natural to hold hands with Dominik Bravnica.

NINETEEN

I woke up feeling like I hadn't slept at all. Pulling on my dressing gown I padded out to the lounge room, stretching out the kinks along the way. Tash was rummaging through her bag at the front door.

"Did you even sleep?" My voice was croaky and she didn't even look up as she pointed to freshly brewed coffee.

"I have to go in and pick up some more books. I managed to find a link to all five Auroras. Something called the Meridian."

I clutched my coffee like a life preserver. "What's that?"

Finally she pulled her keys out of her bag and looked at me. "I'm not one hundred percent sure. My translation of the old text is shaky at best, but from what I can gather it is some kind of goblet. I don't know how it works or even where to find it, but it's kinda important." She opened the door. "I have to go, I'll see you later okay? Behave today." She pointed her keys at me and gave me a stern look before closing the door behind her.

The distraction of work was comforting. The familiar urgency and stubborn determination of everyone working toward a common goal had always been reassuring, but there were few smiles this morning. News of the stolen Auroras had sobered everyone and there seemed to be an underlying edge of uncertainty around the place that left me feeling cold. I tried to shake it off before heading to Bravnica's office, approaching the open door I found him in a meeting with three other high ranking Kaul. I didn't recognise them and didn't want to interrupt so tried to backtrack quietly.

"Ana, please come in. We are just finishing up here."

Smiling like the professional that I am I walked into his office and pretended to be busy at the bookshelves on the other side of the room while listening in to their conversation. From what I could make out there had been another sighting, or non-sighting on the CCTV cameras and they were coordinating more units to begin another search.

Bravnica had his game face on and his voice brooked no argument. "The remaining Auroras in Lameer are secure however I want protection details on the Emir and Vidmar Elite doubled. Make sure all of the dignitaries have made arrangements to leave and advise the Council that I agree to postpone the public funeral service for Vladimir Preseren." He took a breath and continued on. "Also I want to be put in contact with the lead investigator that was on the Drevensek Aurora search after they were killed. If he is in retirement, get him out and back on the job. I want their files pulled out of Archives and on my desk by the end of the day. I need to know the location of their Aurora." Bravnica stood indicating that the meeting was over. "Get those units into the tunnels within the hour and have them ready to be doubled come nightfall. And find out where the *hell* they are."

The three Kaul stood. "Yes Commander."

They spoke in unison and I probably would have found the response amusing if the situation wasn't so dire. They left the room, closing the door quietly behind them.

Bravnica looked at me from across his desk. "I trust you have been informed of the latest situation regarding the Auroras?"

"Ah yes."

His attention turned back to the papers on his desk and started gathering them up. "Okay good. I need you to help coordinate the backup units for tonight and organise a roster for the next two days. And I need you to make sure that Drevensek file makes my desk before you leave. I will be at the Barracks and on the ground with the units for the rest of the day." I nodded in response and he started toward the door. "If there is anything urgent you can get me on my cell."

"Sure." I stepped forward and he halted his exit. "Um, can you please get a message to my brothers?"

His expressions softened slightly. "Of course."

"It's just that I really need to speak with both of them and I wouldn't normally ask but it's important."

His brow furrowed. "Can I help?"

Embarrassed I swiped at my fringe and tried to smile. "Uh, no. Just if you could tell them that it's urgent."

He nodded and started again for the door. "I'll send them to you as soon as I can spare them."

I turned back to the big desk and willed myself not to cry. Sitting in Bravnica's chair I shoved the thought of telling my brothers to the back of my mind. I needed to keep my mind focused.

As hard as I tried, the distraction of the letter kept seeping in. The rosters took twice as long as they should have. In between fielding phone calls and minor interruptions that turned into major distractions, most of the day was gone before I had them completed.

Tash knocked quietly on the open door. "Knock knock?"

I smiled and waved her in. "What are you doing here?"

She held up a thick file. "I hear the Commander is after this; I offered to bring it over. I wanted to see how you are going."

She sat in the smaller chair on my side of the desk and looked around.

"Well this is pretty nice."

I nodded. "It's certainly a step up."

She placed the file on Bravnica's desk and leaned forward. "So, how are you?"

I rested my head in my hands. "Honestly? I don't know. I haven't had time to process any of this."

She tapped the desk in thought. "I'm going to go through the birth records at Archives. There has to be a record somewhere."

I nodded, "Good idea, it'll have to wait till after you come up with something on the Auroras though, we need to prioritise. And right now, there are more important issues than my biological background."

"You sure?"

I smiled to reassure her, "Yes I'm sure."

She nodded and rose. "I have to get back, we're pulling an all-nighter. You should get one of the boys to stay over."

I knew they would both be on shift but didn't want to worry her. "Will do."

She smiled over her shoulder and I followed her to the door. "Don't work too hard. Remember to eat." She waved me off and disappeared around the door.

Letting out a little sigh I turned back to gather my things. There was nothing more I could do today. Locking the file in Bravnica's desk I left him a post-it telling him where to find it and tidied his desk. Pushing his chair in, I slung my bag over my shoulder and headed home, wondering how my brothers would react to the news. I'm sure they would be cool with it, of course they would be. I mean, you can't be siblings one minute and not the next. Right?

Sitting around the kitchen table I waited for a reaction. Garrick's face paled when I let the bombshell drop, Dahrel did a little better and only took a few seconds to recover before speaking.

"Are you sure that letter was for you?"

Garrick nodded frantically, "Yeah, maybe you misread it."

I shook my head and pulled the letter out, holding it up as proof. Dahrel took it and started reading. Garrick leaned in over his shoulder.

Dahrel swore under his breath.

Tears spilled over and I swiped at them, amazed that I actually had any left to cry. Garrick handed me a tissue and I blew my nose.

Dahrel's voice was strong and steady. "It doesn't mean anything." He reached across the table and squeezed my hand, causing more tears to swell.

Garrick scooted his chair around to sit next to me and threw an arm over my shoulder.

"Hey, you're our little sister whether you like it or not. If you think that having different DNA is going to get you a ticket out of this family then you've got another thing coming."

Smiling I let out a little sob. "Oh this… It's all just so fucked up!"

Dahrel smiled and put on his serious voice. "Yes. Yes it is."

We all started laughing. I laughed so hard and for so long that I started to struggle for breath. The boys had stopped and I kept going, silent now my shoulders shook and my throat hurt but I couldn't stop. Dahrel knelt next to me with a hanky and went to start wiping.

Embarrassed I grabbed the hanky out of his hand. "I can do it I'm not a baby."

I cleaned my face as Garrick shifted in his seat. "You sure cry like one."

Dahrel shot him a look and turned back to me. "We have to get back to the barracks." I nodded and he pushed my fringe back to look into my eyes. "Are you going to be okay or do I need to get someone over here?"

I pulled back, letting my fringe fall back into place. "I'm fine really. I don't know what that was all about." I sniffed loudly. "It's just been a full on couple of days."

Satisfied Dahrel stood. "Alright kiddo but if you need anything you get word to me or call Tash."

Garrick stood and mussed up my hair. "Do you want me to get Yari to come over?"

Oh Daska Yari. I hadn't seen him since the night of the ball, I knew he was still pissed at me for what happened that night and he was going to be furious with me for breaching the lockdown. I wanted to see him so bad but I didn't think my emotions could cope with another confrontation.

"No don't tell him. I think I just need to have a quiet evening."

Dahrel nodded. "Okay but promise to call if you need anything okay?"

I smiled and waved them away. "Yes. I promise I will call."

Sitting alone in the apartment I picked at my fingernails. I felt like I had been wound so tight that it would take just one little thing to send me giggling over the edge into crazy land. The silence finally got to me and I got up from the table to turn on the television. I jumped as my phone rang. Picking it up, I saw a picture of Yari smiling at me from the caller ID. I think the flesh version wouldn't be so happy.

"Yari, hey."

His voice was barely contained. "Is it true?"

I bit back the tears and sniffed. "Is what true? The fact that I broke curfew? That there was a break-in at the farm or that I'm no longer a Valinski?" My voice was thick and it broke on my last line but I didn't care.

The line went dead.

"Hello?" Sniffing I stared at my phone. "Well that can't be good." I raced to my bedroom window and parted the curtains. "Shit."

He was running, full tilt across the ovals toward my apartment. His camouflage pants and black tee making him hard to see in the fading light but I knew it was him and I knew he was pissed. I backed away from the window and contemplated dead bolting the door but figured that probably wouldn't stop him anyway. I raced to the front door to unlock it lest he break it off its hinges. Moving back, I positioned myself at the opposite side of the room and hoped that he wasn't going to be too riled.

The door flew open and Yari's large frame filled the space. Chest heaving he stepped forward, kicked the door shut, and threw his phone and keys on the couch. I could feel my heart thumping against my ribs as he pinned me to the spot with a look that was almost wild. I wasn't sure if he wanted to rip me apart or devour me. He said nothing and I could see that he was trying to regain some semblance of control. The tension hung thick in the air between us, I had to say something to try and diffuse the situation.

"Yari I..."

His deep rumble cut my apology short. "You okay?"

Hope bloomed that he might not be mad at me. I shook my head and he moved so suddenly I jumped, crossing the room with long powerful strides he reached for me. Relief swept through me and I stepped forward to meet him, clutching at the muscles on his shoulders as he lifted me clear off the floor and melded my mouth to his. He drank in my groan and I wrapped my legs around his waist as he moved to the kitchen and deposited me onto the breakfast bar.

Breaking the kiss only for a moment he spoke. "It doesn't change anything."

I pulled him back to me. "I know."

"You're still mine."

I caught his lips with mine, I didn't want to talk about it and I didn't want to think about it.

I felt him growl at the back of his throat and the kiss became more and more urgent. He pulled my hips hard against his. I could feel his need pressing against me, warming me from within. I ran my hands down the length of his torso, my fingers skipping over the hard ripples of muscle. I grabbed the bottom of his shirt and started tugging at it. I wanted to feel his skin. Taste it. His phone started ringing from the couch. I stilled and he shook his head mumbling against my lips.

"Leave it." His voice was husky and I loved knowing that I was the cause.

I lifted the bottom edge of his T-Shirt and he took it from my hands, pulling it over his head. I let my hands play over tanned skin and lowered my head to lay a trail of gentle kisses from one nipple to the other. The phone fell silent as his breathing became laboured and his hands moved to the base of my hips. Thumbs following the crease along the top of my thighs his fingers splayed across my cheeks and he pressed me closer still. My head fell back on a whimper and he swooped, curling one hand in my hair he pulled my head to the side, placing a wet kiss on the spot just below my ear, my skin prickled in response.

"Yari." My voice came out sounding urgent and he covered my mouth with his, picking me up off the breakfast bar and taking us to my bedroom. I pressed my chest to his, trying to ease the sudden ache in my breasts. Soft flesh met hard as we fell in a tangle of legs and arms onto my bed. He lay on top of me and I relished in the solid weight of his body on mine. We both stopped our frantic movements as my phone started ringing. Now it was my turn to dismiss the outside world.

"They can wait."

For a second I thought the Kaul in him was going to protest. It could be important. Reaching up to take his mouth with mine, I pressed myself to him. The phone was forgotten, groaning he traced a hand slowly up my ribcage. The anticipation of his touch sent my head spinning. I wanted my skin on his. Breaking the kiss I pulled at my tank top. Yari followed its path with his fingertips as I drew it up my body. His gaze locking on the swell of my breasts he gently traced the lace edge of my bra with his fingertips. My breath was short and shallow, the need for touch was overwhelming and I pressed myself into his hand. Heat radiated and I let out another whimper raising my mouth to take his again when someone knocked on the front door.

Breathless I cried out "No" and let my head fall back on the pillow.

Yari's hands stilled on my body, his eyes were closed and he lowered his forehead slowly so that it rested on mine. Our breath intermingled as we lay there silently catching our breath, waiting to see if the knocking would persist. It did, this time more of a thump than a knock coupled with a muffled voice.

"Yari, get your arse out here now."

Jaw clenched his lip curled in what could only by describe as a growl. "Someone had better be *fucking* dead." He brushed my hair back with his hands and laid a not so gentle kiss on my lips. "We are *not* done here."

He pulled himself off the bed, leaving my heated skin to chill at the sudden loss of contact. I couldn't find my top so grabbed my sheet and wrapped it around my torso before peeking out my bedroom door.

Dahrel stood in the doorway talking to Yari as he pulled his T-shirt back on.

"We've found what we believe to be the breach site with a possible sighting. We need every unit on it. We can't waste any more time. The Commander wants to move on this now. There is a briefing for all Unit leaders above the site in five minutes."

T-shirt back in place Yari nodded, picking up his keys and phone he turned back toward me. Dahrel flicked his eyes at me and I shuffled back as Yari pushed through my bedroom door, wrapping me in arms he let his lips hover above mine.

"I love you Ana."

I was not prepared for his admission and so the time for me to reply came and went with deafening silence. My mouth just couldn't seem to form the words, I knew what I wanted to say but I just couldn't get it out. Half smile in place Yari lowered his lips to mine and kissed me playfully, nibbling on my bottom lip.

"Later 'Lil Bit." Letting me off the hook he followed Dahrel out the door, pulling it closed behind him.

Why couldn't I just say it?

I slapped myself on the forehead and dashed to the window. "I am such an idiot."

Pulling the curtains aside I stepped into the pool of blue moonlight and looked down at the street below. My eyes locked onto Bravnica's as he stood there staring up at me through the window. His eyes travelled over me deliberately before he slowly turned away.

Belatedly I realied I was wearing the sheet. "Shit!"

I jumped back and scrambled for some clothes. My feet caught on my dressing gown and I quickly pulled it on, dashing back over to the window in time to see the tail lights of their military jeep rounding a corner and disappearing from view.

After ten minutes in a cold shower and some rather inventive suggestions of where Bravnica could insert his breach, I figured I may as well go to bed. I wasn't going to be seeing Yari again tonight. Ensuring the newly installed deadbolt was secure and moving my crossbow within arms-reach, I fell into bed enjoying the lingering scent of Yari's aftershave on my pillow, unaware of the complete devastation that would consume me the next time I was to lie here.

TWENTY

The office was reasonably busy with people rushing back and forth and I knew this was the kind of distraction I needed to keep my mind off the varying life crises I was currently wading through. No doubt Bravnica was still in the bowels of the city tending to whatever emergency reared its ugly head last night. That thought brought an uneasy feeling as I remembered the look on his face as he stared at me from the street. Squaring my jaw I sat down heavily in his chair and shook it off. I logged onto his laptop and started archiving emails but had only been at it a minute when Sierra knocked on the open door.

"Ana, hi. I was hoping I would find you here. I was wondering if you could do me a huge favour?"

She wasn't herself, standing in the doorway twisting her hands together. Concerned I motioned for her to come in.

"I need to get an urgent message to the units on the ground. It is strictly confidential and can't be done over the radio. I need you to deliver it to Lt Colonel Levech and wait for a response."

I shrugged, "That's cool, no problem."

She screwed up her face. "That's not all." I waited for her to continue. "Catch is you have to use the secret passageway."

Oh please tell me you did not just say that.

"I'm sorry. You need me to use *what?*"

"I would do it myself but the Emir is holding a meeting and I have to get it set up."

"You're kidding me right?"

"Please Ana, this has to go now and I can't be in two places at once. Please?"

I shook my head, "Daska I can't believe I'm doing this."

She let out an explosive breath. "Oh thank you so much."

I paused, "Is it safe?"

She waved a hand. "Of course it's safe. They're passageways, not tunnels!"

Tunnels? Note to self - never ask Sierra for reassurance.

I followed Sierra, surprised when we left the floor. Apprehension grew as she led me down a familiar hallway and opened the door to Tressilia's office.

I looked around to see if we had been spotted. "Are you out of your mind?"

She threw me a confused look. "What do you mean? This is the entrance." She pointed to the side of the room that housed the infamous cupboard and I cursed my body for its instant and very heated reaction to the memory.

Focus Ana.

Sierra was already on the other side of the room.

"The passage is behind here."

She stood by one of the panels and pushed, putting all of her body weight onto it. I jumped when it made a scraping sound, stone against stone. And then the entire panel shifted forward.

Sierra enjoyed my surprise and smiled, "Just go straight and it will take you directly where you need to be. They are about one hundred metres in. There's a door, you can't miss it."

I gave her a dubious look which she ignored. "You duck in while I hold it open."

She handed me the document. I hesitated for a moment. All my instincts were telling me this was a bad idea but the message had to be delivered. I put my weight against the door and slipped through. Using my foot to keep it open while Sierra grabbed a shoebox sized metal lion and placed it next to my foot, chocking the door open.

"Does Tressilia know we are using this entry to the passage?"

"Of course she does." Sierra paused and swallowed hard. "Do you have your mobile on you so can call me when you're done?"

I patted the back pocket of my pants, suddenly more confident with the security of having a connection to the outside world.

"Got it."

She made to turn away but stopped and gave me a warm smile. "Thanks for this Ana, I really appreciate it."

"No problems."

You so owe me.

I double checked the lion was going to hold the door and then took a couple of steps into the passageway, standing still for a few moments to let my eyes adjust to the dim light. Opposite the door was a very old brick wall.

"Okay Ana, you're fine. You can do this."

Taking a big, deep breath I turned to the left and slowly moved my feet. The air tasted stale and I made a point of breathing through my nose but that was just as bad. I remembered the Mentos in my handbag and contemplated the benefit of hindsight. I was going to eat the entire roll when I got out of here.

The further I moved from the doorway the more uneasy I felt. Looking back in the direction I had come I was reassured by the sliver of light still hitting the back of the passage wall. I squared my shoulders. Giving myself the willies was not going to get this message delivered.

I was struggling to see anything. I took my mobile out of my pocket and activated it, the blue light illuminating my immediate surroundings. I found myself a good fifteen metres down the passage now and at a T intersection.

A little warning bell went off in my head. "Oh Ana, this is so not a good idea."

Backing up the tunnel I turned around, looking for the exit that was my sliver of light.

It was gone.

Blood stormed through my veins in a sudden kick of panicked adrenalin.

"Oh no no no no no."

I ran back to where I thought my exit should be and yelled into the dark. "Hello?" Hands shaking I ran them along the wall in a futile attempt to find the edge of the door.

"Oh no no no no no."

It was all brick and I couldn't tell how far I had come or if I was even in the right place.

"Can anybody hear me?" I pulled out my phone – no service. "Crap. Sierra?" I could hear the panic in my voice.

Who was I kidding? Sierra was long gone and that Lion didn't just prowl off by itself. I imagined Tressilia on the other side of the wall, giggling with the Lion in hand.

Bitch.

I placed my hands on the wall and yelled as loud as my lungs would allow. "Tressilia if you can hear me, I just want to let you know that I am going to make you suffer for this. Do you hear me?" I kicked at the wall. "It's gonna be slow and painful and I'm gonna love every minute of it."

Nothing.

I screamed until my throat hurt and kicked until I had stirred up enough dust to make me cough uncontrollably, compounding the whole sore throat thing. Eyes watering I backed away from the cloud of dust and dirt to regroup. Tressilia was not going to open the door so I was going to have to open it myself or find another way out. I took a deep breath of dust free air and let it out slowly.

"Okay Ana. Think."

Surely there's a handle to pull the door open, I just have to keep cool and find it. Folding the document and sliding it into my back pocket I started back toward the T intersection running my hands over every brick and tugging and poking at anything that seemed out of place. When I reached the junction I worked my way back doing the same thing. I had travelled about a hundred metres in the other direction and knew that I had already passed the point where I had entered the passage. Checking my phone I noted that I had been stuck in here for over an hour now. The darkness was becoming overwhelming and it was getting harder to keep my fears at bay.

"Hello. Can anyone hear me?" I listened to the fading echo of my voice as it travelled down the tunnel and for a second thought that I heard another voice.

I turned my head toward the unexplored end of the passage and held my breath but it was gone. It could have been my mind playing tricks on me but it could also have been my ticket out of here. Someone was using the passages as a short cut. I didn't even realise I had made the decision but I found myself hurrying along in pursuit of the voice. I held my cell out in front of me so that I didn't run into any walls; with my luck I'd probably knock myself out. I ignored the side passages that appeared every now and again, with the rationale that it was better to keep on a straight path in case I had to come back. The passage stopped at a set of stairs that led down and I took them carefully. If I fell it could be hours or days before anyone came this way again.

Another passage, this one wider and older than the one I had just been in; it felt cooler and the extra space made me feel like I could breathe a little easier. Ignoring the uneasy feeling I got whenever I passed the gaping black hole of a bisecting channel I kept on, further into what felt like a labyrinth. The passage took a sharp turn and rounding it, I slowed down to take stock and see if I could hear the voice again but the only sound was the shuffle of my feet.

Damn I need to pee.

I had gone another hundred metres or so when I got the unnerving feeling that the passage was angling down further. and that maybe it wasn't a passage anymore. The thought hit me like a Swedish ice bath. I stopped. Standing dead still, watching the darkness at the edge of my little blue light as my heart tried to thump its way through my ribcage. I was below the city.

Fuck.

Despite the drop in temperature, little beads of sweat started forming on my body. I could taste the dust mingling with saltiness on my lips and wiped at them with the back of my hand, noting the tremors that shook it.

Oh Daska I'm in the tunnels.

Dahrel's words from last night about the breach played over in my head, which then brought to the fore the discussion that took place in Bravnica's office yesterday. There was Kudlak activity down here, proven with the new CCTV sighting.

The CCTV cameras!

If I was in the tunnels, then there would be CCTV, I just had to find a camera and signal to it, someone would come and find me.

With my mission now to locate a camera, I no longer cared about keeping a straight line. Heart in my throat I took several turns before stopping at a large junction, where I found my quarry. The camera was mounted to the ceiling in the centre of a four way intersection. The other tunnels leading off were pitch black and ominous, my breath came fast and shallow as I peered into their impenetrable gloom. I had no choice, I had to expose myself and move into the open space to signal the camera. My knees shook, slowing me down a little as I took three wobbly steps into the middle of the intersection and waved frantically at the lens. It caught sight of the movement and rotated to face me directly, the mechanical whirr crashing through the silence like a freight train. I held my breath and backed up into the tunnel I had just come from, pressing my back to the wall and praying that rescue would come for me before anything else did. I watched the camera as it watched me and could imagine the flurry of activity that would be on the other end of the feed. The colourful language being thrown around in that little observation room right now would be all about me and none of it flattering. I didn't care, I just wanted out.

The minutes ticked by slowly and my back started to ache in spots from the rough wall. I didn't move to try and ease it, the pain was good. It gave me something to focus on other than the building urge to just start running. I counted four more minutes in my head and occupied myself by clenching my knees to try and stop them from shaking, when my entire body stilled as I heard something.

Okay that was not my imagination. Please Daska let it be Kaul.

Holding my breath I listened for more.

I definitely heard something…

The thought froze in my head as the camera whirred and a large figure rushed toward me from the right tunnel. I opened my mouth to scream but he was on me before I could make a sound, covering my mouth with his hand and using his body to hold mine steady against the wall.

"Hey there 'Lil Bit." The voice was hushed and heartbreakingly familiar.

"Yari?" I croaked against his hand.

He removed the helmet from his head and began to strap it to mine. "Now what's a nice girl like you doing in a place like this huh?" I almost smiled as he gave me our standard two taps on top of my newly fastened headwear. Double checking the strap he switched on the small light attached at the side. The helmet was too big but having a light brighter than the eerie blue of my phone made me feel a notch better. I watched as two other Kaul filed in silently behind Yari, guns raised and looking tense.

I lowered my voice to a hush. "I can explain."

Yari held up a hand indicating that I should shut up. I watched as he held the shut up hand to his earpiece and looked back to his team, obviously they were all getting the same message and it wasn't that drinks were on the house tonight. Yari made a couple of quick hand gestures and the team acknowledged him with a small nod each. He then grabbed me by the arm and we moved past the other Kaul who appeared to be staying put. I looked back as each of them took up positions facing the opposite tunnel.

"What are they doing?"

Yari's response was to pick up the pace and we started running. That's when I heard the harsh rattle of a Kudlak as its voice echoed down the tunnel.

"DINNER'S SERVED!"

Yari's grip on my arm tightened but I didn't need any encouragement to pick up the pace.

"That was a Kudlak."

Yari ignored my stunned statement as we rounded a corner at full speed. I almost tripped as I ricochet off the opposite wall but Yari didn't slow, dragging me along until I could get my feet back under me.

"Don't stop and don't fall."

I flinched as the staccato of gunfire started popping behind us and wondered how it was that the air surrounding us suddenly felt as thick as water. Laughter chased us through the tunnels and it was clear from the tones and direction that there was more than one.

Daska help us.

We had only been running for a minute but it felt like an eternity, turning this way and that I was hopelessly lost but there was no hesitation from Yari and no pause in the ruthless pace we kept. The gunfire steadily increased until it roared through the tunnel in a solid stream of noise behind us. It was so loud that I cried out in relief when it stopped abruptly, I went to slow my pace but Yari jerked at my arm and we kept on as raw screams suddenly tore through the silence. The sound was unimaginable and I didn't want to think about the kind of torture it would take to induce it. Bile rose and I swallowed it down, sparing a quick glance at Yari.

Feeling me slow, he jerked my arm again and there was a desperate edge to his voice. "Keep going Ana. No matter what happens you have to keep going."

His tone seemed too final and I was trying to make sense of what he was really saying when the screams stopped. Silence tracked us now and I couldn't decide what was worse, the screams of the dying or the silence of the Kudlak. Two seconds later my mind was made up when a rasp whispering through the tunnels found us.

"Marco...."

We took another turn and I hit the wall hard. Yari slowed to push me in front of him. "Ignore them. Just keep going."

"Polo...."

This came from a different tunnel. I was beyond terrified now as Yari pushed at my back. "See the light ahead?"

"Marco...."

Squinting through the dust and sweat I looked ahead to see the tunnel lighten to grey and made out the foot of a staircase. I nodded. "I see it."

"That's our exit."

Okay Ana push.

Legs burning and completely focused on the stairs ahead, I didn't see the intersecting tunnel to the right until I passed it and felt the rush of air hit me and then a solid force.

"POLO!"

Screaming I flew forward down the tunnel, landing hard on the stone floor. Pain seared through me as I scrambled to my feet. The light on top of my helmet went dead. Standing in the pitch black I heard Yari's gun fire twice and then he was on me, pushing me forward.

"Go, go move, move, move."

My light flickered back on just as we reached the bottom of the stairs before we were hit again, this time from behind, the force so powerful it knocked us both off our feet. The edge of the stairs bruised my bones as Yari landed on top of me. I heard him grunting, wrestling with the weight that had us pinned. I started to crawl out from underneath them and wriggled, just enough to get my torso free and then one leg. The weight on top of me suddenly shifted and I scrambled up a few more steps before a rough icy hand closed around my ankle. Yari's gun fired again and the hand released me as I heard something clatter down the stairs. Regaining my feet I looked over my shoulder to see the Kudlak regarding Yari, who was backing up the stairs toward me, the gun on the floor at the base of the stairs where another Kudlak kicked it away.

The Kudlak closest to Yari tilted its head to the side and gave a chilling smile, voice vibrating in its chest as though a rattlesnake had taken up residence in the rotted cavity.

"You missed."

Yari backing up the stairs didn't take his eye off the Kudlak as he spoke. "Run Ana."

Both Kudlak looked up at me with pure anticipation, their intent clear in their marbled features. They wanted me.

The one closest spoke again with its chilling rattle, "Yeah Ana, run. It'll be fun."

The Kudlak at the base of the stairs threw it's head back and laughed. I flinched and willed myself not to scream in response. A growl escaped Yari and he flew at the closest Kudlak, knocking it backward into the other one as it ran up the stairs after me. They both fell in an awkward heap and Yari turned, already running.

"Go!"

I turned and started running but not before I saw the Kudlak separate and start up the stairs after us. I knew we had no chance. There was no way we could out run them. The top of the stairs was tantalizingly close. I could see it only three metres away now, at the top a large hall, flanked with beautiful tall windows. I looked at the light pouring through those windows with desperation.

I heard Yari grunt and then a dry cold hand grabbed mine, pulling me to a stop so violent that my entire body became inverted. When I hit the deck my feet ended up higher than the rest of me at the top of the stairs. White hot pain seared through my shoulder and a scream tore from my throat.

Yari called out, "Ana?"

I opened my eyes and through my tears saw Yari on his back, wrestling a Kudlak on top of him with one hand and trying to keep the other Kudlak off me with the other. My captor swatted him away, the madness had left its eyes and now it looked at me with alarming curiosity. Sliding up the stairs it brought its face closer to my upturned wrist. I could feel its decaying breath touch my skin and then it inhaled deeply.

A whimper escaped my lips and Yari growled again. "Get your fucking hands off her." My captor ignored him and the struggle that was going on beside him as it regarded me.

Its harsh voice was grating against the skin of my wrist. "That's interesting." Its red eyes widened as it studied me. "And what pray tell are you?"

I tugged desperately at my hand but all that achieved was a blinding pain that shot from my shoulder to the rest of my body. I looked to Yari. If I was about to die then I would rather look at him than the Kudlak that was about to tear me apart. I blinked the tears out of my eyes as Yari rammed something into the chest of the Kudlak above him, it turned to ash coating Yari and the stairs in its grey remains. He was covered in blood from a gaping wound in his arm and one eye was swollen shut but he didn't pause. Scrambling up the stairs he threw himself between me and the Kudlak and grabbed a hold of my forearm pulling it back. Surprised, the Kudlak let go. Its curiosity turning to rage in a heartbeat it hissed at Yari as he pushed me away.

"Run now and do not stop for anything."

The Kudlak smiled at him then and launched, hitting him hard. I heard the breath rush out of his lungs. In the distance I could hear the hiss and screeching of more Kudlak racing through the tunnels toward us, sniffing us out. I scrambled backward up the stairs never taking my eyes off Yari's, I stopped only when I reached the top of the stairs and felt the sunlight touch my skin.

As soon as I was in the light Yari's face relaxed and he gave me his half smile as the Kudlak wrestled with his body.

"Now run!"

TWENTY
ONE

I ran.

Blood roared in my ears, blocking the desperate sounds that escaped my mouth as my legs pumped through the air that felt like it was pushing back at me, fighting me. I had no control of my right arm and it flapped uselessly at my side. I was frustrated with it for slowing me down, but not curious as to why it suddenly stopped working. Oh Daska I needed to go faster but it was like I had switched realities and was now in a dream state. Speeding down the massive hall it seemed to stretch out before me, taking the doors leading to help further and further away. My legs burned and the windows streamed past in a rush of light and shadow, light and shadow.

The vision of Yari looking up at me from the stairs, with the Kudlak poised above him blinded me momentarily and I blinked to clear the vision and the tears that were now streaming down my face. Spurred on I heard myself scream as I slammed into the doors at the end of the hall. Throwing my weight behind my left shoulder I pushed, only to have my feet slide out from underneath me. Scrambling up from the floor I screamed and kicked the door before bracing myself again, I heaved. My body shook with the effort but inch by inch it began to move and I squeezed myself impatiently through the gap, falling onto hard stone outside. I rolled and pulled myself up, crying in frustration at my useless arm as it made every movement clumsy. Panic coursing through me, I half tripped down three large stairs, everything seemed to be tilted at an odd angle as I spun around to get my bearings. I could see the Council Chambers a few blocks to the East and turned to run in the opposite direction. I needed help for Yari now and the best place to get that would be the Barracks.

My breath was coming in laboured gasps now, as I tore down the deserted streets. Not slowing for corners I burst into the next street and then the next. The vision of the Kudlak so fresh in my mind, I ignored the pathetic mewling that kept crawling up the back of my throat and pushing past my lips. Tears blurred my vision but I could see enough to navigate the streets and know that I was nearly there. I rounded the next corner like I had all the previous and felt the breath rush from my lungs in a violent whoosh as I was lifted from the ground by a large body coming from the opposite direction. Instantly my mind screamed KUDLAK and I fought.

Flung over its shoulder I screamed and kicked but the hold never wavered as my captor made a loop and circled back, running in the direction it had come from. Cobblestones raced beneath large black boots and I struggled with everything I had, landing a kick I felt muscles ripple beneath me as the blow was absorbed. I got three more in before we stopped and I was spun around so that my back stretched over its large chest.

"Ana."

I screamed and scratched at the thick forearm that had locked across my waist leaving my feet dangling a foot from the ground. I felt hot breath at my neck and hunched my shoulder in a vain attempt to protect it, a movement that was made futile in the next moment when it placed its free hand on my forehead and pulled back, exposing my throat and the delicate skin that protected my arteries. I screamed as it lowered its mouth to my ear.

"Ana."

I tried to shake my head to break free but it was in a grip that was vice-like.

"LET ME GO." Screaming I bucked but the movement only made the hold tighter.

"Ana stop."

I pushed at the forearm with my good arm in a last ditch effort. My strength had long gone and I knew that anything I did from here on out would be futile. I screamed again but even my voice had deserted me as the sound that came out was more like a wheeze.

"It's me Ana."

I stopped and was instantly rewarded when the grip across my waist loosened a fraction. The fog of fear started to lift as I was lowered slowly to my feet.

"Are you hurt?"

My legs shook under my own weight and I held onto the steadying forearm that I had been fighting moments before.

"You can stop running now."

"Dominik?"

A radio clicked and he spoke again. "I've got her." Slowly he manoeuvred me, pushing me back so that I was resting against a nearby wall.

"Can you stand?"

Feeling the rough brickwork at my back brought the black tunnels rushing back and I could suddenly smell the stench of Kudlak. My body reacted violently and I leant to the side trying to avoid Bravnica as I dry retched. He held me steady as I tried to empty my already empty stomach. My body finally settled and I straightened pushing his hands away as I leaned against the wall, legs shaking.

"You have to go help him."

He responded by fiddling with the strap of Yari's helmet.

"Did you get bitten?"

I looked up at him. His cool exterior was gone and in its place was fear. The strap released and he tossed the helmet to the ground before gathering my hair up behind my head and tilting it this way and that, inspecting my skin.

"I'm fine. You need to go."

I pushed at him but he stood firm tugging at the neck of my shirt he put his hand in the collar running it over the skin at the back of my neck and then over my shoulders. I hissed as he made contact with my right shoulder and I remembered the pain.

"Stop it." The growl took us both by surprise but at least it got his attention. "You're wasting time, go. Now!"

My shoulder was starting to really hurt now that the adrenaline was easing. I swallowed the pain down and begged. "Please. You have to help him. Please."

He took my left arm and flipped it over, running his hand along the smooth skin of my inner arm and then up over my shoulder.

"A Fire team is on its way."

He took my right arm and went to turn it over but I grabbed his wrist and squeezed, stopping the movement.

"Don't."

The look he gave me was knowing and he moved around my arm to check the skin. "Are you sure you didn't get bitten?" Straightening up he pulled me off the wall and ran his hands down my back.

"What the fuck are you doing? I said I was fine." I pushed at him again but I may as well be trying to move a mountain. "Why aren't you listening to me?"

His voice raised a notch. "Because I need to know that you're okay first. What the hell were you doing down there?"

I ignored his question and matched his volume. "I told you I'm fine! It's Yari that needs help."

He nodded and resumed his normal low tone. "Do you know if he was bitten?"

The memory of Yari's bloodied arm came sharply into focus. I knew what he was asking me and that my answer would directly affect his next move.

"I don't think he was bitten." He regarded me for a moment and I felt another tear fall, trailing down the still slick path of the last. "Please."

He stepped back and put a hand to his radio. "Anton, you copy?"

"Roger."

He looked at me as he spoke. "You in position?"

"Affirmative."

"Got a visual?"

"Negative, there's nothing here."

Pursing his lips together he paused for a moment. "Stand by."

Moving toward me he placed one hand on my right shoulder and caught me with the other as my legs folded, I screamed at the shooting pain in my right shoulder and mercifully he let go, propping me up against the wall again.

"Your shoulder is dislocated."

I had never felt so impotent. Glancing up and down the street he steadied me against the wall and worked the radio again, eyeballing my shoulder as he spoke. "This is the Commander, I need a medic at my location ASAP."

Kaul in full combat gear started to fill the street. I ignored them as Bravnica moved closer. Taking my right arm he bent it at the elbow. "Hold your arm here." I obeyed, supporting my right arm with my left, concentrating on his voice as he spoke.

"Brace."

My breath was ripped from me as he rotated my arm back. My knees buckled as my shoulder popped back into place, half on the ground and half in Bravnica's arms, I threw every curse word that I could think of over my shoulder at him. Ignoring my rant he held me from behind, hugging my arm to my body and as much as I hated the contact with him right now, the white hot pain was subsiding and my arm was starting to feel better.

I was not planning on thanking him.

A medic rushed over with a sling and immobilised my arm, Bravnica let go once the sling was in place and I spun around and punched him as hard as I could. He allowed the hit to land on his face without flinching. I shook my now throbbing hand and he just stood there for a moment with his eyebrow raised. Blood began to form at the corner of his mouth and he wiped at it with the back of his hand, ice blue eyes narrowed at me.

"Are we even now?"

I let my anger seep into my voice. "We're not even close. Now send them in!"

"How many are down there?"

"What?"

"Kudlak Ana. How many?"

I blinked. I didn't want to think of the Kudlak I tried to back away from the question. "Umm...I couldn't really tell..."

"I'm not sending anyone in unless I know what they're up against, now give me a number."

The sounds and the jeers coming from the dark filled my mind and I gritted my teeth letting out a frustrated growl. "I don't know. Maybe there was ten, but it could have been double that. It happened so fast and we were running. I couldn't see anything."

Bravnica moved back a fraction and I watched his chest rise and fall on a deep breath, his expression grim. He started to shake his head and I stood taller, eyeballing him. "Don't."

He leaned into me. "Ana..."

"Don't say it. Don't you dare even fucking think it."

He gave me a look of pity and I turned away from it, I didn't want him pitying me, I wanted him to save Yari.

He spoke into his radio again. "Anton do you copy?"

Anton's muffled voice came through. "Copy."

"I have Intel on hostile numbers. You're looking at ten minimum. The chance of more is high. Take two Fire teams but don't go further than the original extraction point. Let me know when you're out so we can start the sweep."

"Roger that. Out."

I glared at him. "Only two teams, are you serious?"

"Ana."

"You're not really willing to help, you've already given up!" I pushed past him. "Don't worry I know some guys that have a little more faith in Yari."

He called out behind me. "Are you going to get your brothers to go in there and die for you too?"

His words hit me like a physical force. I spun around.

"What did you just say?"

My legs shook so hard that my body did a little jolt before righting itself. He approached, standing so close that I could see the fibres in his top, I went to step back but he placed an encompassing hand on the base of my neck.

His voice was low and meant only for me. "Don't do this Ana, let the medics take you back to the hospital and check you over. I can get one of the Lavric Elite to heal that shoulder."

"Don't bother - I don't want any help from you." I tried to shake free but he held firm and lowered his face to mine.

"We are Kaul, it is our job to give our lives to protect the Kresnik people and those men that saved you did just that today. I will not send more men in on another suicide mission when the likelihood is that our target has already been compromised."

My anger started to bubble slowly.

"*Target?*"

I pushed again and he let me go. "His name is Yari and..." I stopped suddenly as my mind replayed his words. "What do you mean *another* suicide mission?"

He let out a sigh of frustration and started steering me toward a nearby jeep. "I don't have time for this Ana."

He was dismissing me and I knew my time for answers was up.

I placed my free hand on his stomach and was pleased when he stopped instantly. "Tell me."

He started us walking again but spoke as he did so.

"We had numerous teams down there when the control room reported an increase in activity with the CCTV cameras and calculated that they were potentially out numbered. We pulled them back with the plan to cover every entrance to the tunnels that hadn't been sealed and get the Preseren Elite to filter fire through the system before sundown. They had just started to pull out when the control room radioed that you were down there. Yari and two of his team where the closest to you, they didn't hesitate."

The world started to tilt again.

This is my fault.

Anton's voice came over the radio again. "Commander, do you copy?"

Bravnica responded instantly. "Go ahead."

"Tunnels to extraction point are clear. They must have smelled our wood and bugged out. We've found two of the original extraction team. Both deceased."

Those men are dead because of me.

"Roger that. Let me know when you're clear."

Bravnica pushed the hair back from my eyes. "I'm sorry Ana."

Mind now racing I looked up at him, trying to make sense of his words. He eased me onto the backseat of the jeep.

"They are all gone Ana, including Yari. There's no sign of him. I'm sorry."

My anger began to seethe and my voice shook as I spoke, "Don't talk as though he is dead." I tried to push my way out of the vehicle but he blocked my exit and I growled in frustration. "You have done nothing to try and save him, how dare you give up without a proper search."

"Ana, you need to calm down."

I couldn't, the edge of my vision started to darken and I pushed frantically at the solid wall of his chest.

"I need air."

The rage surged, white hot and out of control.

"Ana stop." His voice, full of concern, echoed from a distance even though I knew he was right there, holding onto me. Suddenly I felt his presence in my mind pushing gently at the edges trying to find a way in.

Ana, let me in.

Panic flared at the invasion, I couldn't keep him in check and try to regain control at the same time.

No.

Let me help you.

GET OUT!

I don't know how it happened but one second he was there gently peeling back the layers of my subconscious and the next he was gone. I heard him grunt in pain and I looked up, searching for the familiar ice blue. I needed to gain a visual anchor on reality but my eyes kept going, rolling further and further back until everything turned black, it was too late. I surrendered to the energy.

TWENTY TWO

The sound of breaking glass echoed around me and I felt my body shift as a large weight was lifted off my chest. My hips and stomach were still trapped but the weight was warm and solid, more comforting than uncomfortable. I knew that was weird but didn't give it anymore thought as voices, raised in confusion, started calling out in the background.

Feet pounded to a stop nearby.

"Commander, are you okay?"

My body shifted again and I heard Bravnica growl.

"I'm fine, everyone get back to your posts."

There was more commotion in the background but it was moving away now, I cracked my eyelids open a little, just in time to see Bravnica turn back to me. I was sprawled on the backseat of the Jeep with my butt on the edge, and my legs hanging out the door, tangled with Bravnica's who had obviously been lying on top of me and still had me half pinned.

His eyes found mine and it was clear he was shocked at what had just happened. "Are you alright?"

I managed a nod as yet another tear slid down my temple. There was no covering up this one. His brow creased as he followed the tear's descent into my hairline. Bringing his eyes back to mine he stroked my hair back gently and lowered his face to mine.

When he spoke his breath brushed against my cheek. "How did you do that?"

I looked past him. From my position I could see that the windows had been blasted out of the Jeep, leaving us lying in a jumble of glass that tinkled whenever we moved. I didn't need to look outside the jeep to know that the carnage would be widespread. I had never felt this drained after an incident and knew it had been a biggie.

Beyond words I shook my head, that was the best he was going to get out of me and I shifted, indicating that I wanted to get up. He took the hint and slid back, pushing the door wide. As he straightened, glass rained from his back and I noticed for the first time a gash above his eye. The blood had already navigated its way across the arch of his eyebrow and was now travelling slowly down the curve of his cheekbone.

Using my left arm I grabbed the headrest of the front seat and used it to lever myself into a sitting position. Once upright I had to hold still for a moment to allow the world time to stop spinning. Bravnica moved forward supporting me under my good arm.

"You gonna be right to stand?"

I didn't want to nod and set the world off kilter again so croaked instead.

"Of course. I'm fine."

I had no idea if I would be okay but he stepped back again, allowing me the space I needed to shift forward and I braced myself for the physical task of getting myself out of the jeep. Pulling on the headrest I used momentum to haul my body forward, my feet hit the ground and I kept going, unable to stop myself.

The ground rushed at me and Bravnica lunged forward.

"Whoa there!"

The world spun momentarily before going black.

I could feel myself being carried and hear voices around me, the deep rumble of Bravnica's voice through his chest as my head rested on it.

"What the hell was that?" I recognised Anton's voice as he walked beside us.

"We'll discuss it later. In the meantime I would like this to be a *non-event*."

"Alright, won't be too hard to manage with the fire sweep."

I felt Bravnica's muscles tense as he shifted me in his arms, his voice rumbled against the side of my head. "Make sure it isn't. What's the countdown on the sweep?"

"Thirty-two seconds."

A car door opened.

"Thanks."

Finally I was able to push through the fog and command my eyelids to lift. Light filtered through my lashes and I watched a blurry Anton rush away as another Kaul jumped in the driver's seat of the jeep. Bravnica jostled me into the passenger side and I looked up at him while he spoke over me to the driver.

"As soon as she's admitted you are to find Natasha Kovak, pull her out of whatever she is doing and escort her to Miss Valinski. Report back to me when you're done."

"Yes Sir."

Reaching past me he fastened my seatbelt but stopped before pulling back, hovering over me. He looked down and I saw a little flash of surprise when he found me looking back at him. Surprise was quickly replaced with something more. I opened my lips to speak but he blinked, pulling back abruptly and slamming the door shut he banged twice on the roof. We accelerated and my head flopped back onto the headrest. I heard a rumble that wasn't the jeep's engine and the driver steered us toward the middle of the road as orange light raged below us and fire spat out of the drains.

Tears escaped as I squeezed my eyes shut and sent a silent prayer for Yari to be okay.

"Ana, you need to stop this. You are just going to get in the way."

"But Tash, they're not doing *anything*!"

Arm in a sling I had been poked and prodded by numerous sadists claiming doctorate's and was on my way out of the hospital.

"Ana you are to leave it. If Yari is alive, they will find him, you need to trust them. They want him found alive as much as you do."

I gritted my teeth against the helplessness of it all. I may as well be walking around bound and gagged.

"But …"

"*No.*"

She levelled me with a gaze that brooked no argument.

"You have already monopolised enough of the Commanders time with that explosive moment. Time I might add that could have been spent finding Yari."

My face flushed as the truth of her words struck home. Oh I had been such an *idiot*. If I had cooperated with Bravnica and gone to hospital straight away instead of arguing, getting myself into a state and blowing up a bloody Jeep then who knows what he may have been able to do for Yari. Daska he might even be home right now if it wasn't for me.

My hands began to shake as self-loathing settled in.

Who are you trying to kid Ana. Yari would be home right now if it wasn't for you.

All of them would be. Closing my eyes I leaned back in the chair. Two men were dead and Yari was missing and it was all because of me.

"Promise me you will leave this to the Kaul and stay out of their way."

I swallowed hard and nodded my assent as footsteps hesitated at the door.

"Ana?" A nurse was holding out some paperwork. "I've got your discharge papers. You just need to sign and you can go home. It's been approved and an escort is on the way."

We set a beeline for the nurses' station, signed out and turned to the lifts to find our escort in the lobby. The whole time I was desperately trying to block out the screams of the Kaul that I had gotten killed. When the lift doors dinged open we were confronted by the sight of Garrick striding across the foyer toward the lifts. In the back of my mind I knew that someone had been very thoughtful in sending my brother for me, but didn't want to think too hard on who that person might be. I didn't have enough emotional stock left to add grateful to the mix.

Garrick saw us instantly and altered course, charging us down before we could clear the lift doors. I was a little surprised when he asked Tash if she was okay before me but let it slide as we made our way out of the hospital. I was more interested in getting home than navigating the jungle gym that was my brother's head.

Tash threw me a couple of sideways looks as we got to the car and Garrick, in a rare show of gallantry, settled her in the front seat before helping me with my door and lifting me into the back and buckling me up. I was glad for the dark confines of the car and rested my head against the cool glass of the window as my brother steered us slowly through the deserted streets. Eyes closed I listened as Garrick brought us up to date, not that there was much to tell.

No one had heard or seen from Yari since I got out of the tunnels and all Kudlak activity had ceased just before the Fire Sweep. The Auroras hadn't been touched and the only people unaccounted for were the Kaul who had come to rescue me. When speaking of Yari his tone was a little too final for my liking but I didn't have the energy to chip him on it.

I didn't want to talk about it at first. When we got home Tash had made some tea and they had both sat next to me on the couch, refusing to take no for an answer. Outnumbered and out of energy I relented. I was pleased that I had managed to tell the story from start to finish with only two minor breakdowns. The first was when I told them about the screams of the Kaul and the second when I had run and left Yari. They both listened quietly, offering encouragement when I faltered and reserving questions until I had finished.

Tash put on another pot. I could see her mind going a mile a minute but Garrick spoke first. "You did the right thing Ana, when you ran." He took my shoulders and dipped his head to catch my eye. "I know it doesn't feel like it but it was the right thing to do."

Tears welled and I shook my head to clear them. It was so nice to have Garrick back me up.

Tash returned from the kitchen

"What I don't get is why Sierra would have asked you to go. Surely she knew the risks and it seems she put you in the wrong passage."

She settled herself next to Garrick who smiled at her then turned back to me.

"Are you sure you got the name right? Lt. Colonel Levech? Cause I've never heard of him."

I nodded, "Yeah I still have the message. It is the back pocket of my pants." Tash jumped up to retrieve it before I had finished, heading straight for the laundry. "It should have the name of the guy it was for on there shouldn't it?"

She returned moments later without the message. "There's nothing in your pockets, I'm sorry."

I blew across the top of my cup to cool it a little. "It must have fallen out in the struggle."

My mind felt like it had kicked back a gear. "I can't talk about it anymore."

I closed my eyes and heard Garrick speak to Tash. "I'll follow this up later."

It had been three days since my escape from the tunnels and 48 hours since I had allowed myself any sleep. I had slept in on the first morning after Yari disappeared, not waking until ten and was not going to give myself that luxury again, not until Yari was home safe.

I sat quietly on my windowsill, grainy eyes staring sightlessly at the deserted street below. I knew I looked like an urchin but I didn't care. My hair resembled a lazy bird's nest and I'd been wearing the same clothes for two days now. I had managed to avoid everyone but Tash, who insisted on coming in every so often to bring food and make sure I hadn't topped myself.

Bravnica had phoned to check on me a few times and left messages for me with Tash. Thankfully he was using the old fashioned approach to communication rather than trying to get into my head again but the news was always the same, they hadn't found him. I knew that Dahrel and Garrick would be struggling but they had each other to lean on, and the ability to do something to try and fix this mess that I had created.

The city was still under curfew. Only Kaul on duty and escorted officials were allowed to move about after dark. Tash was flat out and apparently Bravnica was demanding answers on the Aurora research and she was being escorted to and from the office at odd hours.

I found myself in imposed isolation, suffocating, but I deserved nothing less and welcomed the silence that surrounded me. I ignored Tash and Garrick's obvious attempts to draw me out. I didn't want to feel better. I should be suffering. Feeding on the guilt over Yari I concentrated on the pain burning inside me.

I had just found a particularly sweet spot of self-loathing when Tash knocked on my bedroom door.

"The funerals begin in two hours. We need to get you looking respectable."

I hung at the back of the crowd wearing a simple black suit, a large pair of dark glasses and looking down so that my hair fell forward and hid my face. I wanted to be there, to pay my respects to the men who had given their lives so that I could have mine but I didn't want to be recognised. The woman who got two Kaul slaughtered. My face burned with shame.

The low key funerals passed in a heartbreaking show of love and respect and with the formalities over, the crowd began to mill around. I was planning on slipping away quietly but Tash gave me a *'don't you dare'* look that I chose not to mess with. I couldn't bring myself to look at the grief stricken families so turned to survey the officials standing on the slightly raised platform. My blood went to an instant boil at the sight of Tressilia on Bravnica's arm. She was dressed dramatically in a skin tight black dress that left nothing to the imagination and a ridiculously large hat tilted at an angle that covered half her face. She leaned heavily into Bravnica as though she was personally affected by the tragedy. I didn't think she could be more disrespectful if she tried.

As if feeling the heat of my gaze she looked up, our eyes clashed and she narrowed hers before excusing herself from Bravnica. Heels clicking she made her way through the crowd toward me and I gritted my teeth against the urge to scream.

Coming to a stop in front of me she cocked her hip and glared, "Don't you think you've done enough?"

Don't cause a scene, don't cause a scene.

I squared my shoulders and matched her glare, "You need to back up."

She missed the warning.

"Is it not bad enough that you killed these men? Now you show your face here among their grieving families?"

My body started to shake as it tried to subdue the anger that was swiftly turning to rage.

"Me?"

"What's going on?" Bravnica's tone was hushed and urgent.

I ignored him and took a step forward, Tressilia wobbled back on her heels and I jabbed my finger at her chest, "You locked me in the passage, this would never have happened if you hadn't closed the door."

"What are you talking about?" She raised a superior eyebrow at me. "Are you on medication, because you should seriously talk to your doctor about upping the dosage."

I launched myself at her, planning to rip that raised eyebrow right off her face but was caught mid-flight by Bravnica, who hauled me backwards as cries of shock rose from the crowd around us. I didn't bother struggling as Bravnica deposited me roughly into Dahrel's arms and turned back to Tressilia, who was being fussed over as though I *had* actually ripped her eyebrow off. Dahrel turned me in the direction of home and shoved me forward. The crowd parted easily for the crazy lady and her brother, and we were soon clear of the throng and moving down the empty streets toward home. Adding insult to injury it started to rain, not too heavy but just enough to frizz my freshly straightened hair. Dahrel said nothing until we reached the apartment and closed the door behind us with a controlled and ominous *click*.

"What is wrong with you Ana?" He shook his head but kept his distance. "You can't put this on anyone else, this isn't about Tressilia. This is about you, about your lack of ability to show any sort of rational thought process for *anything*." He threw his hands out as if to prove the point and started across the room toward me. "I can't understand how you can keep making the same mistakes over and over and over again. It's almost like you are doing it on purpose, which sickens me because your actions have killed my best friend!"

I stepped forward and held out my hand.

"Don't…"

He swatted it away. "Don't give me that crap about Yari still being alive. You know as well as I do that he's dead."

Garrick burst through the door with Tash panting behind him. They had obviously run all the way home. Their dramatic entrance didn't slow Dahrel's tirade.

"Is it not bad enough that you got Yari and his team killed but you have to create a scene at the funeral as well?"

The disappointment in his tone hit hard and I sat heavily on the couch, "That wasn't my fault."

Tash stormed across the room toward Dahrel. "That is enough. Get *out*." She pointed at the door behind him as though he might have forgotten where the exit was. "You are not welcome in my house until you have put some serious thought into your sister's wellbeing and apologised for this disgusting behaviour."

Dahrel looked stunned but recovered quickly and narrowed his eyes at Tash. To her credit she didn't back down and he opened his mouth to retaliate but stopped when Garrick stepped in front of Tash, blocking his view of her.

"I think it best if you go and cool down. You don't want to say anything that can't be unsaid."

Tash piped up behind him. "Well it's a little late for that!"

Dahrel looked past Garrick's shoulder and gave me a long hard stare before turning around and storming out of the apartment, slamming the door so hard that the windows shook. Tash let out a disgusted huff and went for the front door, mumbling under her breath about respect for people's property but Garrick stopped her before she could yank the still vibrating timber open and give Dahrel an earful about door etiquette.

"Just let him go Tash, he needs to cool down."

She cleared her throat and straightened her shoulders, turning around she smiled and came over to join me on the couch.

"You need to sleep Ana. Why don't you close your eyes for a little while? I'll stay right here with you on the couch."

"No, not until he's home." I moved back and turned from her to look out the window. The rain outside started slapping itself harder against the window and I marvelled at how Mother Nature could mirror the mood of an entire city so well.

Tash patted my knee, "Okay, how about a cup of tea then?"

I sighed but didn't turn from the window, "Sure."

Tash and Garrick took the hint and left me alone, I sipped my tea and grimaced wishing it was coffee. Tash refused to give me any because I had been using it to help keep myself up. The tea tasted a little sweet but I figured the glucose would give me a boost. They spoke quietly together, each taking turns at sending surreptitious glances my way as I drank my tea. I ignored them and tried to gain comfort in the familiar surrounds of my living room, settling to stare blindly at one of Tash's throw cushions. My limbs began to feel heavy and I almost dropped my empty cup, leaning over I tried to put it down on the floor next to me. It tipped in slow motion and scraped across the floor out of my reach. Confused I made a grab at it but was stopped when Garrick caught me, pushing me back onto the couch. My head lolled as I watched Tash retrieve the cup and place it on the coffee table.

"Do you think it's working?"

Garrick picked me up easily. "Yep, she's just about gone."

My eyes widened. "Tash whha did yoou pudin my tea?"

TWENTY THREE

I watched my toes, dig into the dirt as I pushed back and forth, back and forth. My white sun dress moved playfully in the afternoon breeze and my childhood swing gently creaked. I could hear a faint gurgling sound that I was trying to ignore. I wanted to concentrate on the warmth of the sun on my skin and I felt like a cat that just wanted to stretch out. The gurgling got louder and louder. Annoyed I let out a sigh and was about to look up and demand whatever was making the sound to stop, when it suddenly fell silent. Relief curved the corners of my mouth momentarily and I looked back at my toes until my peace was interrupted again, this time by a ripping tearing sound. I looked up, my growl of frustration catching in my throat at the sight of a Kudlak in broad daylight.

My knuckles turned white as my grip on the ropes of the swing tightened. Sitting amongst my mother's Roses it cradled

Yari's bloodied body close and tore relentlessly at his throat with rows of needle-like teeth. My mouth fell open on a soundless scream and the air became thick with the stench of death and rotting meat. My lungs seized in protest at the foul air, a protest that I ignored. I had to move, I had to get Yari away from it but I couldn't get off the swing. Panic started clawing at me as I realised I couldn't move, I shook with the effort but it was like a layer of concrete had settled itself over my entire body and I couldn't. No matter how hard I struggled, I couldn't move to help Yari. The Kudlak raised its head to meet my horrified gaze and smiled, showing me a mouth full of dark red flesh. Yari's blood dripped from its macabre grin and an unrecognisable sound escaped my throat. Chest burning I started gulping at the air. Why can't I breathe? Pins and needles started poking at my body and black spots danced before my eyes.

"Look at me." I turned my head toward the steady voice beside me but my eyes remained glued to Yari and the Kudlak.

"Ana. Look at me."

The voice came again, raised this time in authority, I dragged my eyes away from the grinning Kudlak and toward the voice. Dominik sat on a sister swing, motionless. His eyes, unwavering held mine.

"I'm here."

My lungs released and I filled them greedily. He stretched a hand out to me palm up in invitation. I looked at it and then back to Yari. Blinking when I found both he and the Kudlak gone, the flowers swayed innocently in the breeze as though nothing horrible had ever been there. Body trembling I closed my eyes and swallowed hard, concentrating on getting my breathing under control. Opening them again I turned back to Dominik, expecting him to be gone too but he was still there, hand still outstretched, eyes still unwavering.

"I'm here," he repeated.

Tears fell and I couldn't bring myself to respond, instead turning my attention back to my toes.

I bolted upright in bed, heart racing, my brain frantically pushing through the fog of sleep to figure out if the Kudlak was still here and if I was in danger. Looking around my room reality kicked in and I fell back onto my pillow, letting the breath that I had been holding out in a great whoosh. I rubbed at my eyes and turned to blink at my alarm clock, confused when it read 1:15 pm, I grabbed my phone to double check, swearing when it confirmed that I had slept through till lunch.

"Shit."

In a great rustle of sheets and blankets I rolled over and let my feet hit the floor. Sitting perched on the edge of my bed I rubbed at my eyes and thought about the dream, it had been *so* real. The line between fantasy and reality seemed to be getting increasingly blurred for me; so much so that even now I was still on edge, waiting for a Kudlak to jump out of my cupboard when I *knew* it was a dream. In a show of false bravado I strode across the room to my cupboard and yanked open the door, proving that there was nothing there. Closing them quietly I turned and leaned against their hard wood, shaking my head in an attempt to dislodge the image of the Kudlak feeding on Yari. I shouldn't be giving myself the opportunity to dream.

"Wait a minute."

Oh they are so dead.

I stormed into the kitchen firing on all cylinders and ready to give it to whoever was unlucky enough to be around. Finding the room empty I called out.

"Tash?"

Nothing.

I worked my jaw in frustration and headed toward the kettle.

"Seriously, if you're going to drug someone, the least you could do is be around when they wake up so that they can kick your arse." Grabbing my mug and the coffee I placed them roughly on the countertop, calling out. "I'm pretty sure that's in the Roofy handbook people."

Half an hour later, I had worked off most of my steam by channeling my inner turrets and yelling random insults at the walls. I was on a particularly good run when a breathless Tash opened the front door.

"Are you alright? I could hear you from the street."

I stopped awkwardly in mid-rant and spun to face the door throwing my arms wide.

"Well if it isn't the drink spiking Bestie."

Tash rolled her eyes and pushed through the door, dropping her handbag on the couch and heading toward the kitchen.

"Don't be so dramatic, you needed sleep and I needed a break."

I let out a disbelieving gasp. "What! So you just take it upon yourself to *drug* me?"

She turned around and had the grace to look a little guilty but I didn't wait for her to speak.

"Besides, nobody's asking you to babysit Tash."

Her eyebrow shot up in an arch that could rival Bravnica's. "Oh really? And here I was thinking that my best friend in the whole world needed me."

I let out a sigh, realising that fighting with Tash was not going to help matters.

"I'm fine Tash."

"Oh you are so far from fine right now, that I would have to find a really long stick just so that I could poke you with it." My eyebrows shot up but she wasn't done. "You're removing yourself from the world so that you can wallow in your own self-loathing. And yes, I understand that you're feeling guilty over Yari and that you miss him. We *all* miss him Ana."

I shook my head. "You don't understand Tash. You don't know what it was like down there."

"You're right, I don't. I don't pretend to know either. But as bad as that was, at some point, you're gonna have to join us in the land of the living."

My head was going a mile a minute. "I can't deal with this right now."

I retreated to my room, put on a clean pair of jeans and grabbed my riding jacket out of my wardrobe, pulling it on as I stalked toward the kitchen. I picked up my keys and grabbed my helmet and boots out of the hall cupboard before heading for the door.

"Where are you going?" Tash moved towards the front door but I had already pulled it open.

"I need to get out."

"No you're not, not on your own." She flicked her eyes at the clock and then back to me. "Garrick's shift will finish in half an hour, just wait until he gets back and he'll go out with you." She put her hands out to stop me. "Please. I don't want you going out alone. It's not safe."

I didn't miss the concern in her voice and softened my tone a little while I ignored her hands and pushed my feet into my boots. "It's daylight Tash, I'll be back well before dark. Seriously, don't worry about me."

She placed her hands on her hips and shook her stubborn head. "All I seem to do lately is worry about you! Ana, it's these kinds of impulsive decisions that get you into trouble."

I pinched the bridge of my nose in an attempt to alleviate the headache that was threatening. We had come full circle and were back to arguing.

"Sorry Tash. I need some space."

I exited the front door with a blustering Tash following close behind. My hair frizzed as soon as I stepped outside and my lungs worked a little harder at the heavy air. It had been raining all night and for most of the morning. The midday sun had broken through the clouds and heated the ground making the air steamy and thick with humidity. Sweat started prickling its way across my collar bone but I ignored it as I zipped my jacket up and eyed the building clouds on the horizon. We were in for another storm but it wouldn't reach us for a few hours, I had plenty of time to get out, clear my head and get back before it hit. I threw my leg over the bike and settled my weight, aware of Tash standing disapprovingly at my side. I pulled my helmet on and turned to her.

"I'll be back in two hours."

She started to protest but I flipped my visor down and revved the engine. Pulling away from the curb I watched her in my rear vision mirror as she started dialling frantically on her mobile. The line must have connected because she started speaking and pointing violently in my direction, obviously turning me in.

My eyes narrowed. "Thanks Tash."

I decided I would rather not find out who she was dobbing me in to, at least not until I had gotten a decent ride in.

My bike roared as I opened up the throttle. Holding nothing back I relished at the speed and the blur of green as the trees rushed past. It was soothing in a wild kind of a way. This was the oldest stretch of road in the Province, impossible to be accessible from anywhere except Lameer. Surrounded on both sides by heavy forest it led to nowhere and was the last place anyone would choose to go, which is exactly why I chose it.

If Tash had called in the cavalry to come and get me, I wanted to evade them for as long as possible. I just planned to ride the length of it and then back as it eventually petered out at the base of one of the mountains marking the boarder of our Province. Given that I didn't want to go too far it was a good option, especially with my current state of mind. Temptation may have seen me not turn around.

The adrenaline was pumping, masking the pain that sat like a rock, hard and heavy in my chest. I pushed my bike a little harder knowing I would have to slow soon as the mountain and my half way point were approaching rapidly. An hour goes fast when you are running from your own head but unfortunately I knew no matter what my speed, it was a hopeless endeavour. Eventually I was going to have to stop and like Tash said, rejoin everyone in the land of the living; but not today. Smiling, I decided to give it one last burst of speed before I would have to turn and head for home. Letting out a whoop I closed my eyes for a brief moment taking in the rush.

Sliding along the rough grass on the edge of the road everything seemed to slow down and I had a bizarre moment to thank Daska that I wore my riding jacket and boots despite the heat. I watched my bike slide past me on the road and cringed at the damage I knew would be there once she stopped. I eventually came to a stop, and lay still for a moment doing a quick body check. Legs, not broken, stinging pain on my left hip which I assumed would be a graze, ribs sore, back okay, shoulder.... I moved it slowly, praying that it wouldn't pop. No popping but it was tender and I didn't want to press my luck so I tried to keep it immobile as I pulled myself up off the ground and hobbled over to inspect my bike.

"Fuck." I glanced back down the road, cursing at the pothole in the road I hadn't seen until the last minute.

It didn't look good. I pulled my gloves off with my teeth and unbuckled my helmet with shaking fingers before kneeling next to my bike, very aware that my ribs were protesting every movement. The clutch lever was snapped but that wasn't too much of an issue, I could ride without the clutch. What I couldn't ride without was oil. There was a crack along the wall of the crank case that would ensure any oil that was left in there would be gone as soon as I righted the bike. I knew there was no point starting it, without oil the engine would seize in under a minute.

I let out a growl of frustration which turned into a groan as I stood up, I was sore in a few more places than I had originally thought, but nothing that a pair of big panties wouldn't fix. Patting at my jacket pockets I found my mobile phone. My heart soared as I pulled it out and then plummeted when it came apart in my hands. I let out a sigh as big as my ribs would allow.

"How do you manage to do this?" Remembering Tash's warning I kicked at a nearby tuft of grass. "She's always right Ana, you know this. Why can't you just bloody listen?"

I bit at my lip and looked skyward, searching for calm. The only thing I saw was the ominous blue green of the oncoming storm.

"Double fuck."

As if to put an exclamation mark on my foul language the sky rumbled deeply in the distance. I looked down at my bike.

"Okay then, come on girl. We'd better get a wriggle on."

We both groaned as I pulled her up and even though she had spewed out all her oil, she seemed much heavier than when we began this little joy ride. I favoured my left side heavily lest I did anymore damage to my shoulder. I kicked out the stand and retrieved my helmet and gloves before returning to my broken bike and starting the long push back to Lumeer.

Forty five minutes later I kicked out the stand again and slumped to the ground. Breathing heavily as sweat ran down the ridge between my shoulder blades and beaded across my chest. I pulled my hair up off the back of my neck and tied it in an inefficient knot at the top of my head - history would see it fall out and plaster itself to the back of my neck again in about a minute. I was becoming dehydrated and cursed myself for storming out of the house without grabbing a bottle of water, or a hair tie. I had looped my riding jacket through the handlebars and my white tank top was becoming wet with sweat. I plucked at it with my fingers, pulling it away from my chest but it just slapped straight back into place, moulding itself across the top of my breasts.

"Awesome."

Well at least I had a decent bra on, giving me a little modesty so that I wasn't completely exposed when I eventually reached civilization. I looked down the road as it twisted ahead of me.

"If I reach civilization."

It was too far to see Lumeer, I had been riding fast for a solid hour and pushing my bike on foot was slow going. Looking up at the darkening sky I finally acknowledged what I had been trying to ignore since dropping my bike.

"I'm not gonna make it back before dark."

Not that it mattered much. The sun had been completely blocked out by the storm clouds, so anything that was sun averse basically had a free pass right now. My stomach knotted and thunder mirrored my uneasiness, tearing at the sky overhead. I floundered desperately for options but knew there were none. I had taken this road because there was nothing out here, no farms, no houses and not even a bloody woodsman's hut. So basically, unless Tash's cavalry arrived, I was screwed. The glass-is-half-full voice inside my head promised that Bravnica would find me, and as much as I wanted to ignore it, I hoped fervently that it was right.

Having caught my breath I heaved myself up. The movement caused my hair to come undone and I leant my hip against the bike and pushed it out of my face, using the motion to eye the surrounding tree line that was making me increasingly nervous. I felt like it was pressing in on me, toying with me until it got bored and then decided to release its full horror.

"Stop it Ana. Just walk."

The wind picked up, whipping my hair around and cooling my soaked skin. The sky was one solid mass of blue grey and I smiled when the first heavy drops of rain started to smack themselves on the road around me. I paused to tilt my head up, mouth open to catch some droplets and blinking as they slapped at my face. After catching a few I used the bottom of my tank top to wipe my face, smiling at the futility of it. I was not going to stay dry. The storms at this time of year were nothing short of spectacular. Relentless rain with drops the size of walnuts and lightening that would rip jagged tears across the sky, illuminating everything in its wicked white light.

Having rested again I tried to get my bike to make some forward momentum so that we could trudge on but my shoulder and ribs screamed. I looked at the darkening tree line and made my decision. Turning the bike toward the edge of the road I kicked out the stand and gave her an affectionate pat.

"I'll come get you tomorrow."

Leaving my gear with the bike I figured I would make better time with nothing to carry so I took off at a jog, feeling very light. A massive bolt of lightning cracked overhead, making me jump as it lit up the sky and road around me. The silhouette of what appeared to be a tall man left a dark and ominous shadow in the tree line to my right and I swallowed the scream that scrambled up my throat. My heart did a double tap and then settled for an increase in rate as opposed to the full blown attack it desperately wanted to throw.

Shit shit shit shit shit.

My inner monologue closely resembled that of a chuffing steam train as I carried on, pretending I hadn't seen it and trying to act as normal as possible while I figured out what the hell I was going to do. I increased my pace and strained my eyes sideway.

What was that?

Shaking hands wiped at my eyes but the rain was so heavy it was hard to get a clear view of anything.

Oh Daska help. I wonder if Bravnica's mind thingy can work in both directions. Ana to Bravnica, Ana to Bravnica. Come in Bravnica.

Lightening flashed again and the spot where the figure had stood was still in shadow, but the shadow was created by a couple of misshapen branches. I stopped and stared at the spot.

Yep, just a tree.

"Huh. Okay, so I am just scaring the bajeezes out of myself here." I put on my best 'Official Voice'. "Nothing to see here - move along please!"

Despite my bravado, the hairs on the back of my neck simply refused to lie flat and my heart rate didn't slow. I started to jog again, fighting the urge to break into the full blown sprint that my instinct desperately wanted me to do. No matter how many alarm bells were ringing on the danger-metre, I had a long way to go and needed to preserve my energy. I kept my breathing steady as I settled into a moderate pace, counting my breaths to occupy my mind.

In two three, out two three, In two…

My ears pricked at a heavy thump, this time coming from my left. Without breaking my stride I eyed the tree line through sweat and rain, desperate for evidence of a fallen tree.

Nothing.

I increased my pace but before I could get used to the new rhythm I heard footsteps thud on the road behind me. My breathing faltered and panic clawed at me as my heart thudded out a staccato burst that threatened to break my already bruised ribs. Not willing to go down without a fight I spun around, fists shaking but bunched and ready to fly. I faltered, coming to a staggered halt when I was faced with nothing but relentless rain and an empty road. My eyes darted from left to right but saw no one. I wiped at my eyes in a vain attempt to clear my vision and squinting through the rain I shook my head.

That's when I felt it, a presence behind me. So close that their breath pushed at the wisps of my hair on top of my head. Goosebumps pricked the skin at the tip of my head and then ran their way down my body until every hair stood on end. Instinct screamed at me to run but before the message could reach my legs I heard the words.

"Hey 'Lil Bit."

TWENTY FOUR

Everything within me stopped. The pet name that had been used by only one person my entire life and uttered with a gravelling voice, had enough power to simply obliterate all rational thought. Blinking through the rain I slowly turned, my breath catching at the sight of him. I took a couple of staggered steps back.

"Yari?"

Hip cocked confidently it was the typical Yari pose, head dipped his hair fell over his forehead leaving his face in shadow, but it was him. The broad shoulders and strong arms, the long legs encased in battle fatigues, a thumb hooked casually through his belt loop completed the look. Oh Daska I had found him!

Heart soaring I stepped forward hurriedly smiling but paused as he raised his head. It took a couple of static heartbeats to realise something was very wrong. His hair fell to the side to reveal eyes that were no longer the rich brown I remembered but a blood thirsty red. On my sharp intake of breath he shifted his weight and gave me his cheeky half grin, only to reveal the needle-like teeth of my nightmares.

"What? Aren't you gonna give me a kiss?"

His voice rattled painfully down my spine and I back pedalled, tripping over my own feet. I didn't stop the retreat even as I landed hard on my arse. Head shaking, denying what my eyes were telling me as I backed up on my hands, my heels skidding pathetically across the slick surface of the road.

"No, no, no no."

Eyes narrowed, he turned his head to the side bending over at the waist to better watch my awkward retreat.

"What no kiss, huh?" He straightened up and took a step forward. "Oh, well I must say I am very disappointed in that Ana. After all, I am what I am because of you."

I blinked and he was on me. I let out a squeal as he grabbed me by the hair and pulled me painfully to my feet. Busy trying to hold onto the hair that was tangled roughly through his fingers I didn't see the blow coming but knew when it landed. An explosion of pain burst through my cheekbone and radiated out with an intense heat that blinded me on my right side. Stunned I hit the mud at the side of the road and my groan sounded like whooping cough as the air rushed out of my lungs. I rolled onto my hands and knees and tried to get up but the skin across my back tightened in protest at the presence of death as it leaned over me from behind.

"And here I was thinking we could finish what we started."

He punctuated the sentence by thrusting his hips forward with such force that I ended up sprawled in the mud a few feet away, the metallic taste of blood in my mouth now mingled with mud and grass. I spat and tried to right myself but before I could get my feet beneath me he had me again, spinning me around to face him for another backhand. Instead of letting me hit the ground again he held me up. Taking my head between his hands in a crushing grip he studied my wounds as the rain washed the blood and mud from my face.

"Now look what you have made me do. You are bleeding all over the place." He studied my blood soaked tank top and let out a growl of frustration. A deep breath rattled in his chest and he raised his red eyes to meet mine.

"Of course it had to be you didn't it Ana?" He gave me a little shake. "And now I can't have you, not in the way I want." Face screwed up in rage he threw me backwards, I managed to stay on my feet and before I knew it I was running full tilt down the road.

His manic laughter turned my breathing into panicked gulps as it chased me. "Run Ana run.. Ha ha!"

I let out a groan as fear threatened to take over.

"Wait a minute, I'm having dejavu! Ooh ooh, I've got a good one, Marco!"

His demented tormenting terrified me and I ran, knowing full well that he would catch me as soon as he was tired of playing with me.

His breath rattled in my ear. "Polo!"

I screamed and veered away from him but he was lightning fast and grabbed my arm, spinning me to him again. I braced for another blow but it didn't come. My breathing was coming out in short sharp gasps as tears and rain ran down my face.

"Let me go Yari. Please."

His head tilted to the side and he smiled. "You know I can hear your heart fluttering away in there?" It skipped a beat and his smile deepened. "I can smell your fear too."

"Please let me go Yari."

The smile he gave me was almost sad but I didn't get to study it as a voice rattled at us from the tree line. "Let's go, he is waiting."

Yari pulled my arm and started toward the trees that were lined with Kudlak. I pulled as hard as I could in the other direction, knowing that as soon as I was in the cover of the trees there was no hope for me.

"NO. LET ME GO."

Screaming I fought for every inch but I was never going to be able to beat him as his strength was that of a Kudlak now.

The shadows of the trees engulfed me as I lost my battle with Yari. Goosebumps covered my skin and I found myself surrounded by Kudlak. There were at least a dozen, their rattling breath drawing together to create a chilling symphony to accompany me on my death march. I tried to keep my head up as the realisation hit me. That was exactly what this was. I was never going to make it out of this forest alive. Eventually this journey would end and I would be either dinner or having my organs harvested for later.

I had been dragged for what felt like hours but I knew that it had not been that long. Looking up at the clouds I could differentiate them as a slightly lighter grey in contrast to the black bending tips of the trees that had swallowed me up.

My entire body ached but I couldn't afford to indulge in the pain, I was too busy trying to figure a way out. To say that I was used to being surrounded by Kudlak wasn't true, but my urge to vomit with every exhale had subsided, and I now had the courage to eyeball them back when they tried to intimidate me.

The forest was soaked with rain that pooled in leaves and tree roots, creating a little haven for mosquitoes to lay their larvae and spots for me to continually slip in. I slapped at a particularly fat mosquito that had landed on my arm and mumbled a few choice words about bloodsuckers.

Yari chuckled, "It seems I'm not the only one that wants to suck you dry.""

I held up my hand showing Yari the squished bug. "Try it."

His red eyes flared as he crushed me to him, holding his mouth a mere breathe away from my neck and ramming home the message that I was completely and utterly at his mercy.

"Oh you have no *idea,* how badly I want to try it."

I let out a sound of protest as another Kudlak approached Yari from behind and rattled in his ear.

"If temptation gets too great, I will happily take her off your hands."

Yari's response was instant and violent. He had the other Kudlak on the ground before I even realised I was in a crumpled heap at the base of a nearby tree. I made to get up and make a break for it but I was too late, Yari was dragging me up by the hair again. I clutched at it and stood as quickly as I could.

"You could just fucking ask me to stand up."

He gave me a little shake and whispered in my ear, "That's not as fun."

He marched me forward, over the headless body of the Kudlak he had just attacked. The others eyed him warily as they moved back but none challenged him. Yari kicked at the body-less head and it turned to dust causing the headless body to dissipate in a poof of dust as well. I held my breath, not wanting to inhale any of it. We kept walking and despite my lungs' demands, I held my breath until I was sure we were far enough away from where the Kudlak had been before I allowed them to fill. That's when I felt it, the familiar tingle in my head. More forceful than any of the previous times, but I didn't care. Tears sprung into my eyes and I let out an involuntary cry of relief before slapping my hand over my own mouth. Yari gave me a sideways look as I started falling, I heard his growl of frustration but ignored it and surrendered to the silent demand for attention and let Bravnica in.

My surroundings shifted, I was still marching along with my deadly escort but we were in a slightly different area, there were fewer trees and a fast moving stream, a large fallen tree with moss growing over the top of it and, *Kaul*. Heaps of them, armed to the teeth and taking up positions, one by one melting into the forests surrounds. My inner light bulb lit up.

Ambush.

I watched as Taras dragged the bloody carcass of a deer into the clearing, it looked as though it had been attacked by a large animal and abandoned. They must be trying to detract from their scent.

Bravnica?

The vision blurred momentarily before disappearing and my deadly reality returned with a painful blow. I found myself sprawled face first on the forest floor, the vision in my left eye blinded by blood that was pouring out of my brow. I rolled over and found Yari standing over me, staring at the blood, his chest heaving and I realised he was struggling to keep from tearing me apart. His lips slowly started drawing further and further back and my heart rate doubled as I watched him from the forest floor. Moving slowly, I bunched up the bottom of my tank top and dragged it up my body to wipe the blood away. He blinked a couple of times and reached out to grab me by the hair but being a quick learner I jumped to my feet and started moving forward.

Pressing the heel of my hand into my forehead to try and stem the flow of temptation, I scanned the forest for anything that resembled what Bravnica had shown me. I was shaking again and didn't want to give anything away so I tried to keep my breathing and heartbeat normal. Or at least as normal as I could whilst being frog marched through the forest by a bunch of Kudlak that were about to get ambushed by a bunch of heavily armed Kaul. Sending a silent prayer to Daska I swallowed hard and started listening for running water. Ten minutes and several painful trips later I could hear it, bubbling ahead like some sort of beacon of salvation. I swallowed hard and started squinting through the blood and rain at the trees, the sky above still thick with grey rainclouds creating a dark shadow over the forest. I couldn't see anything or anyone, which I guess was what was supposed to happen when walking into an ambush. I nearly tripped when the group stopped as one. Heads raised they all inhaled deeply, the rattle made me want to shrink into myself and I hunched my shoulders against the sound. Three Kudlak at the front took off at a sprint, causing the others to fly off after them. Yari swore. Bunching the back of my top in his fist he pushed me forward and my feet skidded over the slick forest floor as I scrambled to keep pace. The others were well ahead of us when gunfire suddenly cracked through the air.

I jumped involuntarily and Yari let out an animal-like growl through his clenched teeth, hauling me to a violent stop. I fell again and started crawling toward the safety of the gunfire.

"Not gonna happen." He wrapped an arm around my waist and hauled me up backing away from my rescue.

"Let me go!" I kicked and bucked but it had no effect. Taking a deep breath I screamed for help. "DOMINIK!"

Yari stopped and took a hold of my lower jaw. I pulled my tongue back not wanting to taste the skin on his fingers.

"Shut your fucking mouth or I will rip it off your face."

Tears sprung as he slowly started to twist, my knees buckled and I let out a cry of pain.

He smiled, "Good."

Letting go only to start dragging me again, I spat and closed my jaw gingerly as I tripped along behind him. We circled around, giving the Kaul a wide berth and came to the river. I could hear the battle raging to the right of us and was wondering how close I could get if I made a run for it. Yari must have read my mind and his hand closed painfully around my upper arm.

"Don't even think about it."

I stood my ground. "Think about it Yari. I'm slowing you down, you can't stay ahead of them while towing me."

His grip tightened in response. "You're coming with me."

He started wading through the river, taking me with him. I baulked.

"Please let me go Yari."

He turned back to me angrily and I flinched, waiting for the blow I was sure would come. Instead he became unnaturally still. Looking over my head his red eyes were the only things that moved as they slowly swept the forest from left to right.

I twisted in his grip to see what was there. Nothing - just trees. A twig snapped upstream and we both turned to investigate, our heads whipping back when a familiar voice spoke from the other direction.

"I think you should do as she asks Yari." Bravnica appeared beside a large tree, standing sideways with his pistol raised and aimed at us.

TWENTY FIVE

"Have you been bitten?" His eyes never wavered from Yari but the question was obviously for me. I knew he was trying to figure out if he needed two bullets or just the one.

"No."

I felt rather than saw his relief. Yari started backing up toward the river taking me with him and forcing Bravnica out from the cover of the trees as he followed us with his gun.

Yari spoke, his voice dripping with venom. "You won't shoot. You won't risk hitting her." He gave me a little shake just to make sure we were all clear on who he was referring to.

Bravnica approached steadily. Looking deadly in fatigues bristling with weapons, he was still angled sideways and placed one foot in front of the other confidently.

"I think you are more concerned for her safety than you are letting on." Pistol ready he kept coming. "You need her alive."

Yari gave the Kudlak version of a scoff but Bravnica continued.

"She would be dead or infected by now if you didn't."

Yari stilled. Bravnica was too close, my heart rammed away at my ribcage with the knowledge that something deadly was about to happen and I was smack in the middle of it.

Yari made the first move. Picking me up he threw me at Bravnica with a force that ripped the air from my lungs. Dropping his gun Bravnica's arms wrapped around me as I hit the solid wall of his chest. Backing away from Yari I clung to the heat of his body as he whispered roughly in my ear. "Stay back."

He spun, pressing me against the tree where he had first appeared. Our eyes met briefly and there was a flicker of something in the icy blue depths but I didn't have time to analyze it.

Turning back he only had a second to react to the blow that was coming full force at his head. He pulled back enough so that Yari's fist only clipped the side of his head. Incredibly Bravnica absorbed the blow and I thanked Daska for his hard head because the force of it made the hits Yari had landed on me look like love taps. Bravnica spun and landed a kick to Yari's neck, following up with some body blows as he backed him into the river and away from me. A quick leg sweep had Yari on his back in the water.

"Where are the Auroras?"

Yari's response was a hiss as he splashed to regain his footing. Dropping his guard momentarily Bravnica reached over his shoulder, gripping the handle of his sword he was about to pull it free when Yari launched himself out of the water. Attacking in a blur of fists that had Bravnica backing up way too quickly, he stumbled and landed hard on the bank, rolling, before Yari could slam the heel of his boot into his head. Bravnica's small field crossbow became unclipped with the impact of the fall and lay on the ground abandoned as Bravnica regained his feet and drew the fight away from me again.

"What do you want with her?"

Slowly moving toward the crossbow I held my breath, waiting for Yari's answer when the hair on the back of my neck started to rise. Feeling a presence I turned back toward the trees. I screamed and Bravnica's attention shifted toward me and Yari took advantage, knocking him to the ground. The Kudlak was only ten feet away and running toward me at full speed. Launching myself toward the crossbow I loaded the arrow as I rolled to face death. I had a split second to eye my target before letting the oak tipped arrow loose at the Kudlak that was about to land on top of me. Its rattle stopped the instant my arrow pierced its dead heart and its solid mass turned to ash as soon as it landed on me, leaving me in a billow of Kudlak soot. Coughing, I rolled to try and escape the acrid taste of it. Crawling toward the river I blinked it out of my eyes, looking up just as Yari wrestled Bravnica to the ground.

I watched, frozen in place, not wanting either to win the deadly battle but knowing ultimately how this would end. Yari had the advantage now, pound for pound. Kudlak were more powerful when it came to brute strength. That is why Kaul train with weapons, to keep them at arm's length. Bravnica was putting up a good fight but all three of us knew he wouldn't be able to hold Yari off much longer. I had to help him. On autopilot I reloaded the crossbow and approached Yari quickly from behind, they were both struggling in earnest. Yari had his teeth bared and was inches away from Bravnica's straining neck, so intent on the kill he didn't realise I was standing behind him. My hands shook as I raised the crossbow.

Bravnica's ice blue eyes flicked to mine and he growled through gritted teeth, "Do it."

Realising I was behind him, Yari started to stand, turning as he did to defend himself. He was too late. Yari - now facing me, met the arrow with surprise as it imbedded itself into his chest. Covering my hands with his, he dropped to his knees.

Oh Daska what have I done?

"I'm sorry."

Both shocked we stared at each other and I watched in horror as his eyes turned from blood red to warm brown and then ash as his body disintegrated. Numb, I stood bent over at the waist, hands wrapped around the bow in a death grip.

"I killed him."

My mind was skipping on a torturous replay of his eyes, blood red changing to the familiar brown and then back again.

Bravnica pulled himself up off the ground as I repeated myself.

"I killed him. I killed him. I killed him."

I could hear the hysteria in my voice raising an octave with panic. Through my tears I watched Bravnica approach, hands held out in front of him palms down as though he were trying to placate a wild animal.

"Ana, that wasn't Yari."

I closed my eyes and shook my head but the visions wouldn't shift. "His eyes changed. They were brown right before he..."

My voice lodged itself in my throat and I indicated helplessly to the dust that had settled on the ground before us. Covering my hands with his, he eased the crossbow from my fingers.

"Ana, I need you to be alright now. We're still in danger and I have to get you out of here." He was scanning our surrounds as he spoke.

Finding my voice I raised it. "Did you not hear me?"

"Ana, you need to calm down."

"I killed him!" I was yelling now and could feel my face start to flush as the blood roared around my body, heating itself as it went. Tears streamed, joining the rain as it ran down my upturned face.

"Stop it Ana."

I ignored him, I felt like I was about to explode and welcomed the feeling, maybe it would wipe away what I had done.

"Ana I'm sorry, but I can't let you do this."

Something in his tone made me look and my manic smile faltered as he had moved behind me.

"What are you doing?"

He snaked one long arm around my body, trapping my arms to my sides before I had a chance to move away. I tried to break free but he increased his hold, just for a second. I read his silent message, that there was no point, he could easily overpower me.

My helplessness only served to fuel my anger and I levelled my voice. "You should let me go. I don't want to hurt you too."

His response was to cover my forehead with his free hand.

"Dom. No!"

I tried to turn my head in the direction of the third voice but promptly forgot about it when a familiar tickle started picking at the edge of my awareness, I gasped as he eased himself into my mind.

Get out!

Shhhh.

I felt an abyss open before me, black and deep, and senseless. I knew what he was offering me but whether I actually had a choice. I'll never know. I didn't hesitate. A smile touched my lips as I fell forward and let the nothing consume me.

I woke to the sound of hushed voices, arguing above me.

Something wasn't right and it wasn't that we were running for our lives from Kudlak. I couldn't put my finger on it but it was just teasing at the edge of my mind and every time I tried to catch it and look at it, it skittered off to another corner of my messed up head. The angry voices brought me out of my reprieve.

"Are you insane?"

My eyebrows shot up. I had never heard anyone speak to Bravnica like that. Taras was walking a fine line – even if he was the Commander's brother.

I was surprised by Bravnica's controlled response. "I can't explain, but I have good reason. You just need to trust me."

"Okay, well how about you trust me and tell me what the hell you think you're doing?"

I was jostled a little as Bravnica leaned forward. "Careful Taras, I am still your Commander."

"You may be that, but you are also my brother and I sure as shit aren't gonna stand by and let you risk *everything* for her."

Bravnica looked down at me and realised I had come to. Sitting between his legs, he cradled my head in his arms. I tried to smile up at him. "What's the damage?"

"You got knocked out. Do you remember anything?"

I shook my head, "I can't focus, my brain feels like it's been scrambled."

He helped me up. "Forget it now. We need to get moving, we can't stay here."

On cue a burst of gunfire erupted through the woods. Bravnica pushed me toward the river.

"We're leaving."

"Taras, I'm taking Ana to the support crew. Go back and take command. I want an update once you're on scene and I'll get back as soon as I can."

Taras gave his brother a dark look, "This isn't over."

Bravnica ignored his brother as he jogged away and mumbled under his breath. "Don't I know it."

"Is everything alright?"

"Keep moving, we've a long way to go."

I felt like I was missing something and started looking around to see if I'd dropped anything. The forest floor was clear and I started toward the river shaking my head at the ridiculous notion, I didn't bring my handbag to this battle. I stopped at the edge of the water and listened to Bravnica as he spoke to Anton over the radio. The battle was still being waged but they had a good position and were holding firm.

Ending the conversation Bravnica moved toward me stooping low and scooping something up off of the ground without breaking his stride. I narrowed my eyes as he shoved whatever is was into one of his many pockets and came toward me.

I promptly forgot about his souvenir when I entered the river, the ice cold water taking my breath away. Bravnica heard my sharp intake of breath.

"I know it's cold but we have to cross here and then one more time further down. It's the quickest way to vehicles."

Even though it was midsummer, the temperature of the water flowing from the mountains was freezing in contrast to the warm heavy rain. The pull of the current was strong and as we waded in past my knees I put all of my concentration into staying upright and not getting washed down river.

"Just so you know I'm not the best swimmer."

Bracing his feet he twisted back to me, the sleeves of his black shirt were pushed up. Revealing muscles taught under the skin of his outstretched arm, I noticed a few fresh scrapes along the length of it. Palm facing up he reached for me.

"Give me your hand."

I did what I was told and was quietly grateful for the support as his hand engulfed mine and I negotiated a particularly slippery section.

"Thanks."

He gave my hand a quick squeeze before letting go and I sucked in a lung full of air as the next step had me thigh high in the icy water.

"Shit."

"Just watch your footing."

On cue the very next step my foot took landed awkwardly on a submerged rock, I splashed trying to regain my footing but there was no stopping my forward momentum and I went over. The shock of the ice water as it chilled my skin from head to toe was nothing to the pull of the current as it instantly dragged me away. Spluttering I reared up, Bravnica grabbed me by the waist and hauled my body up against his. I wrapped my arms around his neck but my legs were dangling in the water, pulling me at an angle downriver. I heard him swear under his breath as he grabbed my legs from behind my knees and hauled them up. I felt his muscles bunch together as he shifted his stance to compensate for my weight but he didn't say anything as he waded us ashore. Letting go of my legs they swung around and dangled a foot from the muddy bank. I let go of his shoulders and slid down his long body to the ground and as soon as my feet touched we both took a few steps away from each other. Shivering, I sat to pull my boots off. Emptying them I watched him eye the river we had just crossed.

"We need to keep moving."

Shoving my feet back into my boots I stood and hurried into the tree line after him.

He was waiting for me in the shadows.

"Stay close."

I nodded, clenching my teeth against the cold as the wind chilled my wet clothes. I scurried after him further into the forest.

"How far is it?"

"At this pace, probably an hour."

I followed him silently for a while, staying close behind to try and shield myself from the headwind. Stepping onto the trunk of a fallen tree he reached back to help me up. He watched me as I jumped down and I could tell he wanted to ask me something.

"What?"

He turned and started walking again.

"So how do you do it?"

I should have seen it coming, but given my current situation I didn't really care. Things couldn't get any worse, but even speaking about it is an admission.

"You can trust me Ana. I wouldn't do anything to hurt you."

"I don't know."

He shot me a look over his shoulder and I clarified. "I m-mean, I don't know how it happens."

My teeth were starting to chatter with cold but I ignored it, talking about my little condition was a good distraction from the cold.

"It's been happening for as long back as I can remember. W-when I get very emotional - mainly angry, it j-just kind of builds. I can't stop it. Sometimes I blow things up. Sometimes I move shit with my m-mind. I don't choose what happens."

He stopped in a clearing. "Who else knows about it?"

"Just Tash."

I watched as he unclipped the harness that held his sabre and sidearm.

340

"She's been trying to f-figure out what it is."

Placing his weapons carefully at his feet he stretched up and pulled his long sleeved top up over his head.

"Did she have any luck?"

I dragged my attention away from the tight black singlet he wore underneath his jumper and shook my head in response. I hated the way my body reacted to his.

"Take your clothes off."

My jaw chattered. "W- what?"

"You need to warm up. Take your top off and put this on." I moved to take my top off and felt him still, his eyes straying to my soaked top. Looking down I realised what had caught his attention and quickly crossed my arms over my obviously cold breasts. His eyes flicked back to pierce mine and he didn't even have the grace to look guilty.

"Take it off."

Suddenly feeling not so safe I snatched the top out of his hands and turned my back to him. Pealing the tank top off was harder than it should have been. I could hear him behind me making impatient noises but my ribs were screaming and I was wary of my shoulder so the process was near impossible. I got to a point where half of me was out and the other half was twisting awkwardly. Suddenly his warmth radiated across the skin on my back as his voice rumbled just behind my ear making my already taught goose-bumps stretch out even further.

"Let me do it."

He reached around me, his warm hands stilling my movements and I jumped as his fingers skidded up the side of my ribcage while he gently pealed the filthy top from me. It thwacked to the ground at my feet and I felt the chill settle across my back again as he moved away. I quickly pulled his damp but warm top over my head and relished as the rough wool eased my prickled skin. It was huge and I rolled the sleeves up so that I could use my hands to undo my jeans. The top ended mid-thigh so I figured I could still maintain some degree of dignity. I got the sodden denim an inch from my knees and realised the flaw in my plan.

"Ana, we need to keep moving."

"Sorry." I pulled off my boots and waddled a few steps away to lean against a grassy slope and gain some leverage. Hoping on the spot I turned around so that I could sit down on the grass and get my pants off. Letting myself fall backwards I let out a squeal when my arse found little resistance as it hit the ground and then kept going, sending me tumbling back into darkness in a flurry of arms, legs and dislodged tree branches.

"ANA!"

Landing on a dirt floor I looked up at the circle of fading light I had just fallen through. Bravnica dropped through the hole and was beside me before I had a chance to sit up.

"Don't move."

He turned his torch on and started surveying our immediate surrounds. I brushed dust out of my eyes and nearly gagged as the smell of rotting things assaulted my senses. Eyes watering I held my hand up to my nose. "What the hell is that?"

"Shhhh."

Bravnica completed a couple of sweeps with his torch before turning back to me. He lowered his voice. "You just found the nest."

I matched his whisper. "What?"

Without answering, Bravnica moved to stand in front of me. He pealed the material off my damp skin and left it in a bundle on the floor. Standing slowly I studied our surrounds and whispered.

"It looks empty."

The light bounced off the walls. The room we were in being about the size of my bedroom with a sloping floor that led to what looked like a larger space. The ground was littered with bones and the rotting carcasses of animals that had obviously been used as snacks. Bravnica pushed me to stand behind him as he stepped silently to the other side of the door. Watching my step I tried shifting around him so that I could get a better look but Bravnica was having none of it. Without taking his eyes off the opening he reached out and grabbed me by his oversized shirt, pressing me against the wall behind him.

"Don't move."

He couldn't have seen my nod so must have just assumed obedience as he moved through the arch. I took a couple of tentative steps forward and when his head poked back through the arch I jumped about a foot.

He raised his eyebrow in question before speaking. "It's clear, there's no-one home."

Relieved, I followed as he moved toward the nest opening and disappeared through the hole. I made to follow but stopped when he tossed my boots down.

"Put those on."

Ducking I threw him a dirty look as they landed on the ground just beyond where I stood. He ignored the look as he jumped back down, striding past me into the larger room. I sat down on the rough earth and wrestled my boots on. Bravnica emerged from the large room carrying two sports bags.

A tremor shook my body and I wrapped my arms around myself.

"Are you still cold?"

I stood up and shook my head. "No just…" I threw around for a word that could describe the wrongness I was feeling but came up with nothing. I waved the sentence away. "Nothing, don't worry. It stinks in here. Can we just get out?"

"Yes, are you right to climb?"

I looked up at the hole I had fallen through and then down at my shirt that stopped mid-thigh.

Letting out a long suffering sigh Bravnica dropped the bags and linked his hands to create a stirrup.

"I'll give you a leg up."

With as much dignity as I could muster I placed my foot into his hands and clambered out of the hole. Whilst dusting the dirt from my grazed knee, Bravnica dumped the two bags onto the grass next to me and started emptying the contents of one.

"Why are you doing that?"

Without looking up from his task he mumbled, "Kudlak usually run with the clothes on their back and that's it. They don't usually keep belongings or anything that will weigh them down or slow them up. They are wired to hunt and feed only."

"Yeah, so?"

He raised an eyebrow and indicated to the bag in his hands. "So what is so important to a nest of Kudlak that they would change centuries' old behaviours and go against their predatorial instinct?"

Looking at the other bag sitting on the ground I tilted my head to the side.

"Good question."

Turning the second bag on its side I unzipped the back pocket to reveal a small hessian bag, smiling I pulled it out and emptied its contents. Two heavy chains fell into my hand, entangling my fingers as they snaked themselves into my palm, at the end of the chains were two pendants. They landed heavily, their jewels catching in the torchlight.

"Wow."

Bravnica looked up and was on his knees at my side in an instant. Smiling he took one of the chains. "Ana, these are the stolen Auroras!"

I grinned holding one of the chains up so that the pendant twinkled as it spun around and around.

Smiling over my find we didn't notice the large figure as it strolled over the rise of the hill but both froze when we heard the unmistakable rattle.

"Tut, tut little brother. You know, you shouldn't play with things that don't belong to you."

TWENTY

SIX

Bravnica stepped forward, blocking me from the large figure that boiled with hostility. He reached behind himself and pushed at me. I knew he was trying to get me to run and I had no intention of arguing. His reaction was enough to tell me that this was not your regular Kudlak. I didn't want to turn my back with death only a few metres away so started backing up, but my tired legs caught on a knarled tree root and I overbalanced. Bravnica's arm snaked out like a whip, his large hand wrapping around my arm as I stumbled sideways.

I heard it chuckle as I righted myself.

"Ah Dom. Always the hero."

Dom?

I made the mistake of looking up and got a clear view of the Kudlak's face.

Oh Daska.

My body seized and I stood there, mouth agape, frozen in the fading light. My eyes flicked back and forth from the Kudlak to the Kaul protecting me, as Tash's story about the missing Bravnica brother replayed through my head in double time. All the while I tried to deny what my eyes were screaming at me. The features were identical, same strong jaw line, same broad shoulders and same cocky swag. The intense stare mirrored Bravnica's, everything the same except for one thing. Its eyes were red - wild with anticipation, dark with hate and baying for revenge, blood and death.

Shit.

Bile rose and I swallowed hard, clenching my shaking hands at my sides. So this is what had become of the brother. Bravnica remained steady, gun aimed at his dead brother's heart. He held his ground and his poker face.

"You behind all of this Nikoli?" Bravnica cocked his head, indicating the Auroras as he spoke.

A disturbingly familiar smile met the question.

"Surprised Dom?"

He stepped closer and I rocked back on my heels, pointed teeth flashed as anger seeped in and Nikoli raised his voice. "Didn't think I had it in me?"

His head swivelled in my direction and a small noise escaped my throat as Nikoli spoke directly to me. "I don't blame him. You see, I was always different, not special, not Enlightened like them."

Nikoli used air quotes over the word Enlightened, but the weirdness of that didn't register as panic ripped through me.

He leaned toward me without moving his feet. The motion seemed to defy gravity and was unnatural enough to snap me back to attention.

He flashed a smile meant to chill and continued. "The only Bravnica in history born without power, not the best way to be remembered is it?"

Watching, he seemed to be waiting for me to respond but when all I managed was to open and close my mouth a couple of times he moved on, turning slowly to smile at his brother.

"I'm faster now."

He feinted to the left and leapt to the right. The move so fast I was looking in the completely wrong direction when he chuckled clearly amused at his little game.

Then the smile fell and his voice rattled low. "Stronger! Superior! Ironic isn't it? How's the back by the way?"

The look of disdain it levelled at Bravnica was telling. I always thought that Kudlak were devoid of feeling, but that one look proved otherwise. I backed up a few paces and Bravnica spoke.

"Why are you doing this? What do you want with the Auroras?"

Red eyes flared. "I WANT IT ALL!"

I stumbled back a few steps.

"I want power. I want revenge and I want what is rightfully mine."

He pointed a finger menacingly at Bravnica. "He will fall Dom and when he does, I will take my rightful place."

The last was said so quietly that it was more chilling than anything he had said previously.

Bravnica spoke low and steady. "You know I can't allow that Nikoli, no matter who you are, were. I am the future Emir."

Nikoli erupted. "But *I* am the first born."

The shout was drowned out as noises started rushing toward us. Gun fire ripped through the air as the echo of voices raised joined the sound of rushing feet and breaking branches. I glanced around but it was becoming harder to see as the blanket of night settled around us. I reached out behind me feeling the rough bark of a tree as I backed away a little further. I could see gun flare spit through random breaks in the forest and knew the battle was getting closer. My breathing was becoming laboured and I tried to swallow my panic, clinging to the solid trunk, willing Bravnica to end this. As if hearing my silent plea, he stepped forward.

"I have the Auroras Nikoli, so whatever your plan was, it's not going to happen now."

Nikoli's eyes flashed. "Ah, but everything I need is right here." He spread his hands out wide and cocked his head to the side. "You brought it straight to me, one of the last pieces of the puzzle."

He was talking in riddles. Smiling at what he knew. "It won't be long now brother. It has started and there is nothing you can do to stop it."

Bravnica stood firm. "Without the Auroras it's just a plan isn't it Nikoli? You have nothing, you are nothing."

A stray bullet whizzed through the air and imbedded itself in a tree next to Bravnica's head. The thud of bullet penetrating wood drew everyone's attention and that's when Nikoli moved. Hitting me at full force the impact knocked the air out of my lungs and stars burst in my head as I glanced off the tree behind me and landed face down on the rough forest floor. I tried to blink my vision back but a second later Nikoli landed heavily on top of me, pinning me with his weight.

He whispered. "Ready for the future? This is gonna hurt."

In a weird moment of dejavu I felt my hair pull as he grabbed a handful, pushing my head forward into the ground. I squeezed my eyes shut and opened my mouth to scream but only choked on the decaying leaf litter of the forest floor and then I felt it - the acid burn of his needle-like teeth as they sunk into the back of my neck. The pain was incredible but lasted only a second as the next moment he was gone. The force of his exit rolled me over and I let out a delayed yell as the realisation of what had just happened sunk in. Bravnica landed hard at my side.

"Ana. Did he hurt you?" He brushed at the dirt on my forehead.

I wiped at my mouth before looking up into the ice blue eyes that looked almost desperate. Tears were threatening but I took a deep breath, killing me was the last thing he needed to worry about now.

I am going to die.

"No. I'm not hurt, just… shaken." Tasting dirt as I spoke I wiped at my mouth again before giving a weak smile to try and reassure him.

He let out a deep breath and turned in the direction his brother had disappeared. "I have to go after him."

I nodded, "You go. I'll get the Auroras and find help."

Handing over the torch from his gun belt he gave me one last look before taking off into the forest after his dead brother. I wanted to cry.

The back of my neck was starting to throb, the bite mocking, making sure I was aware at all times of my fate and forcing me to acknowledge it. Giving in I raised my hand to feel the broken skin at my hairline, I turned on the torch, my fingers were covered in dark sticky blood. I swiped at the wound in a vain attempt to remove any residual venom.

"Fuck."

Alone with the truth I rolled over and emptied my stomach, heaving until there was nothing left. I sat in the darkness for a while, not moving not doing anything, just breathing.

Suicide had never been something that I had cause to think about, but as I stood to recover the dropped Aurora's I started going over my options.

I would never become a Kudlak.

It took me at least three minutes but I managed to squeeze back into my wet jeans. I knew my night was far from over and decided I would rather face what was to come with pants on. Auroras secure I zipped up the bag and headed out in search of the support vehicles, taking the same direction Bravnica had originally been leading me and hoping I didn't get it too wrong. I came along the stream again, remembering Bravnica had said we would have to cross twice. I was going in the right direction. After washing my mouth out and scrubbing the back of my neck, I rolled up my jeans and stepped into the freezing water. Wading through this time without any problems I was thankful the water was only knee deep. Reaching the other side I repositioned the bag slung over my good shoulder, and ignoring the chill of the wind as it whipped around my legs, I stumbled on, determined to reach my goal before it was too late.

It was completely dark now and I had lost track of time. Doubting my sense of direction I started to contemplate heading back. Standing still I looked around at grey on black, the light of my torch only going so far I turned it off, preferring to let my eyes adjust to what little moonlight had managed to slip through the forest canopy. It took a full minute for my eyes to adjust. I stood on the spot and turned in a slow circle, stopping suddenly when I caught a glimpse of light peeking through the forest to my right. I moved closer to get a clear view, my eyebrows shooting up in surprise. I had found the support vehicles.

Raising my hands above my head I moved directly into the beam of light. Squinting, I approached at a slow but steady pace. I couldn't get shot just yet.

I received the typical Kaul greeting but as I explained myself the gun barrel I was staring down slowly lowered.

"Follow me."

I followed him. Reaching one of the jeeps my gruff Kaul offered me a bottle of water which I accepted with a smile and drank greedily while he opened the jeep door and sat behind the wheel, one foot still outside the vehicle. The pose was so Kaul it reminded me of my brothers. I felt the tears well and dug my fingernails into the palm of my hand to try and stop them. Blinking hard I shook my head and focused on the Kaul in front of me as he spoke into the jeep's radio.

"Bravo Team One this is Gypsy's Nest do you copy?"

We both stared at the radio waiting for a response, I jumped when it came.

"Roger Gypsy's Nest this is Bravo Team One, go ahead."

"I have a civilian that has stumbled upon our position." He gave me a look that said I should be dead before continuing. "This will compromise the logistics of the prisoner transport. Please advise? Over."

"Roger Gypsy's Nest. Stand by."

The Kaul looked at me. "This could take a little while - you might want to get comfortable."

I eyed the backseat of the jeep with longing. I was so cold and so tired. But I didn't trust myself to lie down. I knew I would fall asleep and I was so exhausted that I would no doubt sleep till dawn and by dawn it would be too late.

"Gypsy's Nest this is Bravo One do you copy?"

"Roger Bravo One this is Gypsy's Nest standing by."

"Roger Gypsy's Nest. Prisoner transport is to stand down. The Commander has ordered everyone back to base so you will have incoming Kaul in the next twenty. The civilian can return with the first group out."

"Roger that Bravo One. Gypsy's Nest out."

I shook my head, "But what about Nikoli?"

The Kaul's brow furrowed and I realised I had spoken out loud. "Who's Nikoli? Do you have a friend still out there?" He was reaching for the radio again and I stepped forward to stop him.

"No! It was just me. I just..." I stepped forward. "Look it's not important. What is important is that you give this to Commander Bravnica when he gets here. He will be looking for it."

I pushed the bag at him so that he had no choice but to take it. Confusion was clear on his face.

"What?"

He moved to give it back to me but I opened the back door of the jeep creating a barrier between us. "I'm really tired, I'm just gonna lie down here until it is time to go. Do you mind giving me some privacy?"

I could tell he wanted to argue and I held my breath hoping that he would let it go. He nodded slightly and walked away. I climbed into the back of the truck, pulled the door shut behind me, crawled across the bench seat and went straight out the other side. As long as Bravnica thought I was safe, he would not come looking for me.

I took refuge in the nearby scrub and stilled when I heard Bravnica's voice crackle over a nearby radio. I couldn't catch every word but deciphered most as he let the troops know the Kudlak threat had been taken out and the Aurora's recovered. I smiled when he signed off with a 'job done boys'.

Wanting to ensure that Bravnica was safe and that he would get the Auroras I settled in to wait. It didn't take long for the first group to arrive. They were battered and bloodied but had only a few serious causalities. These were loaded into the first few trucks and I watched as the jeep I had pretended to seek shelter in drove away, its tail lights winking at me as it trundled its way through the dark forest.

There was a commotion at the edge of the clearing and Bravnica arrived. Taras was with him, limping slightly but keeping pace. A medic rushed over but Taras waved him away, they both looked a little worse for wear. It was clear this had been a rough day for them. Taras would know by now what fate had befallen their long lost brother and that he had been plotting against them.

My gruff Kaul approached Bravnica with the bag. I watched as he explained himself and then pointed in the direction my jeep had taken back to Lumeer. Bravnica smiled his thanks, relief clear on his features. I wondered if that smile was because he had the Auroras back, or because he thought I was safe - not that it mattered anyway.

I watched through bleary eyes as he set his shoulders and signalled for the final group to move out. One by one, all of them weary, they climbed into the jeeps. Bravnica was the last to get in and he scanned the forest one last time before slamming his door shut. The head vehicle led the way out and a tear escaped as I watched the last taillight disappear from view.

All of this for me and it had been in vain. I'd been dead for hours.

TWENTY
SEVEN

I was alone and the silence weighed heavily on me. Having had my last glimpse at friends and familiar faces it was now time to go. I knew the venom was flooding my veins, slowly poisoning my heart as it pumped the toxin through my body, changing it bit by bit it into something else. My eyes had adjusted to the dark and I stepped out of my hiding spot. Dusting myself off I started walking further into the rugged forest and as far from Lumeer as I could get before sun-up.

The sound of my own breathing started to annoy me after half an hour so I decided to distract myself by singing quietly. The first song that popped out was a lullaby my mother used to sing to me when I was little. By the end of the song my voice was thick with tears so I sat heavily on the ground and looked up at the stars, wishing that I could have had a chance to say goodbye to my family. I knew the boys would never stop looking for me and the guilt was crushing because they would never know what happened to me. And neither would Bravnica.

I let out a feral scream, angry and frustrated with myself. "Stop it Ana, it has to be this way!"

I had to stop thinking of loved ones, I had a job to do and if I didn't get it done then that would be worse for them, worse for everyone. They would never forgive themselves if they knew I had been turned. Wiping at my tears I eased my aching body off the ground and pushed on.

Mind numb I didn't notice a change in the vegetation until it started slapping and scratching at my face. I swiped at the branches as they added insult to injury. The forest was becoming thicker and it felt like I had been walking for hours and I was starting to feel a little shaky and out of breath. I didn't know if it was because I was starting to turn or just the feeling of dread that lay heavy in the pit of my stomach. I paused to take a break but didn't sit down. Instead I leaned against the trunk of a nearby tree. I was scared that if I sat I wouldn't be able to get back up again and I had to keep on going. I looked up to the sky to try and gauge how much longer I had. The stars twinkled back at me innocently, their stage lightening slowly from pitch to black. I was on the downhill run now.

Motivated I pushed myself off the tree and stumbled on. I had only gone another fifty metres or so when the ground opened up beneath me. A massive gash scarred the landscape and I stumbled back, tripping over my feet and landing on the forest floor. I wasn't sure how deep the ravine was so I crawled forward slowly, the echo of running water bouncing off the sheer walls.

"Well I guess this is as good a place as any."

I expelled the last of the energy in my battered body and crawled to a comfy spot, clear of the edge so that I could settle in and watch my last sunrise. Sighing I allowed myself to relax a little, letting the memories of my life start to filter into my still scrambled mind. Smiling I closed my eyes and allowed myself one last look at the past, knowing I had no future.

I took a deep breath and let the sweet smells of summer fill my lungs as I fiddled with the rough rope of my old swing. Back and forth I took comfort in the familiar surrounds. Tash was giggling with Garrick as they tried to corner a runaway hen and Dahrel was helping Mum plant another rose. I couldn't see Dad but could hear him tinkering in his shed. The breeze lifted the happy sounds up into the air and suddenly the comforting scene became eerie, everything slowing down as if someone had pressed a button on a remote.

"Something's wrong."

I looked around and everything seemed in place but I knew it wasn't.

"There's supposed to be something else here."

I looked around trying to lay my finger on what was missing. Instead I found Bravnica.

I smiled at him but he didn't return it, his face was full of concern. "Ana, where are you?"

"I'm right here."

He looked straight through me as though he were blind. "Ana? I know something is wrong. You have to tell me where you are."

I looked out, spreading my hands wide to encompass our surroundings. "Look I'm right..." I looked back but he had disappeared. "...here."

Turning back to find my family I realised that everyone was gone, the sky was turning grey and a storm had begun to brew on the horizon.

"No."

I ran to the house scared that I had lost them but when I pushed through the front door the place was empty. Not just empty but untouched, it didn't look like anyone had set foot in there for years. The furniture was covered with sheets and a thin layer of dust carpeted the wood floor. The windows were grimy stopping any sunlight that may have filtered in. The place was cold and dark and not like home at all, I had to get out. Rushing to the door I caught sight of my reflection in the hall mirror as I passed. The reflection stopped me dead in my tracks. Turning I walked back down the hall until I was level with it, turning slowly to face the mirror. I let out a scream at the sight of my own eyes, Kudlak red, staring back.

Crying out I sat bolt upright.

It took me a moment to gather my bearings. I was still at the ravine, waiting for my last sunrise. I rubbed at my face and scooted toward the edge.

"Not long now."

My voice sounded foreign and my hands began to sweat. Maybe that was the first signs of turning? I felt the back of my neck, the wound had already sealed, a scar raising the surface of my skin. The vision of myself as a Kudlak was raw and sweat pricked through the pores of my skin, my heart knocking against my ribs in an odd rhythm. I swallowed hard and concentrated on my breathing to slow the adrenaline.

"That's not going to happen."

Smiling I watched my end start peaking its way over the horizon. I stilled and decided that if the pain got too much I could always throw myself over the edge of the ravine. The second option gave me a little comfort, as like magnesium, the sunlight slipped and slid its way over the terrain toward me. I sent up a silent prayer for my family and took a deep breath as the rays washed over me.

My eyes squeezed shut against the intense light and I took another deep breath waiting for the burn. Muscles braced I sucked another breath through gritted teeth. And then another.

Shouldn't it be quicker than this?

I opened my eyes to find my body bathed in sunlight. "What the hell?" I felt for the scar on the back of my neck and found it, angry and raised.

"But he bit me."

Stunned I sat for a few minutes just trying to wrap my head around the fact that I wasn't dust. I dragged a finger across the sharp edge of a rock and hissed in pain as the skin opened and blood began to seep out. I was still alive, but it made no sense. There was one basic law when it came to Kudlak and that was if you get bitten, you turn.

But I haven't.

I knew something in me felt different, not evil just different. I couldn't name it, but I knew it was there and I didn't like it. I tried to ignore the feeling as I turned my attention to the most pressing question.

What next?

I sat for awhile, my body was beat. I had to take small breaths to stop my bruised ribs form sending sharp stabs of pain through my chest, my shoulder felt like it was going to pop out at the slightest of movement. My feet were blistered and swollen in their boots. Given all this I smiled anyway as the realisation that I could go home and see my family again finally hit.

Using the mountains as my guide I headed in the direction I had come the night before. Glad that I had taken the path of least resistance by skirting the base of one of the larger mountains. Following it back, my progress was slow and I had to stop frequently, slowing my breathing to compensate for my ribs. I was getting tired and the sun was already directly overhead, the day getting away from me and I was beginning to doubt if I would make the road by nightfall. I pushed away the negative thought and distracting myself, started to think about the circumstances that had landed me here in the first place, trudging through the forest after trying to kill myself because I had been bitten.

A shudder ran through my body at the thought of Nikoli, the calculated way he looked at me and the manic way he spoke about power and revenge. His jealousy had driven him to the top of the food chain of the most savage race on the planet. I had no idea how Bravnica was feeling right now, seeing a loved one changed so radically. Into something so evil.

My mind instantly scrambled when I tried to remember further back. I couldn't quite put my finger on it. Flashes of tunnels appeared like a movie in my mind, the rattle of the Kudlak and there was someone else - a figure, standing in the shadows. I shut my eyes to concentrate but the harder I tried the more confusing everything became. Shaking my head I moved on, the trees cleared up ahead and I could hear the tell-tale bubble of running water. Landing on my knees in front of the stream, I knew I was dehydrated and began to drink slowly, desperate to rehydrate my parched body. It had been over twenty four hours since I had last eaten and my energy levels were dropping rapidly. Allowing myself time to rest I let my stomach settle before attempting to cross the river. The icy water brought temporary relief to my swollen feet as I slowly waded to the other side. Carefully, I moved, trying not to slip on the slick rocks because if I went down there was little chance of getting back up any time soon. Clearing the stream I looked skyward before heading back into the cover of trees as the sun was angling to the West and I was running out of time. I kept on.

They would be looking for me by now. My brothers would be tearing Lumeer apart.

And Bravnica.

"Oh Daska."

I closed my eyes at the memory of my confession, but stopped before I became too despondent. I had spent my entire life trying to keep my little episodes hidden. It was natural to feel apprehensive about someone besides Tash knowing. But it wasn't just anybody, it was Dominik Bravnica. I trusted him, I knew he wouldn't use the information against me.

I slipped on a loose rock and came down hard on my side, jarring my ribs painfully. Tears pricked as I dragged myself up again, I didn't know how much longer I could go on. But I did, finding the second river crossing I must have come upon it at a different spot. The water was still fast flowing but shallow and I managed to cross without incident. The sun's angle was getting deeper but I was so close now I that I refused to give in. My body was starting to disobey me, my feet not lifting high enough caused me to stumble more than walk and I had to use my good arm to keep from glancing off the trees. I went on like this until my hand was raw and then kept on, leaving bloodied palm prints on tree trunks like a trail of bread crumbs behind me.

All of a sudden the trees disappeared. With nothing to lean on I stumbled forward, just managing to get my feet under me before I fell into the verge at the side of the road. It was flat and solid under my feet and if I had the energy I would have let out a whoop of joy but I didn't, so I settled for a smile.

Turning toward home I could see my bike in the distance, parked on the side of the road where I had left it. I focused on the bike and started forward, trying to keep my feet up. I made a deal with myself that I could stop when I reached my bike but not before. I trudged on, my eyes were starting to blur, I rubbed at them with filthy hands to little effect. I tried to dismiss it as the angle of the sun on the road but I knew better. With my goal so close I couldn't stop now, my lungs heaved and my ribs screamed and I pushed myself till I thought I would collapse. I was only metres away now.

Nearly there.

I staggered to a stop leaning hard on the seat of my bike, my bottom lip cracked and blood starting to flow when I smiled. I ignored it, too caught up in the enjoyment of my small success. I could stop for awhile and recover. Sitting on the road I rested my back against the bike and reached up with my good arm to angle the side mirror down so that I could see myself. Signature green eyes stared back at me and I let out a relieved sigh before dropping my arm and letting my head roll to one side. I knew I wasn't far from unconsciousness and I stared down the road to Lumeer, willing myself to stay awake. The sound of a wolf howl echoed in the distance and my eyelids dipped several times but I kept opening them stubbornly, until I no longer had the strength to heave them up.

They closed, missing the outline of a Kaul jeep as it appeared on the road ahead. Racing toward me, a pair of ice blue eyes locked onto my broken form.

www.ingramcontent.com/pod-product-compliance
Lightning Source LLC
Chambersburg PA
CBHW061522050726
47503CB00015B/2374